Praise for Marianne Fredriksson's
#1 International Bestseller
Hanna's Daughters

"Brilliant . . . *Hanna's Daughters* outlines the lives of three generations of women and their complicated relationships with one another."
—*USA Today*

"I loved *Hanna's Daughters* from the very first page, and I absolutely could not put it down. . . . Written with grace and wit, this novel deserves to be read, discussed, and cherished by future generations of mothers and daughters."
—JUDITH GUEST
Author of *Ordinary People* and *Errands*

"An uplifting family saga . . . Fredriksson provides a satisfyingly complex . . . chronicle of women and the burdens imposed by their family history, their gender, and themselves. . . . Its message of reconciliation is transcendent."
—*People*

"With uncommon wisdom, Marianne Fredriksson spins a generational tale about the inner lives of women and the ties that bind. . . . *Hanna's Daughters* is a generous, consuming, and deeply satisfying novel."
—CONNIE MAY FOWLER
Author of *Before Won*

BY MARIANNE FREDRIKSSON
Published by The Ballantine Publishing Group

Hanna's Daughters

S IMON'S FAMILY

MARIANNE

FREDRIKSSON

Ballantine Books

New York

SIMON'S FAMILY

ONE

"*A*n ordinary bloody oak," the boy said to the tree. "Hardly fifteen meters high. That's nothing much to boast about.

"And nor are you a hundred thousand," he said, thinking of his grandmother, now nearly ninety and nothing but an ordinary shrill old woman.

Named, measured, and compared, the tree retreated from the boy.

But he could still hear the singing in the great treetops, melancholy and reproachful. So he resorted to violence and crashed the stone he had kept for so long in his pocket straight into the trunk.

"That'll shut you up," he said.

The great tree instantly fell silent, and the boy knew something important had happened. He swallowed the lump in his throat, disowning his grief.

That was the day he said farewell to his childhood. He did so at a definite moment and in a definite place; thus he would always remember it. For many years, he pondered over what he had relinquished on that day far back in his childhood. At twenty, he would have some idea, and then would spend his life trying to recapture it.

But at this moment, he was on the hillside above Äppelgren's garden, looking out over the sea, the fog gathering around the skerries before rolling in toward the coast. In the land of his childhood, the fog had many voices, the fog singing from Vinga to Älvsborg on a day like this.

Behind him was the mountain and the meadow. At the end of the meadow, where the ground opened up, were the oak woods, the trees that had spoken to him over the years.

In their shade, he had met the little man with the strange round hat. No, he thought, that wasn't true. He had always known the man, but it was in the shade of those great trees that he had actually seen him.

It no longer mattered.

"Just a load of shit," the boy said aloud as he crawled under the barbed wire of Äppelgren's fence.

He managed to avoid the old woman, Edit Äppelgren, who used to tear out the couch grass in her dead-straight flower beds on early spring days like this. The foghorns had frightened her indoors. She couldn't stand fog.

The boy understood that. Fog was the grief of the sea, as infinite as the sea, almost unbearable . . .

"Oh, shit," he said, for he knew better, and had just resolved to look on the world as other people saw it. The fog was the warmth of the Gulf Stream rising when the air grew cold.

Nothing more than that.

But he couldn't really deny the sorrow in the long drawn-out wail of foghorns over the harbor entrance as he slanted across Äppelgren's lawn and slipped into his kitchen, where he was given hot cocoa.

His name was Simon Larsson. He was eleven, small, thin, dark complexioned. His hair was coarse, brown, almost black, his eyes so dark sometimes it was hard to distinguish the pupils.

What was strange about his appearance had hitherto evaded him, for up to that day, he hadn't been given to comparisons and had escaped a great many torments. He thought about Edit Äppelgren and her difficulties with the fog. But he mostly thought about Aron, her husband. Simon had always liked Aron.

Simon had been a frequent runaway—one of those children, like cheerful puppies, who follow the temptations of the road. It could begin with a colorful toffee paper in the ditch outside the gate, continue with an empty box of Tiger Brand and a little farther away a bottle, then another, a red flower, and farther on a white stone, then perhaps a glimpse of a cat.

In that way he ended up farther and farther away from home,

and he remembered very clearly one time when he had realized he was lost. That was when he saw the tram, large and blue as it rattled out of town. It frightened him terribly, but just as he was opening his mouth to bawl, Aron was there.

Aron bent his tall figure over the boy, and as he spoke, his voice seemed to come from up in the sky.

"Good gracious, boy, running away again, eh?"

He heaved the boy up onto the carrier of his black bicycle and started walking home, all the time talking about the birds, the fat chaffinches and cheeky great tits, the gray sparrows hopping around them in the dust on the road.

He said he had nothing but contempt for them, those flying rats.

It was spring, so they cut across the field and the boy learned to distinguish the song of the lark. Then, in his tremendous voice, Aron sang a song that went rolling down the slopes and echoed against the cliffs.

"When in spri-i-i-ing among the mountai-ai-ains . . ."

Best was when Aron whistled. He could imitate any bird, and the boy almost burst with excitement when Aron got the female blackbird to respond to him, lustily and willingly. Then Aron grinned his good big grin.

The birdsong that surpassed all others in the hills at the mouth of the river was actually the *skriek*ing of gulls. Aron could imitate them, too, and could tease them into such rage, they would dive-bomb down onto the boy and the man.

Then Simon laughed so much he almost wet himself, and the neighbors on their errands hastened past along the road, but would stop and smile at the tall man who was enjoying himself as much as the little boy.

"Aron will never grow up," they said.

But Simon didn't hear that. Right up to this very day, Aron had been king in his world.

The boy sat at the table with his cocoa, seeing Aron as other people saw him, realizing that the man's amazing ability to rescue him coincided with Aron's working hours. Simon had run away after his midday meal. Aron often finished work early and had just caught the tram when the boy reached the tram stop and realized he was lost. Aron picked up his bicycle there, and that was where he came across this strange little boy who was so often getting lost.

Simon could now see the contempt, the sly grins and half words that were always around Aron. He was the bouncer at a disreputable pub down in the harbor and had a nickname Simon didn't understand, but was so foul it made his mother turn scarlet with indignation.

As Simon swallowed the last bit of bun and scraped around the cup with his spoon, he reckoned Aron had never taken the step he had taken that day. Aron Äppelgren had never stood up on a hillside and said good-bye to his childhood.

The boy slept on the wooden kitchen sofa every night. The spacious, sunny kitchen had large mullion windows facing west and south, with white curtains and flowering potted plants, and old apple trees outside. Below the south window was the zinc-covered bench with the cold-water tap in the angle and a double-burner Primus stove. Along the long wall below the window was the kitchen sofa, painted blue like the chairs, and the big kitchen table covered with oilcloth for everyday and an embroidered cotton tablecloth on Sundays.

The kitchen was full of slow cooking, often meat soup. Coffee. Baking, a good smell on Wednesdays, baking day. Gossip. You could absorb it from the wood box if you made yourself small and invisible, the almost endless going over, just who was expecting and whom to be sorry for.

There were many to be sorry for—most, in fact. Listening to all that turned him into a socialist. The boy learned to be sorry for them, not think ill of them. In that way, he lost his rage so early, he never really found it again. It existed, shouting out occasionally through his life, but always too late and often in the wrong place.

Simon became a good boy.

Things were good for him. He also learned that early, and so well, that throughout the years there could never be any thoughts of him feeling sorry for himself.

There was Hansson, who was unemployed, so had to beat his wife on Saturdays when he'd bought strong liquor from the store. There was Hilma, with two daughters at the sanatorium and whose youngest had died of consumption. And then there was Andersson's beautiful girl, who always had new clothes and walked the streets in town.

But when they came to what she did on the streets, they sent the boy out. The women were always aware of the children.

The men weren't. That was what was so good about sleeping on the kitchen sofa. The men sat in the kitchen in the evenings, drinking beer rather than coffee, talking about politics instead of people, and inevitably that damned vehicle that had broken down again.

His father and uncle had a haulage business, which meant they owned a truck. In the daytime, it took timber and materials to the building sites around the growing city, and food to the houses. At night they mended it, for the bearings were worn, the valves had to be reground, and the gearbox was all shot to hell.

They were skillful mechanics. The day they came across a six-cylinder engine to replace the worn-out old four-cylinder one, they were happy. But the switch forced them to lengthen the shaft and give it an extra coupling. Because they stubbornly stuck to the sturdy cogwheel transmission, they soon had a vehicle that could crawl up the steepest of all the steep hills in the city, even when they were icy.

The vehicle gradually became a piece of craftsmanship in almost every detail. It said Dodge on the front, but in the end it was questionable whether there was anything left from Detroit besides the red shell.

Perched on stools at the foot of the kitchen sofa, they took a break at ten o'clock every evening, listening over a beer to the late news bulletin on the radio. At the head of the sofa, Simon lay under a pink tent and was thought to be asleep.

That was how he heard about the terror creeping out of the

heart of Europe called Hitler. Sometimes Hitler himself bellowed on the radio and Germans yelled their *Heils*, and afterward his father said that sooner or later it would all go to hell and everything the workers and Per Albin had built up would soon be smashed to smithereens.

One day a man came with specially forged nuts, nuts he had made out of the goodness of his heart, the boy's mother said after his father had thrown him out.

"Goodness of his heart," raged his father. "A Jew-hater, a Nazi in my kitchen. Are you mad, woman!"

"Don't shout like that, you'll wake the boy."

"Worse things could happen to him," said his father, but then his mother started crying and the quarrel gave way to calmer words.

Lying under the tent on the sofa, the boy was frightened. The man had said some bad words before Simon's father threw him out. Those same words had been flung at Simon at school a while ago. His father had turned pale when Simon had told him, and one unusual but wonderful evening, he had taught the boy how to fight. Hour after hour, they had practiced in the basement—straight right, swift left hook, and an uppercut if the situation demanded.

The next day, the boy had used his new skills at school, and ever since, he had never heard those words again.

Until that evening.

T W O

Simon's mother was a good woman.

That could never be forgotten, for her goodness was somehow always present. It shaped the world in which the boy grew up.

She was also beautiful, tall, and blond, with a large sensitive mouth and startlingly brown eyes.

Her goodness was not the cloying kind. She was strong in herself, not threatened by growth in other people. Karin was one of those rare people who know that love cannot be cultivated simply with nourishment and water.

She also understood that almost nothing could be done about the fear running through people's lives and that no one can help another person internally. And that makes the need for consolation endless.

So she became the person everyone turned to. There was no ill-treated woman or man not given coffee and comfort in her kitchen, not to mention all the children who were allowed to cry it out and then given cocoa.

She neither dried their tears nor found any solutions.

But she could listen.

She wasn't a woman to get satisfaction from other people's sorrow. Her patience and great heart gave her little joy. In fact, all the misery in life she confronted in her kitchen only increased her own sorrow. But from it she found new fuel for her socialist convictions. She avowed that people treat each other like animals because *they* are treated like animals.

Like all good people, she did not believe in evil. It existed, but not in itself, and was only an outgrowth of injustice and unhappiness.

Simon was well treated and happy. Then he took to damming up the outlet for his dark sorrow, his need for revenge. Denied, they thrived and were nourished by his guilt.

Mrs. Ågren had eight children and hated them all. Simon was probably the only person in the village drawn to her, even going so far as to make friends with one of her sons, no easy friendship, for like all the Ågrens, the boy was sly and suspicious.

But his friendship gave Simon entry to the Ågren kitchen, and as he was good at making himself invisible, he was able to see and hear that hatred, so forceful, it kept boiling over and enveloping them all.

"Bloody cow!" she would yell at her eldest daughter doing her hair at the kitchen mirror. "That's no use. You're like some wretched heifer, so skinny you wouldn't be worth even the butcher's fee. Don't you go thinking anyone'll want you."

She was worst toward her daughters, simply scolding the boys as if in passing.

"I've got you for my sins," she would cry. "Get out of my kitchen, so I don't have to look at you."

One day she spotted Simon, and he suddenly became the focus of her hatred.

"Little bastard, you," she said slowly, quietly, drawing it out. "You just go to hell and take your damned sanctimonious mother with you. But by all means don't forget to ask her where she got you from."

Simon drew a deep breath as he felt her rage arousing his own. He could find no words, but rushed out and ran down to the shore and the rocks by the bathing place. It was autumn, the sea gray and angry, which helped him find the words.

"Bitch," he said. "Evil bitch."

That didn't make him feel better, so, in his mind, he cut off her breasts and gouged out her eyes, then kicked her to death.

Afterward he felt strangely pleased.

Mrs. Ågren was not old. But she had had four miscarriages and eight children in thirteen years, and she had hated every single one of them from the moment they were inside her. They devoured her, swallowing her life, breaking up her nights, and filling her days with bilious resentment. They robbed her of her self-esteem and all joy. Only anger kept her going, keeping food on the table and clean clothes for her man and children.

"She's an overfertile woman," Karin said. "That's her misfortune."

The woman herself blamed her husband, Ågren, the lecherous bastard, yet he came home on Fridays with his wages, so she didn't dare start on him.

She had married early, a kind man in good circumstances, a crown servant, a customs officer. Though many considered her lucky in life, perhaps she herself had once had dreams of life in a new house by the sea.

One spring the eldest daughter walked into the sea. Only sixteen years old, but when the police found her body, she turned out to be pregnant. At the grocer's, Mrs. Ågren said it was just as well the girl had the sense to do away with herself, otherwise she, her mother, would have strangled the damned little whore.

But then she went home and had a miscarriage.

By winter, her belly was again swollen, but this time it was no infant. In her thirty-seventh year, Ågren's wife died of a cancer raging through her just like her hatred.

Simon grieved for her, and when Ågren soon married again, an ordinary submissive woman, who kept the house clean and baked cakes, the boy stopped going there.

Now it was the evening after the day Simon had decided to be grown up. The fog had lifted toward afternoon, and the light May sky dyed pink by the red-and-white-checked cloth on the kitchen sofa as he lay there thinking about his decision.

He had done it for his mother's sake, that was clear. But he hadn't found the words that would explain it to her. So he had lost his reward, that of seeing the sorrow disappearing from her brown eyes.

That sorrow was the only truly alarming thing in the boy's life, the only unbearable thing. He would not understand until much later, when he was an adult and she was dead, that her sorrow had little to do with him.

He could make her happy. Over the years he had thought up a great many tricks to get that laughing glint in her brown eyes. Subsequently, he always thought he was the cause of both her happiness and her sadness.

A few days earlier, they had learned that Simon had gotten into high school, the first in the family to be allowed to study. Although only eleven, he had filled in the application form himself and cycled alone on the long road to that stuck-up school, as his parents called it, when the time came for the entrance test.

The boy had seen the glint in his mother's eye when he had returned with the news that he had passed.

The light went out the moment his father spoke.

"So you're going to be something, are you? And I'll have to pay, of course. Are you sure we can afford it?"

"We'll handle the money," his mother said. "But the rest you'll have to do yourself, Simon. It was your idea."

A few years later, in puberty, he would hate them for the words spoken in the kitchen that evening, and for the loneliness that followed. But later in life, he came to understand his parents, understand their ambivalence toward the middle-class school that devoured the bookish children and ate at the working classes from within. Later he would also have some idea of their feelings as they sat over dinner and wondered if the boy would now outgrow them.

But on the other hand they wanted their child to have the very best.

So one night, when Karin cleared the table and wiped the oilcloth clean, Erik took out his account book and, looking worried, asked about school fees, calculating the cost of books and tram money. But that was all largely for show, as there was no real shortage of money.

Only the eternal terror of poverty.

His mother hardly gave money a thought, but she was not in a good mood and her eyes darkened with the weight of her words. "Then all these dreams'll have to come to an end."

Perhaps her anxiety had nothing to do with whether Simon could cope with school. Perhaps she was worried her boy would now become one of the kind who was neither one thing nor the other, one of those people who were always searching for something in themselves.

But Simon only heard their words, and he lay there on the kitchen sofa thinking how pleased she would be if he could somehow tell her that he would be like the other children, but more so and better. For he had noticed she was proud of his good marks and the teacher's words at the end of term last year.

"Simon is very gifted," his teacher had said.

His father had grunted, suspecting the very word, then had been embarrassed for the teacher. Saying things like that when the boy could hear, that was crazy.

"The lad could get uppish," he said as they walked slowly home. "Gifted," he went on, savoring the word, spitting it out.

"He's clever," said Karin.

"Of course he's clever," said Erik. "He takes after us."

"And you talk about being uppish," his wife said, but her laugh was happy.

The boy had always been bookish, as they say. It was a quality that was accepted, like his smallness and his black hair.

Simon had devoured all the books in the house that first summer holiday. He remembered when one woman found him on the sofa in the parlor with *Gösta Berling's Saga*.

"Is the lad reading Lagerlöf?" she said in a disapproving voice.

"You can't stop him," said Karin.

"But he can't understand a book like that."

"He must understand something or he'd stop reading it."

His mother hadn't sounded apologetic, but nevertheless the woman had the last word.

"Believe you me, nothing good can come of it."

Did a shadow of unease come over Karin? Perhaps, for she must have told his father.

"Don't you go thinking the world consists of upper-class misses and mad priests," he said. "Read Jack London."

Simon read the collected works of Jack London, brown marbled editions with red borders on the spines. He would remember these characters and images for some time—Wolf Larsen, a priest who ate human flesh, the mad violin player, that long leafy lake in the sun, and the East End slums.

The rest sank into his subconscious and flourished there.

At the age of eleven, he had found his way to the public library in Majorna, his thirst less urgent now, as happens in someone who knows he always has access to water. He had also become more cautious, seeing the anxiety flitting over his mother's face as she asked herself whether there might be something seriously different about her boy.

"Get on outside and run around before the blood rots in your veins," she would say. It was a joke, but beneath it lay an unease.

She once found him in the attic, deep in Joan Grant's book on the Queen of Egypt. He stared at Karin from Pharaonic heights, not even hearing what she had said. Not until she shook him back through the centuries did he see she was frightened.

"You mustn't lose your grasp on life like that," she said.

It still hurt whenever he remembered that.

That evening on the kitchen sofa, he questioned himself: Was there something seriously wrong with him?

But the next day he had almost forgotten it completely. He went with his cousin in a canoe out toward the harbor mouth, lay there with the paddle, waiting for the ferry from Denmark. It came so regularly, you could set your watch by it. It was nowhere near the largest vessel on its way into the harbor, but unlike the American ships and the white ships from the Far East, the ferry had to pass the river mouth at full speed. She made a great wash, and the boys had become skilled at steering the canoe up onto the first wave and riding with it into the shore.

There she came, swift and handsome. Simon heard his cousin shout with excitement as they balanced on the crest of the wave. But they were out of line, the canoe tipped over, flinging them out, and they slid with the wave down into the depths.

For a moment, Simon felt a stab of fear, but he was a good swimmer, as was his cousin. He knew what he had to do to prevent himself from being sucked under by the next wave, and he floated with it, unresisting, and the next, and the next.

As the sea calmed, the boys swam over to the canoe and towed it ashore to where the gang was waiting, scared as well as scornful. But his cousin boasted about the enormous wave, higher than any other, ever—this was accepted, and honor was saved.

Simon had something else on his mind: the image of the man he had met on his way down into the depths. The little man had been there, the old man he had said good-bye to forever the day before.

Back at home he was scolded and given dry clothes, then he climbed the hill and ran across the meadow toward the oak woods. He found his great trees, silent, just as they should be. Their agreement held, that was good, that was all he wanted to know.

But in his sleep that night he met his little man again and sat on the seabed, carrying on a long conversation with him. When he awoke in the morning he felt strangely strengthened.

Later on in the day, after he had handed in his math test at school and had a free moment, he remembered he had forgotten to ask who the man was, nor did he remember a single word that had been said.

It was an unusually hot summer, heavy with unease. The adults in the kitchen listened to every news bulletin.

"It's getting darker," said his father.

"We need rain," said his mother. "The potatoes are shriveling and the well drying up."

But the rain didn't come, and in the end they had to buy water and have the well filled from a tanker.

THREE

*H*e started school that autumn, the same day the German diplomat Ribbentrop went to Moscow.

Simon was the smallest in the class and the only pupil from a working-class home. He didn't know how to behave, failing to stand up when the teachers spoke to him and saying yes and no without saying thank you.

"Thank you, thank you, thank you, sir," his classmates said, which Simon found silly. But he realized he had to learn—for school—and keep things apart. At home, they would laugh their heads off.

You were grateful at home, but you didn't say thank you.

He was the only one to apply for a reduction of the term fees, but like all the others he was given a German reader and a German grammar.

The way back home was nearly four miles. Simon was unused to Göteborg traffic, heavy trucks, and large trams, so once back home he was in need of some comforting.

But Karin was worried about Erik, sitting there in front of the radio in the kitchen, facing a shattered world. His political acumen had never included Soviet Russia. The Russo-German Nonaggression Pact signed in Moscow was a betrayal of the workers of the world. Simon didn't understand how serious it was until Karin fetched the schnapps bottle from the larder on a perfectly ordinary weekday.

By the evening, the liquor and Karin's many comforting words had done their work. Erik had slightly repaired the ground he stood on and had ascertained that the Russians had signed the pact to give themselves time to arm for the great and decisive battle against the Nazis. Karin could breathe a sigh of relief, look at her son, and ask the question.

"Well now, how was the new school?"

"Good," said the boy, and nothing more was really said over all the years through middle school, high school, and university.

He didn't take the German textbooks out of his backpack that evening.

It happened the next day during the first break.

"Little Jew bastard, you," said the tallest and fairest boy in the class, a boy with such a grand name, a murmur rose when it was read out at registration.

Simon struck out, his right arm shooting straight from the shoulder, swiftly and unexpectedly, just as he had been taught, and the tall boy fell, blood spurting from his nose.

Nothing else happened before the bell rang. And it never got worse, for Simon had acquired respect, yet he also knew that great loneliness was now his, here as in his junior school.

But he was wrong there.

As the boys ran up the stairs to the physics lab, an arm was put around his shoulders and he looked up into a pair of rather sorrowful brown eyes.

"My name's Isak," the boy said. "And I'm Jewish."

They sat next to each other in the physics lab, just as they came to sit next to each other all through their school years. Simon had a friend.

But he didn't understand that all at once. His surprise was much greater than his delight. A real Jew! Simon looked at Isak during the lesson and simply couldn't understand. The boy was tall, thin, had brown hair, and looked kind.

Just like any ordinary person.

In the long break, Isak took Simon home with him and offered him sandwiches. They had a maid rather like Mrs. Ågren, and she put thick slices of liver pâté on the bread and pressed tomatoes on them.

Simon had never seen a maid before, and had rarely eaten tomatoes, but that wasn't what struck him. No, it was the large dark rooms, the heavy velvet curtains at the windows, the red plush sofas, the endless rows of bookshelves—and the smell, the fine smell of wax polish, perfume, and wealth.

Simon absorbed it all, and as he cycled home that afternoon, he thought now he really knew what happiness was like. He had met Isak's cousin, as grand as a princess and with long painted nails. Simon wondered whether she ever needed to pee. Then it occurred to him that Karin would ask questions if he came back with his sandwiches uneaten, so he made a detour around the oak trees and ate them there.

The trees were silent.

Down the slope to Äppelgren's garden, he met one of his cousins, the backward one, and was ashamed of him, of how dirty he was and how unbearable his ingratiating grin was.

I hate him, Simon thought. I've always hated him. Then he was even more ashamed.

They were the same age and had started school at the same time. But his cousin had soon ended in the special class, and the school had now given him up. He spent most of his time in the cowshed at the Dahls', working for the people who still had a small farm among the houses in their growing suburb. The Dahls got a laborer who was simpleminded, but a good boy and strong enough for the hard work of the farm.

At home, Karin had brought a folding bed down from the attic, and she showed Simon how he should unfold it every evening and make his bed up in the parlor. She had cleared a shelf in the oak sideboard for his bedclothes. Then she had taken the cloth off the big table by the window and arranged a box and a shelf for his books. He was to move out of the kitchen into the parlor. All this was an acknowledgment of the seriousness of school.

That first long week came to an end and Sunday arrived, a Sunday the world would never forget. Hitler's troops marched into Poland, Warsaw was bombed, Britain declared war, and all of it was somehow a relief.

It was most noticeable in Erik, who straightened up as he said, "At last," and in the voices as people gathered around the radio in the kitchen. Only Karin was more sorrowful than usual as she helped Simon make his bed that evening.

"If I had a God," she said, "I would thank him on my knees that you're only eleven."

Simon didn't know what she meant, and felt nothing but guilt, as always when his mother was sadder than usual.

Something had also changed at school the next day, as if the air had cleared and things had simplified.

Their first class was history, but there was a delay before opening their books. The teacher, young and despairing, considered it his task to explain to the boys what had happened. Nearly all of them came from homes where children were protected from reality. And because Göteborg was the country's major port in the west, facing the sea and England, there were few Nazis here.

To Simon, however, it was mostly familiar—Fascism, Nazism, persecution of the Jews, Spain, Czechoslovakia, Austria, Munich. Suddenly the kitchen sofa was of some use. He was the one who knew, who faced the teacher and soon found himself in a dialogue.

"It's good to know there is at least one of you who knows what it's all about," the teacher said finally. Behind his words was a challenge to the others, to the middle-class boys whose world map had been given its first realistic contours that morning.

Isak didn't say much, but the teacher's eyes rested on him occasionally, as if knowing the person with the greatest insight had remained silent.

Simon sat at his desk thinking there were bridges between his two worlds, and much of what Erik and Karin stood for also had some value here in this grand school. Thinking that everything didn't have to be denied, or be shameful.

Simon realized that what was worst in all this new world was that he was ashamed of his kin. That afternoon he was able to ask Isak whether he would like to come to his house after school.

But how Isak came to find Karin, her comforting arms, and sturdy ground to stand on in her kitchen is a later story. At that moment, the teacher spoke.

"Whatever happens in the world, everyone has to play his part. Open your books. Now then, history begins with the Sumerians."

Suddenly Simon was there, no longer in the classroom. Never could he have dreamed of anything so amazing.

They read Grimberg: "In our day, Mesopotamia is a land of the dead and great silence. The Lord's restraining hand weighs heavily over the centuries on this unhappy land. The words of the prophet Isaiah, 'How hast thou fallen from the heavens, thou destroyer of peoples,' ring like a lament of the dead throughout the fallen walls . . ."

Simon didn't understand, but was caught up by the torrent of words. Then Grimberg came to the Sumerians, those broad-browed, squat people, reminiscent of the Mongols.

"They discovered written characters," the teacher said, and went on about the innumerable hieroglyphics in the great temples. For the first time, the huge ziggurats rose before the boy's eyes and he followed the teacher down into the tombs of Ur and found the dead.

Many years later, he came to believe that his interest in prehistory was born at that moment, spurred on by his success during the first half of the lesson, or perhaps it had affected him so much because it was such a tremendous day, the first day of the war.

But the eleven-year-old knew beyond the words that the world now opening to him had something to do with the meadow back at home.

He weighed the heavy knife in his hand, and the blue stones of the lapis lazuli spoke their secret language to him, giving strength to the hand. His gaze was fixed on the long golden blade.

The tool was good.

But it wouldn't help him if he couldn't stay in the approaching mo-

ment and make himself timeless. He walked toward the great temple hall, sensing rather than seeing the upturned faces of the thousand people united in prayer for him.

But the bull was massive, and in the decisive moment, time caught up with him, as did that great ally of time, great fear. As the bull raced toward him, he knew he was going to die and he screamed . . .

Screamed so that he woke Karin, soon there and shaking him awake.

"You've had a nightmare," she said. "Get up and drink some water. You always have to make sure you wake up properly after you've had a nightmare."

One day, before Isak ended up in Karin's kitchen, Simon was sitting at Isak's dinner table with Isak and his father, his mother and the cousin with the painted nails. He had trouble with the many knives and forks, but soon learned by observing and hoped no one had noticed his uncertainty.

He had been invited to dinner. At home, people were never invited to dinner. If people came at the time of their midday meal, they just joined in. Invitations were to a party.

Isak's father was one of those rare people always intensely present. There was a suppleness in his body, and the finely chiseled features were lively, always shifting. He had a quick smile, light and friendly, his eyes brown and sparkling, a curiosity in them, and something else. Fear? Simon could see it, but didn't want to, so he dismissed the feeling.

Ruben Lentov had created a life for himself in Sweden based on books. His bookshop in the city center was the largest in town, and he had branches in Majorna, Redbergslid, and Örgryte. He was known all over the world, with contacts in London, Berlin, Paris, and New York.

In his youth, he had been a seeker, lured to Sweden by Strindberg's plays and Swedenborg's writings, and he had endured hardship until his business had begun to grow.

His departure from Germany had been a matter of rebellion,

against far too much maternal love and too strong ties to his father. But the family back in Berlin had never wanted to see it. They thought of him as the first clear-sighted one, who, long before 1933, had realized what was going to happen. They supported him with money and bank contacts and looked after his wife and their little son.

In the mid-1930s, his wife had followed him, by which time he was well established and she was frightened to death. In the early years, he had been confused about his wife's tendency to terrible visions and her ghoulish interpretation of things.

But more recently he thought he understood.

The doctors she went to in this new country talked about persecution mania. These were words that could be used in the daytime, but never after dark, for a many-thousands-of-years-old ghost was there.

At his dinner table was Simon, this Swedish boy, his son's friend. Ruben was grateful for every hand that could be clasped in this new country, and he had listened with great attention when Isak had told him about the history lesson and the boy who was so politically aware and who hated the Nazis.

But he was disappointed, and ashamed of that. He had not expected this dark little boy, but a tall fair-haired Swede. That would have felt better.

His miscalculation was banished during their conversation, and Simon relaxed. Ruben realized the boy was Swedish working class, and although his voice was that of a child, the source of it was an increasingly powerful social democracy. They disagreed on the communists, and Simon lost his foothold for a while when Ruben eagerly maintained that the Soviet Union was a slave state of the same ilk as Hitler's Germany. Then Ruben stopped, realizing he had no right to get carried away and wreck things like this.

Ashamed, he offered Simon some more ice cream.

Simon would never forget that evening, not only because of what he heard, but even more because of what he saw of the anxieties and unhappiness in the middle of all this wealth. And because he was so frightened of Isak's mother.

Simon had never before come across anything so contradictory. Her mouth and her fragrance tempted him, but her eyes and the sounds she made frightened him. Her bangles tinkled, necklaces rustled, and her gaze was burning with anxiety. She clutched him to her and pushed him away. Hugged him, kissed him, shoved him away, observed, and said uncomprehendingly, "Larsson, but it can't be true."

Then she forgot him, no longer even seeing him, and Simon realized she had banished him from that moment and from her mind, and he understood the sorrow in his friend's eyes, the sadness he had noticed that very first day.

The next weekend, on the Saturday, he made an attempt to build a bridge between his old world and the new, and at the kitchen table he told his parents about the grand family that had invited him to dinner.

"They were so . . . nervous," he said, fumbling for words that would explain the unease in the big apartment in town.

But Karin found them.

"They live in terror," she said. "They're Jews, and if the Germans come . . ."

But autumn went by and the Germans didn't come. Something else happened, something that from Erik's point of view was almost worse. On the thirtieth of November, the Soviet Union bombed Helsinki.

The Winter War.

God, how cold it was that winter, when the earth nearly died of the wickedness of man. There were days when children were kept indoors, when the radio announced the schools were closed. Simon sat in the parlor, where Karin lit the stove and the coal smelled dry, and Erik came home with frozen ears and said that if this went on, they would soon be able to drive across the ice to Vinga.

The next Sunday they did just that, and it was an adventure

never to be equaled. The ever lively, ever present, unconquered, and immense sea was clapped in irons by the hideous wind from the east, which blew at thirty degrees below zero and twenty meters per second.

Russians and Finns died like flies, of cold and bullets. Death took about 225,000 lives, they found out later, once circumstances made it possible to start counting.

In Simon's home city, Göteborg, the great shipyard was working overtime and the workers gave their earnings to Finland. In Luleå up north, houses were blown up and five committed communists lost their lives.

In February, it was all over and Karelia had lost its domiciliary rights in Scandinavia. That was when Karin said that in the spring they must try to rent a field from the Dahls and grow more potatoes. And vegetables.

The shortage of food began.

FOUR

*F*or a long time afterward, Simon would wonder whether he had sensed something special that morning. He had awoken at dawn and heard his mother weeping in her sleep.

Karin had premonitions.

But he felt much the same as usual as he cycled off to school. The city had awoken to what seemed to be an ordinary day, and from the top of the hill at the city boundary he could see all four cranes in the harbor moving like long-legged spiders dancing. As usual, he cycled past the tram taking his better-off friends to school, and as usual, he felt a certain triumph. The sun was out above Majorna and there were streaks of warmth in Karl Johansgatan.

As usual, he did his German homework during morning prayers in the hall. He had still not been able to bring himself to take his German textbooks home, so he did not do well in lessons. As usual on Tuesdays, they had chemistry in the morning, and as usual, Simon was not very interested. But in the third lesson, in the middle of history, the caretaker, his face blank, went from door to door saying curtly that they were all to assemble in the school hall.

What he remembered best afterward was not what the headmaster had said, but the mindless terror he induced when the boys were sent home. He said they were all to go straight home to their parents, for the school could not take any responsibility for them that day.

That was the ninth of April 1940, and Simon's legs went like pistons as he cycled home to Karin, only to find her weeping at the kitchen window. But as she lifted the boy up and put him onto the kitchen sofa, her arms around him, he felt a child's assurance that nothing really bad could happen as long as she existed.

Out of the radio an excited voice chattered on about the Norwegians sinking the battleship *Blücher* in the harbor entrance to Oslo. Karin said it would have been better if the Norwegians had done what the Danes had, and capitulated immediately.

Erik came home with the truck. The prime minister spoke on the radio, saying that the defense of the country was good, and in many households, his safe south-country voice perhaps induced some confidence. But not in the Larssons' kitchen, where Erik said it just as it was, "He's lying, he has to lie."

A few days later, Erik was called up for military service and disappeared to some unknown place. Karin and Simon dug up the field they had rented and planted potatoes.

In Simon's dreams, wild mountain people with drawn swords rushed down high mountains, spreading like locusts over great fields of crops, burning, killing, and flinging dead bodies into canals and rivers. The images of the night had little to do with the war raging around the world, for he knew what that looked like from newspapers and newsreels. In the daytime, his terror contained swastikas, boots, and black SS uniforms, but at night they took on the form of colorful fat madmen cutting his throat with oriental voluptuousness and flinging him into the river, where he floated about among thousands of other dead, the water turning red, and he saw Karin with her head smashed in floating beside him, and it was her, although it didn't look like her.

As an adult, he would often wonder what the war did to the children, what effect this terror had on them. What he remembered most was the longing every morning for the day to come to an end without anything happening, that day and the next, and the next, an always present painful desire.

Five years is an eternity when you are a child.

His generation became the generation of impatience, those who couldn't stay in the moment, but lived for the next day. And yet, there was an everyday. School reopened, and like Simon, many of the boys no longer had a father at home. Only for Isak was it different, for in his home it was his mother who had disappeared. On the night of the tenth of April, she tried to poison the children and set fire to their apartment in Kvarnsgatan. Isak and his cousin had been taken to a clinic and had their stomachs pumped. When they returned home, his mother had gone, admitted to the mental hospital on the other side of the river, where injections were given to her to make her sleep, and gradually they turned her into an addict. Isak would never have his mother back again.

At night, Ruben Lentov paced through the big silent apartment, from the bookshelves in the library to the hall, through the row of four rooms, back and forth across the thick carpets. He had always been a man of action, and now he found himself powerless. A caged animal. There was still one door to flee through. Jewish friends had kept the flight open to London, and from there, on to America. He could sell his business, take the children and his money, and escape.

He thought about his brother in Denmark, the one who had delayed too long.

But most of all he thought about Olga, locked up in the mental hospital in Hisingen, nothing but a shell, drugged, beyond all contact, but still his wife and Isak's mother.

The door of the cage had slammed shut and he knew it.

Yet he paced there night after night as if he had to make a decision and needed those long hours to arrive at some clarity.

To Simon, the terror had names, and so it could be more or less controlled: the bombs, the Gestapo, Møllergatan 19. Isak knew the words, too, but they were of no use for sorting out and distancing. His terror was of another kind, all-embracing and wordless, as terror is when we have had it within us from very early on and we are unable to or cannot bear to remember.

Karin understood and noticed the very first time she saw the boy. Once she went so far as to talk to him about his fear.

"We can do no more than die, any of us," she said.

It was a simple truth, but it helped Isak.

To him, Karin and her kitchen and her food, her sorrow and

anger became what there was to live for. Through Karin, he had order and she made life tolerable.

All that spring term, Isak had brooded in her kitchen while his
mother at home was becoming more and more confused and frightened. That Sunday in May when the Norwegians capitulated and
the king and his government left Norway, Isak went out to help
Karin and Simon with the weeding.

He had been to visit his mother in the hospital, and she hadn't
recognized him.

The next day Karin put on her best clothes, the pale blue coat
she had made herself and the big white hat with blue roses on the
brim, and she took the tram to Ruben Lentov's office.

They sat in silence for a long time, looking at each other, and
Ruben thought that if she didn't soon turn her eyes away, he risked
beginning to cry. Then she looked away and gave him time to say
something about the weather before she came out with her message.

"I thought Isak might come and live at our place," she said.
"With Simon and me, for a while."

Ruben Lentov at last returned to the thought he had rejected for
weeks now, that the terror in Isak's eyes was like Olga's and that
things could go very wrong for the boy if nothing was done.

"I'm so grateful," he said.

Nothing much more was said. As he went with her through the
office to the outer door, he thought he had never seen a more beautiful woman. Later in the afternoon, it occurred to him that he must
pay for the boy's expenses. Larsson was a workingman and couldn't
be all that well off.

But there had been no trace of the lower class in Karin Larsson,
and when he phoned her in the afternoon to take up the question of
payment, he could find no words. He was glad about that later,
when he realized that what Karin was offering couldn't be paid for.

So it had to be gifts instead, coffee and preserves, books for Simon and presents for Karin, which he took with him once a week
out to the little house at the mouth of the river by the hollow moun-

tain where the military stored their oil. Like everyone else, he was welcomed into the big kitchen and if he was looking particularly miserable, he was offered a drink.

He didn't like schnapps, but had to admit Karin was right in that it helped against melancholy.

Then it turned out that Isak was able to pay his own way, as he liked physical work, was practical, patient, a friend of the ax, spades, wrenches, and hard toil, and to a great extent, he took over Erik's tasks. That meant contributing a major share in the home, much more than Simon with his bookishness.

"It's as if we'd exchanged boys," Karin said to Ruben Lentov one Sunday, when Erik was home on leave and Ruben had come out to see him.

Erik was thinner, though just as voluble, and in the depths of his Swedish soul, he was disturbed about the state of their defenses.

"We've vehicles but no gas," he said. "On the other hand, we've got ammunition but no guns."

A look from Karin stopped him, and he noticed the anxiety in Ruben's eyes increasing.

That evening Ruben told them what he knew from secret sources about the fate of the Jews in Germany. The boys were sent out of the kitchen, but Simon crept back in for a drink of water, and he would never forget the look in Erik's eyes.

His father was frightened.

And Karin was so very pale as she made up the boys' beds in the parlor that evening. But what scared Simon most was a telephone conversation he happened to overhear.

Erik was calling someone. He was in a hurry, as he had to catch a train back to his unit. It was not his haste that sharpened his voice, however, but the note of something immensely important.

"You must burn the letter. . . . Yes, I know I promised. But I had no idea then that— . . . You must see that if the Germans come, then it concerns his very life."

Simon listened, sitting straight up in bed to hear better, though he had no real need to make that effort, for the telephone was in the hall just outside the parlor and every syllable came quite clearly through the wall.

Questions swirled around in his head. Who was Erik talking to? What letter? Whose life was in danger?

Then he felt a knot in his stomach as he realized he knew the answer to the last question. It was his own life.

Isak was asleep in the bed next to him. That was good, for he wasn't to be upset.

But Simon felt very lonely as he sat there trying to make it all out, without getting anywhere. He heard Erik saying good-bye to Karin, then picking up his pack.

"Bye then, Karin, take care of yourself and the boys."

"Bye, Erik, take care of yourself."

He could see them in front of him as they rather clumsily took hands.

Then, just before the door closed, she asked, "Did you get her to understand?"

"I think so."

Simon was angry, as children are when they don't understand. His anger gave him confusing dreams—meeting Mrs. Ågren, now even more horrible dead than she had been alive, and she chased him along the shore, screaming at him, "Go home and ask your mother."

But he had forgotten the question, dropped it, couldn't find it, and searched in despair as if his life depended on it.

He awoke crying and stayed there in the twilight realm between sleep and waking. He went to the trees, the oaks, and managed in the end to find the land that is but doesn't exist, and met his man, the little man with the peculiar hat and the mysterious smile. They sat together for a while, talking as they had over the years, wordlessly and beyond time.

In the morning, he stood for a long time in front of the kitchen mirror above the cold-water tap, gazing at those alien eyes, his but unlike everyone else's, darker than Karin's, darker even than Ruben's.

But he asked the image no questions.

Nor did he ask Karin.

Daily life took over. In the hassle of making porridge, packing his lunch, gathering his homework and books, the telephone call and the evening before faded away. It lost its contours and seemed to him unreal, a dream.

That day, Simon failed his German test. Isak was worried.

"Do you think Karin'll be miserable?"

Simon looked surprised. School was his responsibility. Karin wouldn't even ask.

"No," he said. "She doesn't bother about school."

Isak nodded with relief, remembering that when Ruben had asked her about Isak's homework, he had heard her say that you should trust your children.

"I could help you with your German. After all, it is my mother tongue."

Simon was so astonished he almost choked over the toffee he had bought to console himself after the test.

Isak didn't go to German lessons. Somehow, Simon had taken that for granted, that he was excused just as he was excused from Scripture lessons because he was Jewish. Now he realized for the first time that Isak had no need to learn German, as he already knew that frightening language with all its harsh commands: *Achtung, Heil, halt, verboten . . .*

Then the kitchen walls, over the years familiar with Hitler bellowing, now heard another German voice, a softly rounded Berlin dialect.

It was strange, and even Karin was surprised how deft the Nazi's language could sound. Simon learned quickly and soon became proficient with the language. He passed the next test and got a good term report on the very day the Germans marched into Paris.

Meningitis had broken out in the district. On the same night that the British shipped 300,000 men in small boats out of Dunkirk, one of Simon's playmates, a girl he had always found difficult, died.

That small death became more real than all the dead of the big war. Simon felt guilty.

Only two weeks earlier, he had called the girl a silly bum in an angry and meaningless squabble. She had been red-haired, and clever like him, the middle child in a big family, where the bricklayer father drank and the mother wept.

"She was caught in the middle. She didn't want to be part of it any longer," Karin said.

But she kept a watchful eye on the boys for the next few days and was very worried one evening when she thought Isak had a temperature.

Simon came to remember very clearly yet another event of that spring. Karin woke one morning remembering a vivid dream, and she told the boys about how she was in a bomb shelter and had seen a crucifix hanging on the wall. As the bombs fell, the figure came alive, raised his arm, and pointed with a palm branch at the roof, which then opened up. Karin saw the sky was blue and endless above the little planes.

"Both the planes and the bombs were toys," she said, then added that the dream had comforted her.

The boys felt strengthened, too, especially when Edit Äppelgren came into the kitchen to fetch some scissors Karin had borrowed, and was given coffee and told the dream. She was a devout Christian, so she knew about Pentecost, which they had just celebrated with the first daffodils on the table. It was a reminder of the outpouring of the Holy Spirit in the human world.

They had just had coffee when they heard the antiaircraft guns up on Käringberget firing. They rushed out just in time to see the German plane with the swastika on it and the German pilot in flames like a torch before he and his machine disappeared into the cool of the great sea.

Simon cried, but Isak was excited, strangely pleased.

Despite everything, it was a good summer for the boys out there on the meadows between the hills where the great river flowed out into the sea. Light summer nights, tents down on the shore, girls to tease, boys to fight with, canoes and sailing dinghies.

Erik came home and told them how in secret they had helped Norwegian Jews across the border.

One Sunday, Erik took the truck to go to see Inga, one of his cousins. She had a small farm several miles north of the city.

Did Simon want to come, too?

No, he disliked Inga. She was fat and slow, smelled of the cow-shed, and never dared look at him.

But Isak said the outing must be important as Erik had used his precious gas ration, and that made Simon uneasy.

Then he forgot all about it. Isak and he stood on ladders around the house and painted it white with paint Ruben had provided. The paint was a present to Erik, and Isak sang as he painted, "Cold is the wind, cold storm from the sea."

Simon hated it when Isak sang, but he had to agree, nothing much seemed to be going to happen that summer of 1940.

FIVE

*T*he sea could just be glimpsed from the bedroom, in the autumn when all the leaves had fallen, but also in the spring, when the sea could be heard breaking itself free of the ice. Facing south, the house was no bigger than a cottage and lay on the slope with the mountains behind it. The view was magnificent, though less magnificent than it had been when there had been able-bodied men to control the undergrowth and keep the view to the sea clear.

A few meadows, some fields, potatoes, no grains any longer, but four cows in the cowshed, two pigs, and twenty or so hens, and inside the cottage, two very old, confused, and feeble people. Of the family in the city, all except Karin avoided thinking about how lonely Inga was.

Like everyone else, Inga had made her way into town in her youth, taken a job in a family, then later in a shop. They had been good years, full of meetings and people, experiences and events. She was good-looking, fair-skinned, and plump in a soft attractive way.

She could probably have found a man as her sisters had, but she had been the eldest of seven children and had seen too much of love and what that could do to a woman.

She was careful.

So when the old people could no longer manage to keep up the farm she was the one who had to go back and was kept there by their terror of the poorhouse, nowadays called the old people's home, but still considered worse than death.

She never even objected and soon gave way to guilt, defenseless against duty and the fourth commandment.

It would have been easier if there had at least been some affection, or a way of talking to her mother. But life had not even given her that. She had been regarded with disfavor since birth as the cause of her parents' having to marry. She arrived too early, barely a month or so after the marriage, and the shame stuck to her all through her growing years.

The first long winters after her return as an adult, her impulse had been to poison the old people and set fire to the farm. She knew where the henbane grew and remembered how Ida, the witch of their childhood in the village, had extracted the poison from the capsules.

Then she realized that these thoughts were making her insane. She knew that you can go mad from thinking, that her thoughts would only lead to the lunatic asylum in Hisingen.

So she decided to stop thinking, and after a few years she had managed that quite well.

When her father went blind, the newspaper was canceled. The family was not given to writing, so only holiday postcards came. And although this was the late 1920s, electricity had still not been brought over the hill to the cottage, so there was no question of a radio.

Her brothers and sisters sent money, but there were long gaps between visits, which was good, for when they did come, especially the brothers, their mother grew more uneasy than ever and that had an effect for days and days afterward.

Her cousin Erik was the one who came most, as he had his truck. And his wife Karin had helped Inga find a job in the bazaar in town and was so kind. Kind and strong at the same time. That had always amazed Inga.

They came because they felt sorry for her, Inga realized that. Karin once said straight out to the old people that Inga had a right to a life of her own and old people nowadays were well cared for in the local old people's home. But then the mother's heart started to pain her and Erik had to go for the doctor, who indeed found nothing wrong, but nonetheless said that you had to be very careful with people who were so old.

Then no more was said on the matter. Inga could see Erik was angry and realized Karin would be reproached for what she had said.

Then came that spring when a fiddler was sitting by the stream.

It couldn't be true, thought Inga afterward. He must have sprung from her dreams. But that evening, he was quite real, and the next, and the next, right up until the light midsummer nights, when he vanished.

It was a fairly modest stream, which had a long way to go through the forests and much trouble making its way through the hills to reach the sea. At the end, it could do nothing but hurtle over the last rocks before the slope down to the shore. For such a small stream, the waterfall was quite an achievement, particularly in the spring when it was both strong and cheerful.

To Inga, the waterfall was a joy. And a liberation.

She looked after the old people, struggled with the potatoes, milked the cows, and kept all the creatures in good condition. But she was not the kind to grow close with animals, to see what was unique in each of them, so her labors did not give her much pleasure.

No, she went from mute animals to mute human beings. Her father had not said a word for many years now, and her mother would occasionally burst into long and increasingly incomprehensible harangues.

She was bad-tempered, had always been, Inga thought.

But she mostly thought about the waterfall to which she would go and wash herself clean after the old people had gone to bed and the animals had been shut in. Long into the autumn, too, she would go there every evening, undress and stand in the waterfall, feeling cleansed and free of troubles.

One evening in the spring, the fiddler was there, simply sitting and looking at her as if she were a creature from some heathen saga.

She wasn't frightened. It was all too unreal. She just went straight up to him, naked as she was, and lay down with her head in his lap. He took out his violin and played for her, and the one was no stranger than the other.

His music was wild and beautiful, just as it should be.

It could be said that it would have been better for Inga if it had been the man from the dairy, who came to fetch the milk every other day in a tanker. But he was ugly and gruff, and married.

Perhaps the fiddler also had a wife, but she never found out, for they couldn't speak to each other. He was a foreigner. Later on, Erik found out that he was Jewish and a music teacher at a college on the other side of the lake. When the term came to an end, he went back to Germany and there was a name and address in Berlin.

But no one ever wrote to him. Inga knew that he had never really been of this world, and she stuck to her Father Unknown.

All that happened much later, though, long into the winter when Inga finally had to admit she was with child and that the man by the waterfall had been of flesh and blood.

They made love, made love half the nights that spring, and Inga at last understood why people were able to give up everything, dignity and prosperity, for the sake of love. She had had no inkling of what her body could experience when caressed like that by experienced hands, nor had she realized how beautiful a man could be. He was slender, finely built, but his member was large and stiff and she could never have enough of it. Nor of his eyes, which were as dark as the forest lake.

He talked, and his voice was full of tenderness. But as she couldn't understand the words, he had to express his feelings to her with his violin, and every evening he played her almost insane with desire.

Afterward she remembered that he was very sad that last evening and that his violin had been full of pain. So she wasn't surprised when he didn't come the next evening.

Only infinitely sad.

But she told herself that she had known all the time that this would happen, that it had been a dream and that people like her sooner or later had to wake up and get on with life.

She was clumsy and ungainly as she lifted the potatoes in the autumn, yet gave no thought to there being a child inside her. Erik and Karin came at the time of the first snow to help her get the sacks of potatoes into the earth-cellar, and Karin immediately saw what the situation was.

"Inga," she said. "You're going to have a child."

"What the hell have you been up to?" said Erik, his voice so shrill it struck Inga like a whiplash.

But Karin intervened, swiftly and harshly.

"Hold your tongue just for once, Erik Larsson," she said.

Then she went with Inga up to the attic bedroom, and slowly and tentatively, Inga began to remember and was able to tell her.

If that great belly hadn't been there, Karin would have thought that Inga had become crazed in her loneliness, and that wouldn't have surprised her. As things were, she had to believe the story of the dark-eyed fiddler by the stream.

"It'll be the death of Mother," Inga wept, and Karin kept quiet, although she thought that would be for the best. Erik and Karin were practical people. Inga, too. And Inga was able to make herself clear. No one was to know of her shame. No one in the village, none of the family, and never, ever, her parents.

Erik talked to the old people and told them Inga had a serious stomach illness, and as things were, she would have to go to a hospital in town. He didn't know how much they had understood.

But the middle sister, Märta, understood all right when Erik appeared in her apartment kitchen in town and said that as her child was big enough to manage on her own, Märta had to go back home and look after the old people while Inga had her operation.

She objected, but in the end gave in; people did give in to Erik. And she believed him when he said Inga would die if she wasn't looked after, so she packed her bags and went back home to the old ones.

But she couldn't stand the loneliness out there in the cottage for more than a few weeks, so in early spring, the parents went to the poorhouse, where just what they had said would happen, happened. Both of them died within the course of a month.

By that stage, the child had been born and had already been adopted by Karin and Erik.

Inga returned to the farm, although she no longer had to, and Karin again undertook to help her find a job in the bazaar.

"She's become antisocial," said Erik. "She no longer dares go back into ordinary life."

Karin nodded, thinking things were probably not that simple.

As Karin stood there with the newborn babe in her arms, the nurse saying that the mother hadn't even wanted to look at the boy, in the depths of her heart she felt she had no right to the child. She hadn't conceived him in bliss and anguish, nor given birth in pain.

She gazed into the boy's eyes and found that the melancholy from the long twilights over the lake was there, but also something else, a great loneliness.

That's from Inga denying him, Karin thought, from nine months of unacknowledged existence. Then Karin thought about Inga's words up in the attic, how she had thought the man with the violin was really a water sprite.

But the man had clearly existed, thought Karin, admitting what she had already seen, that this was a very Jewish child. A stranger's child that was to be hers. Not that she was thinking about difficulties over his difference. She loved the boy. And as she was a practical person, she knew beyond all doubt that her love would move mountains and change the skies if it became necessary to make the child feel secure.

She had powerful and strange thoughts.

Children are of the earth, she thought, with the ancient history of the earth in their cells and the entire wisdom of nature in the circulation of their blood.

She saw that he possessed the truth.

All children do, she thought. For a brief time, the children know. Perhaps every new child is the earth's attempt to give expression to what cannot be understood.

Inga decided on his name. After her parents' funeral, she went straight up to Erik in the churchyard.

"He's to be called Simon," she said.

Karin realized they had no choice but to comply, and as she stood there with the child in her arms, she thought that after all, he had been given a name, the water sprite.

S I X

*K*arin had been an afterthought, the youngest of a batch of six, the others all boys, the youngest already at school when it was clear yet another babe was coming to master tailor Lundström's cottage opposite the railway in the Värmland industrial community.

Her mother wept and cursed her fate and the child growing inside her. She was over forty and had thought she was free. Driving the child out of her was a three-day-long struggle, and she nearly died. As she lay there with the newborn infant at her breast, she still had tears in her eyes.

But this time she was weeping because the child was a girl, another poor thing condemned to slavery and painful births.

All through her childhood, Karin heard how unwanted she had been, and how she had nearly cost her mother her life. It was an oft-repeated story, and she sympathized with her mother.

On the other hand, she never understood the sorrow that had struck deep roots in her heart and grew and branched out with such force that she would never manage to tear it out.

She should really have given up early on, as did other unwanted children afflicted by tuberculosis in that area. But she survived, grew large and strong, and it was all due to her father.

Petter Lundström was over sixty when his daughter was born. He had been married twice and had two batches of children. The first lot had long since grown up, all sons, except one daughter, a little one who had died of consumption at seven.

What was amazing was that this dead little girl was Petter's link with life, with what was alive within him. He had loved her. His sons from his second marriage had also heard a great many stories about how strangely sweet she had been and how exceedingly fond he had been of her.

It had been a great joy to him when this new little girl had been born toward the end of his life. It was as if he imagined that his first daughter had come back to him to be a comfort and light in his increasingly gray life.

He worked from home, and from the very first day, he made the child his own. She lay in a box on the big table in his workshop, and he prattled to her, smiled at her, and sang for her.

People came and went, and in among them Petter sat with the child Karin, his angel child, sweetness of his life, apple of his eye. True, some laughed at him and his boundless love, but this was Värmland, where oddities were accepted. The child was pretty, and neither troubled anyone nor got in the way when people came for fittings.

He knew a hundred songs, a thousand sagas, and even more crazy stories. All this he gave to her, and she floated on a wave of warmth and subtle wisdom, learning early most things about the foolishness and sagacities of people, about how nearly all wished for the good and ended to the bad.

Petter had always been very neat. His workshop was now so clean and tidy, people said you could eat straight off the floor. He got hold of a book from Karlstad and learned everything about what small children need. It contained a great deal about cleanliness, nourishment, and fresh air. Nothing about tenderness and love, and as far as Petter Lundström was concerned, that didn't matter at all.

That was how Karin acquired her strength and insight into how incomprehensible life was and how it could be grasped despite that.

By the time she started school, she had long learned to read and write, so she was put ahead a class, much to Petter's immeasurable pride.

Her mother? Well, she was there, coming and going in the workshop, weighed down by the image of herself as a patient beast of burden, prematurely worn out from too many childbirths and all the hard work of cooking and cleaning. She was the guilt in Petter's life. He would never escape the fact that it was he who had given her all those children and, as she so often said, had sent his first wife to an early grave.

She had died in childbirth.

All he could do was submit to his wife's laments and constant weariness, but that had also come in useful since Karin had been born. The mother couldn't demand the girl back and had to admit that he did what he could to lift this last burden off her shoulders.

He no longer touched his wife in bed, and she dimly realized that there was a connection, that his need for closeness was satisfied as long as he was allowed to be with the child.

The discord grew worse as the girl grew older and the mother thought Karin should help with the household chores. Petter could not deny her the help and loaned out the girl, but only for short spells. She never became domestic and was often clumsy at the stove. Her mother once struck her across the back with the poker.

This event became one that no one in the tailor's house would ever forget, for the kindhearted Petter went straight for his wife with the same poker and struck her, too.

"So you know what it feels like," he said, white with fury.

The mother never forgot, neither the humiliation nor the pain, both of which went deep, and that was not good for the girl, as she turned out to be the one who had to pay for it.

When Karin was nine, Petter died, seated there on his table and falling forward like an open pocketknife.

The child didn't understand. This couldn't have happened. She ran off into the forest and stayed there all night, then woke in the morning under a spruce and remembered. She went deeper into the forest and found a clearing where there was a stream. Slowly she took in what had happened and saw that the stream was too shallow to drown herself in.

In the dawn light, a flock of waxwings appeared on their long journey from the high mountains in the north to the warm southern rivers. They settled around the child, who had never seen these strange shimmering birds before, nor heard their calls, halfway between rejoicing and sorrow.

The girl sat very still, knowing her father had sent her a message, that he was still there around her and always would be.

So she decided she would live after all.

Her mother sold the tailor's business and moved to Göteborg with those children who were still at home, two almost grown sons and this little girl whom she scarcely knew. There she again was able to play the part of the tormented beast of burden. She worked in a factory that took all her strength but provided her with money for the tiny one-room apartment in Majorna and food for her and the children.

Then came the First World War, shortages of food, and people with fading desire to live dying like flies from the Spanish flu. Karin survived thanks to those waxwings. One or two teachers had taken to this unusual and gifted girl, and when Karin was to be confirmed, the priest came to see her mother to say her daughter ought to be allowed to go on to the high school.

A mockery, he could see for himself, as he stood there in the kitchen of this old widow.

"Whims and fancies," she said after the priest had left. "Your silly father made you think you were someone."

When the sons came home, she told them about the crazy priest and they laughed loudly. Spend money on a girl, they'd never heard of anything so stupid. But the quiet one said afterward that if Dad had been alive then . . .

That was when she realized why they hated her.

At thirteen, Karin took a job with a family, at fifteen, she worked in a dressmaking shop, and at sixteen, in a shop in the great bazaar. The waxwings followed her everywhere. When she was eighteen she met Erik, saw that he resembled Petter, became a socialist, and even dared to believe what he said to her, that she was very beautiful.

Erik was the only son in the one-room apartment in the great block in Stigberg. He was his mother's hope and the support of his younger sister. The sister was delicate, one of those forced to live with a punctured lung after the ravages of tuberculosis at the age of six, denied both personality and a life of her own, growing slowly and crookedly in the shadow of her mother.

His mother was strong, handsome, bitter, and very religious. She had married late and hated love with such fury, she frightened her shadowy husband out of the marriage bed as soon as she had given birth to her children.

She acquired an outlet for her desire by beating the boy with the carpet-beater on his bare red backside. His childhood was not easy, but there was a respect for Erik, for his sex, the man in the boy, who had inherited his mother's intelligence and force and was to realize her dreams.

That respect gave him sufficient strength gradually to take a stand against her, against her opinions at least, and her dark Christianity. Much worse was everything that he had acquired so early and that was invisible.

All his life, physical love remained linked with sin, and no one ever helped him understand the strange connection between desire and cruelty in his fantasies, of which he was terribly ashamed.

When his mother no longer ruled him with the carpet-beater, she got him to obey by constantly threatening him with a heart attack.

Her heart grew sick at the same time as he reached puberty.

He should have been allowed to continue his schooling and was one of many of his generation who could have gone far, as they say. But perhaps what happened was best.

As a fifteen-year-old, he started work at the Götaverken factory and came home every evening after a ten-hour workday to evening classes and his books. There, in his books, he found the tools to understand the cruel world he had grown up in and learned how oppression functions against those who are weaker.

Sometimes he even understood his mother.

Just as he understood the dreadful sense of humiliation attached to his shoes. Every Christmas through his childhood he had to accept a new pair from the parish priest, who in his turn had received them from a charitable organization that called itself the Älvsborg Christmas Gnomes.

At sixteen, he told his mother that God didn't exist and that her church was no better than liquor when it came to keeping the working man down.

She clutched at her heart and threatened to die, but that failed to have any effect, as the boy was already out the door on his way to his next meeting. His mother, mortally afraid that her son would desert her, pushed the girls he fell in love with out of his life.

When he met Karin, he was nearly thirty and realized as soon as he looked into those gentle brown eyes that this was serious. His longing was so great and his fear so immense that he prayed to heaven.

Dear Lord, help me with Mother.

But he had been mistaken about those gentle eyes and soon found that behind Karin's meekness was a strength that easily matched his mother's. On her very first visit to his home, she said straight out what the situation was.

"Erik and I are getting married."

"You'll be the death of me," said the old woman, turning so pale as if about to put the threat into action there and then at the kitchen table. But Karin laughed straight into her face and said that was the point of life, that the old were to die and leave room for the young on this earth.

Then she left and took Erik with her. The mother survived and remained a great affliction to Erik and Karin for a great many years.

Erik never realized just what a fate Karin had saved him from. But he did realize that evening that his woman was as strong as his mother, and, frightened, he brushed aside the thought that he had escaped from one female trap only to fall into another. The challenge now was to maintain his manhood so as not to become a shadow like his father.

They married that spring, the two mothers both weeping, Karin's mother because her daughter was now moving into the inevitable fate of constant pregnancies and awful births.

So they set up house and were childless. He made their furniture himself, armchairs, sideboard, dining table, and linen cupboard. She sewed.

The home they made was both different and beautiful.

But they remained childless, much to the delight of their mothers-in-law.

At a birthday gathering, his mother openly mocked Karin, and for once Erik resorted to his great rage against the old woman and told her their childlessness could be blamed on him. He had had a shameful disease, the kind you get when you have to go to whores because you are not allowed to have a girl of your own. Couldn't she see it was basically her fault, his mother's?

As they went home that evening, Karin took Erik's hand in hers and said that as his mother hadn't died on the spot that evening, she would certainly live to be a hundred.

She lived until she was ninety-six.

Karin never dared ask whether there was any truth in the story Erik had told. He'd been magnificent. That was like him, a man to be trusted. Not like Petter, she now realized, much less secure, more pugnacious and vulnerable. But that was good. Petter still lived his life in her heart and no one could threaten him there.

So they received their son, and what did it matter that this longed-for child was not of their own blood.

Erik was as proud as a king: He drew out his savings and bought a plot of land at the river mouth, where the child would have fresh air and open space.

He built his house with his own hands. It became an amusing house, its structure shaped by the scraps of material he could acquire cheaply as he drove his truck around town. He knew all the builders, and returned home with slatted windows and fancy carpentry, handsome tiled stoves from patrician houses being modernized in the Allé, and beautifully made old doors from some manor house being rebuilt in Landvetter.

It became a delightful house, full of surprises and warmth, and they were never happier than they were that summer. They trudged around in the mud outside and slept the hot nights in a great crate Erik had found in the harbor, which was no more reliable than a tent.

Their mothers-in-law didn't know where the child had come from and moaned about bad blood and poor heritage, but Erik frightened them into silence. Karin and he believed in the socialist idea of the importance of the environment to human development.

Sometimes Erik felt a twinge when he looked into the dark eyes of the infant, but he pushed aside the fear and made the boy his own, and soon no longer saw the darkness in those eyes or the rough hair. Simon was his, therefore first class in every respect.

Erik had a good and loud singing voice, trained early in church and later in the labor movement. As he couldn't bring himself to prattle to the child, as Karin constantly did, he used to sing the *Red Flag* so that it rolled around the hills, and he almost burst with pride when the boy gurgled with delight. When he ran out of campaign songs, Erik hummed the old hymns, without the words, of course. There was no mistaking the boy's delight, and even Karin saw it and was surprised.

Karin nearly always had the child in her arms, but in the spring when the garden began to take shape, she had to sow and plant, so Erik made a cradle and hung it up in the big pear tree that had been there long before they had arrived. The boy slept there and woke to the hum of bees and the rustle of leaves, white blossoms falling like snowflakes onto his bed.

SEVEN

*T*he sea was always present in Simon's childhood, flavoring the air with salt, filling the air with its song from its wide expanses, and coloring all light between the houses and hills.

Gray days became impenetrably gray. Blue days became bluer than the sky, days when the sea became a mirror for the great sky, multiplying the light and reflecting it back over the land.

The child took this light with him all through his life. It penetrated his skin, through flesh and bone and into his soul, where his longing was born.

A blue yearning for freedom and infinity.

Wherever his yearning sought for a fixed point in reality, he was drawn to the huge ships making their way past Oljeberget and on to the great harbors. Nearly all of Simon's childhood friends went to sea, despite the war, many of them before he was even halfway through high school.

They signed on the neutral ships with their yellow and blue flags painted on their plating. Some of the boys never returned, vanishing into the depths with their ships and their longing for freedom.

Others came home with something hard to fathom in their eyes, and in Karin's kitchen their mothers talked of the nightmares their sons had at night.

Simon and Isak were also attracted to the ships in the great harbor, where life had largely fallen silent, wasting away from lack of nourishment. Sweden was blockaded.

So were the quays, guarded by the police.

The harbor had never contained so many ships as now, so many giants shackled to buoys and anchors, condemned to silence and inactivity. Despite the closed quays, they couldn't be hidden and the boys soon found that the best way to see them at close quarters was to take the ferries across the river.

They started at Sänkverket and went back and forth. Then they found their way to Fiskhamnen, took the ferry to Sannegården, and stood on deck gazing at the huge sides of the ships looming like ghostly mountains.

Many of them were Norwegian merchant ships, some brand new. They had sailed straight from the Swedish shipyards to their anchorages, having never even completed a job.

Others had sailed the oceans of the world and, worn out, had been approaching their home country the spring the Nazis raped Norway. In despair, the ships had altered course and headed for their still-free neighboring country. There they remained, lying silent, unemployed, impounded.

But early that spring rumors flew around town that the Norwegian ships were being loaded with ball bearings and arms, preparing for departure, and that explosives were being brought on board so the ships could sink themselves if necessary.

On the night of March 31, the city by the river held its breath while ten Norwegian ships slipped past the fortress and out toward Rivöfjorden. It was foggy, but that was no help to them. On board were hundreds of men who never saw the dawn, for the German naval forces were sitting waiting out by Måseskär.

Three of the ships were sunk by their own crews according to the suicide plan, three went to the bottom after being hit by German torpedoes, and two managed to turn and make their way back to safe harbor in Sweden.

Only two of the ten ships broke through and reached England, a small tanker, and then the swift sixteen-thousand-ton *B. P. Newton*, which on the third of April entered a harbor in Scotland, escorted by the HMS *Valorous*.

It was a grim day for all sea-minded people in town, and one of the blackest days of the war.

There were whispers of treachery.

Simon sat through lessons at school, but like the others, he was not really listening. The teachers were equally despairing, but no one spoke of what had happened. The hours crept by and the rituals were observed as long as was possible. Open your books to page ninety-eight.

Toward the end of the day, the weight inside Simon detached itself and he was the first to slump over his desk and weep. They were having a Swedish lesson and their woman teacher also broke down and wept silently at her desk.

No one said a word.

Then the bell rang and the boys slowly got up and slowly and silently dispersed, sniveling and blank-eyed.

When they got out into the corridor and put on their jackets, Simon noticed that Isak hadn't wept and there was something in his eyes, an expression he found difficult to grasp.

They should have gone to the library, but Simon saw they had to get home as quickly as possible, to Karin and her kitchen. As they crossed the school yard on their way to the bike shed, Isak walked like a mechanical doll, and Simon realized that they should take the tram that day.

Isak followed him like a dog, but all the way, his eyes never met Simon's, as if he didn't recognize his friend. When they came to their stop, Isak couldn't find his way, and Simon was so frightened he felt a knot in his stomach.

He wanted to run, but he took Isak by the arm and they walked up- and downhill, along the route Aron Äppelgren had taught Simon to love.

They arrived home and Karin was there. She at once saw what was wrong and the cramp left Simon's stomach, although he heard Karin's voice sliding and saw a flickering darkness in her brown eyes as she spoke.

"Outside with you."

He flew out of the door and ran to the oaks, to the land where everything was simple.

Gently and cautiously, as if there were a risk of him bleeding to death, Karin took off Isak's jersey and shoes. Then she sat down in the rocking chair with the big boy on her lap, rocking slowly and stroking his head as she prattled.

He grew a little warmer, but his rigidity remained and it was obvious that he didn't recognize her.

She sang an old nursery rhyme . . . and though he grew a little less rigid, when she tried to meet his gaze it was clear that Isak Lentov no longer knew where he was.

I ought to phone Ruben, she thought, but every attempt to get up and loosen the boy's grip increased the terror in him. So things had to remain as they were until Helen came with the milk and Karin could give her the number and whisper, "For God's sake, hurry."

Ruben Lentov managed to find a taxi, but his arrival changed nothing. Isak did not even recognize his own father.

When Isak was four, his mother loved him the way one loves something that gives meaning and dignity to an anguished life. This love forced him constantly to respond to her needs and prevented him from feeling his own emotions, the emotions he would need to evaluate and understand.

Isak became a good boy, a quiet child.

But he sometimes had incomprehensible outbursts of rage, and then he ran screaming around the large Berlin apartment.

His father was in a faraway country, his mother said, and she spoke with a longing that all through his life would color the boy's image of Sweden. But he had a grandfather, Ruben's father, and he was God, the boy had understood that much, for Grandfather had a voice that thundered like the Lord's. On Saturdays, when he walked to the synagogue holding the little boy by the hand, he was clad in majesty and dignity. Just like Job's Lord.

And he punished just as God did, and his blows fell heavily on the righteous and unrighteous, and the boy never even tried to understand, for he had learned at the synagogue that the counsels of the Lord are incomprehensible.

The boy never remembered those moments when he raced

around the apartment screaming, tormenting his mother. She would then appeal to the Lord, who in turn with heavy heart and a hard hand would punish the child.

But one sunny spring afternoon in Berlin when he was between four and five, he had hurt his mother again with his screams and was sitting under the dining room table with its thick cloth embroidered in red and gold, and its faint smell of wax polish and stale wine. On that particular day as he was listening to his mother crying in her room, and waiting for the Lord, who was to come and beat him, he experienced an emotion.

In it was a rage of the same kind he had when he ran around screaming. But now he was aware of his anger and that gave him hope, because he could think clearly, and he thought he would run away and go to his father in that distant country.

He would find his way there. He knew the address.

He took off his shoes and crept out into the hall, then stood there for a moment looking at the coat stand, thinking that perhaps he would need an overcoat on the long walk to this new country where it was said to be so cold.

But he couldn't reach it.

He managed to open the door and close it behind him without making a sound. Then he made his way down the stairs and out onto the street, where the sun was shining and people's faces lit up at the sound of military music and the regular tramp of the Hitler Youth boots.

He would forget how they caught him, those tall men in brown shirts and swastika armbands. But he remembered their nostrils quivering with delight and how they laughed as they sat him up on the counter in the nearest beer hall and pulled his trousers off to see if he had been circumcised, to see whether he was a little Jewish swine, sent their way by friendly forces on this sunny open day, so full of hope for all those who had seen the birth of the Third Reich.

They pulled his little member until it turned blue, and the boy sank into the dark of unconsciousness in the middle of it all, which took some of the fun out of it for them. Nevertheless, they did not stop until blood spurted and the barmaid intervened, picking up the child and putting him down behind the bar counter.

She was tall and blond like Karin. She had recognized the child, and in the evening, once the cheerful marching had ceased, she took him back to the Lentov apartment.

When the boy came to his senses, he realized that his grandfather was not God, for he was weeping with terror and despair. The doctor, himself a Jew, came with bandages and medicine, and was so frightened the syringe trembled in his hand.

While the boy slept his drugged sleep, they sat there, his grandfather and his mother, hating each other in their mutual but silent attempts to put the blame elsewhere.

It's you, you damned stupid goose, with your tears and your behavior. You made me beat him.

It was you, you old devil, frightening the life out of him.

But they said nothing, and the old grandmother crept around with wine and consolation, searching for whatever she could find in the fourth commandment.

"Children forget so easily," she said.

Gradually they got through the shock and hatred, and became allies in an agreement: Ruben Lentov was never to know what had happened to his son.

As they each went off to their rooms to try to sleep, they must have been slightly uneasy that the boy himself might tell. They could have saved themselves the worry, for when the boy awoke he was mute.

He neither spoke nor cried, perhaps only a little whimper when the doctor came to rebandage his injury.

"He's in shock," said the doctor.

He was still in shock a month later, when Ruben Lentov came to see them and, full of rage, demanded to know what had happened. The two conspirators stuck to their agreement, but they hadn't reckoned on the doctor, who was still coming and going, increasingly worried about the state of the boy.

For many years afterward, Ruben Lentov made an effort to

forget his horror and guilt that night after his conversation with the doctor. He never even thought to ask why the boy had run away. In this drama there was only one guilty person, and that was him.

When the day dawned, with all the strength of despair, he set out to do what he should have done long ago. He wore out the stony streets and waiting-room chairs of Berlin, was insulted and humiliated, but prevailed because of his Swedish credentials.

Then he stood there one day in the boy's room with all those stamped documents and lifted up the child.

"You're coming with me to the new country now."

The strength in his father's voice and the warmth of his arms were forceful enough to penetrate the boy's paralysis, and Isak revived and at last was able to think. He concluded that he had succeeded after all, that running away had led him to his goal.

He wept quietly all that day, refusing to let Ruben go. In the evening he began to speak, but only to his father, screaming loudly from the darkness within him as soon as his mother appeared in his room. Ruben finally understood and realized his burdensome duty in the future would be to protect the child from his mother.

The next morning, as they stood with their suitcases in the hall of their old home in Berlin, Ruben told his parents that he hoped they would soon follow him. But he felt an immense and guilty relief when his father said that they would stay in the Germany they loved, that this Nazi business would soon be over. The boy didn't even look at his grandfather, had already obliterated him from his mind.

The elder Lentovs' other son made his way to Denmark and the only daughter went to America with her husband and children. The old people stayed, as they had decided, and in the very spring the sequestered ships were sunk and Isak fell ill, they had likely gone to their deaths in one of the huge camps in the east.

Ruben sat on the train, listening to the thump of wheels over the joints and looking at his wife, even daring to think it would have been better if she had stayed behind in Berlin. The cousin, an eleven-year-old girl he had promised to look after, was sitting beside her, and despite all her self-absorption, she was nevertheless good with the little boy.

They were lucky with the weather, and after changing trains at Hälsingborg, the early summer countryside opened out before the boy's eyes, light and beautiful.

In his new home, a maple was flowering outside the window of the boy's room, and the child would stand there for hours, practically inside the great crown of the tree, listening to the buzz of bees and smelling the scent of honey from the thousands of pale green flowers.

This distant country smelled good.

But the best of all was that they spoke another language.

There was a large girl named Ulla in the bookshop. She had been to a high school for girls and could speak German, so was too grand to be a nursemaid, but when Ruben saw how fond she was of the boy, he increased her wages and hired her as a governess.

She was the kind who loved songs, poems, and fairy tales. For three years, she devoted herself to the boy and was soon singing both Bellmann and Taube. Isak loved the new language with such passion that he had to make it his own at furious speed. After only a few months, he had a larger vocabulary and was more voluble than he had ever been in German.

Ruben was astonished and pleased, for the boy was not as slow as his mother and grandfather had feared, though he realized that this was not just a matter of words for the boy. Through the language, Isak had found the way to his own emotions and had been given a history and coherence.

The boy never spoke Swedish to his mother.

EIGHT

*F*inally, Isak fell asleep in Karin's arms in the rocking chair. Simon and Ruben put Isak into Erik's bed. Ruben slept as best he could in the kitchen on Simon's old kitchen sofa, but it was not his discomfort that kept him awake all night.

Karin lay beside Isak with his hand in hers. He slept so soundly, he didn't even wake when Simon went to school the next morning, or when Ruben went back into town to see to what was most urgent at the office. He was to be back about twelve, and Karin whispered what food he was to buy and other practical details. He nodded from the kitchen door and said that if Isak ended up like his mother . . .

Then Karin forgot to whisper and said that Isak was not going to any madhouse as long as she, Karin, had any say in the matter.

"I'm strong, Ruben," she said. "Go on, now."

But at heart, she was much more frightened than she cared to admit.

Then, quite undramatically, Isak woke up, looked at Karin, and recognized her. But he was frightened, gazing around the room as if expecting to find someone else there.

"Who are you looking for, Isak?"

"Grandfather," said Isak, just as surprised as she was, almost smiling at his own foolishness.

"Why are you afraid of your grandfather?"

"He used to beat me when I had been away like this and couldn't remember."

Fragile, oh how fragile was the ice Karin had to walk on; don't be afraid, don't hesitate for too long, or think too much. Just calmly take the next step and have trust.

"What happened yesterday?"

"During the lunch hour, we cycled to, you know, the railway station in Olskroken and looked at them."

His eyes widened and the terror took hold of him. Karin's mind worked quickly and clearly, for she knew what the boy had seen, the German trains rolling through Sweden. At Olskroken they stopped for a rest, to stretch their legs.

"It hurts," cried Isak, his hand over his crotch.

"You probably need to go," said Karin, at once knowing she had put a foot wrong.

But he accepted her diversion and disappeared out to the privy in the backyard. When he came back, she had cocoa and a honey sandwich ready for him. She knew he liked that, but his eyes were flickering and she was worried that he was about to glide away from her again.

"What happened next, Isak? After you'd been to Olskroken?"

"I don't remember."

The ice was brittle, but her voice was warm and safe.

"Of course you remember, Isak."

"We got to school and there they told us . . ."

"Told you what? Isak!"

"I don't remember. Bloody hell, I don't remember."

"Yes you do, Isak. They told you about the ships."

"Yes," he shouted. "But shut up now, for God's sake."

But Karin wouldn't let him go. The ice was safer now, and held.

"About the ships trying to break out and the Germans waiting for them."

He threw himself backward on the sofa, clutching at his crotch and crying out.

"It hurts. Help me, Karin, help!"

"Does your member hurt?" asked Karin.

"Yes, yes."

"What happened to you, Isak?"

"I don't remember."

"But you can see in front of you, Isak. Open your eyes—look."

That was when the boy realized that he had to go down into it. He had to see and experience it yet again. He clung to her, changed languages, cried out in German, the words pouring out of him, and the tears and the terror.

It was just as well Karin could not understand it all, because if she had been able to see the event that morning being relived in her kitchen, her terrible wrath would have run away with both her and the boy. As it was, she understood most of it yet managed to keep calm, with deliberately careful steps on thin ice and clear cold reason.

When Ruben came back, most of it was over. Isak and Karin were sitting on the kitchen sofa holding hands, both of them crying, their tears full of misery, yet cleansing at the same time.

Without much ado, Karin told Ruben what Isak had told her. She asked about what she hadn't understood, and Ruben, scarlet with shame when not pale with guilt, filled her in. Isak's gaze went from one to the other, and there were words for everything and everything could be told.

It was all a great relief, especially when Karin said that the Nazis were indeed swine, but she reckoned both his mother and his grandfather were simply damned monsters.

Later that evening Isak went with Simon to the oak trees, and Simon told him how the trees had spoken to him when he was small.

Isak understood and thought it a pity Simon had forced them into silence.

"Oh," said Simon. "Trees can't talk. It's just something you get in your head when you're a child."

But Isak said he knew trees could speak and that the maple outside his window had had a lot to say to him the spring he had come to Sweden.

"What?" said Simon eagerly.

"I suppose it was about nothing being really harmful," said Isak, and Simon knew that something important had been given words.

*   *   *

Karin knew she needed some air, so she went with Ruben to the tram. She could also see he needed comforting, but her energy seemed to have run out.

"Did you know his grandfather beat him?"

"I should have realized."

"What makes me most angry is your wife," Karin said. "What kind of mother tells on her own child and then looks on while he is abused?"

"I had a mother like that myself," said Ruben.

Then Karin was ashamed, but he didn't notice, for suddenly in the March twilight on the road, he saw his mother through Karin's eyes and knew that he hated her.

Then he thought about the extermination camps.

It was a long and difficult spring for Isak. He stayed away from school all that spring term because that was what Karin wanted. Most of all he wanted to sleep, and every time Karin made him wake up, he wept. Sometimes he thought the grief in him had no end.

He had no energy and no desire to live any longer.

Nothing really changed until Erik came home and the two of them, Erik and Isak, started building a boat.

NINE

*T*hey built the boat out in Norden.

Isak helped, and the frame was stretched under the great tarpaulin Erik had erected over a skeleton of demolition timber.

She was to be carvel-built, with mahogany cabin tables, the finest double-ender in the river mouth. How Erik had acquired the mahogany in the blockade year of 1942 only he and God knew. But one day it was off-loaded into the backyard between the house and the hillside and lovingly covered.

Erik had returned from military service and, like so many others, was unemployed. Yet Erik was pleased.

"We'll be all right, you'll see," he said. "Now those bastards have got their hands full and old Sweden will be a hard nut to crack."

He was a Swedish tiger, so of course he would believe that, but it turned out that order, people, weapons, and a damned good will to fight existed along the borders of the country nowadays.

The Larssons held a party in their garden that early summer night, and friends and neighbors raised their glasses to drink to Hitler's death, the courage of the Russians, and the American Flying Fortresses.

Ruben Lentov drank deeply, strengthened and comforted. The year before, he had realized that Erik had political sense. Erik had only been on a short leave that midsummer, but had rung the bell one evening to Ruben's apartment and stood there in the hall.

"I thought I'd look in and tell you that things are turning now, the whole damned war's turning."

Ruben had been more pleased by the visit than the news. He

had taken out a treasured bottle of French brandy and tried to keep his voice steady.

"What in the name of God makes you believe that?"

There was little hope at the time, only that the British had curbed Hitler in the Battle of Britain.

"England's never lost a war," said Erik. "And it looks as if something's going to happen soon in the east."

Ruben couldn't remember how much of the brandy they had managed to consume by the time they switched on the news. But he remembered staggering slightly in the middle of the library floor and the excited radio voice announcing Operation Barbarossa, Hitler's surprise attack on Russia that broke their nonaggression pact and ended their alliance. He would never forget Erik's yell of delight that the Russians would now be fighting on the proper side and how he had almost hugged the breath out of Ruben.

"You've got a cruel, just, old god, haven't you! Pray now, Ruben Lentov, for a hellish winter of snowstorms and temperatures of forty below."

Then they had laughed like madmen and finished off the brandy while talking about Napoléon and King Karl XII and how their campaigns were defeated by the harsh Russian winters.

As the ice piled up around the coasts that winter and the two men met, they joked about it. When Erik read in the paper that the icebreakers in the Baltic had had to work hard right into June, he said to Ruben, "See, what a bastard you are for getting your prayers answered!"

For a while the building of the boat had been a sensitive issue. Ruben had commissioned the boat to give his son new courage. He drew up a comprehensive contract, which included a decent wage for Erik. But when he brought the papers, silent ghosts started moving through the Larsson kitchen. Or perhaps they were the Älvsborg Christmas Gnomes, the charity that, out of its unfathomable goodness of heart, had presented Erik with a pair of shoes each year all through his childhood.

"Go to hell, and take your money with you," Erik said. Ruben bowed his head from the blow, just as his people had done throughout the ages.

But then his submissiveness turned to anger and he said he had earned the money honestly and it was clean, even if it had come from the pockets of a Jew.

"You must be damned crazy," said Erik. "This has nothing to do with Jews."

But he was deeply ashamed and, afraid Karin would come, hurriedly suggested they should go fishing.

They took the dinghy, set sail, and anchored in Rivöfjorden, where they fished for mackerel and drank home-brewed brandy. That was when Ruben learned about the Älvsborg Christmas Gnomes and Erik's dream of a boatyard of his own.

"Times might be good after the war," Erik said.

During the following week, they formed a company at Ruben Lentov's lawyer's office, laying the foundation for activities that were gradually to make Erik a respected employer and other things not associated with a man of his kind.

But this summer the keel was laid for the first double-ender. Simon got left out, preferring to pore over his books rather than work on the boat. He hated Isak for the collaboration between him and Erik, and he hated himself for hating it, for things were terrible for Isak, and they should all be pleased about his interest in the boatbuilding and his friendship with Erik.

As Karin put it.

Nor did she take much interest in Simon that summer. He was just her own secure boy. Things had always been good for him. Her thoughts were on Isak, constantly looking for signs of him again sliding away into no-man's-land. And Isak, whose mother had never really known him, basked in Karin's concern.

But she did notice Simon when she found he had shot up and was outgrowing all of his clothes. She made some trousers for him out of an old pair of Isak's, not noticing the rage in Simon's eyes as she made him try them on.

He ran to the oaks and cried like a child, but then went down to the sea and murdered Isak in his mind. He was not all that successful at that, either, as it gave him no relief and the little man of his childhood had long since disappeared. He considered running away, which gave him some pleasure, thinking about how miserable Karin would be, and how she would have regrets and wring her hands in despair and cry out that she had driven her son to his death.

For they would find him, killed by his own hand.

There was only one snag in the plan, and that was that Simon didn't want to die. Once he realized that, he was ashamed, for Isak had had a bad time, and Karin was an angel. Ruben had said so, and Simon had always known it.

He went home with his tail between his legs and was pleased Karin no longer noticed him, for if she had seen his black thoughts, he would die.

He was sure of that.

That night he dreamed about the forest and a far-flung lake. He recognized it all, knew he had been there and that the melancholy in what he saw would become wild anguish. He existed, but no one noticed him. He cried out, wept, kicked, all in his need for someone to notice him. He was in a cave. With furious determination, he found the way out, narrow though it was, his whole body in pain as he forced his way through, but the person who had to notice him to enable him to live wasn't there, and his rage ebbed into a huge weariness, and he died. Then someone saw him, and it was Karin, and her eyes were brown, like loyalty, and full of love, but his misery over the one who had not noticed him remained and would follow him all his life.

Then it was morning and no one noticed that Simon was strangely pale as they sat over breakfast. As usual, Erik and Isak were occupied with paper and pens among the coffee cups and porridge plates, making new sketches of how to solve this or that detail inside the cabin. Karin was worrying about food for dinner. She had used up all her meat coupons, last's year's potatoes were poor, and her imagination was exhausted.

But she noticed Simon wasn't eating much.

"Finish up your porridge, boy," she said. "You need it, growing so fast as you are."

Simon looked at his mother and hated her.

Then he was saved by his cousins coming to the Larssons' kitchen to ask Simon to go fishing with them. It was a gray day, the clouds low and heavy with rain, so Karin made him put on his oilskin and boots. Then he was free, escaping from both her and the boatbuilders and their constant nagging at him to at least come with them to fetch and carry.

For once, they had land wind and headed for a while toward Danska Liljan, found lee behind Böttö Island, and dropped the grapnel. Simon usually didn't enjoy fishing, but today the long wait in the dinghy suited him.

He was frightened by his hateful thoughts about Karin at breakfast, so, as he stared at the line on the surface of the water, he told himself he hadn't meant it. He had meant Mrs. Ågren, and Isak's bloody mother, and Mrs. Jönsson at the grocer's who had once caught him stealing sweets, and crazy Mrs. Äppelgren, who did nothing but housework and had once accused him of stealing apples from her garden.

That bitch, he thought, remembering that the apples had tasted sweet and forbidden.

Then he thought about Aunt Inga and felt he hated her most of all, although she had never done anything to him. He could see her fat face in front of him, her eyes always evading his.

A slut, he mumbled to himself, and was surprised how fierce was his loathing at the thought of her, over there on that filthy farm. But then he remembered the long lake there and heard the sighing in the trees, and the next moment his heart beat faster and he knew he was touching on something very dangerous.

They had a bite and the pull was so strong he almost fell off the thwart, but he hauled in hard, as one had to for cod, and it was a giant of at least five kilos. The line only just held, but the boys got the whopper over the railing and jubilantly killed it.

The sun came out as they were on their way home and a friendly wind blew up, drying the sail and coming from the right direction, from the sea. They were able to sail free and quickly all the way in, and Simon looked with gratitude at the cod that had revived him and given him a good day. Karin would be pleased and he would be welcomed in the manner due a man who brought food home in bad times.

It turned out just like that. Karin hugged both the cod and the boy, overcame her caution and dug up some new potatoes, although that was straight wicked, for they were still very small and could have grown twice as big if she had waited a month or so.

They phoned Ruben and told him that thanks to Simon, there would be a party in the kitchen, and could he come, and had he a dab of butter they could melt? He came, bringing with him both butter and a bottle of wine.

He also had news for Isak. He was to start extra lessons the next week to make up for what he had missed when he had been ill during the spring term. Ruben had already spoken to the teacher. Isak was to go for lessons three hours a day for the rest of the summer.

Erik look surprised, but said nothing. Karin was silent, too, though she thought it unnecessary—what was important now was that Isak was enjoying himself.

Isak himself went scarlet with anger, but didn't dare say anything. Only Simon was pleased.

But then Erik said that Simon would have to help with the boat the hours Isak was away, and Simon knew what would happen. He was all thumbs, as Erik used to say.

TEN

*R*uben Lentov went to concerts and occasionally tried to get the Larssons to come with him, but Erik had looked embarrassed and Karin said that was probably not for the likes of them.

"To me it's a way of surviving," said Ruben.

"Well, everyone has some way of doing that," said Karin, and Ruben hadn't the courage to ask her what hers was. But he knew her so well now, he could see her sorrow, that sorrow that was perpetually there.

One Saturday evening he had to leave early from the Larssons' and the boatbuilding because Berlioz's *Symphonie fantastique* was being performed. He took Simon with him.

No one thought much about how it had happened. Perhaps Ruben sensed Simon's loneliness and wanted to comfort him. Perhaps Simon accepted just to challenge Karin. Or because he was flattered. Perhaps it was all just chance.

Or perhaps destiny moved the determining piece in the game of Simon Larsson's life.

At first it was unpleasant. The great concert hall, the grand people with their dignified expressions, and the solemn men on the platform scraping away on their instruments and looking like magpies—it all gave him such a sense of alienation. If he'd dared, Simon would have fled.

But then one of the black-and-white figures raised a baton.

And Simon heard . . .

. . . the grass singing in another country and in another epoch, when the world was still young and full of hope. The sky was rent asunder by

the wild cries of birds, endless like the grass, and each bird in all that blue had its individual character, just like the grass on the ground.

Life encompassed everything. The wind moved over the plain and touched it all, challenging fiercely sometimes, gentle and tender the next moment.

But there was also pain and a great yearning, an impatience and a dream. And a man who carried all this within him. He sat by the great river and gazed at the shores as if he could never have enough of their beauty and gentle footholds.

He had two mothers. Ke Ba, the priestess of the goddess Gatumdu, had given birth to him in secret. She was still beautiful and her reputation among the people was great.

But Lia, who had brought him up, he knew nothing of anymore, for she had disappeared among the people, into the gray faceless multitude. They both loved him, as mothers do, and perhaps, after all, their love was what he lived off of.

Others came, people with increasing expectations of him, and he received their ideas and knew that it was his destiny to give shape to their dreams. His agony increased almost to madness, for like the river, his disposition was gentle and he had no desire for violence. But then the wind grew into a storm and drove him to the decision.

The storm had drawn swords, coming from the mountains in the east, intoxicated by death, by the joy of killing, and blood washed over the fields.

When the storm had moved on across the plain, the survivors flocked around the man and put all their expectations into his hands. He spoke to them of a god whose temple had been destroyed and whose name could no longer be mentioned. But the most amazing thing was the language he spoke, an ancient language that had slept for centuries.

He intended to restore them both—the weighty language that had belonged to these people for thousands of years, but had been trampled on and forbidden, and the old god, exiled from the people's hearts.

As he stood there on the shore and spoke, he felt that the old language was also the language of the river and the grass, the language of peasants and peace, heavy with earth and toil. He looked across the plain, saw the canals patterning the landscape with their silver threads and carrying the water out over the fields. Like the language, they were under the foreign domination of the Akkadians.

Although it was forbidden, he sang the old hymns to the people, songs of the sanctity of the earth and the love of the water, of the river that gave life to the earth, the great mother.

The old men and women standing there still knew the words, and they fell in with the singing. The young, hoping they had gained the right to their mother tongue, sensed that the language had the power to go past the head and touch the heart.

Their joy rose to the sky, occasionally sounding like a dance, a game from vanished times when everything was simple and people's hearts were wide open to the earth, given color and strength by the endless sea of grass and the yellow waters of the gentle river.

He resurrected long-since-forgotten images, the man who was speaking and singing by the river. His beautiful words aroused a sorrow so great it had had to be denied for hundreds of years. The wrath, that mindless rage, had slumbered during the sorrow, and now awoke.

"Death to Akkad," the people cried.

Then he wandered away alone, and his fear was great, but greater was his grief, for he knew the price of this action of his. He prayed to the forbidden god up there in the blue sky to be released from the assignment, and the god answered him with birdsong full of freedom. The man realized that he could reject great actions and live a small life of restraint and peace.

When dusk fell, he was still down by the river, resting under the great tree in whose branches the birds were settling for the night. He spoke to the birds of his great doubts. But all the birdsong could tell him was that life was good as it was and people's actions were madness. The tree spoke to him about the wordless joint creation beyond good and evil. That gave him strength and he took it to mean that he must go beyond the border guarded by guilt and shame.

But the river sang through the night about a change, a movement independent of man.

You are nothing but a guest of reality, so you do not see it. You see nothing but the named parts, never the connection from which grows the whole.

That was the river's message, and the man was irresolute. But when dawn came with the first glint of sun on the river and the first birdcall from the sky, he had made up his mind. Defiantly, he replied to them all, the trees, the river, and the birds, that he was a human being and had to go the way of human beings, which is the way of action and the mind.

The new war was as grim as the first. The waters of the river turned red with the blood of the many who lost their lives for his sake, because his great idea that simply desired rebirth also sowed hatred and harvested death.

On the day of victory, he laid the foundation stone of the temple while his tired soldiers returned home. Their footsteps were as heavy as death's, and the grass died wherever they trod.

He saw it, but banished the sight from his memory. He had overcome the straitjacket of subjugation and stood alone beside the god whose honor he had restored and whose temple would be the largest in the world. It rose in its stunning beauty up to the sky, containing fifty lesser temples, one for every one of the sons and daughters of the great god. Hall after hall was clad in gold that gave luster to the hymns and the old language. So great was his victory, so vast, that all that was unobtrusive and providential was obliterated. The walls of the temple were so massive that the wind dashed itself to oblivion against the stones; the walls so well made, no bird could find foothold there.

The drums thundered their weighty rhythms over the town in the evenings, carrying the news of peace to the people at last speaking their own language, but they could find no peace in their hearts because of the many dead, the divisions and the fratricides, the treacheries and betrayals that also followed in the tracks of the war of liberation.

The people did not know the art of rejecting memories. In every home, shame stamped on the threshold and guilt stood watching over their beds at night. The days were not much easier to bear, for then sorrow wept in the wind and everyone heard it except the man in the huge temple, the man who had killed his memory.

In town it was whispered that the divine king could not sleep, that he bore their guilt in endless walking around the walls of the new temple. And it was true that he walked there night after night, in constant combat with the questions of what stood between him and the god whose realm he had restored to earth.

He received no answer and he trembled at the unheard-of thought that God was dead.

But his astrologers were full of hope for the new kingdom and songs were written in his honor. And the people's sorrow was subdued by great ceremonies, spectacles of unimaginable magnificence.

In burdened moments, he considered returning to the river, to the trees and the birds, but he had come so far from the truth now, he thought they would no longer listen to him.

And that he could not endure.

Then finally his last sacrifice came, the night in spring when he was to meet the long-horned bull and thrust the golden knife into the great animal's heart. He knew the action depended on freedom from fear and had to be pure of every thought.

He had had a long training. He had performed this sacrifice year after year at the time when the birdsong rose again over the reborn grass and over the fields, where the first seeds were already shooting out of the red soil.

But in this, his last moment on earth, the guilt rose out of his memory, burst open the door he had sealed with multitudes of locks, and the horns of the bull ripped his body in two. His heart fell out and shattered.

Then all the people saw that only the surface of the heart was stone and that it was as thin as an eggshell. And inside was the dark sorrow, so overwhelmingly great that it could at any moment have burst the fragile shell.

ELEVEN

*R*uben observed Simon during the concert, at first with delight, then with some wonder, and finally with anxiety. The boy was as white as a sheet and, for a while toward the end, seemed to have difficulty breathing.

It had been decided that they would stay overnight in town at Lentov's apartment. Neither of them said a word as the tram rattled them out to Majorna. A plate of sandwiches covered with a white cloth had been left on the dining room table, but Simon shook his head and went straight into Isak's room and fell into bed. Ruben had never seen a person fall asleep so immediately; the boy had time only to get his clothes off.

But Simon smiled at Ruben in his sleep, and a few hours later, after Ruben had digested the impressions of the evening with a cognac, Ruben could hear Simon laughing in his sleep and crying at the same time.

"Why did he have to die?" said Simon at breakfast.

"Who?" said Ruben from behind a newspaper.

"The one in the music, the king or the priest, or whatever he was called."

"Simon," said Ruben. "I saw no priest. The music isn't about anything special. Different people experience it in different ways."

Simon was astonished.

"So that, what's his name, the man who made it up . . ."

"Berlioz."

"Yes, Berlioz, him. He never saw the priest?"

"No." Ruben, feeling the boy's intensity, carefully folded the paper and answered, unsure of the right words. "Art, Simon, comes to people who listen or read or look at a picture. It arouses something, emotions there are no words for."

Simon made an effort, screwing up his eyes as he always did when he was intensely preoccupied with trying to understand. Ruben thought, as he had before, that there was a fire within the boy.

"So it's not real, then?"

"That depends on what you mean by real. You read a lot, so you must have realized that people in books aren't real in the same way as you and I are, and what happens to them hasn't happened in what we call reality."

Simon had never thought about the matter and had taken for granted that the worlds he stepped into and the people he met in books had existed and looked just as he saw them. Things seemed to be sliding around in his head. He screwed up his face and bit his lower lip with the effort of getting his thoughts into some kind of order.

"Don't use your head, Simon. Use your heart," said Ruben.

Simon's face smoothed out and his eyes opened wide as he stared far away into the unknowable, and he remembered the trees that had talked to him in his childhood, so clear and yet so impossible to remember afterward. He thought about the man and their conversations under the oaks, about how much strength he had been given. Without ever remembering what had been said.

Ruben saw the change and finally risked a question. "Can you tell me?"

"I recognized the man in the music, the priest or king. He was with me when I was small."

Ruben nodded and smiled. "I see. He once existed for you and the music reminded you."

"But he really did exist."

"I believe you. He was once part of your reality, your inner world. It's common for children to create fantasy figures as a solace against loneliness."

Simon felt both relieved and cheated, for something was wrong with what Ruben had said, he felt it.

Then the maid came and cleared the table, and Ruben had to go to visit Olga in the asylum. It was one of those rare days when hot water was allowed, and Ruben urged Simon to take a bath before taking the tram back to Erik and Karin. Simon nodded, but washed only as skimpily as he usually did.

After Ruben had left the house, the boy went around the apartment to look at everything. There were large paintings, which Erik used to joke about, daubs representing nothing. Simon stood looking at them for a long time, thinking perhaps something would come into his heart—but nothing did.

Then he went home and everything was just as usual, all was focused on the boat, and no one had time for him, nor did anyone ask what he had thought of the concert, a fact for which he was largely grateful.

But Ruben couldn't get the boy out of his mind, the way he had disappeared into the music. On Sunday evening he phoned Karin and told her he had reason to believe that Simon was musical, and that he would very much like to see the boy develop his talent. He, Ruben, had a friend who was a music teacher and Simon could go for a test.

"I may be wrong," he said. "But it wouldn't surprise me if there were another person, perhaps a violin player, in Simon."

It was just as well Ruben Lentov was unable to see Karin's expression. All he could hear was that her voice quavered as she replied that Simon would have to decide for himself, but they couldn't afford music lessons.

The boy was lying up in the attic with his nose in a book as usual. Despite Lord Jim having just made his fateful leap from the rusty deck of the steamer *Patna* in Joseph Conrad's novel, Simon was not there, not really present in the entrance to the Persian Gulf. His mind was roaming in the country where the grass sang and the river spoke its gentle wisdom to people.

The priest-king had talked about resurrecting a language that had been forbidden and forgotten.

Simon made an effort to understand. He remembered what

Ruben said about remembering with your heart, and he could hear the river and the people's voices.

But then his head took over. What had they called out? What was the secret of the forgotten language?

Karin came up the creaking wooden stairs.

"Uncle Ruben has got it into his head that you're musical and wants you to learn the violin."

For once he didn't hear the reproachful concern that usually went straight into the marrow of his bones. He was so overwhelmingly pleased as the idea exploded in his mind.

If he could play, then he would be able to re-create the miracle himself.

As always, the boys slept up in the attic in the summer. Isak slept heavily from exhaustion, so only Simon was awakened by the quarrel down in the kitchen. Erik was shouting at Karin that she was bloody crazy and that he, Erik, had certainly had quite enough of that mysterious fiddler.

As usual when they quarreled, Simon's guilt increased, and this time he was quite certain it was his fault. He sat up in bed feeling sick, and as the voices rose and the abuse grew worse, tears came. It became unbearable, so he went downstairs, opened the kitchen door, and stood there crying, saying he didn't want to have violin lessons.

To Karin, it was as if the boy had struck her in the heart, and Erik was so ashamed he had to go on shouting.

"Go back to sleep, you damned good-for-nothing!"

But Simon heard nothing, as he was in Karin's arms and four years old again, and she paid attention only to him as she dried his tears and comforted him, assuring him that both she and Erik wanted nothing more in life than that he should be happy.

"But you only care about Isak," said Simon, and the next moment he was asleep.

It was a difficult but enlightening moment for Erik, who resolved to take a week off from work on the boat and go fishing with

Simon. For Karin, too, as she tucked the boy up in his own bed and looked back on the spring and summer and everything that had happened since Isak had gone mad.

After that night, Simon was visible once again in the house by the river mouth.

The next morning, after Simon had gone off for his music test and Isak to his extra lessons, Erik and Karin were able to speak to each other. Not about their unpleasant quarrel, nor their fear of the hurtful words, nor their mutual guilt over the boy feeling left out. And least of all about why Ruben's suggestion had upset them so much.

All those touched on emotions, and with emotions there were only angry words. But if they stayed with the facts of the matter, they could articulate what was strange in Ruben's idea.

"Simon has never liked music," said Karin, remembering how they had laughed when Simon had come home from junior school and said that he couldn't stand the song they had to sing every morning. "Do you remember he said it made him feel sick when the kids sang at the end of term and the teacher played the organ?"

"Mm," said Erik, nodding, as he also remembered the way the teacher had played, what the children had sounded like, and that Simon had curled up in misery even when he was small whenever Karin had sung to him.

Karin was mercifully tone-deaf.

"He never liked the portable gramophone, either," said Karin, and Erik thought about those warped records and awful ditties, how he himself had found them hard to bear when some singer was bawling even worse than usual because Karin had forgotten to wind up the gramophone.

Then he remembered the time he had been making a wooden truck for the boy, who was no more than three at the time. Simon was perched on the workbench as Erik chiseled away, whistling the Toreador aria from *Carmen*. Suddenly the boy, small as he was, had taken up the tune and sung it.

As clear as a bell.

Even then the thought of the boy's origins had disturbed Erik.

Hair flattened with water, in a newly ironed shirt, tram money in his pocket, Simon walked the old way to the tram stop. He was feeling as lighthearted as long ago when he had sat on Aron Äppelgren's bicycle carrier, having just been saved from getting lost.

He changed trams at Järntorget and gradually found his way to his destination, a large strange apartment in Park-Viktoria, where an irascible and impatient man was expecting him.

But Simon was not easily scared that day.

Yet the visit was a disappointment. The man had long hair and shouted in broken Swedish, and did nothing but tinkle on his piano, wanting Simon to imitate the notes. There was no violin to be seen, though the longhaired man was nicer toward the end and muttered something about being interesting.

"Very interesting," he said.

"Not much," said Simon when he got home and Karin asked him whether he had enjoyed it.

"So, you're not interested?"

Simon was well aware of her concern and answered no, he probably wasn't.

But an hour or so later, Ruben phoned and told them that the man at Park-Viktoria had said that Simon had something called perfect pitch and that was very unusual.

"But he doesn't want to take lessons," said Karin, and Ruben could hear she was relieved.

"Can't be true," said Ruben. "I'll come and talk to the boy."

So they sat in the parlor that evening, alone, Ruben and Simon.

"You'll have a new language," said Ruben.

Simon thought about English, which was fun, and German, which had been hard going, and he couldn't understand why he would want to learn another language.

"What use would that be?"

Ruben looked downcast when he said he'd suspected that Simon had a predisposition to the language and would be able to express a lot of what he had inside him . . .

The boy vanished like lightning, so quickly Ruben never even had time to see the surprise and pain in his dark eyes.

Simon never became a violin player.

TWELVE

*T*his was when Simon began lying. He found it so easy, it was as if he had had a slumbering talent for that, too.

It was like the time he had run sixty meters at the Nya Varvet athletics ground. Faster than anyone else, he had won a prize and been the center of interest.

He was soon quite masterly at it. Lies ran off his tongue, the first providing the second, which gave birth to the third, which in its turn spawned the next and the next.

He couldn't stop.

His lies gave him a place in the sun, at school, at home, in Karin's interest and Erik's appreciation. Yet he was lonelier than ever.

In the house by the sea, life was simple, for there were clear boundaries between black and white. Lying was black, and therefore simply unacceptable.

Simon was a liar, and the realization allowed guilt to fasten its claws into him. And fear. He thought that if Karin happened to expose him one single time, her love, on which he lived, would cease to exist. With growing anxiety, he trained his mind to remember what he had said and never to contradict himself. The effort tied his insides into knots.

It began with Dolly, the girl on the upper floor of the neighboring house, the girl he had loved for as long as he could remember. She had eyes like forget-me-nots and a cloud of fair curls, carefully set once a week by her hairdresser father.

Dolly was an only child and as stuck-up as her mother and father. When they moved into the Gustafssons' apartment next door, they decorated the walls with flowered wallpaper and covered the floors with colorful oriental rugs. Period furniture was lined up in dead-straight rows, and chandeliers tinkled from the ceilings.

Dolly had a room of her own. That alone was so remarkable it gave her a special luster.

Her father had gone around the houses, holding his daughter by the hand and pointing out the ones where she was allowed to get to know the children and play in their kitchens. Not at Olivia, because gypsies lived there, nor at Helene, because they had had consumption there.

The houses had women's names, like ships.

The Larssons were approved, fortunately for Dolly, because that meant access to Karin's kitchen, her reality and good wholesome food.

Ten years later, Dolly would become the district's most elegant whore, but no one could imagine that when she and Simon were fourteen and loved each other.

It was not clear whether Dolly ever really loved anyone, but Simon was quality. He went to a posh school and his father's boatyard was growing in influence and grandeur. Simon had also grown tall and good-looking; the darkness that had marked him when he was little was now attractive.

From the half-moon window in the Larssons' attic, it was possible to see right into Dolly's room. Neither of them ever said anything to anyone about it, but Dolly slowly and voluptuously undressed every evening—with the ceiling light on and without drawing the blackout curtain.

Simon stood in the attic with his hand firmly around his member, and they soon managed to coordinate their activities. Once Dolly had got her panties off, she would put one foot up on the windowsill, thrust her hand into her crevice, and push her hips back and forth at an increasing pace.

Then Simon would come, desire straining in him and exploding for one dizzying second, his hand filling with warm sperm and his heart with gratitude to the girl for so generously offering herself to him.

Whenever they met, they avoided each other's eyes. Not a word was uttered, for Simon was tongue-tied. But one Sunday he told the local boys that he had done it with Dolly in the kiosk down by the bathing place. He hadn't really expected all the interest this aroused. They all wanted to know more, and he obliged. Lie spawned lie as he painted exciting and colorful pictures.

Yes, she had hair on her cunt. And a birthmark on one buttock, which she wanted you to bite. No, she hadn't bled much, that virginity business was just so much fuss about nothing. Yes, you could suck her breast.

Simon's own surprise at what he said was so great, he didn't really notice the murmur in the air. But he soon came to enjoy the admiration apparent in the wide-open eyes all around him.

So one Monday he tried his story out at school, with the same results. Even Isak was struck dumb with surprise and pride in his friend.

During the break, they walked around the girls' school in the cold, looking at the tittering bunches of girls inside and hating them all because they had everything boys need, all those holes that all their dreams were about, those soft, moist secret places.

"Imagine having a hole to yourself you could do what you like with," said Isak, and Simon was scared and worried. They had never put this into words before. Now, after his story about Dolly, he realized everything was possible.

"Did you stick it in her?" said Isak.

"No," said Simon. "Just a finger."

Then he cursed himself, sensing a wall rising between him and his friend and wishing he could knock it down. But there was no going back.

One early spring morning when the weather was stormy, he took the sea way along the shore and sat on the cliff, hoping the storm would blow him clean of all this falseness. So he was late for school and had to knock on the door and apologize. That had happened before and he never usually made any excuses, accepting the bad conduct mark without protest. Karin used to sign it without reproaches.

This time, he said, "I was involved in an accident."

Then he described the squealing brakes of the truck, the woman who had been run over, and the blood pouring down the gutter in Karl Johansgatan, and how he had only just managed to stop his bicycle and had been questioned by the police as a witness.

They had Rubbet for math, a big man in his fifties, used to decades of seeing through boys. So he didn't join in the murmur of surprise running around the class, just told Simon to sit down and do his square roots.

There was distrust in Rubbet's cold eyes, and Simon felt his stomach contracting. His story could be checked, and Rubbet looked as if that was what he was going to do.

But Simon learned that the wickedness in him had allies. The next day there was a report in the newspaper on an accident in Karl Johansgatan, and Rubbet took the matter up again.

"You were wrong, Larsson," he said. "It wasn't a woman who got run over, but an elderly man."

Then he expounded on the psychology of witnesses, how the agitation of witnessing an accident distorts your vision.

"Witnesses are often wrong and rarely to be relied on," he said.

At first, Simon felt only relief, a touch of triumph, but later his terror came creeping back, fastening in his midriff this time, not in his stomach.

The Devil sees to his own, Erik used to say.

Simon knew that was true. The Devil helped him, again and again. Simon told Erik that he was the only one in the class who had dared climb the rope right up to the ceiling, and the gym master had been astonished. The Devil you did, the gym master had said.

Erik lit up with delight.

Otherwise afraid of heights, and somewhat faintheartedly, the next day Simon climbed right up to the ceiling, and the gym master, a ridiculous bowlegged old cavalry officer, said, "The Devil you did."

He told Karin he had been to see his grandmother, and Karin was pleased. The next day, he realized he would have to go and see the old thing. He took flowers with him, flowers he'd bought with money borrowed from Isak, to whom he said he had lost a bet he'd made with Abrahamsson in Scripture. He didn't have to safeguard that story, because Isak never went to Scripture lessons, so never met Abrahamsson.

But Simon received great appreciation for the flowers, which touched his mother's heart.

One afternoon as he was walking home from the tram stop, someone had chalked on the baker's wall that Simon loves Dolly, with a heart and an arrow. Simon felt the back of his neck stiffen with the effort of not looking at it.

As he sauntered along the road up to the garage, he saw her sitting there below the hedge. Dolly. Her cheeks red, her eyes blank.

"Did you read it?" she said.

He nodded.

"Is it true?" she said, and he wanted to die, or at least have the earth open up and swallow him, thinking of Nordenskjöld and *Vega*'s route through the Northeast Passage and the great expanses of ice in the Arctic night. His mouth was dry—he didn't even dare meet those forget-me-not eyes.

But she persisted. "Is it true?"

Afraid Karin might hear, Simon nodded and said almost inaudibly, "I suppose so."

You're not supposed to hit girls, he thought. Suppose she leapt on him and scratched. But she looked extremely content and said that if they met after dinner down by the bathing place, where no one could see them, he would be allowed to kiss her.

He had no desire to go, but didn't dare stay away. So it happened that when he kissed a girl for the very first time, it tasted of lies and yellow terror.

All his love ceased with that kiss. He detested the girl he had dreamed about all through his childhood. When he realized she would soon be making demands on him and he would have to do all the things he had already said he had done, he was almost panic-stricken.

Then, as usual, the lies came leaping out of his mouth to rescue him. Dismally, he screwed up his eyes.

"I'm going to die soon," he said. "You see, I've got TB, though no one knows it yet. But I cough up blood all night."

Dolly fled.

Fear of consumption was stronger than the desire to conquer, stronger than lust, stronger even than vanity. When the ten o'clock news was switched on in the kitchen, Simon went upstairs as usual to watch Dolly undress. But this time she had drawn the blackout curtain across.

Simon was relieved.

A week later, Karin said, "Aunt Jenny was in and said you had a bad cough. I hadn't noticed anything, but she looked so frightened, I was almost worried."

"Oh," said Simon. "I had a bit of cold one day and happened to cough on the same tram as Dolly."

Karin smiled, then she sighed a little at the thought of their grand neighbors in those neat rooms with bacteria crawling all over the walls.

Then spring came with strong west winds blowing clean between the mountains, the grass green and people's voices ringing more clearly than for many years, full of hope.

When the apple blossom was out, they launched Isak's boat, and it was just as Erik had imagined, the finest double-ender in the river mouth. She was moored to a buoy and anchor inside Oljeberget and was given a ballast of granite instead of the lead that could not be bought for money. They were delayed by the sailmaker, until one day at the end of May, they were able to test-sail her.

She flew, cleaving the sea as if dancing, and in his happiness to get her up in the wind, Isak forgot his dreams of that moist hole. She turned out to be excellent close to the wind. They named her *Kajsa*, after Karin and the west wind.

On D day, when the great invasion force established its bridgehead in Normandy, Isak and Simon took their exams, did well, and Simon was awarded the Premium, the school's literary prize.

He had written an essay on the peasant who farmed the fields inside the Oljeberget, a sour-eyed old man of whom Simon had always been afraid. But in his essay he made the old farmer into a man with great gifts, a master at runes, who knew the influence of the old signs, was familiar with the powers, and put the evil eye on people, but also cured them of serious and rare diseases.

His teacher, Kerstin Larberg, read the essay aloud in class and said it was a wonderful story.

"Is there any truth in it? Or is there a writer hidden there inside you, Larsson?"

Her words flashed like lightning through Simon's head, and with one relieved breath, he said, "I made it all up."

For a while he acquired the nickname the Poet, but he ignored it. He thought a lot about Uncle Ruben and what he had said at the concert about there being a reality based on lies but possessing the truth.

Before he fell asleep he decided to write out all his lies. All summer, he would write stories about women and breasts and holes and about Arctic explorers and death down there in Europe. He would write about Karin as one of the Fates sitting by her spinning wheel in her kitchen, spinning people's destinies into a thread, and about the little man in his dreams, the man who had such a strange hat and fought wars in the realm of the high grass and died when he was trying to sacrifice a bull in the temple. And he would write about Dolly, the faithless slut, betraying the man who loved her, and about Aunt Inga up there on the lonely farm by the blue lake. The latter surprised him. What the hell could he invent about Inga?

But he didn't worry about it. Tomorrow he would ask Uncle Ruben for notebooks, a whole stack of them.

Then summer came with its free delights, enveloping the two boys, now no longer inseparable.

Isak sailed and Simon wrote.

Karin worked in the garden, Erik sang, laid the keel of his third double-ender, and the Americans and British liberated Paris.

When summer was at its best, the lies stopped running off Si-

Isak lifted up the floorboard and extracted beer from the keelson, secret beer stolen from Ruben.

They drank.

Trying to calm down.

"Did you hear what she said when we left?"

Oh yes, Simon had heard. Come back tomorrow at the same time.

Every evening that hot summer when thirty thousand Balts were fleeing across the Baltic in small boats, they went back and rejoiced, as Maj-Britt put it, learning everything boys need to know about making love to girls. Both of them became good lovers, and they often sent grateful thanks back to the wonderful Maj-Britt on the mountain.

One evening, as they slipped around the corner of the house as usual and knocked on the basement door, a sailor in nothing but his jaunty bell-bottoms opened up, a man as broad as a hatch cover and tall as a flagpole.

"What the hell do these kids want?" he said to the just-visible Maj-Britt on the bed in the cool of the basement. Simon had not forgotten his skills from the previous winter and collected his wits.

"We're selling Älvsborg Christmas Gnomes," he said.

"In the middle of the summer?" said the sailor as Maj-Britt's laughter came rolling off the bed.

On their way home, they tried to hate the sailor, but that didn't work very well. They were grateful for what they had been given, almost satiated in fact, and they had known all along that this incredible business could not go on.

THIRTEEN

*T*hen it came, the longest spring of all. Never before had time been so slow, the days creeping by toward evenings, when nothing happened, either.

The Swedish diplomat Wallenberg disappeared in Budapest.

In Germany, twelve-year-olds were being conscripted into war service.

Important men met in Yalta to carve up the world among them. Then Roosevelt died, and with fierce resentment, Karin said it was not fair.

For a while, time stood still after Hitler shot himself in the Berlin bunker and peace had still not come. The radio ticked over in its corner, the old kitchen clock refused to budge, and Karin found herself shaking it. There was nothing wrong with it, but time itself seemed to have stopped, driving the waiting people mad.

But the waiting came to an end eventually. Germany surrendered that seventh of May, just as the birches began to come out. There was a smell of wet earth from the garden and the birds should have been singing. But no one had any energy. They gathered as usual around the radio in the Larssons' kitchen and listened to the jubilation in Oslo, London, and Stockholm, but they couldn't share in their joy.

Wallin sat on the kitchen sofa staring stubbornly down at his huge workingman's hands lying so still in his lap it was as if they would never come to life again. Ågren had feverish red patches on his cheeks and kept swearing. Damn and blast the bloody bastards.

For once, Erik was silent, looking with envy at Äppelgren stalking like an awkward crane to and fro across the kitchen floor, tripping on the rag rug, not even attempting to hide that he was crying like a baby.

Karin was also quietly crying.

Simon and Isak had squeezed together on the wood box as usual, and Simon was thinking that tonight no one was killing anyone else in Europe. He wanted to cry, too, but he was too old for that now. The excitement went to his legs and feet, now drumming on the wood box until Karin begged him to cease. "For God's sake, Simon, stop it. Be quiet!"

Isak was beside him, as strangely still as Wallin was. His heart was burning but his head was cold and empty, his body so rigid it could have been frozen. Not until Johansson the postman, a fisherman by birth and as large as a house, said they should now boil all the Nazi bastards in oil and make sure they stayed alive and were tormented as long as possible, did the tension in Isak's body give way.

He drew a deep breath, realizing that hatred had been knotting his muscles. Burning in his heart was the realization that revenge was possible and sweet.

In the middle of it all, Helen arrived with the milk, looking rather solemn. She looked at them all and said challengingly, "I think you should all come to the chapel and thank God for peace."

At that, Erik came to life and leapt to his feet.

"And who the hell do we have to thank for the war and all the dead?"

"War is the work of man," said Helen, without losing an ounce of her gravity.

"You're crazy," said Ågren, but then Karin broke in and said that at least in her kitchen, people should show consideration for other people's views.

Her words were familiar, but her voice lacked force.

Toward evening, Ruben appeared, something inscrutable in his eyes, great relief mixed with unbearable pain. When Karin's eyes met his, she took out the schnapps bottle and the footless glasses, then poured out a full measure for everyone.

"Let's drink to peace, then, shall we?" she said in a voice as thin as paper.

They drank, Karin too, swallowing the horrible drink in one go, and if it hadn't been such a momentous and remarkable moment, the others would have probably noticed and been both surprised and appalled.

As it was, they were all absorbed in themselves.

But Karin had to go out to the old privy in the backyard and throw up. She stood leaning against the plastered wall, white in the face and sweating as the nausea kept washing over her.

But worst of all was the pain in her chest.

She was surprised at herself. And annoyed. Why should she have pain now that it was all over and people could breathe out again?

The pain churned around inside her, as if someone were twisting a knife in there. She tried to think about Petter and the wax-wings, but failed. At the moment her mother and her bitter eyes and sharp tongue were in Petter's place. Something was being dislodged in Karin's heart, the old and safe sorrow moving, tearing at the roots.

Karin thought the war had also taken the lives of the waxwings.

She stayed there until dusk, gradually realizing that time had reverted to its usual pace and she had to go back in, get the men out of her kitchen, and begin on dinner. Her hand clenched beneath her left breast, she set about her ordinary everyday chores.

Over the past winter, they had altered the house, raising walls on the upper floor and abolishing the attic. Simon had a room of his own, and there was plenty of space for Isak, too. They had made a guest room with a view over the sea for Ruben, who increasingly stayed out there with them, tired as he was of his brother's family and all the refugees he had given shelter to in his apartment in Majorna.

The Larssons now had a bathroom and an indoor lavatory.

It was marvelous, and Karin and Erik had been happy all winter.

They had raised the sink cabinet in the kitchen and replaced the zinc with stainless steel. They had central heating and two kinds of water. Karin hardly dared believe that the end had now come to smoky tiled stoves and heaving wood and coal about. Or that she only had to turn on a tap and hot water came rushing out, warming her hands and making things clean. A handsome refrigerator had been put in the place where they used to stand and wash themselves in the kitchen.

Karin had a great deal to be pleased about. She thought about it late that night when they were on their own and dinner was on the table. As she put some potato into her mouth, she was at last able to admit that she detested potatoes—boiled, fried, grated, baked, and boiled, especially boiled potatoes. It was over now, her worries about food soon to be a dismal memory like the coal and the cold privy in the backyard.

Rationing would cease and there would be fruit again.

Bananas, thought Karin, remembering that Simon had loved bananas when he was small. He had probably forgotten what they tasted like now.

She looked at Eric and saw how his pride had grown on him like a cock's crest. Things were going well for him and his boatyard, the list of orders for double-enders long, and he now employed four men. They supported four families now, as Karin liked to put it. She liked the money, too, that was there when needed.

As always when Karin ran through all the things she had to be grateful for, she hopped over Ruben and saved Simon till last.

The boy who had brought her so much joy.

He'll soon be an adult, she thought. And he had changed and was almost handsome, like a strange bird that by some wonderful chance had settled here in her kitchen.

She was still uneasy, and again she felt that stab in her chest. Always sensitive to her moods, Simon noticed the pain flitting over her face.

"You're tired, Mom," he said. "You go on to bed. I'll do the dishes."

She nodded, but when she met his anxious eyes, she knew that all her gratitude had not helped her this evening. Her abundance of riches was no defense against what was tearing inside at her.

What is the matter with me?

Erik had gone to the boatyard, so Karin had the bedroom to herself. She stood among the roses on the new wallpaper and looked at herself in the mirror. She had always been content with her appearance, liking the firm and fine features of her face, her big mouth and straight nose.

She studied her features for a long time, as if wondering whether they had anything new to tell her. An answer, maybe. And she could see that her brown eyes, always surprising in contrast to her fairness, had acquired new depths.

What was down there in the depths?

Fear?

No, Karin denied it. I've got a few wrinkles, and my hair's faded to the color of straw. I'm not yet fat, but heavier, sturdier.

It'll be gone by tomorrow, she said to herself. As long as I can get some sleep.

Next morning, as they all tore down the blackout curtains and cleaned the windows in the spring warmth, she was almost happy.

But then came the evening when Ruben brought with him the first English newspapers with eyewitness accounts of the liberated concentration camps in Poland and Germany. He sat at the kitchen table and read from them. Isak's eyes rolled up at the ceiling as Ruben translated. Erik was white in the face, and the blue in his eyes darkened. As always when he was afraid, Simon's eyes sought Karin's.

The next moment, he snatched the newspaper out of Ruben's hands and cried out that that was enough, and through his great weariness, Ruben looked from the boy to Karin and saw that she was close to fainting.

He was deeply ashamed, then frightened.

But she said it as it was, that if his relatives had had to experience it, then at least she could cope with hearing about it.

Yet from that evening on, it was quite clear even to the others that there was something wrong with Karin. They tried to spare her. Erik took the radio to the workshop, and Simon smuggled the newspaper out in the mornings. But Karin was drawn to what was terrible, and went into town to buy magazines with pictures of corpses, stacked up in piles.

When the white buses came to Malmö, Karin went by herself to fetch the morning papers with photographs of people who had seen evil and should have been dead, not staring like that at her with lifeless eyes.

Then Karin realized she, too, would die. And she welcomed that knowledge.

A few days later, Ruben said to Erik that this would no longer do, and they took her to a heart specialist Ruben knew. He listened for a long time, and troubled by the ragged clatter in her chest, he said she must rest completely if things weren't to get worse.

Karin was admitted to his private clinic, so tired she hadn't the energy to protest. She was given medicine and sleep. In her sleep, she was again faced with her mother and dared to see that her mother had hated her from the day she was born.

Just as her mother had hated Petter.

Like a huge black crow, her mother came tearing toward Karin in her dreams at the clinic, croaking and shrieking, swastikas flashing around her, flying in and out between them, and they were suddenly in the tailor's workshop at home. Karin saw Petter crouching below the swastikas. He was strangely like the people pouring off the white buses in Malmö, who should be dead, and the horrible croaking went straight into his heart and hurt so badly that in the end it broke and he died at his tailor's table.

Her dreams came and went, and Karin let the images speak their clear language without resisting or seeking explanations. Her mind had to be washed clean before she could leave. The hurt was good, but somehow necessary.

In waking moments, she carried on a conversation with her mother.

"How did you come to be like you were?"

But her mother croaked away, poor me, poor me, and Karin turned her head away with distaste, realizing that she had always denied evil because she had grown up in its shadow.

Then, half asleep, she heard herself croaking over Simon, poor me, poor me, and saw those anxious eyes of his that always followed her.

Then she cried out loud and the doctor came, told her she simply must not worry about things. She was given tablets to banish her worries.

The next night Petter came to her, and her sleep was deep and peaceful. She thought it was all over now, and she would be allowed to follow him and escape having to wake to another day. He was there all night, cradling her in his arms, singing to her, and there was no evil, and Karin was as safe as a child.

She knew there was something he wanted to tell her, but she was too tired to listen.

Dawn came and when Karin became aware of the sunlight coming through the crack between the blind and the window frame, she realized it wasn't all over. She was still there, alone. While they washed her and persuaded her to eat some gruel, she thought about what Petter had wanted to tell her. But not for long, for she couldn't collect her thoughts.

Then suddenly, Simon was there and it was night again, and difficult to understand, but Simon was quite real and holding her hand so hard it almost hurt, and she heard the anger in his voice as he spoke.

"Don't leave me, Mom."

When Karin next awoke, it was light again. He was sitting by her bed and she realized he was right. She mustn't leave yet.

"Simon," she whispered. "I promise to get better."

His delight was so great, it went straight into Karin, warmed her and gave her life.

After he had left, Karin wept quietly for a long time. She had no idea she had so many tears in her, or where they came from, but she sensed where they went, straight into her heart, warm and soothing.

Simon cycled wildly through town, the slanting morning rays of sun glittering in the harbor and on the sea as he raced to the boatyard and Erik.

"Dad, she's going to get better. She promised."

Ordinarily, Erik would have taken little notice of such a statement, but he was in such a state of fear, he simply took Simon's words as the absolute truth.

They were almost as tall as each other now, Erik and Simon, as they stood facing each other across the half-finished double-ender. They were crying, both of them, the same kind of healing tears as Karin's.

Then Erik went inside, washed the sawdust off his neck and hands, shaved, and put on his best suit, wintery and dark blue. There was no ironed shirt, but Simon picked all the tulips from the garden into a huge bunch.

Erik felt slightly foolish as he stood there in the corridor of the clinic with all those flowers. Karin could see his uncertainty, his worker's fear, the unironed shirt, and her tenderness was great as she saw she had to stay for the sake of this fragile creature.

FOURTEEN

*T*he days of recovery were peaceful.

Ruben brought roses, and she found she was able to tell him.

"I had decided to go."

"I've long seen you going around with some great sorrow" was all he said.

Karin was surprised, as she had never seen it like that, but it struck her as the truth, and she told him about Petter and the waxwings, as well as about her mother and the evil she had always denied.

He didn't say much, only, "Nothing is ever simple."

Much later, Karin found herself thinking about those words.

She wanted to ask him about the God he went to every Saturday at the synagogue, which, after all, must give him some strength to live through misfortunes.

But she could find no words.

Then, as he was leaving, he said, "You really must try to live, Karin. For my sake, so that I can cope."

She could see that had been difficult for him to say.

Then he had gone, and Karin lay there watching the sun trickling through the dark spruce outside. A tram rattled around the corner, and when the nurse came with dinner, Karin noticed she had brilliant blue eyes.

The veal tasted of dill sauce, strong and good, and the apple puree afterward freshened her mouth. The world seemed to have acquired a new tangibility.

For a while that afternoon, she tried to feel ashamed of burdening Ruben with her sorrows, for he had quite enough of his own. But there was no conviction in the feeling, so she gave it up.

Perhaps I've lost my conscience, she thought.

When Simon came that evening and she saw how pale and thin he was, she realized that was not true.

"I hope you're all eating properly," she said, guilt stabbing at her in the same old way.

"Where's Isak?" she said as he was leaving. "Give him my love and tell him to come tomorrow," her voice now containing all the old weight of responsibility.

Simon nodded, but his expression was so odd, and she saw she had missed something important.

Simon cycled through town, strengthened by Karin apparently being herself again, forceful and demanding as she usually was. But he was also worried. And angry.

Bloody Isak, he thought.

Simon knew where to find him, down in the harbor out at Långedrag, where Ruben had rented a mooring and Isak had become the king of handsome double-enders. Simon could hear the racket from the cabin from quite far away, and his anger reached boiling point when he saw beer bottles bobbing about in the water around the boat.

They were smoking, the air thick as Simon opened the hatch into the cabin.

"Get the hell out of here, you lot," he said. "I want to talk to Isak alone."

The boys didn't leave at once, and there was some jeering, but a quarter of an hour later, Simon and Isak found themselves alone. Simon took the net, fixed it to the boat hook, and fished up the empty bottles that hadn't already sunk, emptied ashtrays, swilled down the cockpit and deck, then turned to Isak hunched up on the bunk.

"You have to go and see Karin tomorrow," said Simon.

"I can't."

"She's better now. She's well. Do you understand?"

"Because of the beer," said Isak.

"For Christ's sake, she doesn't drink beer," said Simon in astonishment. "Are you crazy? Or just drunk, you bastard?"

They stood there staring at each other, and deep down in Isak's eyes was an emptiness Simon recognized from the war, when those ships had disappeared into the depths. All Simon's anger ran out of him, and he was truly frightened as he thought that this time there was no Karin to cope with this and he would have to do it himself. He flung his arms around Isak, and with no idea where the words came from, he said, "For God's sake, Isak, Karin's illness has nothing to do with you."

He could see he had said the right thing, for Isak relaxed, and when their eyes met, the frightening emptiness had gone.

The next day Isak was at the hospital and could see with his own eyes that she was almost herself again, and as always, he could talk to her.

"I was going to boil them in oil, twist their pricks off, you see. I was going to sail up Oslo Fjord because the papers said that a lot of Germans were still there, and I was going to find them and . . ."

"And what?"

"Well, then you fell ill."

In a few words, she managed to get him to understand that what had made her ill was her grief over everything that had happened, and what had been disclosed by peace, and that his wicked thoughts were just a breeze in a gale of evil deeds.

"Perhaps it was good for you, Isak, to fantasize about revenge," she said.

He told her about the beer, the boys on the boat, and how they laced the beer with brandy Isak filched from Ruben's cupboard. That put an end to all gentleness. Karin sat up in bed and looked him straight in the eye.

"Isak Lentov, you must put a stop to that kind of thing. Swear you will now, at once . . ."

Scarlet with shame, Isak hunched up at her fury.

"You must learn to distinguish between fantasy and reality, Isak. Maybe you need to have horrible ideas of revenge, but if you caught some terrified German boy running away from Norway, you should cry with pity. Revenge is only sweet in your imagination, don't you see?"

Isak said nothing. He did not believe her.

"Stealing drink tempts other people to ruin, that's reality. And you must stop it."

Isak solemnly promised, and he left, ashamed yet happy.

Karin lay there thinking how stupid and selfish she had been. It was obvious she had to go on living and make life comprehensible to the people she was responsible for. The thought pleased her so much, she fell asleep and slept all night without sleeping pills. Strangely enough, she thought least about Erik, who had it the worst of them all.

He came one day for a talk with the consultant, who had weighty words on the importance of sparing Karin. Strong emotions had to be avoided, the doctor said. The responsibility for Karin's staying calm rested with Erik.

"If she gets angry or frightened, the result could be disastrous," the heart specialist said.

Erik was intimidated, his shirt button sticking into his larynx, class hatred rising in him as he thought, Here we go again, that old sense of inferiority.

Bloody hell.

When he at last got away and slunk in to Karin, he was distraught and scarcely present. He had planned to tell her about the car he had bought, expecting her protests with some pleasure, her arguments about extravagance, then her delight when he would finally say he had bought it so that she could get out and about in the world.

But nothing came of that.

Nor did he take any pleasure in the handy Fiat Balilla as he cruised home through the Avenue and along the quays, where the cranes were again dancing as in the old days. He drove up toward Karl Johansgatan and went in to buy a whole bottle of spirits.

That afternoon at the boatyard, he was curt and restless, and he noticed he was upsetting people.

The kitchen back at home looked terrible, smelling of garbage and dirty dishes. Simon was going sailing with Isak.

"You go on out," said Erik, his tone more friendly than he felt, and he thought that appropriate. Just why, he didn't really know until he had locked the door and taken out the bottle.

After his third drink, he thought about his mother, how she had threatened and frightened him with her heart all those years. He was back there again, but now it was for real, the trap had slammed shut and there was no way out.

For a long spell, he hated Karin because of her heart, then was bitterly ashamed. Karin was nothing like his mother. She never threatened.

But then he was furious about that, too. Karin was more cunning than his mother. She didn't frighten, didn't give any warning, but then just gave out.

No quarreling, the doctor had said. Nothing to upset her. Go with it, agree with her.

God Almighty.

What hadn't his rebellion cost when he'd left the congregation and joined the union. But his mother hadn't died as he'd thought she would. She was still alive and kicking even today. Karin, however, might die at any moment.

There were medical terms for that.

Erik had strange thoughts as he sat there on his own, drink eliminating the boundaries. An old curse would be fulfilled, a penance demanded.

He tried to pull himself together and heated up some coffee. He could see things were the same as when he was a child. He had always known that the weak heart inside his mother was all his fault, and had always had to behave so that it kept on beating.

Oh, God.

The next day he spoke to Anton, the carpenter at the boatyard, about his wife, Lisa. Erik was embarrassed, but the wages he was offering were better than usual, and Anton was pleased and said he would speak to Lisa. They needed the money and his wife hadn't so much to do now that the children would soon be gone. She was good at cleaning and at keeping a place tidy, and she wasn't a bad cook, either.

Erik built ramparts against the darkness ahead, went to the hospital, and was so nice it made him sick, while Lisa meticulously cleaned every corner of the white house and made it shine. But nothing helped Erik against his anger, that great wrath burning in his chest that he understood only when he drank.

Soon that would come to an end, too, for Karin would be back from the clinic and he knew what her eyes looked like when he drank.

Oh, hell.

It was a trap and he was racing around in it like a mad rat.

FIFTEEN

She came home at midsummer, and Erik paid the bill that amounted to half the profit on a double-ender. He did so with bitter satisfaction, as if he had bought himself free.

They had a festive meal with new potatoes and smoked salmon. Ruben brought wine, and friends and neighbors came with flowers. Karin was happy, deeply and quietly happy.

She was also happy about the car Erik had fetched her in. And, naturally, the spotless house.

But when life returned to normal, there was the matter of Lisa, who was so nice yet Karin found her rather difficult. She had to admit the house had never been so tidy as it was now, and she was also happy to find cupboards cleaned out and neat piles of linen, not to mention the men's shirts all ironed, the windows cleaned, and the plants cared for.

Karin had once been a domestic servant and had learned from that how to be a housewife. But nothing about how to *be*.

So she felt inferior now.

But she had to admit she was tired and couldn't really cope with the house, and that Erik was kind to have engaged Lisa. She also soon came to see it was irrevocable when she realized Anton and Lisa, who had always lived on the poverty line, had already adjusted their dreams to the level Lisa's new wages brought them.

Karin had to put up with it.

As she grew stronger, she found a solution and told Lisa she thought it would be enough with hourly help. So it was settled that Lisa would come at eleven in the morning and finish every day at three after having cleaned, done a quick wash, and prepared dinner.

Thus Karin had the mornings to herself in the kitchen, with coffee within reach and neighbors dropping in, just as it had always been. The afternoons were hers, too, when she took a nap, did a little sewing, and read a lot.

In the evenings she was even heard joking that she was becoming an upper-class wife.

But best about the new order was her walks. When Lisa came at eleven and took over the house, Karin set out. She went along the river, out onto the rickety jetties creeping through the reeds, stopping to listen to the water and gazing at the funny little gray bells of the knawel. Then she went on around the hill, through the overgrown wild garden, and out toward the sea, the sea that made everything grandiose and easy to comprehend.

On her way home, she roamed the hills, sat on smooth warm rocks, and spoke to the wind and the harebells. She once found her way to Simon's old oaks, and after that she went there every day, greeted them, and made friends with the great trees.

For the first time in her life, Karin had time and space for a great many thoughts, the difficult ones, too, thoughts that could no longer be chased away with household tasks.

They were mostly about her mother. She talked to the oaks a great deal about the old people and her childhood. The oaks listened with great seriousness and taught her that she did not have to understand.

Understanding was not necessary.

It was a human misery that we have to explain everything and thus come to misunderstand everything.

They said what Ruben had said. It's not that simple.

The sloes were angrier and brought up all those old injustices, reminding her of the malevolence in that bitter childhood.

Then Karin went to the sea and sat there looking at its endless expanse and listening to its message about life being so much greater than sloe thickets and with many more flavors than the bitterness of sloes.

In Anderson's meadows, the hay had been stacked, and the strong scent tickled her nipples and loins, making her flush like a seventeen-year-old, unfamiliar as she was with feeling her own desire.

She picked a bunch of summer flowers, cornflowers and oxeye daisies, swaying lacy cow parsley, put them in a vase in the bedroom, and tempted Erik into bed when evening came.

It went well, but Karin couldn't help seeing he was anxious. Afterward they tried to talk.

"You know, the doctor warned . . ."

Karin laughed her forceful old laugh.

"Oh, to hell with the doctor."

Erik laughed, too, even daring to believe that at least there would be excursions out of his trap and into the open air, and he fell asleep like a comforted child, his hand on her heart, now beating quite calmly and steadily.

One day Karin pulled herself together and dressed to go see her mother. After putting on her new white summer coat, her gloves, and the big hat with blue roses, she stood in front of the mirror and thought her new thinness suited her. She even took out a lipstick and reddened her lips.

Then she went to the boatyard to tell Erik where she was going. He climbed down from the mast of the boat he was rigging.

"You shouldn't go see her by yourself. Wait a minute, and I'll change and drive you in."

As Karin sat on the bench outside the porch, she realized with some astonishment that Erik understood a lot more than she had imagined.

Things went better than expected at her mother's. She was genuinely pleased to see Karin, and fussed over how thin she was.

"Goodness me, you look wretched!"

Karin could hear her anxiety and was able to eat the horrible pork sandwiches her mother made to ensure Karin would put on a bit of weight.

Erik talked more than usual, and Karin noticed how pleased her mother was. She remembered her mother had always liked her son-in-law. He talked about the home for pensioners being built in

Masthugget, and the old lady was interested. Suddenly Karin realized that her nightmare of her mother living with them was not going to happen.

Her eldest brother appeared, and Karin rather liked him—that was new, too, for she had been estranged from her brothers for many years.

They all left together, as her brother wanted to see Erik's new car.

On the stairs, Karin said, "Mother was really quite nice today, wasn't she?"

"She's been worried about you, you must see that," said her brother.

Karin thought that was quite enough.

"I've never known her to care for me."

Her brother looked embarrassed, as men do when women get emotional.

"You took Dad away from both her and us," he said, not without anger. "So it wasn't all her fault."

Karin stopped on the stairs, her heart beating fast, and Erik intervened.

"Now shut up, you. Karin's not to be upset."

The men went on down, but Karin heard her brother speak as he got to the entrance.

"Then things can't be all that easy for you."

In the car, Karin put her hand on Erik's shoulder, Ruben's words swirling around in her head.

Nothing is that simple.

SIXTEEN

*O*n the sixth of August, they dropped the bomb.

Hiroshima, a lovely name. It must have been a lovely city, thought Karin.

They talked about three hundred thousand dead.

The number was too great to take in. Her head couldn't take it in and her heart had had enough.

Erik read aloud from the newspaper that the world would never be the same again. Man now knew that he could exterminate himself as well as everything that grew on earth.

Karin couldn't take it in. Her world had already changed, but the boys sitting there in the kitchen listened to Erik and froze in the warmth of summer. Isak thought about Hitler and that you have to recognize early on the lunatics in the world. And Simon reckoned that his world had already shifted from trust to unpredictability that night in the hospital when he had sat with Karin, thinking she was going to die.

School started again, first year at senior high, and everything was the same. No war or atom bombs could change that.

Boredom sat in the very walls, thick layers of it, dripping down into corners where it collected, then creeping inexorably along the rows of desks, smelling of chalk and sweat, burbling out of the Latin master's mouth and crunching between the math master's teeth. Boredom penetrated everything. It was there in German, and in their own language.

There were moments when Simon was frightened, thinking he would soon be as dead as the old men up there at the master's desk.

Boredom would fill his lungs, poison his blood, and turn his body rigid.

It's a disease, he thought, and the worst of it is, you die from it without knowing it. You go on as before, your legs moving and your mouth babbling irregular French verbs.

Some of the dead had ended up in hell and become demons whose only joy was malice.

"It would help if you had something in your head, Svensson, that could fasten on to these verbs. As it is, they are just rattling around in a vacuum."

Svensson, Dahlberg, and Axelsson belonged in Stretered, the math master said. That was the city's institute for the mentally retarded.

Larsson did not, for he found everything easy. Too easy. He didn't have to chew over the knowledge that had been turned into hay by teachers who presumed boys were ruminants. Chew, swallow, regurgitate, chew again, swallow, regurgitate.

Boredom crept out of the classroom along the corridor into the science labs. It stopped at the library door, but then crept on up toward the school hall.

A handsome hall, but boredom made its way in and found nourishment in all those edifying speeches on peace and God, who was particularly thanked for sparing their country. The priest had the best of the boredom, as he came to morning prayers once a week and spouted forth astounding stupidities to four hundred boys trying to memorize words slipped inside their hymn books.

Perhaps the boredom would have broken Simon in the end if he hadn't had the good fortune to find a book in the library about yoga, and learned, among a lot of other things, how to get his mind to leave his body.

He had to concentrate on a point in the upper part of the brain, the imaginary breaking point between a line drawn straight in from the right eye and another drawn from the right ear. With a little

practice, it wasn't difficult to find that point. Then he sat still for
two minutes and assembled his mind there.

The next step was trickier, for he had to charge his mind with
energy. But Simon learned that, too, and was soon able to cautiously pilot his mind out through the seam between his temple
bone and his skull.

His mind wandered out into the world, flying across the Atlantic to the skyscrapers of New York and whirling with astonishment around the Empire State Building. Then it went west across
the prairies, turned sharply to the Pacific coast, and took the route
back to Europe. Across the Mediterranean it went, to the sultan's
harem in Istanbul, and Simon realized with delight that it also
moved freely in time. For now it was the seventeenth century and
the harem was wonderful to behold, and he fell in love with a belly
dancer wriggling like a snake in golden veils. By that stage he was
forced to put his school textbook on his lap so no one should see he
had a hard-on.

On the rocks by the bathing place at home, Karin sat gazing at the
great river flowing into the sea, wondering whether the river grieved
for its waters now lost. But she thought not. Instead it was probably
a fulfillment and a liberation.

The water itself probably knew it had served its purpose as it
joined the sea, raging down with thunderous force through the Trollhättan falls, swirling through the channel past Lilla Edet, providing
the turbines of man with power and the calm shores with greenery.
It brought with it the sweetness from its long run through Lake
Vänern, the banks of the Klarälven, and the glaciers of the Norwegian mountains. And the sweetness would be smelled and tasted
right out to Rivö Huvud before becoming lost in the salty sea.

She thought about that spring when she, too, had been about to
join what was infinite, and how she had stopped herself that night
Simon had sat at her bedside.

She was not like the river water, for she hadn't yet completed
her task.

Simon had a right to know, she thought.

Again and again that summer she thought about it, and it was so obvious and threatening that it appeared like a mountain wall in front of her. Steep, with neither hand- nor foothold.

He had to be told.

Guilt assailed her. He should have been told long ago.

But she parried the blow. There had been reasons.

In the beginning, they had meant to tell him as soon as he was old enough to understand. But then in the 1930s, anti-Semitism had appeared, taking root here and there, poisoning the air, and frightening her and Erik into silence.

She remembered a peddler, one of a whole series of tramps and hawkers she had given coffee and a sandwich to in her kitchen over the years. He had thought himself superior to the others, as he had a niece who was a film star.

Karin had bought a packet of needles from him, not noticing that the man was mad until Simon, rosy-cheeked and dark-eyed, had rushed into the kitchen for a drink of water. He had always been thirsty as a child, as if on fire and needing cooling.

She could see it all before her like a play at the theater, scene by scene: The boy stopping, bowing, and politely greeting the man. And the man's face twisting with hatred.

"A bastard Jew," he had said. "Christ, woman, you've got a Jew-boy in your kitchen."

Then the scene blurred and she couldn't remember how she got the man out of the house, only that she had flung the packet of needles at him and threatened him with the police if he came back. But the picture of the boy's pale face and the many questions in it was quite clear, as was the memory of how she had sat there at the kitchen table with the boy on her lap, trying to explain what was inexplicable.

She also remembered that evening when Erik drove the truck into the garage. Before she could intervene, Simon was asking the question.

"Dad, what's a bastard Jew?"

Erik had stiffened, then collected his wits.

"There's no such thing," he said.

But Karin knew Simon had seen the fear in Erik's eyes.

That evening, they made the decision that it would be best if the boy didn't know.

There were whispers and Karin remembered her anxiety over Mrs. Ågren's poisonous tongue, and how Simon had come home one day to say that Mrs. Ågren wanted to know where she, Karin, had found him.

Then war came and the spring of 1940 when all the insidious ill will changed to threats. Oh, those warm April nights as the Germans were invading Norway and she thought they would be at her door at any moment, pointing at the boy.

My heart had pained me then, thought Karin, surprised she hadn't remembered before. She had also understood Ruben's anguish. And Olga, the mother whom she had never seen, the woman who had chosen madness.

I should have talked to Ruben, she thought.

The sea beyond the fortress was turning gray. They would have rain before evening. Karin rose. It was past three, so Lisa would have gone home and Helen would have come with the milk. She would have time for a nap before Simon came back from school.

But Karin got no sleep. As she lay on her bed with a blanket around her, that mountain wall again appeared before her.

He had to be told.

Her memory went back again to the war years, to the evening when Erik and she had remembered the letter. Inga had received a letter from the violin player, a long letter in German, which none of them could read. But they had decided that Inga should keep it and eventually give it to Simon.

She remembered the telephone call, Erik's voice urging Inga to burn the letter. Afterward, fear of the parish register had haunted Karin—what was in it and who had Inga given as father of the child?

She had hoped Erik would reassure her when he came home on

leave, telling her she was blowing it all out of proportion. But her fear had aroused his, and using his precious gas coupons, he had driven all the way up to the parish where Inga had been registered.

That simply made things worse. Erik had told the whole story to the priest, a middle-aged man, who had licked his lips.

"The damned priest was a Fascist," said Erik when he got back. "I didn't realize it until he started gabbling on about keeping the Aryan race pure."

They had quarreled.

"I could have killed him," said Erik.

In the parish register, it stated *Father Unknown*.

Karin opened her eyes. There was to be no midday nap. Her gaze fell on the rocking chair where she had sat with Isak when all those ships had been lost and Isak had lost both himself and his mind. Everything had combined to keep her fears alive. But the memory of Isak at the time nevertheless gave her strength.

I managed, she thought.

Then Simon came in, flung his schoolbooks on the stairs, and stood there, intense, full of life.

"Hi, Mom. How's things? What's for dinner?"

Karin laughed, trying to remember.

"Meat loaf," she said. "Are you in a hurry?"

"Yes. Going to a dance at Långedrag."

Karin looked at the handsome youth and thought she would like to be young and going out to dance with him.

It's been good for him not to know, she thought as she got up to see about dinner.

"Is Isak going with you?"

"Yes. Ruben's driving him here. He sent his regards and said he'd like some coffee."

That's good, thought Karin, and after dinner when Simon went up to his room to change, she said to Erik, "We must tell him. He's seventeen, and has the right to know."

Erik suddenly looked ten years older, but he nodded.

"Mm," he said. "I've been thinking that, too."

"It's difficult," said Karin. "Perhaps we should consult Ruben."
She could see that Erik disagreed.

"Everyone close to us must be told, anyhow," she said.

"Mm."

When Ruben came, she served coffee in the parlor so that he would at once know it was not going to be an ordinary evening. They talked, sluggishly, feeling their way at first, then more and more eagerly, Karin and Erik almost at the same time. Karin had always known Ruben was a good listener, but she hadn't realized how good it would feel to be able to tell this whole long story. The October dark closed in on them so they couldn't even see each other. But when Erik finally got up to light the lamp, they saw Ruben's eyes were glistening.

He didn't say much, only, "So it was not chance that you were able to help Isak."

"We were in the same damned boat," said Erik.

There was a long silence before Ruben spoke again.

"I did wonder a little at first," he said. "He didn't look particularly Swedish."

He remembered Olga saying, *Larsson—but that's not possible.* But he didn't tell them that, just said that over the years he had often thought Simon was like Karin and Erik.

"He's got the same temperament as you, Karin, the same purity, if you see what I mean. And he's like Erik, too, eager and intense."

That helped.

But how did Ruben think Simon would take it?

Ruben sighed. "It won't be easy. But I don't think it will do any real harm. He's got such good foundations."

Then Ruben said they should be natural, not throw the truth into the boy's face, but wait for a suitable moment.

"When would that be?" said Karin in surprise.

"You'll know when the moment comes," said Ruben, so confidently they had to believe him.

When the boys came back from the dance, they sat in the kitchen as usual over a beer and a late sandwich. Ruben embraced Simon and thumped him on the back.

"Oh, my goodness, boy," he said. "If you only knew what I've ordered for you from America for Christmas."

The next morning the fog was like cotton wool around the houses. As on so many mornings before, Simon woke to the wail of foghorns and thought they sounded more ominous than usual. Karin seemed as burdened as the fog as she put out breakfast and said she had to go over to Edit Äppelgren's before the fog drove the woman mad. Simon was to leave his bicycle behind and take the tram.

"You can hardly see your hand in front of your face," said Karin.

He had to run the last bit to the stop, the blue tram appearing like a phantom out of the fog, its warm interior welcoming him with its friendly incandescent lights.

The parish minister, the stupidest of all the priests to bless the school with morning prayers, was on the platform in the school hall, so boredom soon crept up on Simon. Right at the beginning of the Lord's Prayer he managed to step out of his head, but found to his disappointment that this time his mind had gone straight home.

He found the kitchen empty, Karin already gone to the neighbor's. Simon's mind then went to the boatyard, but halfway there, he stopped it. They were having a break, Erik and his men, and Simon could hear Erik bragging over his coffee, talking about the bomb and the changed world, the men all listening respectfully.

He's happy, thought Simon, at his worst and best and greatest.

Simon thought he hated and despised his father. Just as his father despised him, the boy who was all thumbs, his head full of useless whims and fancies. He would never be a true worker.

God, how tired Simon was of the house. And the boatyard. And the bragging about boats. And politics. And everything sterling and reliable.

Simon's mind turned to the garden path, where he met Karin coming toward him in the fog, and he saw her with new eyes. She wasn't particularly beautiful, and the expression around her mouth of ardent self-satisfaction was detestable. She, the angel, had done her good deed for the day.

He hated her, too. He could never carry on a sensible conversation with her. She was uneducated and stupid and had never understood him.

Then it started again: Thanks be to you, O Lord, for what . . .

Simon's mind had to recross the boundary again, and he felt sick as always as the loud and out-of-tune singing went on all around him.

He never sang a note.

Then his stomach started to ache because of all these horrible thoughts. Later in the physics lab, where Alm was droning on about some idiotic experiment and there was plenty of time to think, he remembered the evening before, that something special had been going on when he and Isak had come back from the dance.

Something peculiar. Erik had looked tired.

But the memory of Erik fired his anger. Simon again started loathing Erik, his coarse hands and simple truths.

Karin was also thinking about Erik. The fog lifted later in the day and she went for a walk as usual.

Erik had not had an easy evening. The decision they had made during the war not to tell Simon where he came from turned into not thinking about it at all. Refusing to know.

Erik was good at not knowing.

He had always been more sensitive than she when it came to Simon's background. He had been the one to react badly each time they were reminded of it, such as the time when Ruben had thought Simon should become a violinist.

He was a man who created his own reality, Karin thought. He constructed it himself, stone by stone, never owing anyone anything. Anything that did not fit in with what he constructed was thrown away or denied. Thus others had to re-create themselves so that they could be fitted in. Simon fitted in less and less well.

There was trouble in the air. Karin knew that, even if both Simon and Erik said nothing so as not to worry her. This wasn't just about Simon's being impractical, but much more. Erik's superiority was necessary to protect his reality. He had to be superior, the marvelous only son of his mother. Otherwise what?

"Well, then he'd die," said Karin straight out aloud, angry as always when she glimpsed this inheritance from her mother-in-law.

Now Simon had gone ahead of Erik in many ways, in acuteness, in knowledge, in swiftness. Erik felt threatened and took to scorn.

"Give us a hand here, boy, unless you're afraid of dirtying your hands, of course."

Simon was upper class and had to pay for it. That was school, of course, but something else, as well. He was born upper class, Karin thought, but the next moment she thought that foolish.

Could it have anything to do with race, that the essence of Simon was Jewish?

No, Isak was about upper class and Jewish, and in him was everything Erik demanded, cleverness, a good hand with nails and screws, and most important of all, a great admiration for Erik and an obvious admission of his leadership.

The sun came out, the light silvery white from the fog, and Karin went to the oaks. There, beneath the largest tree, heavy and golden in the early autumn, she realized that it was herself she was protecting with all these thoughts about Erik. She didn't dare take her own fears out into the light of day.

It might break now, the umbilical cord that had given nourishment to her life.

When Simon is told, he will be free, Karin thought. She wasn't his mother, so he could choose to discard her. She knew that there were moments when he despised her.

She felt a pain in her chest, and no tears came to heal it.

In the mirror at home, she saw that her lips had turned blue, but she took her pills and slept. She dreamed she was giving birth in great pain to a son, and it was Simon who came out of her womb. She swaddled him and took him to his father.

It was a long way to go to the man waiting for her up on the hill, but with great dignity she went and held the child out to him. He took the child in his arms, and not until then did she look at the man, up into his face, and she recognized Ruben.

SEVENTEEN

"*I*s that Mr. Ruben Lentov?"

"Yes, speaking."

"My name's Kerstin Andersson. I'm the welfare officer at Söråsen Sanatorium."

She named the town, and Ruben was vaguely able to place it somewhere in the Småland Highlands.

"Oh yes. Good morning."

"Good morning."

The voice on the telephone appeared to be doing everything to seem assured, but not succeeding.

"Is it possible that your wife's name was Leonardt? I mean, her maiden name, before she married you?"

"Yes." Ruben was now feeling threatened.

"Olga Leonardt?"

"Yes. What can I do for you?" His tone of voice was so formal, the other voice lost all confidence.

"Perhaps I could speak with her?"

"No," said Ruben. "My wife is mentally ill."

"Oh, I'm sorry."

What the hell's this all about? thought Ruben, but he already knew that the inevitable had caught up with him. The voice went on as if its owner had heard what he had been thinking.

"We have a girl here, one of those rescued from Bergen-Belsen. Her name is Iza von Schentz, and she says she is your wife's niece, daughter of your wife's sister."

The walls of the spacious office began to close in on him, the room growing smaller as images raced through his head. Iza, a lively five-year-old. She had been bridesmaid at his wedding once upon a time in another world. Oh God, he thought, God of Israel, help me, and he put the receiver down on the desk and managed to get to the window facing Norra Hamngatan and open it, drawing a deep breath and noticing the sea was white right up to the harbor channel. Stormy weather over Göteborg.

Then from so far away it was as if from another universe, he heard the voice on the telephone.

"Hello, hello. Are you still there, Mr. Lentov?"

He pulled himself together, picked up the receiver intending to ask questions, but found he could find none.

"Iza," he said. "Little Iza."

Kerstin Andersson's voice had regained strength now.

"I realize you need time to think," she said. "Perhaps you could ring me back a little later."

She gave him her number, he wrote it down, and as he put down the receiver he found he was very cold.

The room had reverted to its usual size as he went over to close the window and tell those in the office that he didn't want to be disturbed for the next half hour. Then he went to lie down on the black leather couch, a newspaper over his head.

He tried to remember the child, see her face. Couldn't.

One of the dead millions had returned, but she had no face. Was she like her mother? Ruben suddenly remembered what it had cost him to try to forget Rebecca all these years in Sweden, trying to forget the girl in Berlin he had once loved.

Rebecca Leonardt.

She had married a German officer. Ruben couldn't find an image of von Schentz either, but he very clearly remembered a conversation in a café in Paris, where Rebecca had tried to explain her engagement to the German.

"He's kind, von Schentz," she had said. With his help she was going to get herself out of the Judaism that was ensnaring her, imprisoning her.

"I can't breathe in the women's gallery at the synagogue."

He, Ruben, had not shown his despair, but had been generous and understanding.

So the marriage hadn't helped her, he thought. He got up and fetched a mineral water to quench his sudden thirst.

She was a writer, and up to the end of the 1930s, she had sent letters and signed copies of her books to Olga. Ruben had never been able to bring himself to read her books, but he knew she had a good reputation.

I married Olga to be near her, he thought.

No.

Yes.

The two daughters of wealthy Dr. Leonardt, one of whom had had everything, talent, beauty, and a large open mind. While the other . . .

Ruben felt an almost wild tenderness for Olga now, the younger sister now in a mental hospital, playing with dolls.

The image of his wife and her dolls brought Ruben Lentov back to reality, to the late autumn of 1945 in Göteborg, to action and responsibility.

I never even asked how the girl was, he thought. He sat down at his desk to phone, but his finger dialed Karin's number, and when he heard her voice he realized what he had always known but never dared see, that Karin was like Rebecca in every respect.

"But, Ruben," said Karin. "How wonderful. We must get her better, and she'll like it here in Sweden."

That was right. That was what he needed to hear.

"First of all you must find out how ill she is. She's presumably got tuberculosis, as she's in a sanatorium. Talk to the doctors. You must go there."

"Yes."

"And you must ask about her family, her mother."

"Yes."

"Ask the welfare officer, not the girl. Oh, goodness, Ruben, it's a miracle."

He could hear Karin was upset, and thought about her heart.

He wanted to say something calming, but was struck again with the realization that he had recognized Rebecca in Karin the very first time she had come to his office.

"Ruben."

"Yes."

"We'll make her glad to live again."

Both of them would remember those words as they gradually came to understand that Iza was a person with a ruthless, burning desire to live.

"How old is she, Ruben?"

He worked it out. He had married in 1927, so she must have been born in 1923.

"She's twenty-two."

"Oh, good," said Karin. "I think the young mend more easily."

He still had some of Karin's confidence when he spoke to Kerstin Andersson again.

"A few patches on her lungs and they healed well," she said. "Iza is a survivor. She goes to school here, learned the language, and is tremendously inquisitive about her new country. But this business with you will be difficult," she added.

"What do you mean?"

Kerstin Andersson told him her patients found it difficult to cope with great joy. She told him about a woman who had had a good prognosis but had died when she got a letter from a surviving sister, now in Palestine.

Ruben tried to understand.

"Is that why you haven't tried to contact me before?"

"No," said Kerstin Andersson. "Iza has been talking all summer about an aunt in Norway, but she couldn't remember what the aunt's married name was and we didn't really take it all that seriously."

She didn't know what my name was, thought Ruben. Rebecca obliterated me just as I obliterated her.

"Then one day she saw an advertisement for your bookstore in the paper."

Ruben remembered the advertisement, autumn news from England and America, books that had once again reached his shops.

"She recognized the name and went quite crazy. Her temperature shot up and she scared the doctors. I didn't really believe her story, but the specialist thought I should check it out. Mostly to calm her down, you see. So I phoned you."

"Does she know anything about it?"

"No, I must try to talk to her this afternoon."

"I thought I'd come this weekend."

"Good, but wait until you hear from me."

"Yes. Is there anything she'd like to have, do you think?"

A laugh came over the phone.

"She wants everything," the voice said. "Clothes, shoes, makeup, sweets, books, handbags, stockings. They all want everything."

Ruben couldn't laugh. He collected himself for the most difficult question.

"Is anything known about her mother?"

"Yes, she was gassed in Auschwitz. Both children saw her being taken to the gas chambers. Iza's brother died in Bergen-Belsen a week after it was liberated."

"Oh, no."

"Yes, that was hard for Iza. But a lot gave up at that stage. There were a whole lot of diseases, too, typhus and so on."

Her voice was tired, and there was a brief silence before she went on.

"Your wife, is she very ill?"

"She has no contact with the outside world. She's in a mental hospital. But you needn't worry, I have a son and friends. I'll take good care of Iza."

"Oh, I didn't ask because of that. I just wanted to know what to tell the girl."

In the end, Ruben managed to say something soothing, for he realized he had been speaking to someone whose life was not easy.

Erik rang later to say he'd be glad to drive Ruben to the hospital on Saturday. Train services to the Småland Highlands were poor, and he knew Ruben didn't like driving long journeys in the country.

"I can find the way," Erik said. "I was admitted there once myself, when I was young."

Ruben thanked him, for that was a great relief all around, but he was surprised.

"Did you have consumption?"

"Yes, for a spell in my youth, after a broken heart."

Broken heart sounded odd coming from Erik, but he presumably couldn't think of another way of putting it. How well they knew each other, thought Ruben, and how little they knew about each other.

Kerstin Andersson put down the receiver with a bang and stayed seated. She knew that the entire women's ward was already simmering with excitement at the chance that Iza had relatives in Sweden, rich ones, too. Everyone's hopes had been ignited by Iza's.

She's as fragile as a reed, Kerstin thought. But she won't die. Despite everything, this was no personal tie. Iza couldn't remember her uncle. But a tie was a sign that one belonged, and more, a link back into the world.

Kerstin got up, went over to the bookcase, and took out the file she had kept after her talk with Iza. Yes, she remembered now, the father had been a German officer and had shot himself with his own service revolver when the Gestapo had come to fetch his wife and children.

She remembered Iza's astonishment.

"He died, you see, right in front of us."

The girl seemed to have forgotten it and suddenly remembered, this first death of the thousands she had seen.

There had been a younger sister, too. She had died on the way to the camp.

"It was best for her," Iza had said. "But Mama couldn't take it. They had to wrench the child away from her."

Then the usual, but through all that hell they had managed

to keep together, Iza and her brother. When he died after the liberation, Iza had fallen ill and had hovered between life and death.

Kerstin sighed, put the file back, and as she had so many times before, she wondered whether she could go on with this job. There were tensions over Iza. She acted superior. At the sanatorium they were mostly Polish, grown up in the ghettos of Łódź and Warsaw, and Iza challenged them with her good German, her grand name, and her manner.

And her ruthlessness, Kerstin thought with some reluctance.

But she looked like the others, awful.

I must prepare Lentov for her fatness and loss of hair, Kerstin thought.

She went off to look for Iza and found her in the schoolroom with a book, a Swedish novel, Moberg's *Ride This Night*.

"Isn't that a bit difficult for you?"

"No, it's exciting."

Kerstin thought about the strange eagerness with which the girl tackled the language, and in fact everything that was Swedish. She remembered Iza reading newspapers, starting on the front page and reading everything, advertisements, death announcements, radio programs, reports of lost dogs and lost wallets, and personal ads. Everything surprised her, delighted her. She asked about every word she didn't understand, making the nurses, the assistants, Kerstin, even the doctor himself, explain.

Kerstin asked Iza to come with her to her office, gave her a chair, and stayed standing as she briefly and factually told her about Ruben Lentov, that he had remembered Iza and her mother, and he would be glad to look after her.

Iza's triumph was boundless.

"I knew it," she cried. "I knew it, but you didn't believe me." Then nothing would stop her. She flew down the corridor, from ward to ward, calling out.

"I've got an uncle in Sweden, a rich uncle, and he's going to look after me."

The excitement rose everywhere and dreams flourished. They forgot she was so grand. A miracle had happened to her, so miracles could happen to them all.

Now I'll be in trouble again, thought Kerstin as she saw Sister coming toward her, dignified as usual but more forbidding than friendly.

"I've told you the patients mustn't be upset. They'll all have temperatures tonight, and it'll be your fault."

Kerstin hurried after Iza.

"Now come with me. Put your coat on and we'll go out on the grounds."

As soon as they were outside, Kerstin said, "Your aunt is sick, mentally ill."

"Why?" Iza stopped in midstep.

"What do you mean? No one knows that kind of thing."

"How silly," said Iza. "Here, in peace, with food and a rich hus- band, and then to go mad."

She was angry, and afraid, for she realized this changed her po- sition. Ruben Lentov was no blood relative, and she was only his wife's niece.

"You said he was going to look after me?"

"Yes. He seems to be a trustworthy man."

Iza calmed down, her voice less sharp.

"Is it true he's rich?"

Kerstin thought about her poverty-stricken student years at the Institute of Social Studies in Göteborg, when she and her friends had slipped into the elegant bookshop in the city center, with its soft carpets and smell of fine books.

"I should think so."

They set off early on Saturday morning in Ruben's old Chevrolet, which had been laid up during the war and was now purring like a contented cat along the narrow winding road to Borås, growling with delight up the hills, and generally enjoying being able to go out into the world.

"Quite a car," said Erik. "They don't make them like this any longer."

But the car gobbled gas, and it began to snow in Borås. Erik filled her up, and bought some chains when he was told the weather would be worse up toward Ulricehamn.

Simon was in the back with Isak, who, after some hesitation, had decided to go with them to meet this cousin returned from the kingdom of the dead. In the trunk was Olga's fur coat, a new hand-bag of the finest patent leather, a bag of cosmetics Karin had bought, bars of chocolate, and a heap of books.

"She reads everything she can get hold of," Kerstin Anders-son had said.

They wiggled out of Borås and began the climb up the Småland Highlands and into the kingdom of snow, its bluish mountains, miles and miles of forest, its white spruces.

"It's lovely here," said Ruben. He was nearly always surprised by how magnificent Sweden was whenever he got out of town.

But Erik muttered about worn tires, changed into second gear, and crawled, but eventually had to stop to put on the chains. Isak helped him while Ruben and Simon went into the forest to relieve themselves. Then Ruben stood stamping his feet for a while to keep warm, watching Erik quickly and skillfully affixing the last chain.

Ruben suddenly remembered what Otto von Schentz had looked like.

As they went on, he thought about the German, the girl's father. He might be still alive, perhaps in a Russian prisoner-of-war camp.

It was quiet in the car, all four of them now rather ill at ease, thinking about the accounts they had read and the photographs they had seen, and they realized that none of it had been real to them.

Not until now.

Then they were there, driving into the courtyard, the sun shin-ing, the snow sparkling, and perfectly real people swarming around the car, fat, amused, inquisitive. Livelier than ordinary people in Sweden, yes, more childish, more openly affectionate.

Did they have any food with them? Bread?

No, were they hungry? Didn't they get enough to eat?

Erik felt his anger rising, but then Kerstin Andersson was there, a tall gray-eyed girl who said briefly that everyone there got double rations of everything, but nothing was ever enough for them.

"You can see how fat they've gotten."

Simon thought she was horrible, but the patients laughed and said that was the worst thing of all, that they could never get enough food. They spoke a mixture of German and Swedish.

Erik didn't find it difficult to understand, and feeling quite unreal, he was soon sitting with a pot of coffee and a coffee cake, together with ten fat women. But he was pleased and in a good mood.

Iza was waiting for Ruben in Kerstin Andersson's room. The last few days had changed her. She had turned quiet, tried to eat less, had washed her hair, and wept in despair when it kept coming out in chunks. Alone in the schoolroom, she spent hours trying to remember what to do, how to speak and behave in the salons of decent people. She had borrowed some nail polish from a nurse and that had strengthened her, for she had lovely hands. But she didn't dare look in the long mirror in the gym.

Her temperature had been high that morning and Sister had looked cross, but Iza was pleased because in her pocket mirror she could see that it had put color in her cheeks and a gleam in her eye.

Like Olga. Not like Rebecca, like Olga. The same nervous craving around her mouth, the same slightly curved nose and high narrow forehead. Even the fine slightly bluish network at her temples was there. And the same restless eagerness, the same hunger that nothing could satisfy.

"Iza, my dear," he said.

She saw in a flash that she wouldn't have to make an effort, that his guilt was so great that he had to accept her as she was.

"I want to get out of here," she said. "Now, at once."

"I quite understand," said Ruben. "But the doctor decides that."

"I hate him," she said. He was astonished at the intensity in her voice, and the hatred. "He's a Nazi, the same kind of bastard as the Germans in the camp."

She may be right, Ruben thought, and he was frightened. But he didn't want to pursue it, so he changed the subject.

"Kerstin Andersson told me about Rebecca," he said.

"I don't want to remember."

"I can understand that."

Her reply came like lightning. "No, you understand nothing."

Ruben lowered his head. "Do you know anything about your father?"

His question was tentative, but he had to know. It went right into Iza, making her open and genuine and surprised, like a child.

"He shot himself," she said. "Right in front of our noses. We just stood there, and then he shot himself."

Her eyes looked back in time to that moment when all those incomprehensible things had begun.

"Why?" whispered Ruben.

"When the Gestapo came to fetch us, Mama and us."

Her eyes turned back into the room and onto him. She laughed. "Can you imagine such a coward, the bastard."

Ruben didn't dare look at her.

A little later, he opened the door and called to Isak, asking the boys to bring the presents. She barely looked at her cousin and didn't even glance at Simon. She had eyes only for the presents.

"God, what a wonderful fur."

She tore it out of the bag and tried to squeeze into it, only just managing, though it would not button.

"I'll get slim again," she said. "I will, I will."

As Simon was helping her take the coat off, he saw the number, clumsily tattooed numbers on her arm.

It was a moment outside time, a second containing everything anyone ever needed to know. He read the huge number and saw the many dead, knowing they would not hold the living responsible.

They had ceased whispering in the wind.

But he also knew that the dead created the silence on earth and everything that could not be comprehended.

As he took his eyes off the girl's arm and met her eyes, he saw she was angry, and he knew her anger would make his life real, and so he would have to endure it.

Isak had also seen those numbers.

"Why do you go bare-armed in winter?"

But she wasn't listening. She was busy with the marvelous patent leather handbag, the lipstick, and the perfume.

Kerstin Andersson came to tell them that the doctor would like to speak to Ruben. A Nazi, Ruben thought, as he uneasily followed the tall girl along corridors, knocked on a door, only to find himself eye to eye with a very old Jewish friend.

Olof Hirtz!

They were equally astonished.

"I had just been told about a rich uncle."

"And I'd been told about a Nazi doctor."

They hugged each other.

Hirtz was a leading medic, specializing in tuberculosis. He was married to a psychiatrist, and Ruben remembered that he had always been interested in the psychology of tuberculosis, the connection between the disease and grief and the lack of the will to live.

But he had to ask.

"What are you doing here?"

"I took a sabbatical from Sahlgrenska Hospital," said Olof. "You know, you want to do something. And also, this is very interesting study material."

His words were deliberately cynical, and he emphasized that with a grimace.

"But these cases can't be representative," said Ruben, feeling his way. "I mean they've contracted the disease in absurd circumstances."

"That's what I thought at first," said Olof Hirtz. "But I'm beginning to wonder. These people were just ordinary people. They were brought up, loved, hated, had good and bad mothers, cold homes, warm homes, siblings, poor parents, rich ones."

"Yes, of course, but . . . but then . . ."

"Yes, they landed in hell, were humiliated and abused to an extreme, and reacted in different ways, regardless of background and any strength they had been given in childhood."

"They're not so different. Is that what you mean?"

"Yes, but they are clearer now because they've been tested. They have an unconscious knowledge of what is real and what is semblance. We ordinary mortals are seldom allowed to know that."

"That's true," said Ruben.

"Maybe we'll be allowed to experience it when in extremis, when we're to die, I mean. If we're not so drugged that we miss out on it."

Olof sounded angry, so Ruben did not say what was on the tip of his tongue—that then it wouldn't matter. He also remembered that Olof Hirtz was deeply religious, and Ruben had no desire for a discussion on extremes.

"Iza," he said. "I came to talk about Iza . . ."

"She'll be all right," said Olof. "It actually surprises me that she contracted TB. She's one of those hungry for life, the ones who owe their survival to their actual will to live. Perhaps it's typical that the disease made a late appearance, and was only in the early stages when it was spotted in the quarantine ward in Malmö."

"I don't really understand."

"She had strength as long as the battle lasted. When it was over, she could give way to her weariness. Then her brother died and she could no longer hold back her sense of being abandoned in childhood."

"What do you mean?"

"Iza didn't have an easy childhood."

Ruben felt as if something had attacked his heart.

"Her mother was a wonderful person."

"Possibly. But Iza was to a great extent her father's daughter, and he . . ."

"And he?"

"Well, a Prussian officer."

The words hung in the air, and Ruben reckoned Olof knew more than he wished to tell.

"Anyhow, she must stay here this winter," Olof went on. "We'll make another assessment in the spring. There's a risk we'll have to operate. One lung is gassed, perhaps you knew that?"

No, Ruben knew nothing about the treatment of tuberculosis, but he reacted to the word. Gas!

"You can have complete faith in us. She couldn't have better care than she gets here."

"No, I'm quite sure of that."

His words restored the old warmth between them. They talked for a while longer about mutual friends and books Olof wanted, which Ruben said he would get for him.

"You would help Iza if you can bring yourself to say no, and make demands on her. You'll have to watch out with your formality," Olof said.

"What do you mean?"

"I mean you probably have a touch of the Christian veneration for suffering, and that's no help to survivors of concentration camps."

Ruben expected a scene when he had to tell the girl that she still had to stay in the hospital.

But there was no scene. She shrugged, so perhaps she already knew.

Trying to sound firm, Ruben said, "The doctor is an old friend of mine, a famous medical man and a humanist. He is no Nazi. He's Jewish."

"I know more about Nazis than you do," said Iza. "And I despise Jews."

"Just as the Nazis did," said Isak, his voice like the crack of whip.

She looked frightened and said she hadn't really meant it, that she was so tired of all the talk and she had a temperature.

Nor was there much talk in the car on the way home. Erik was really the only one to speak at first, about how strong people's will to survive was, and how surprising it was to find sick people with so much joy in them.

"They really do believe in the future," he said.

Ruben nodded, but was thinking that a life directed only at survival would probably find great strength in simplicity.

Simon sat in the back feeling ashamed of Erik. Isak wasn't listening.

They drove to the house by the river, where Karin was waiting for them with dinner, veal with pickled gherkins and compote of strawberries.

"How was she?"

"Full of life," said Erik. "And anger."

"Frayed," said Ruben. "Hectic and frayed."

"She's a bloody cow," said Isak, dropping his fork onto the floor.

Karin looked from one to the other and thought about those ghosts getting off the white buses and how she had felt they ought to be dead, just as she herself ought to die, and how she had decided to survive just as Iza had. But she said nothing.

"You make things simple for yourself, Isak," snapped Erik.

Ruben was thinking how like Olga the girl had been, and he said nothing.

Later, when Karin was alone with Simon, she took up the question again.

"But what was she like, Simon?"

Simon looked at Karin for a while, thinking she would never understand, but he tried to answer.

"Lively," he said, hunting for words. "Affected." Then he added, "Open. She's open to everything, hungry. And sometimes she's got those eyes, you know, like Isak had that time."

Karin nodded.

Empty, she thought. Perhaps eyes that have seen too much had to be emptied.

EIGHTEEN

*T*wo days before Christmas Eve, surprisingly and in the middle of the morning, Ruben turned up in a hired truck at the house by the river mouth.

He was so pleased, he was glowing.

"What on earth?" said Karin, and she could hear from his laugh that she had said the right thing.

The driver helped him ease off a large heavy wooden crate, stamped *Handle with Care*. Ruben had spent all morning at customs, but now he was here with it, his Christmas present to Simon.

After the truck had gone, Ruben went to the boatyard to ask Erik for some help.

"What in heaven's name is that?" exclaimed Erik.

"I'm so nervous. I'll put the coffee on," said Karin, but by then Lisa had already set about it.

They had coffee while Ruben continued to glow over his surprise.

"Upstairs with you, women," he ordered. "Go and do Simon's room."

"It's already been done, I'll have you know," said Lisa.

"No," said Ruben. "I mean the long wall opposite the bed has to be cleared."

Karin laughed, infected by his delight.

"All right, we'll do as you say, Ruben," she said, and she and Lisa went upstairs to move things.

"We'll never get that up the stairs," said Erik. But then he measured, calculating angles, and finally said yes, they probably could.

"Have you any electricians at the yard?"

"No, I do that myself," said Erik. "Is it a machine?"

"Well, yes, you could say that."

It took a lot of sweat and half an hour to get the crate up the stairs, which was just as well, for Lisa and Karin needed the time to move the bookcase over to the short wall, taking things off, then putting them back.

The men were given a beer each as they stood panting on the top landing before they set about the crate, levering the lid off with a jimmy.

"Careful," said Ruben.

Wood shavings and paper came out, and Lisa reckoned she would have waited with the cleaning had she known about this. Then finally it was revealed, a terrifying cabinet of fiery shiny walnut with garish gilt moldings and silvery material in front of loudspeakers.

"It's not beautiful," said Ruben.

"It certainly is," said Karin. "It's handsome. But what is it for?"

Erik's smile ran from ear to ear as he plugged it in, wondering whether that was what Ruben had wanted an electrician for.

"Wait," said Ruben. He pressed a button, then twisted a knob. A symphony orchestra thundered out as if the players were all in the room with them.

The house held its breath. It had never heard anything like it, and it took some getting used to. Erik screwed up his face. Karin sat down on Simon's bed with a gasp of surprise, and Lisa almost dropped the vacuum cleaner on her way up the stairs.

"That's not the most important part," said Ruben. "Where in heaven's name is the phonograph?"

None of them could hear what he said because of the music. Ruben turned it down and looked at them with satisfaction.

"Now listen, Erik Larsson. You're a technical genius. Please find the phonograph and connect it up."

Erik nodded.

"You must be able to open it somehow," he said, fumbling around the piece of furniture named Victrola.

"Switch it off!" cried Karin. "It might explode!"

That provided the house with a story that caused a great deal of laughter.

"You're crazy, woman," said Erik, and Ruben laughed so much, he also had to sit down on the bed. He hadn't had so much fun in a long time.

Erik was a good hand with things, even the newest and unfamiliar, so it wasn't long before he found the button that made one half of the top rise like a lid. The turntable, heavy and sturdy, was in place. But the tonearm had been removed and lay there neatly in pieces in a carton, with instructions on how to assemble it.

Ruben started slowly translating, but Erik impatiently took the leaflet away from him, and glancing at the drawings, he put the tonearm together and got it into place.

"Now," said Ruben, taking out a record. "This is for you, the two others for Simon."

Jussi Björling sang about Sweden through the hideous speakers, and the atmosphere in the room grew quite solemn.

"Christ, that's good," said Erik, and Ruben could see his eyes glistening, and again thought how little people knew about each other.

They went down to the kitchen afterward, and Ruben said they should wait for the boys, and as soon as they saw them coming up the drive, he, Ruben, would go upstairs and put on the Berlioz.

"What's that?" said Karin.

They laughed at her again, and she laughed herself, saying it was a good thing she wasn't easily offended.

"I did bring some smoked salmon and wine with me," said Ruben. "But what did I do with it?"

"I expect you left it in the truck," said Karin, and they all laughed again.

"We'll go and get some more," said Ruben. "We must have a party."

While Karin was setting the table, Ruben told her that he and Isak were going to Copenhagen for Christmas, to his brother's. They were to fly from Torslanda on the morning of Christmas Eve, taking Iza with them. She was on leave from the sanatorium.

"We talked a lot about it when they were staying with me during the war," said Ruben. "About celebrating Christmas in Copenhagen. It was a dream my brother had."

Karin nodded. That made sense. Ruben couldn't look after the girl on his own. He needed help from his family, so he was trying to get Iza to become a joint Jewish affair. That won't be easy, she thought, remembering the brother's family.

"Isak was pleased," said Ruben. "He finds the Danish family difficult, not to mention Iza. But he was persuaded, largely, I think, because he very much wanted to fly."

Silent ghosts again went through the kitchen as Karin thought about Iza, whom she had now met. Karin had seen those unnaturally large eyes and thought Simon was wrong. Iza's eyes were not empty, but were filled with every degradation and horror they had seen. In their depths, they were burning, a hunger deep down that no one and nothing could satisfy, but would devour anyone who got in its way.

She doesn't know it herself, Karin had thought. She thinks she is going to take back everything she has been robbed of.

"And what did you do during the war?" Iza had said to Karin. "Grow potatoes and worry about dinner?"

"Yes. What would you have done in my place?"

Karin had been neither angry nor sad. But she had felt it in the air that the girl was sowing divisions, and when Karin looked at Simon and saw how bewitched by her he was, she was frightened.

But Karin put her thoughts on Iza aside, for this was a happy day. The truck came back again, and the driver knocked on the door.

"You forgot this," he said, handing over the salmon and wine.

An hour or two later they heard the boys coming up the drive on their bikes, and Ruben shot upstairs, found the record, and turned the sound up to full volume.

He'll have a stroke, thought Karin, but then Simon was there in the hall, the music rolling down the stairs. He stood stock-still, a shimmer of happiness around him, then slowly went up to his room and lay down on the bed, still in his outdoor clothes.

Little was said down in the kitchen as the music filled the house. They seemed to understand that Simon had gone into another world, a land that was his and to which he had always longed to go.

Ruben knows, Erik thought, ashamed of the time when Ruben had wanted Simon to learn the violin.

I've known, too, he thought reluctantly, made uneasy by the music still pouring through the house, strange and unfamiliar.

Silence fell eventually, and Simon came down and stood in the kitchen door looking at Ruben.

"You're crazy, Uncle Ruben," he said.

Everything lay in his words, not just gratitude for the gift. Ruben felt honored, touched as so many times before by the forbidden thought—if only the boy were mine.

Late that evening after Erik had driven Ruben and Isak home, as they sat in the kitchen, hearing the music from upstairs, they were able to ask the question they had wanted to ask all day.

What had the Victrola cost?

"The freight from America alone," said Erik. "You know, the freight and customs alone . . ."

"But he's rich," said Karin, and Erik thought about the profit Ruben made from his investment in the boatyard.

Then he said so to Karin, and they overcame the great problem of what the music had cost Ruben.

They didn't see much of Simon that Christmas. He made brief excursions into their world, for food and to give Karin a hand in the kitchen, and he was physically present on Christmas Eve, opening parcels from the two grandmothers, containing knitted socks and other things he didn't want, but he didn't disdain the old people as much as usual.

On Christmas morning, not sparkling, but gray everywhere, he did the dishes while Erik demonstrated the Victrola to the neighbors, who all said it was as if Jussi Björling himself were there in the room.

Simon wasn't angry with Erik for boasting, nor did he hate the piles of plates with sticky remains on them. Everything was as it should be, and when Erik had finished with the neighbors and the kitchen was clean and tidy, Simon went back to Berlioz's *fantastique*.

The first time he played his record, he was back in the great grassy realm and saw the man speaking the forbidden language, the war, the building of the temple, and death on the great bull's horns.

But gradually, those images faded, and Simon was able to sense the great sorrow in the long notes at the beginning, and the painful beauty when the first movement started in all its splendor. In the middle of the liberating storm, he became aware of the thumping darkness in the background, its solemnity giving order and power, frightening and wonderful, to the world. He experienced space and the heavens, the vast heavens, neither naming them nor seeing them, like light flowing in from the west, white and liberating, followed by the sun playing with the wind in the seas of grass, where the images appeared again, colored by brittle joy.

Then he was filled with wordless melancholy.

He put on the first movement over and over again and made a strange discovery. If he let his mind go free, roaming where it wanted to go, yet at the same time experiencing emotions without naming them, a fusion occurred. Then thoughts and emotions ceased, obliterating each other.

Eternity, he thought. The Kingdom of Heaven. But as soon as he tried to rationalize, it was all lost.

He put on the first movement again and disappeared. When he came back he was lying on the floor, knowing he had recognized the oaks, the land that is but doesn't exist.

Suddenly he thought about his philosophy teacher, one of the few at school who managed to dispel his boredom. He had talked about thought, the mind. Was the mind unlimited? he had asked. Or does the mind set the limits? Simon had thought that stupid at the time, as it was so obvious that the universe could be conquered by the mind.

His teacher had talked about Einstein and Bohr, the theory of what is not manifested. He had said something amusing, something they had laughed at, but what? Simon began rummaging in his notebooks, remembering he had written it down because it was so contradictory.

He found it, some quotes, but Simon hadn't bothered to note down who had said it.

"Every attempt to understand what is not manifested leads to self-deception. You think about it, and the next moment you have formed an idea of it, and thus you have lost it."

A little farther on was another quote, carelessly noted down and hard to read.

"The mind can ask all the questions on the meaning of life. But it cannot answer one of them, for the answers are beyond the mind."

"That's true," Simon said aloud, astonished.

He put on the first movement again.

It took him nearly the whole of the Christmas holidays to conquer the symphony and make it a familiar route toward its own source.

Before he fell asleep at night, he thought with secret delight about the other record, the one he hadn't yet heard. "Mahler's second symphony, easy, more earthy. I think you'll like it," Ruben had said.

Simon listened to it on Twelfth Night, when Karin and Erik went to a party.

For a while that evening, he thought he would go crazy with his delight in the music, the humor, what was young and untamed, the freedom flying through the great forest. It was easier to let the images go this time, and he did so almost with a sense of loss, for they were full of cheerfulness.

When he went beyond the content in Mahler, too, the next afternoon, he felt like a king, splendid and victorious.

Angry, too, filled with wrath. But no guilt, no fear.

Erik had had enough, and closing his eyes to the appeal in Karin's eyes, he yelled up the stairs.

"Can't we have a moment's peace from that damned music."

Simon switched off the phonograph, gathered up his nerve, and went downstairs.

Now, he thought, now.

He stood in the kitchen doorway, tall and slim, looking at them, his eyes burning, as if the music had darkened them even further. As he turned to Karin, there was more sorrow in his voice than anger.

"What the hell's wrong with the music? What are you afraid of?"

Tears came into his eyes when he remembered the time they had tried to stop him from learning the violin.

"What were you quarreling about that evening when Ruben wanted me to learn the violin?" he said. "What was so awful about it?"

It was snowing outside, the flakes as big as a child's hand, and as always when it snowed, the house was bathed in a vast silence. All three of them heard it, and Karin knew the moment Ruben had mentioned had come. She could see that Erik knew it, too, but was reluctant, and would soon escape to the boatyard if she didn't keep him here in the kitchen.

"We must talk about it now, Simon. Let's take our coffee into the parlor."

Simon knew then that something tremendous was on its way. He was so frightened, he felt sick and he, too, tried to get away.

"Can't we go for a run in the car?" he said to Erik.

But they both went into the parlor and sat down on the uncomfortable armchairs, listening to Karin clattering with the coffee tray. Erik did not meet Simon's eyes, but spoke when Karin came in with the coffee.

"Make sure you take your heart pills before we start."

NINETEEN

*I*t was all so momentous, there was no room for small and careful words.

The thing is, Karin said, she and Erik couldn't have children. They had never been able to. Simon was adopted and had come to them when he was three days old.

Simon's gaze wandered from Karin's face to the window. It was still snowing, the light going. Everything that was happening was beyond reality.

I've always known, he thought, I've somehow always known. I've never belonged.

It was an old idea, belonging in unreality, to fantasies.

"But who am I?"

Karin took a gulp of her coffee, swallowed noisily, and Simon felt he had loathed them for a long time, Erik and his boasting, Karin and her simplicity. But that feeling also belonged in his fantasies, that secret world he created when he was angry and miserable.

Karin started telling him about the fiddler, the Jewish violin player they knew so little about.

She's invading my daydreams, he thought. This is crazy, shameful somehow.

"Inga believed it was the water sprite," said Karin.

"Inga," he said.

That didn't fit, didn't match his dreams. He turned icy cold and looked around the parlor. Everything seemed unbelievable, although it was all taking place in reality.

No.

"She was young and lovely then," said Erik.

"They fell in love in the forest by the waterfall," said Karin. "But they couldn't speak to each other."

The preposterous story calmed him. It simply couldn't be true. He gave Karin an appealing look, then heard himself ask a question. "Doesn't Inga know his name?"

"No," said Erik.

"It's probably Simon," said Karin. "He was a music teacher at the college on the other side of the lake, but he came from Berlin and was Jewish."

"A Jewish bastard," said Simon, and then it was finally true, for the words brought confirmation.

The snow kept falling, but the silence between them went on until Simon broke it.

"But I'm not like Inga."

"No, you're like your father. At least, if one can believe Inga."

"So we're related anyhow, you and me?"

"Yes," said Erik. "Slightly."

"Dad," said Simon, now hoping to stop them, get them to say to hell with all this, let's go back to reality so everything is the same again. "Why have you never told me?"

They both spoke at once, telling him about the creeping anti-Semitism, the Nazism, the Germans in Norway hunting out Jews in second and third generations.

Then at last Simon knew it was true.

"I remember a telephone conversation, in the spring of 1940. I heard you say that someone should burn a letter."

Oh God, he thought, I already knew then it was about me.

"We were so frightened."

That was Karin, but Simon felt no pity for her.

"There was a letter?"

"Yes." This time it was Erik. "Inga had a letter from Berlin, but none of us could read it. We decided to keep it to give to you when you were older."

"Someone could have translated it," Simon almost shouted.

"Yes, but it was all so shameful out there in the country, and we had promised Inga we would tell no one."

That didn't make sense, Karin saw that herself, but Simon went on.

"Was the letter burned?"

"Yes, as far as we know."

Erik told him about the parish register and the Nazi priest. But Simon heard just the words *parish register*.

"What did it say?" he said.

"Father Unknown," said Erik, his old bitterness washing over him. "You see, I had revealed you to that Nazi bastard."

Silence, like the snow, again. Simon was cold, so cold he was shaking.

But he looked at them, from one to the other.

"So I'm supposed to be grateful, even more grateful?"

Karin could find no words, her mouth like sandpaper.

"To us you were a gift from God."

That was Erik. Simon was so surprised for a moment, he was shocked out of the present, for his father's words were so unlike him, and because of the great truth the words contained. He knew.

"Sorry, Dad," he managed to say.

Karin took another gulp of coffee. She wanted to tell him about the nights when he was an infant, the thoughts she had had, those strange thoughts about all children being children of the earth.

"You were only three days old" was all she said.

"You said so."

Long silence. Then Simon spoke again. "Does anyone know?"

"Yes. Ruben. We've talked to him."

"What did he say?"

Karin's thin voice stopped fluttering as she recalled. "He said children belong to those who love them and care for them."

"He said something else, too," said Erik. "That you're like Karin, that you have the same temperament as she has."

Simon was so cold his teeth were chattering, so Karin went to fetch a sweater. As she started draping it over his shoulders, he shied away from her touch, and she had to put it on the arm of the chair. He pulled it on and looked at Erik.

"Then I don't have to be as clever as you are?"

"Good God, Simon, you're much cleverer."

In the end, they appeared not to have anything more to say. Simon seemed collected, but was still shaking with cold. Must be this damned parlor, thought Erik.

The boy went into the kitchen for some water and drank glass after glass, then stood in the doorway looking at them.

"In a way, I've always known," he said.

A moment later, they heard the phonograph again, the incomprehensible music filling the house. But it soon stopped, and when Karin slipped upstairs to look in on him, he was fast asleep.

It was almost disappointing.

"It went well, didn't it?"said Erik.

Both of them were so tired, they went straight to bed without supper.

There was school the next day and the usual madhouse in the kitchen over breakfast. Term report. Simon found it. Karin wrote *Have read* on it and signed it.

But that was hardly true, as she never looked at Simon's marks.

"You all right?"

"Of course, Mom. Don't worry."

But he came home a few hours later with a high temperature.

Nothing odd about that. Half the city had the flu. Karin tucked him up in bed, made a honey drink, and took his temperature. It was high, and that scared her.

"Does the back of your neck hurt?"

He managed to shake his head and smile at her. Then he fell asleep.

At the time, all mothers had a terror of polio, which hovered like a chilling threat over everyone with a high temperature and a stiff neck. So Karin rang their old doctor, who said it sounded like influenza and she should phone again the next day if his temperature hadn't gone down.

A girl was running alongside Simon in the kingdom of long grass, birds making a nest in her hair, and she said, "Nice, isn't it?"

He desired her and had her, could do anything with her as long as he was careful about the bird's nest. He undressed her, sucked on her nipples, kissed everything that was her, her appetite as wild as spring, and he couldn't have enough of her as he saw she was more beautiful than any earthly woman. The grass played the second movement of Mahler's first symphony, the rhythm striking its waves with theirs, and when he stepped toward the unknown, the drums beat as if obsessed and he was obliterated, crossing the border into the land where nothing has shape and everything is comprehensible and perfect.

She was with him and with no words asked him if he understood what he had always known.

Then he saw there was an egg in her bird's nest, shimmering white and almost luminous, and he knew the egg was life and the chick soon to leap out of the shell would take on his shape and he loved the egg—it was as precious as life.

Then Karin was there with clear soup, saying it was important to drink, and if he didn't improve soon, she would have to get the doctor to come. He swallowed obediently, hearing her say how good it was for him and making himself get it down, thinking it was good for the egg, for the chick that was soon to be hatched.

But he wanted to return to the grass, to the endless sea of grass and the girl with the bird's nest in her hair. But he couldn't find her, and his fear was as great as the sea of grass as he ran, crying out her name. She had no name, he knew, yet he could hear it rolling over the plains and echoing in the mountains far away.

He was almost mad with fear. Didn't she understand that he had to get back to her and the egg if everything was not to disintegrate and life, his chance of life, be lost?

But she had disappeared.

He was now standing at the foot of a cliff and could see, high up near the sky, a large bird had settled, and he knew it was the bird of wisdom and it possessed knowledge of where the girl and the egg were. Using the last of his strength, he climbed up the mountain and prayed. Dear Lord, don't let me frighten the bird away.

But the bird stayed, as if waiting for him, and when he got close, he saw she was sitting on an egg, and realized the egg she was keeping alive with her warmth was his egg, his life.

The next moment, he heard a violin playing a strange tune, full of melancholy, and when he turned to look down the mountainside, he saw the girl, saw that she was a man now, a young fiddler wandering along with his fiddle, and the loneliness around him was great.

The big bird was looking at Simon with Karin's eyes and then he saw it was the bird of sorrow, not of wisdom, and he could be sure of his egg, the life inside its fragile shell and those thin membranes.

The bird of sorrow was faithful and loving. And strong—no harm was to come to the chick.

"But, Simon, you must calm down," the bird cried.

The bird gave him an aspirin and his temperature died away into a great sweat, then the bird got cool clothes on him and wiped his body and his forehead.

Karin was really frightened and called for the doctor, although it was ten o'clock at night. He felt and pinched and shone with his light, listening and calming them down.

It was only an unusually severe bout of influenza.

"Has something happened to him?" said the doctor as he was leaving. "He's showing some signs of shock."

Karin put her hand to her forehead and thought what an idiot she was not to have realized.

Erik took the old camp bed into Simon's room, and Karin slept beside the boy. But he slept all night and awoke before she did. He lay there looking at the bird of sorrow who had watched over his life.

Then he must have fallen asleep again, because when he awoke the next time, Erik was there with tea and sandwiches. Simon ate with good appetite, and Erik and Karin sighed with relief. Simon looked at Erik and thought it was good that he was as he was, earthy and unyielding.

Limited, restricted to a little piece of land you have made your own.

Simon was able to walk unsteadily to the bathroom, and when he came back, Karin had changed his sheets.

"I can hardly remember how many times I've done this now," she said, with some grateful thoughts for Lisa, who would soon come and do the washing and clean the house.

She found an old bedspread for the camp bed and a blanket, then lay down on it as if she had known that she and Simon would be able to talk now. The words were there, forming perfectly natural sentences.

She told him about the winter when she had gotten up in the night to give him an extra meal, how she had sat in the kitchen with him in her arms and had so many strange thoughts.

"I was probably terribly presumptuous," she said. "I was so sure I could give you everything you needed to become a strong and happy person."

"But you were right," Simon found he was able to say.

Karin had to cry a little. She also found words for all the happiness he had brought them, how they had found strength from him to get themselves out of the grasp of their mothers-in-law and the world of the poor, buy a plot of land and build their house.

"They thought we were conceited, and predicted it would all end badly," she said. "But we both knew we had to have a house in the country for you."

A nest by the sea, thought Simon.

She told him about the peddler, the Jew-hater with his packet of needles, the way he had looked at Simon and hissed *little Jew-boy* at him.

"He frightened me to death," said Karin. "Do you remember?"

"No."

Simon remembered the tramps coming and going around the houses, but recalled only that there was something strange, something frightening about them.

But he remembered them shouting at him at school. Jew bastard. And how Erik had turned white and taught him to fight.

"Well, I didn't really approve," said Karin. "But it did help you. It was a useful lesson to me, too, for I was made to see I couldn't protect you all the time, that you would have to be strong enough to manage on your own."

They talked over several days, reestablishing his childhood.

On the morning of the sixth day, the sun shone over the snow and Simon disappeared as usual into his music, while Karin went for a walk along the river and out toward the sea.

She stood there a long time, watching Vinga shimmering like a mirage in the crystal clarity of winter.

"I've done my bit," she said to the sea.

When she went back home, she was tired, but not in that hopeless old way. Her heart was beating calmly and regularly.

A few days later, Ruben came to see them. Isak went to the boatyard, so Karin could tell Ruben they had talked it out, that no one had died of it, but Simon had been delirious with the flu.

"It'd probably be good if you spoke to him," she said. Ruben nodded and went up to Simon's room.

At dinner, all five of them were able to talk about Simon's background, so long concealed, carefully hidden and terribly dangerous.

It was a relief.

Erik had not only concealed but had also tried to forget, and he clenched his teeth when Karin said, "I thought perhaps we ought to try to find out if Simon's father is still alive."

"He was a musician," said Ruben. "A lot of artists left Germany before it was too late."

He was thinking about the Jewish organizations still working to reunite scattered families.

But Simon was seeing the back of the young fiddler walking below the mountain with his violin and he was heading straight for the gas chambers, their chimneys just visible on the horizon.

"He's dead," he said. "He's one of those numbers on Iza's arm."

Simon was so definite, no one protested, though Isak thought, How the hell can he know that?

"He was probably a good man," said Karin, taking up the conversation again.

Good. Simon had to smile at her.

"He was lonely and miserable," he said.

Isak couldn't stand it any longer. "How do you know? Perhaps he was wild and happy."

Simon laughed. "That, too, perhaps."

"I was thinking about genes," said Karin, but Ruben explained at great length that nowadays it was acknowledged that environment was the important thing.

"We inherit certain physical features, and a talent or two, like Simon's musicality," he said. "But goodness isn't in the genes, Karin. It depends on how much security a child has."

Simon wasn't really listening, but mostly thinking about what Ruben had said upstairs, that all young people dream about being changelings, and that they all have to despise their parents by rebelling and disliking them.

"I used to wonder sometimes why I'm not as practical as Erik," he said. "But I might not have inherited it from him."

Ruben had laughed. "What about Inga, then? Your biological mother. I've always heard she ran the farm as well as any man."

Simon didn't like this kind of talk, but he had to smile like the others.

"Didn't you ever wonder why Isak isn't as well read or interested in books as I am?"

"No," said Simon.

"Perhaps every son has to vanquish his father," said Ruben. "He's likely to choose a field in which the father does not excel, in which the son can defeat the father by a wide margin."

Over that long spring Simon sometimes found the fear hurt him as it crept from his stomach up his throat, making it hard for him to breathe.

He thought about Inga, but pushed away the decision to go to see her. He thought about roots, that he had none, but he didn't truly understand it.

He also thought about the girl waiting for him at the sanatorium, like the spider waiting for the fly. Calm in the knowledge that he would let himself be caught, that it was only a matter of time.

TWENTY

*T*hen his last school summer holiday came. They were all to remember it, Simon because he was cheated and Isak because he met love.

Iza had been discharged from the sanatorium and was living with Ruben. She found the apartment cramped, the city dull, and Ruben himself hopeless, just like his friends, all middle-aged and bookish men. She also refused to go with them to visit Karin and Erik.

"Karin's an old cow, just like Mama," she said, oblivious to Ruben's reaction.

He tried to give her contacts with Jewish families in the city, appealing to mothers and daughters. But despite their attempts, no one could cope with her, and her anguish grew as she went in and out of shops on the Avenue and Kungsgatan, buying things to get relief. Isak was so frightened of her that even before the end of the term he had moved out to the Larssons' and the boatyard.

Karin appealed to Ruben.

"We have to understand him. The girl reminds him of what happened."

She reminds me of something else, too, thought Ruben. Of Olga. He had sensed it himself, that restless trotting around the apartment in high heels, the tinkle of bracelets and necklaces, the heavy perfume in the air, but most of all the unease reverberating through all the rooms.

There was really only one thing that interested Iza, and that was Simon.

"There's something mysterious about him," she said, and Ruben tried to be dismissive.

"He's just a kid who hasn't left school yet."

"I've nothing against little boys," said Iza.

She had become as slim and pretty as she had intended, and she talked to Simon about the camp and all the horrors.

"She needs to talk it out," Simon said to Ruben when Ruben interrupted them.

"No, she doesn't," said Ruben. "She wallows in it, and now she is tying you up. Watch out, for God's sake, Simon, just watch out."

This was one late afternoon after school. Ruben had found Simon in Iza's room and had as good as driven him out, then followed him down to the street.

Simon hung over his bicycle, staring at the man he admired more than anyone else, his eyes dark with misery.

"I can't escape, Uncle Ruben."

But as he cycled home, he had already forgotten both Ruben's and his own fears, now simply feeling how drawn he was to her, those red lips and that delicious body with all its incredible memories.

A week later, just before the end of the term, Iza was sent to convalesce at a spa in Switzerland. Olof Hirtz, her doctor and Ruben's friend, had arranged it all, along with therapy with a famous psychoanalyst in Zürich. Iza was pleased, for she wanted to go out into the world. Simon *was* just a kid, she thought, for after all, Ruben's words had sunk in.

"Was it necessary to send Iza away?" said Karin when she heard about it.

"You know as well as I do it was damned necessary," said Ruben.

Simon felt cheated, but also some relief mixed with his disappointment. The air around him had become fresher since the girl had gone.

After midsummer, Simon and Isak went sailing and were at sea for almost a month, cruising along the Bohus coast and into the Oslo Fjord. Then they came to the city where the Nazi boots had tramped.

"I can almost hear them," said Isak.

Simon stopped and also listened for the rhythmic tramp of boots on the stone streets.

"Let's go, Isak."

So they didn't see much of Oslo, not even the Oseberg ship that Isak had dreamed of, nor the Nansen museum to which Simon had wanted to go.

They returned home, proud of their sparse beards, brown as Indians, dirty, their hair bleached by wind and salt water. Karin laughed at them and sent them packing to the bathroom with razors.

"If you want beards, you'll have to wait until they grow more evenly," she said.

When they saw themselves in the mirror, they admitted she was right.

They took up the boat, scaled her, and cleaned her interior, for Erik and Ruben were now going off on a long trip. They wanted Karin to come, too, but she declined. Ruben thought she was afraid on account of her heart, while Erik thought she didn't want to leave the boys on their own.

But Karin didn't want to be in such close quarters with Ruben.

So one high summer evening, the boys set off to a dance on a quay down by Särö Island.

Isak met Mona.

Isak saw immediately that she was one of those rare people who make the world comprehensible.

She was pear-shaped, all her weight below the waist, and she had straight rather sturdy legs that always, wherever she was, kept her balanced at the center point of the earth.

No one had noticed she was tremendously beautiful until Isak saw it and made it obvious to the world. She looked at him with Karin's eyes, though strangely enough hers were blue, and she loved him from the very first moment in a great and calm way.

She had been mother to two small siblings, and that had helped her see life as something tangible. She had been deeply hurt the day her mother died, when Mona was just fourteen, yet she had been stable, secure, and straightforward, like her mother.

There had been no time to grieve or brood over fate. Little children had to have what they needed, every day and every moment.

If it hadn't been for an aunt, her mother's sister, things might have gone wrong, but her aunt maintained with some force that Mona also had a right to a life of her own.

So the fish dealer's daughter had gone to the girls' high school, after all, and that summer she had left school and was going to Sahlgrenska Hospital to train as a nurse.

She brought with her a slight contempt for men. She had never considered they were worth taking seriously. She may have read about love in some magazine or other, but she hadn't really believed in it, and it had never occurred to her that she might be afflicted by it.

So she was really tremendously surprised.

So was Simon. He had come across great love in a thousand books, passions sweeping people with them, driving them mad with despair or happiness. But he hadn't really believed in it, either, and he had never seen it in real life.

Now he saw it happening in front of his very eyes. It filled him with astonishment, jealousy, and something else he gradually had to accept as envy.

"They're nuts, Mom," he said to Karin. "They seem to be in a trance and see nothing but each other."

"I hope he'll bring her here soon, so I can see this miracle," she said.

But both Karin and Simon had disappeared from Isak's world.

He slept in town, in Ruben's apartment, got up every morning and drove the old Chevrolet, without a driver's license, to Axelsson's grocery store at a crossroads in Askim, where she was waiting. She was even more beautiful than the day before, and the car took them to the woods in the south, the rocks at Gottskär, the freshwaters of the Del lakes, and the thick spruce forests of Hindås. They found soft mossy banks to lie on, new meadows to wander across, and fresh flowers to pick.

Simply and without fuss, Mona gave herself to Isak, and he was gentle and tender, blessing the rock-blaster's daughter, Maj-Britt, for the experience and confidence she had given him.

Mona was a virgin, yet it was neither difficult nor painful. The next day, she went without hesitating to a doctor and learned how to fit a pessary.

Isak did not remember there was anyone else in the world until the end of a brilliant week after their meeting on Särö Island. Karin and Simon had some right to know that he was alive and what he lived for.

Not to mention Ruben, who was due to return a week later.

As soon as they met again, he said to Mona, "We must go and see, well, not exactly my family, but those closest to me."

She nodded. This was inevitable.

Then he tried to explain who he was, and he was overcome with shame, his head empty of thoughts, his mouth of words.

"I don't even know your surname," she said.

"Lentov," he said. "Isak Lentov."

She closed in on herself, and he sensed it, fear shuddering through him.

"I'm Jewish," he said.

She laughed. "I'm not an idiot, and I've read all about circumcision."

And his fears left him. He had to stop the car and kiss her. But there was still a stiffness, a surprise, and an absence.

"What's wrong?"

"Lentov," she said. "The rich Lentov with all those bookshops?"

"Yes. Anything wrong with that?"

"No," she said, but she was rigid, no doubt to hide her delight. If Mona had ever had any dreams in life, they would have been about money, wealth, and lovely expensive things.

"It's all so impossible to believe," she said. And then she added in a voice thin with unease, "What'll your father say?"

"My dad'll love you," said Isak.

"Now, don't be silly. You must know he'll want a grand rich Jewish girl for you."

"You don't know Ruben Lentov, " said Isak. "He'll dance for joy at our wedding."

She wasn't surprised that marriage had been mentioned. That had been obvious from the start. But she didn't believe in the father Isak had painted for her.

First it was Karin and Simon, though, only a quarter of an hour's car journey away, but it took several hours. There was so much to tell each other.

It was impossible to explain who Karin was if he didn't pluck up the courage to tell her about that time in Berlin, when the Hitler Youth were on the march.

Mona cried, good child that she was, hugged him and comforted him, good mother that she also was. I'll never abandon him, she thought. Not even if Ruben Lentov disinherits him.

Then she could tell him about her mother, about when death came one night and wrung all the blood out of her mother, about all those sheets stained red, and her own peculiar thoughts.

"You don't believe it," she said. "It goes on there in front of your nose, dying, and yet you don't believe it. Isn't that strange?"

No, Isak didn't think so.

Then he thought about Olga and knew that had to be told, too.

"My mom's in the loony bin," he said. "She went mad the night the Germans took Norway."

"Poor thing."

"It could be hereditary," said Isak, knowing he hadn't even dared think that until he met Mona. But he was not going to hide anything. "I've also got a cousin who seems mad. But she's been in a concentration camp."

Mona was crying again.

"We'll have four happy kids," she said.

So finally they were there on the kitchen sofa at Karin's, not saying very much but lighting up the whole kitchen. They're like sunlight, thought Karin, looking out of the window at the pouring rain.

"You'll stay to dinner, won't you?" she said.

"Yes, please."

When it stopped raining, they went out into the garden to pick strawberries for dessert. Simon came back from the lake where he'd been fishing from the rowboat. He was pleased to see them.

"You two are the most amazing thing I've ever seen," he said after watching them for a while.

They all had to laugh.

Karin took Simon with her back to the kitchen while the two lovers went on picking strawberries.

"Do you see how bright it is all around them, Simon?"

"Yes. Is it wise, Mom?"

"Wise?" said Karin. "I have to tell you that not even in my wildest imagination, trying to find something great for Isak, could I have created that girl."

"I like her," said Mona to Isak out in the strawberry bed.

"Of course," said Isak.

"But Simon's jealous."

Isak laughed. "Serves him right."

He put a strawberry into her mouth and kissed her.

They slept in the guest room in Ruben's narrow bed, and Karin lent Mona her very best nightdress.

I've got a daughter, thought Karin as she went to bed and heard the girl phoning home and calmly lying.

"I'm staying overnight with a girlfriend in town. Tell Dad, will you."

They must be a good family to have such a nice girl, Karin said to herself before falling asleep.

They had a few days to get to know each other before Ruben and Erik came home. Karin managed to keep Isak busy so that she at least had a few moments with the girl on her own.

The first morning she sent Isak off home with the car. "Put it into the garage. But clean it first. And not a word to Ruben about you driving without a license."

He obeyed, and Karin said just what Mona's own mother always used to say.

"Oh, men!"

As the boys took the car into town, Karin and Mona went to the bathing place. Karin took a cautious dip as usual, but Mona swam like a seal.

She seemed to have nothing to hide. She told Karin about her mother and that was difficult, then about her little brothers and sisters, now big enough to look after themselves.

And her father, the fish dealer.

"He's not up to much," she said. "Troublesome and easily offended, lots of toes to be trodden on. Stupid, too, and stingy. But you have to accept it. He's the father I've got."

Karin laughed. "How will he take Isak?"

"Well, there'll be a row, of course."

"Because he's Jewish?"

"Yes, that, too, but mostly because Dad'll lose his slave."

"Isn't he religious, a nonconformist? They usually are, out in the islands."

"Yes, there'll be a bit of shouting about Antichrists and so on. But religious people are only like that on the surface." Mona's eyes glittered as she went on, "But all that'll soon be over when he stops to consider the money."

Not even my own daughter could have been so like me, Karin thought, amazed and pleased. But Mona frowned.

"Not so good with Isak's dad. What he'll say."

"No," said Karin. "He'll like you."

"How do you know that?"

"He's a good man."

"That's a strange thing to say," said Mona. "Will that help me?"

"You'll see," said Karin.

Erik rang from Marstrand on Saturday to say all was well on board.

"We'll be there tomorrow as arranged," he said. "I'll go to the boatyard to take the provisions ashore. Are you well?"

"Fine," said Karin. "Love to Ruben and tell him we have a big surprise for him here."

"None for me?"

"No, I'm afraid not," she said, thinking about Simon and Iza. "But we have to take life as it comes."

She sounded just the same as ever. A Weird Sister spinning destinies in her kitchen, looking out for broken threads or tangles, but accepting that the fabric of life was complicated, not easily sorted out.

"How's your heart? I hope you've been taking your medicine."

"Erik, I don't even feel it."

"You never even worry about it," said Erik.

But he sounded happy. They had talked a bit, he and Ruben, about Karin getting so much better after her talk to Simon last winter, and the doctor had been pleased on her last visit.

As the handsome double-ender rounded Oljenäset at full sail, Mona, who knew about boats, drew a deep breath of admiration.

"That's my boat," said Isak, his eyes gleaming.

They let the big sail go, but the foresail flapped in the wind as they dropped anchor and lowered the dinghy. Erik stayed on board while Ruben rowed to the jetty.

"Where's my surprise?" he called out to Karin.

"I'll come down," said Karin.

So young he is, thought Mona, and handsome, every inch upper class. Her heart thumped and her sweaty hand clutched Isak's.

They couldn't hear what Karin was saying to Ruben down on the jetty, but Isak knew her well enough to imagine, and he knew he couldn't have had a better messenger.

"Great love, Ruben. And she's everything you need, Ruben."

Ruben was so taken aback, he had to sit down on one of the piles.

Over the years, he had come to rely on Karin's judgment, so he was already convinced before he went up to meet the girl. It was a gray day, and he at once became aware of the light around the young couple.

He looked at the girl, took in what was the core of her being in one single look.

"Heavens? What does one say?"

Then he took Mona into his arms and laughed.

"You're a wonderful surprise."

Then he gave Isak a long look, and they all sensed the tenderness in his gaze as he said, "My boy."

Things went much as Mona had predicted with her father. He was furious. She was too young. A Jew! Was she crazy? What would people say! And the congregation?

But then, when he heard the name and thought about the money, a mild reflection of the gold glowed in his mind and he calmed down.

"The Jews have been punished for two thousand years," he said. "Maybe the debt has now been paid."

They became formally engaged at the Gardening Society's restaurant on the Sunday before school started.

In the morning before the party, Ruben took Mona with him to meet Olga, the first time in years Ruben had not made that weary journey on his own.

He was also grateful when he saw how naturally and without fear Mona faced Olga, the way she made contact through the dolls, and he saw a glint of life in Olga's eyes.

On the way home in the car, the girl said, "She's not unhappy. In a way, that's what's most important."

Ruben nodded. He had thought the same himself, that Olga was now happier than during all the years when she had been well and mercilessly exposed to her fears.

"It's true," he said. "But that doesn't console me much."

"Yes, I can understand that," said Mona.

When Ruben met Mona's father for a drink at the restaurant before they went in to eat, he thought that life and people's way through it was more mysterious than any psychology could ever explain.

How in heaven's name had the girl managed to grow up in the shadow of this man?

Erik made a speech, stating the essential.

"You've found a Karin. Take care of her. They're rare."

TWENTY-ONE

Simon and Ruben went out to listen to the Göteborg Symphony Orchestra play Gösta Nystroem's *Sinfonia del Mare*. And Simon heard . . .

. . . *Gentle Indian women washing their children at the source of the river, where a wave was born, a wave that went to the sea, taking with it the memory of the smell of human children. The wave also remembered the smell of the mud and the moss of trees, the great trees that could halt the course of the river with their heavy roots and sing the eager water to calmness for a moment or so, before the wave had to go on to be reborn in the sea.*

At the outlet, the wave met salmon on their way upriver, obsessed with their love of life.

Yet the wave soon forgot the playful fish for its fear, the river water's terror of losing itself in the limitless sea.

But the wave was not obliterated. It froze to ice and its imprisonment in the cold almost took its lust for life away.

Then spring came one day and the wave broke free from the ice, knowing it had survived, that it was still itself while at the same time a part of the whole sea. The wave began its long journey eastward, and great ships divided it and great winds played on its surface.

The wave loved the winds: the strong wind that gathered up its strength and invited the wave to take part in the dance; the sun-wind that rocked the wave to sleep with dreams of the sky; and the huge clouds, too, that added to the life of the wave through mists and rain.

On the southern tip of Greenland, the wave met the icebergs, swung around in surprise, and stopped. It murmured at the transparent green

veins of water trapped in the smooth precipices and felt them exploding in-
side the iceberg from their longing to be away from the frozen solidity.

As the wave went on, it took color from the meltwater and a knowl-
edge of the sorrow that existed in everything that allowed itself to be
shaped.

Between Iceland and the Shetlands, the wave became heavy with
salt and learned to hiss, finding enjoyment in the constant exchange be-
tween white crests and its green base. It raced across Skagerrak in heavy
breakers, rounded Lister, slow and mighty, aware of its strength.

Then one day in the autumn it was smashed to pieces on the rocks of
Bohuslän, meeting its gray death, yet finding it could not die, rather
that all these experiences had to be handed back to the sea. The wave
was reborn and, with new memories of deep fjords and heavy granite,
headed north again along the Gulf Stream toward the ice and the tre-
mendous wind.

Simon stayed in the concert hall as the audience was leaving, until
finally Ruben put his hand on his shoulder and said, "I think we
must go, too."

Olof Hirtz was there and came up to speak to Ruben. Simon
managed to put into words his new insight, right in the face of this
stranger.

"The wave doesn't die," he said. "It can't be obliterated, because it never falls for the temptation to separate."

Olof Hirtz was pleased, in that way you can only be from
unique encounters.

"Come back with me for a late snack," he said.

They had only a few blocks to walk and were soon in the spacious kitchen of an old apartment. There was Maria, one of the Indian women from the source of the great river. She had a strong
curved nose, wide cheerful mouth, eyes that were black and far too
large in that triangular face, and a boyish haircut like a black helmet.

It's not true, thought Simon, but he realized it was, and that
Maria was Olof's wife and also a doctor.

"Psychoanalyst," said Ruben as he introduced them, and that was just as astonishing as the fact that she was wearing trousers and a red velvet top, her handshake firm and her smile broad and inquisitive.

While Simon was helping her take smoked salmon, cheese, bread, butter, and beer from the larder and refrigerator, he could hear Ruben phoning Karin.

"We'll be late," he was saying. "So don't wait up for Simon. Maybe he'll stay overnight at my place."

Olof Hirtz was back working at Sahlgrenska Hospital, doing research and teaching again after his years at the sanatorium in Småland. His experience with the suffering of the concentration camps had marked and absorbed him. He and Ruben often met now over talks about Iza, and their acquaintance had matured into great friendship, as happens when one has to talk about sensitive and personal problems.

Ruben had told him about the Larssons, how Karin and Erik had helped Isak over the years, and about Simon, the boy who was so lonely in the middle of this happy family.

"He's attracted to Iza," Ruben had said.

"If the mother is as good as you think, perhaps he needs to singe his wings," Olof had said, adding the usual wise words about all young people having to have their own bitter experiences. "All we can wish for them is the strength to endure their fate."

As they sat at the table in the spacious old-fashioned kitchen, Olof felt the same need as Ruben to protect Simon.

But he was no fool, so not a word was said about the girl. Instead, he told Maria what Simon had said at the concert hall, that he had increasingly come to believe people's misery was due to their striving to create an identity that distinguishes them from others.

"But that's necessary," said Maria.

"It just makes us lonelier."

"But we are alone," protested Ruben. "We're born alone and we die alone. We're not waves in the sea. Anyhow, there's great satisfaction in being an individual."

"Not on a deeper level," said Olof. "A personality can never find the meaning of life, or have any peace of mind."

Simon looked at him in surprise, but Ruben didn't give in.

"Other things can give life meaning," he said. "The struggle, the joy of striving for a goal and winning, all those things that require you to have a personality."

"Power and money?"

"Those, too," said Ruben, then when Olof laughed, he added, "Anyhow, that keeps fear at bay. And helps a bit against guilt."

Olof turned serious then, too, and said he had thought quite a bit in recent years about guilt upholding the myth that we are separated from others. He told them about his patients, the camp people with lung troubles, and how they had feelings of guilt over all they had to endure.

"But that's crazy," said Simon.

"No, it strengthens the sense of a destiny of one's own and clarifies the borderline with the executioner."

Ruben's face turned red with suppressed anger. "If it's guilt that allows me to escape feeling solidarity with the Nazis in Buchenwald, then I'll pay that price. God, Olof, we are separate."

Maria laughed. She had a way of tossing her head back, and her laugh was as dark as the primeval forest. Indian, thought Simon.

"Olof," she said. "I know you don't like talking about the Fall of Man, but it did actually happen, and the separated person is so fiercely forced to eat from the tree of knowledge. You know as well as I do that all children have to have an identity, a self with which they can hold their own. Otherwise things go wrong. Then you can lament that the identity or the personality, as you call it, is so vulnerable and that fear and guilt require so many defenses. But that doesn't change the actual fact that the experience of self is the destiny or task of humankind."

Ruben smiled this time. "Eve," he said. "The eternal Eve, an earthly woman keeping our feet firmly on the ground."

Olof was also amused but persisted. "I think the Fall of Man is a delusion and the identity a defense mechanism against nonexistent threats. Separation concerns only a small part of everything a person is, namely the intellect."

"You forget the body," said Maria.

"We aren't bodies," said Olof.

"I certainly am," said Maria, and there was a frosty element in her smile.

As always when Simon had to make an effort to understand, he screwed up his eyes and tightened his face muscles. So many of their words went over his head. For fear of being left out, he started telling them about the wave born to the Indian women.

They listened with interest. That gave him the courage to talk about the kingdom of grass.

"Somehow I've always been in that country," he said. "I was there all through my childhood, and now I'm there in my dreams."

He told them about the girl with the bird's nest, the precious egg, and the bird of sorrow.

Maria was profoundly taken by his story. "When did you dream that?"

"When I was ill and had just been told I was adopted."

Maria nodded and said he was one of those who have thin walls against the subconscious and he should be pleased that that was so.

Simon didn't know what she meant, but he was feeling encouraged and told them about Berlioz's symphony, the one that had taken him into the grassy realm's hour of destiny, and about the priest-king he had known ever since childhood.

"A little man with a funny round hat," he said.

He was so eager, he avoided looking at any of them so as not to be stopped by their surprise. He talked about the phonograph and how he could play movements over and over again in order to be free at last of the images and all content.

"Where are you then?" said Olof.

"In reality," said Simon, so surprised himself that he had to look straight at Olof so as not to lose his foothold. But Olof just nodded as if Simon had said something quite natural.

"That's a good expression. Others call it God."

"No," said Simon, and the others had to make an effort not to smile.

"I do," said Olof, and seeing Simon's astonishment, he had to explain. "I'm not one to go to church or synagogue. On the contrary, I try to think as little as possible about God, but I constantly want to be in Him."

"Like the wave in the sea?"

"Yes, that's a good image. That's why I was so interested when you said the wave couldn't die, because it avoided separating itself from the sea. I think the same condition applies to human beings, requiring them to relinquish the self."

"But they have to do their bit on earth first," said Maria. "Human beings have to take responsibility for their lives and their world, cope with their relationships, be good parents and decent householders."

Simon wasn't listening to her, as he had turned to Olof.

"How do you get rid of self?" he said. "What do you do?"

"Well," said Olof. "How do you obey the will of God? It's the same question, isn't it?"

It wasn't to Simon, but he made no protest.

"One way is to do what you did and go beyond the images," Olof went on. "But that's not easy, for anyone with a strong ego has a great many images. He has to make images for himself of everything he has detached himself from."

"That would mean that if you have some idea of God, then you separate yourself from Him," said Ruben.

"I think so. You can only obey the will of God if you have no image or any concept of Him whatsoever. That's what you've learned through music, Simon. You just use other words. And words are of no significance."

Ruben could see the boy was on fire.

"Many people have described the same experience as you have, Simon," he said. "Seekers and mystics have gone the same way. They've used prayer or meditation, whereas you've used music."

Simon had never been so surprised in his life. He thought about his endless lessons in religion, the morning prayers at school, and how he used to ask himself how anyone could be so stupid as the priest up there in the pulpit. Was it possible that he was the one who hadn't understood?

He told them about the priests at school.

"So, I'm an idiot, then?" he said.

They laughed again.

"No," said Ruben. "You're probably not the stupid one. Religions create a system that makes people stupid."

"All answers make people stupid," said Maria.

"Yet you have to ask questions," said Olof. "I think everyone seeking answers to questions on the meaning of life is religious. You are, Simon."

There was a long silence, as if they all needed time to think. Then Maria spoke.

"I have learned with my patients over the years that to understand another person, you have to ask yourself in what direction that person is seeking the answers, what is that person's secret religion."

"But many people never even get as far as the idea," said Simon. He was thinking of Karin and Erik, living their lives as something self-evident.

"Many more than you think," said Ruben.

"But, Uncle Ruben, think about Mom, Karin!"

Ruben smiled so brightly, it lit up the table.

"Karin's one of those who don't have to question. She lives in the answer."

Maria smiled.

"There are people like that," she said. "A few."

"But all the others, who just live from hand to mouth," said Simon.

"Some become strangers to themselves and others," said Maria. "Others try to reach the goal of their yearning by regressing."

"What? What does that mean?" said Simon.

"Well," said Maria. "Children have an answer in their way, beyond consciousness. I think so."

The oaks, thought Simon.

"But that's not good, regressing, is it?"

"No," she said. "It's always a miserable business."

"I suppose there's no way back," said Olof, and Ruben laughed.

"Maybe you remember from school that paradise is guarded by angels with raised swords," he said.

Simon had never given a thought to the creation story, but he remembered the stone he had smashed against the trunk of the great tree, and he realized that his farewell when he was eleven had been necessary.

Then Maria said that most people were actually obsessed by the dream of a mother's breast, and that made Simon uneasy.

But Maria made coffee and found a box of chocolates. Her ordinary everyday activity calmed Simon, and they talked about language, the tool and obstacle of humankind, and that we can never just let things be as they are, that we can never stop trying to describe them.

"Imagine being in an open relationship with the world," said Olof. "Being observant and sensitive but not evaluating."

"No measuring, no weighing, no judging," said Ruben.

"Exactly," said Olof, and he sounded so appalled that Maria had to laugh at him.

"Have a bit of this good chocolate," she said. "I know you value it highly."

"Simon," said Maria as they were leaving. "Don't take too much notice of these old men. There are words that free you. And you're welcome to come again. It's been nice meeting you, if I am allowed yet another evaluation."

Ruben phoned for a taxi. He wanted Simon to come back with him, but Simon had left his bicycle outside the concert hall and he also needed to be alone.

He flew through the sleeping city, out toward the sea, right out to the farthest quay at Långedrag. He stood there and let what had been said that evening run back and forth through his head until he was certain he would remember it.

The wind had risen and he could hear the sea roaring out there among the skerries. Storm clouds were racing past the moon, and all the scents of the sea wafted over him.

What does the sea smell of?

As he got back on his bicycle and set off home with the wind behind him, he thought he would write a poem about the sea tonight. He crept up the stairs, found pen and paper in his room, the sea symphony roaring through him, and he tried to describe the wave born of the Indian women at the source of the river.

But his words turned to ashes until he went straight to his question.

> *What does the sea smell of?*
> *Turn your face to the storm*
> *out there, bringing to you all the scents of sea,*
> *filling your nose, your lungs.*
> *Start with sturdy words.*
> *Seaweed. Salt.*
> *There is no answer to the words.*
> *What does the sea smell of?*
> *Try the other words, the harder ones:*
> *Force, freedom, adventure.*
> *They fall to the ground, limit the unlimited.*
> *Ask the question yet again:*
> *What does the sea smell of?*
> *And at last see that the question has no meaning.*
> *When you have stopped asking,*
> *then perhaps*
> *you can experience the sea.*

It was past two in the morning, but Simon wasn't tired. When he went to the bathroom, he must have woken Mona and Isak in the guest room. He could hear them laughing, softly and passionately, and he stopped in the hall listening until he heard Mona's half-suppressed bird-cry.

Then he was ashamed, but only for a moment, and as he finally crawled into his lonely bed, he felt how much he hated Isak.

But then he remembered his poem and thought about how he could make it acquire strength from the music, the rhythm in the symphony.

Simon went on writing his poem about the sea all through the whole of his last year at school. And hating Isak.

TWENTY-TWO

*T*hey left school in the spring of 1947. End of term was no great day, for neither Simon nor Isak put much stake in the rituals of final school exams. The only important thing was that they were going to be free.

No more compulsion, thought Isak.

No more boredom, thought Simon.

Nor was it a tense day, for neither ran any risk of failing.

Ruben threw a party in his apartment in town, which pleased Karin, for a student celebration in the hills at the river mouth was challenging. It was enough that for a few days Simon tore around the roads out there, his grand new cap apparently glued to his head. Then it was forgotten.

Isak was going on to Chalmers University of Technology. That was no problem, as his marks were sufficient. Simon wanted to study history at college.

Erik and Karin were not pleased with Simon's choice. What use would that be, and what kind of profession would it lead to?

But Ruben laid down the law, talking about research, and that in a few years Simon could be a teacher.

That comforted Karin, but Erik thought Isak had chosen the better way. He would become a civil engineer, which was what Erik had always wanted to be.

"Just as I wanted to be a historian," said Ruben, which made them all laugh again at the old joke about their reversed sons.

But first the boys had to do their military service.

Karin was secretly pleased, for then Simon would be out of

Iza's reach for another nine months. Iza had come back and been given an apartment in Stockholm, where she was to go to art school.

Erik was worried about the army—for heaven's sake, they were still only kids.

"Remember to look on it as a game," he said. "Don't take it seriously, just obey, and realize it'll soon be over."

Simon nodded. He knew what Erik was trying to say.

But Isak stated with great solemnity that he thought it was important, and anyhow, he wanted to learn how to defend Sweden.

Karin and Mona smiled, Karin gently, Mona proudly. As they sat over coffee at the table outside, no one noticed Erik's uneasiness.

The moment went by. Isak started singing the battalion song, and as always when he sang, Simon winced.

"It's a miracle I've put up with you all these years," he said, and he told the others about being awakened from his dreams at morning prayers by Isak bawling away at the top of his voice.

They all laughed. Mona sang the old song. Erik joined in and they sang it as a part-song. Simon approved and told them that it should sound like that.

"I couldn't hear any difference," said Isak.

But for some reason Karin wasn't amused, affected as she was by Erik's uneasiness.

Forwaaaaard match! Halt! About . . . turn!

The unmentionable was out to get Isak, creeping through his whole body from neck to midriff, where it hurt, emerging in his arms and down into his hands, which prickled from within as if from a thousand pins, reached his legs, and they refused to obey.

"Lentov, for Christ's sake, keep time . . ."

"Preseeeeent . . . arms!"

"Crawling by numbers!"

"Up. Down. Up. Down."

The unmentionable was in the air he breathed, in the measured tramp of the straight ranks. It clung to him, conquered him, and when it reached his head, he knew he had to obliterate himself in order not to die.

But then Simon was there, close by.

"For God's sake, Isak, you'll get used to it. You'll soon get over it."

Perhaps that would have been possible if Lance Corporal Nilsson's mother hadn't died and his place been taken by a sergeant by the name of Bylund, who hadn't chosen this occupation by chance, for his great delight was in tormenting boys.

There he was, in front of them, a large tall man, not bad-looking, but he had a quick and peculiar smile.

Like a wolf, thought Simon, who had never seen a wolf. It came and went, that smile. Bylund was pleased. Two bloody Jew-boys in his platoon, sheer bliss.

"You there."

"Who, me?"

"Yes, Sergeant, for Christ's sake."

"Yes, Sergeant."

Then it hailed down. Crawl, up, down, crawl, left turn, halt. Lentov, you put us all to shame, but that's to be expected.

That dry rattling laugh.

Bylund was amused. This would be a happier summer than he had reckoned on when Nilsson's damned mom had gone and died. Hilly terrain, sheltering rocky slopes between him and the lieutenant, who didn't like Jews, either, so would no doubt look the other way. Bylund smiled his wolf-smile at life.

He sniffed, smelling the scent of weakness, of corpses, in the air. I know him. I recognize him.

But Isak did not choose obliteration, not immediately. He got through the day, crawled, wriggled, was humiliated, shouted at. Simon went almost mad with rage. And with fear, for when they were in the canteen in the evening, he noticed Isak was becoming more and more mechanical.

Inaccessible.

Like that day in the school yard.

He got Isak into bed in the hut among six others who didn't dare meet his eyes, then he went to the lieutenant, managed to stand to attention, and spoke.

"Isak Lentov . . ."

"Number and name." The lieutenant didn't shout, but his voice was icy cold.

Simon managed to get out name and number, and also to say briefly and concisely, "Isak Lentov was badly damaged by the Nazis in Berlin when he was a child. He was ill later, mentally ill. He isn't able to stand the kind of treatment he's getting from Sergeant Bylund."

The lieutenant's blue eyes narrowed. "Are you reporting him?"

"I just wanted to . . . tell someone. It could be harmful."

Simon was being painfully civil.

"Didn't you understand my question, man?"

"Yes . . ."

"Yes, sir . . ."

"Yes, sir."

"So you're not reporting him."

Then Simon saw the derison in those blue chinks. The bloody man was amused. Despair washed over Simon, and he turned on his heel and left.

Lieutenant Fahlén suppressed his impulse to call Larsson back and teach him how to take leave of an officer, but discipline would have to wait for another time.

Damned unpleasant business, he thought. Bylund was known, his methods notorious.

Why the hell do they have Jews in the service?

Larsson, but hardly Swedish, him, either. More Jewish than the other one.

Lentov, son of that rich book Jew, of course.

But he let it rest.

The next day he kept Bylund's platoon in sight and made sure the sergeant was aware of his presence. But then he forgot all about it.

Bylund took it out on Simon when they had exercises out in the terrain, and Simon let it happen, suddenly seeing a way out. He was careless, messed things up, drew Bylund's hatred onto himself, absorbed his rage, crawled, wriggled, let himself be humiliated, every moment conscious he was sparing Isak. That wasn't really so much fun for Bylund, who knew in his guts that he couldn't break Larsson, but he comforted himself—the summer was long and he had plenty of time for Lentov.

That evening in the barracks, Simon saw the emptiness had crept into Isak's eyes. Perhaps it was no easier for him to see Simon being tormented.

God, what should I do?

There was a telephone down on the jetty. He had seen it when they arrived, an ordinary public telephone. But he was locked in.

The fence?

The guards were good shots, they said.

But he must get a message out.

The next morning Isak went on parade like a puppet, was shouted at, but took nothing in. They were to have exercises in the terrain again, and suddenly Simon had an idea.

At their first break, he made sure he was alone with Isak behind a stony hillock. Bylund was out of sight for a second or two, so Simon picked up a stone and struck Isak's lower arm with it as hard as he could.

"Isak," he said. "Sorry, but I couldn't see any other way out."

Isak smiled at Simon, as if he had understood and as if the pain had brought him back to himself.

"You'll end up in sick bay now, anyhow," said Simon, but Isak wasn't listening any longer. He had gone away again.

Simon ran over to Bylund.

"Sergeant—" Stand to attention, name and number, he remembered everything. "—378 Lentov has broken his arm."

"What the hell?"

Bylund looked anxious for a moment, though perhaps it was disappointment that the mouse had slipped out of his hands. But he obeyed orders—stretcher, transport, sick bay.

Simon went with Isak.

"Stay here, Larsson!" yelled Bylund.

Simon went on walking beside the stretcher.

"Halt!"

Simon went on.

"Halt or I'll fire!"

But Bylund didn't fire, for he was suddenly aware that the other six in his platoon would jump on him if he drew his gun.

Isak was unconscious now. The doctor was a captain, a man called Ivarsson. Simon went into the treatment room with Isak, and while the arm was being examined—yes, it was fractured—and plastered, Simon told him about Bylund, Isak's childhood in Berlin, and the risk of psychosis.

"But why didn't you say something before?" said Ivarsson, who was more of a doctor than a captain, and was now very upset.

"I reported it to the lieutenant."

"Oh, God," said the doctor, and then Simon realized the man was frightened. But then the captain assumed his doctor's demeanor and barked, "Larsson, leave the hospital immediately."

Simon went out into the sunny parade ground and saw at once that they had forgotten him, saw his chance and took it. He got his wallet out of his locker in the barracks, prayed to God that there were some coins in it, then flew over the fence down to the jetty and the telephone.

"Uncle Ruben, it's me, Simon."

His voice was shrill and sliced straight into Ruben.

"You must get Isak out of here. They're killing him. I've broken his arm, so he's in sick bay now, but he's gone away, you know, like he did during the war."

He managed to tell Ruben the doctor's name before his money ran out and the line went dead.

Ruben's emotions switched off and his blood pounded as he dialed the number of Sahlgrenska.

"Professor Hirtz, please. It's urgent."

"One moment."

"Olof, it's me, Ruben. You know what happened to Isak in Berlin . . ." Then he briefly related what Simon had told him.

"Have you the phone number out there?"

Yes, Ruben had it in his pocket diary.

"I'll phone and ring you back."

"Thanks."

A minute later, Olof got through.

"Dr. Ivarsson, this is Professor Hirtz at Sahlgrenska. I'm a friend of Ruben Lentov's, who's just had a worrying message about his son."

Ivarsson had been to Hirtz's lectures and admired him.

"An uncomplicated arm fracture, there's no danger."

"I want a psychiatric assessment."

"Not so good. He's fairly distant, preoccupied."

"He's to be sent here immediately. He needs special care."

"Yes, Professor Hirtz."

Ivarsson himself supervised Isak being put into the ambulance, then ordered Simon to go with him, though Lieutenant Fahlén looked as if he were about to protest as he stood watching.

As the ambulance left the barracks square, the doctor looked steadily at the lieutenant for a while. He's a Fascist, too, he thought. Both men sensed the quiet of the great parade ground and both simultaneously realized that every man knew what had happened.

The doctor walked heavily over to the regimental commander's office.

"Lentov. He's rich," said the commanding officer.

"And influential."

The regimental commander groaned, that damned Bylund, why the hell was he on duty again?

Ivarsson didn't know, but told him what Simon Larsson had reported to Lieutenant Fahlén.

Fahlén was ordered in.

"He didn't report anything, not formally. He stammered something about Nazis and that the boy couldn't stand Bylund. I didn't take it all that seriously."

"Lieutenant Sixten Fahlén," said the regimental commander extremely slowly. "If there's a court-martial on this and a scandal, and there probably will be, then you'll be the one, Lieutenant, to hang for it. You've brought shame to the regiment."

Fahlén clicked his heels and left in search of Bylund. But the sergeant had vanished.

The ambulance climbed through the twilight up the hill to the great hospital, Simon holding Isak's hand, though Isak was far away.

At the entrance, the driver asked for Professor Hirtz and was given directions. Ruben was there, but Isak didn't recognize him, so the stretcher was taken straight to the psychiatric department.

While Olof examined him, Ruben, Simon, and the driver waited outside in the corridor.

"I did what I could," said Simon, his voice breaking.

"I know, Simon."

"It was a sergeant," Simon began, but couldn't go on.

The driver took over, and Ruben was given a detailed account of what had happened, of Bylund and how Simon had tried to take on his rancor, and the report to the lieutenant.

"He's a Fascist, that Bylund, notorious," said the young driver, now so agitated that he was trembling. "Crack down on him, crack down on all those bloody bastards.

"He almost fired at Simon Larsson," he went on. "The boy in hut eighteen said Bylund almost fired his gun just because Simon went with Isak when the accident happened."

"Accident," said Ruben, glancing at Simon.

"Yes, the broken arm," said the driver, but at that moment Olof Hirtz came back.

"Shock. Impossible to make a diagnosis, possibly prepsychosis. He's to stay here."

"Phone for Mom," said Simon.

Olof nodded. Ruben thought about Karin, about how she had once said that Isak was not going into any loony bin, and she would see to that.

"Can she stay with him here tonight?" Ruben said.

"Yes, we'll put him in a single room."

Ruben went to the telephone and stood holding the receiver for a long time, trying to find the right words.

"You'd better come with me," the driver said to Simon. "Otherwise you'll be charged with desertion."

Simon nodded, and when Ruben came back he was already by the door.

"I don't know how to thank you."

"Huh," said Simon, and left hurriedly.

An hour later, Karin was there, Mona with her. She had fortunately been in the house when Ruben had phoned. Karin was pale, but calm and collected as she sat down by the bed and exchanged a few words with Olof Hirtz.

"I'll phone," she said.

She wanted him to go, and as soon as he had gone, she told Mona to get into bed with Isak.

In the corridor, Olof shook hands with Erik, who was as white as a sheet and was saying to Ruben that it was all his fault.

"I knew what it was like. I ought to have realized."

"But he wanted to go," said Ruben.

Erik was unconsoled.

"I've no damned insight when it comes to people," he said. "How will he get on?"

"I don't know yet," said Olof. "We'll see when he wakes. Karin's managed to put him back together before."

Erik sighed.

"Should I drive you back, or are you staying the night, too?"

"Thanks," said Olof. "I think we'd all better go home and try to get some sleep. Karin'll call me when the boy wakes."

"As long as those bastards don't take it out on Simon," said Erik on the way home.

Ruben felt his stomach contract. He was tired. And frightened.

"I'll call Ivarsson in the morning," said Olof Hirtz.

He did that, but it was too late then. Hours and hours too late.

TWENTY-THREE

*I*n the ambulance, Simon was so tired his whole body ached. He had been unable to think from the moment he had handed Isak over to Ruben.

"Lie down and have a nap, boy," said the driver.

Simon lay down on the stretcher bed and immediately fell asleep. When the driver woke him an hour or so later, he was feeling sick. The barracks square was deserted, and the one thought in his head as he jumped out of the ambulance was bed.

But as he stood in the dark corridor of the hut—God, how dark it was—he caught the scent. Fear collected in every muscle in his body, ready to leap, and before he even saw the sergeant's shadow, Simon knew where Bylund was and that his life was at stake.

Simon was fully visible in the light from the door, so he quickly shut it.

Don't let on you've sensed the danger. Go straight in and hit him.

His mind worked like lightning, Erik's old instructions still there. His straight right was precise, swift, and strong, and so was the smashing left jab, hurting his knuckles, but he ducked the blow that came, and as he rose again, his mind said, *Only as a last resort, Simon, kick him in the crotch as hard as you can . . .*

He kicked, and was almost happy to hear the roar of pain, then he struck again, into the man's stomach this time, horribly and effectively. Bylund bent double, and Simon struck him again, his head this time, and the sergeant fell.

At least fifty pairs of eyes were staring at him in the light that suddenly poured into the corridor. But Simon didn't see them. All he could see was Bylund's front teeth in a pool of blood on the floor, and he thought, He's dead, and he felt a wild joy.

The ambulance driver had seen the light go on and had taken over.

"Put it out!" he yelled.

They obeyed, then his voice came out of the dark, "Two men take him into the washroom and give him a shower. The rest of you get back to bed. Not one bloody one of you has seen anything. Understood?"

The whispered yes was enthusiastic, and the two who had been to the showers returned to say that Bylund was alive.

"Is he the duty officer here?"

"Yes, he changed with Fahlén."

"Oh, God," said the driver.

He got Simon's uniform off and put a bandage on the damaged knuckles.

"Put Bylund in the duty officer's bed." Then he said again, "No one's heard or seen anything."

As he got Simon into bed, he added, "You injured your hand when you jumped out of the ambulance. I can testify to that. Got it?"

"Yes."

It'll never work, thought Simon, but he was much more preoccupied with his own pleasure in having killed Bylund.

I'm crazy, too, he thought.

"Is he dead?" he whispered.

"Not bloody likely. He'll go on plaguing the life out of new rookies."

In all his relief, Simon was disappointed, but he soon escaped all his contradictory thoughts and slept like a log.

At reveille in the morning, Simon was ordered to report to sick bay, where he found the driver at the entrance.

"Not a word," the man whispered.

To the nurse he said, "This is the man who injured his hand when he fell out of the ambulance yesterday."

She was pretty and asked no questions as she bandaged his hand. Ivarsson came in for a moment.

"Arm in a sling," he said. "Off sick for a week."

His eyes did not meet Simon's.

This is crazy, thought Simon. They haven't found Bylund yet.

But the driver whispered, "They stitched up Bylund as well as they could this morning and took him to the nearest hospital. Suspected concussion."

"But they must know."

"They haven't set up an inquiry. They seem to be going to hush it up."

The regimental commander in his office two floors up was striding back and forth like an angry tiger.

"Lieutenant Fahlén, did you not realize Bylund's intentions in taking over your guard duty?"

"No, sir."

The old man stopped and gazed at the fair-haired lieutenant.

"You're no fool, Fahlén. You're something much worse."

Fahlén left, and the old man sat down at his desk and dialed Ruben Lentov's number.

"I need hardly say that I'm sorry about what happened to your son. How is he?"

"He's in the psychiatric department at Sahlgrenska."

"I'm sorry."

"Did you phone just to say that?"

"No."

Long pause. Simon, thought Ruben, now it's about Simon.

Then the voice came back again.

"Simon Larsson almost killed Sergeant Bylund last night."

Ruben found it difficult to breathe, but his voice remained calm.

"It must have been in self-defense."

"Possibly. But hardly a scratch on himself, so he must have used much more violence than necessary. Bylund's in the hospital with teeth knocked out and a concussion."

Ruben could say nothing.

"Mr. Lentov, perhaps you understand this might mean prison for Larsson, and for quite a stretch, too. If we don't hush it up."

"What's the price of that?" said Ruben, although he already knew.

So they settled the matter in a businesslike manner, silence on everything that had happened, on both sides.

"I'll arrange for Larsson to go on patrol duty out on the coast," the colonel said.

Ruben phoned the boatyard, directly to Erik.

"Christ Almighty," said Erik. "What a lad."

There was no mistaking the pride in his voice. They agreed not to say a word about it to Karin, Isak, or Mona.

"He's being sent on some patrol duty out in the islands," said Ruben. "So he won't get any leave for a while."

In the colonel's office, Captain Viktor Sjövall, commander of the patrol service, listened to the old man's story with increasing displeasure.

"Good Christ," he said.

"You can look after the boy."

"Yes. Must be a fine fellow."

"Devil of a fighter," said the colonel with some admiration in his voice as he took out Simon's papers. "An A student," he went on. "Highest marks we've ever had on the IQ test when he came. He ought to have been an officer."

Sjövall laughed. "No doubt we've gotten rid of any such desire now. If he ever had any."

The old man sighed.

Simon was asleep in sick bay, but was awakened in the afternoon, discharged, and sent off to a patrol boat down at the quay. They're going to drown me in their silence, he thought.

In the boat was a captain, with warmth and understanding in his eyes as he told Simon to sit down.

"I'm Viktor Sjövall, and you're to spend the rest of your military service with me out in the archipelago."

Simon had heard about the patrol service and knew it was much coveted.

"I know what happened, Larsson."

He's almost human, thought Simon, but he stayed on his guard.

"Yes, sir."

"That is, I know what happened to Bylund last night, but no one else knows, nor do you. Understood?"

"Yes, sir," said Simon, but when he saw the corners of Sjövall's mouth twitching, he added, "Perhaps I may tell you on some dark night at sea."

Sjövall laughed, and Simon relaxed.

"Sir, do you know how Isak Lentov is?"

"No, but you can phone home by radio as soon as we're at sea."

"Thank you, sir," said Simon, but then couldn't stand the man's warmth any longer and had to struggle to hold back his tears. Viktor Sjövall noticed.

"This has all been a bit too much, hasn't it, Larsson?"

"It was worse for Isak, sir."

"I understand that."

"I don't think anyone can understand," said Simon, and as the boat made its way through the islands, he told the officer about the sequestered ships, and about Isak and the Hitler Youth waiting for the four-year-old one May morning in Berlin.

When he had finished, he looked up at the other man and saw that he was moved, and also that he resembled Erik.

An hour later, the telegraphist said, "Your mom's on the line, Larsson."

Karin had never had a radio phone call before and thought that with no lines she had to shout.

"Isak's all right. He's coming home tomorrow."

"Oh, Mom," said Simon.

"He's going for treatment with Maria Hirtz."

The Indian woman, thought Simon, and he shouted back, "Great, Mom."

For the first time in a great many days, Simon felt he was back in reality. But then she said, "How are you?" and all became unreal again.

"Fine," he said. "I'm at sea."

But he thought that if she knew, if she ever found out that he had nearly killed a man and that he had enjoyed it . . .

His life became simple, a jetty, a few huts, boats for patrolling, guard duty.

But his unease kept gnawing at him.

Sjövall noticed.

"How are the nerves, Larsson?"

Then Simon told him the situation.

"I need to talk to my father."

The next day, Simon went on a transport that had an assignment at Nya Varvet. The skipper was told to put Larsson ashore at Rivö Huvud for two hours' leave.

Simon phoned his father and told him the time and place. "Bring Ruben with you if you can, but not Karin, do you hear, Dad, not Karin."

"Understood," said Erik.

They were there in good time, and anchored the double-ender on the wind side so that she was fully visible from the sea.

The wind was fresh, pulling on the grapnel.

"We'll have to keep an eye on her," said Erik.

Then they sat there, Ruben and he, staring out toward Vinga, waiting for a torpedo boat, but what came was a fishing smack and it was a moment before they noticed she was flying the patrol service flag. She yawed up, crept up against the cliff, and Simon jumped aboard.

They both noticed—he had become an adult, all soft boyishness gone, and there was a new and bitter awareness in his eyes.

They shook hands as if they were strangers, then Erik spoke formally and in that mawkish way Simon detested, "Bloody proud of you, I am, boy."

Simon's eyes darkened and his mouth twitched.

"Steady on, Dad. You don't know the worst yet. I almost killed the sergeant."

"Yes, Simon, we know."

Ruben told him about the telephone call with the colonel, the mutual threats, and the settlement.

"Christ," he said. "Christ Almighty, Uncle Ruben, what if you'd been any old poor bastard? Isak would be in the bin now and I'd be in prison. It's nuts."

"Yes," said Ruben. "It's nuts."

All three of them sat down in the lee of the wind.

"Does Mom know?"

"No, we're keeping her out of it, you know—her heart."

A moment later, he put his head down on Erik's lap and covered his eyes with his bandaged hand.

"Does it hurt?"

"No, it's getting better, just stings like hell in salt water."

He took his hand down and looked at Erik, his brown eyes looking right into the blue of Erik's.

"Just think, Dad, every punch went just where it should've."

Erik ran his fingers through Simon's hair, just as he had when the boy was small.

Ruben went over to the boat.

"I'll get the coffee and sandwiches."

As they ate, Simon told them in detail what had happened in the corridor when Bylund had been waiting there for him.

"He'll have false teeth as a souvenir for the rest of his life. And by Christ, that pleases me."

He looked at them as if expecting protests, but they laughed, the same satisfied laugh as his own.

"Later," he went on, "when the ambulance driver had put me into bed, I thought Bylund was dead, that I'd killed him. I was so happy, as if I were in heaven. Then I thought I wasn't all that different from Bylund."

They laughed again.

"We've probably all got a little sergeant in us," said Erik.

It was simple, even for Ruben, a matter of course.

When the fishing smack appeared again, they shook hands.

"See you soon," they said, and Simon went on board feeling he was now an adult, on an equal footing with both men.

"He never asked about Isak," said Erik as they set sail and reefed in the double-ender a little.

"No, thank God for that," said Ruben.

Isak had woken up at about four in the morning in his hospital bed, warm from Mona's warmth. He had felt her presence all over him and hadn't dared believe it.

Then he'd heard Karin's voice.

"Time to come back now, Isak."

Without opening his eyes, he had said, "Explain it to me, Karin."

"Well, Simon broke your arm to get you away from the sergeant."

Isak remembered, the stone, Simon's eyes. But then Bylund's voice came and everything went empty again.

Karin continued, "Simon managed to get to a telephone and called Ruben."

"He got over the fence. Bloody brave of him."

Karin went on, keen that he should understand the whole context, and then she started asking questions, trying to drag the whole wretched story out of him, bit by bit, over and over again.

"Who was he like?"

"Don't know."

"Isak, you do."

But the Nazis in Isak's childhood merged together and he couldn't distinguish one face from another.

"It was something about his nose, Karin. He sniffed. Then laughed. Oh God."

He screamed with terror, wept, begged them not to send him back there, back to the regiment and Bylund.

They promised.

Then Ruben was there and Olof Hirtz with Maria. Isak looked at her and thought about Simon, that Simon was fond of her.

Then he must have fallen asleep, because when he awoke only Maria was with him. His tears had gone, for the terror inside him was far too great for tears.

"Am I going mad?"

She hadn't snorted like Karin, nor consoled him.

"There's a risk, Isak," she said.

Then he wanted to return to the unmentionable, the silence in obliteration. But Maria's face wasn't like Bylund's, so she couldn't frighten him over the border, although she said, "You must stop running away, Isak. I think I can help, but you must stay put in your anguish."

"Then I'll die," he shouted.

But all that was long ago now, many weeks ago. He had been discharged, gone to Karin and Erik's, but the strength from them and their house no longer helped him.

Sometimes he got rid of the terror for a few hours, mostly when he was needed at the boatyard and his hands obeyed him. But usually he didn't know what to do with them and would sit gazing at them for hours.

Mona came and went, and he could see she was also growing more and more frightened, and in a moment of clarity he thought that at least he could do that, release her.

He gave her back his gold ring and told her to go. But she refused, and then he hated her. Just as he had hated Karin for the dark anxiety in her eyes and Ruben who had aged so, shrinking for every day that passed.

Maria came out in the evenings. They sat in Simon's room, and he occasionally made an effort to find a thread in the tangle that was the terror inside him. But when they pulled at the thread, nothing was sorted out, it all became even more tangled, more unendurable.

One day he ran away, just left, ending up on the Onsala peninsula. He stood there on the smooth rocks where he and Mona had made love only a year ago. He thought the boy who had made love to the girl had never known himself, and it had been someone else who had been so happy and so full of hope. He thought about putting an end to himself by diving down into the water from the rock.

But he was a good swimmer.

He remembered a cat they had once drowned, he and Simon. They had put it into a sack with some stones and flung it into the river, and the cat had howled for a long time in their dreams.

Even though it was an old wild cat that was hurt and would be better off dead, as Erik had said when he had asked them to do it.

Dreams. Maria kept going on about dreams.

I've never dreamed in all my life, thought Isak.

He couldn't remember how he got to the main road, but when he saw a grocer's shop, he went inside and phoned Karin.

"Heavens, Isak. Ruben has just been talking to the police."

"The police? Why?"

"You've been missing for three days."

He was surprised, but it didn't affect him much.

"I'll make my way home now."

He got a lift to Käringberget and walked the rest of the way. They were waiting for him in the kitchen, but he couldn't face them and turned toward the stairs. But then he stopped and went back.

"Perhaps it's best to give up," he said to Karin. "And put me in the bin."

Karin looked straight at him. "Maria says you'll get better, and the worse you are, the more certain it is that you'll get better."

"She's crazy, as well," said Isak.

The next day when Maria came, he nevertheless asked her, "How much worse am I to get?"

"I don't know," she said. "But I'd be pleased if you trusted me."

Then he felt that he did, and that he could tell her so.

They pulled at another thread, the memory of drowning the cat. But the tangle just got worse, became hard, and the thread snapped.

"Can't do it," he said.

As she was leaving, she told him that they could have him admitted again.

"What for?"

She told him straight out, so that he didn't run away and do himself harm. He could feel himself going rigid, and that night he did have a dream. He was stuffing Maria into a sack and filling it with stones and she was crying and begging for her life, but he drowned her, and as the sack sank, he thought now he would never have to pull at threads any longer.

That was a great relief.

In the morning he remembered the dream but knew he would never dare tell her about it. He stayed in bed while Lisa cleaned the house and Karin went for her walk.

Then he realized he had to get away and he would take the boat this time. Right out into the western sea, he thought, and there was freedom in the thought, a moment's freedom from his terror. He couldn't find his bicycle, so he took Simon's out of the garage, stopped for a while to pump up the tires, but was soon down at the jetty in Långedrag, and there she was, *Kajsa,* his double-ender.

What an idiot he was not to have thought of her before.

He cruised westward, past Vinga, due west toward the sunset. When the summer night that had no darkness crept around him, there was nothing but the sea and the boat, land now out of sight.

But then he must have fallen asleep at the rudder, for suddenly there was a fishing boat there and some man shouting.

"D'you want any help, boy?"

The sail was flapping like mad and he couldn't get her into the wind.

"Rudder's failed," he shouted.

They flung over a rope and took him in tow. Must be fated, he thought, that he was not to sail to his death either. They towed him between the skerries and reached Korshamn Channel early in the morning, where the skipper pointed over to the boatyard and its crane on the north side of Brännö, saying he could get help with his rudder if he went there.

He untied the rope and shouted his thanks across the water, which was now so still it seemed to be holding its breath. At this stage, he knew, of course, there was nothing wrong with his rudder, but was ashamed they might see, so he rowed into the yard and stayed there for an hour or two.

There wasn't a living soul there at this time of day, for which he was grateful.

In the end he set the foresail, slipped along the hillside until he found a bay in the lee, moored, crept down into the cabin, and slept. I'm not even any good at taking my own life.

It was late evening when the rain pattering on the deck woke him, and he was in a worse mood than ever. No grocer's shop here with a telephone to ring home to tell them not to worry.

The loony bin for me, best for everyone, he thought as he set sail. He took the course toward Långedrag, but carelessly went too far north and at Kopparholmen ran onto the barrier that was there to defend Göteborg in 1914.

The impact sounded like a pistol shot and then there she was, on the stone barrier, shuddering as if he had wounded her dignity. He came out of his fright and went into action.

She was too hard aground, and he got her afloat with the aid of the boat hook and headed at full sail for the boatyard and Erik.

She was taking on water.

For a moment he thought he might turn and sail out to sea again and sink with her. But the boat was expensive, irreplaceable, and had been built when he was sick and she had been his lease on life.

So he went on toward the river mouth.

They were in the kitchen waiting for him as usual, but there were more this evening, Olof and Maria, too, and Mona, who was strangely hunched up.

But Isak had eyes only for Erik.

"I went aground at Kopparholmen. Smashed the bottom. She's leaking like hell to the fore of the starboard side."

Erik simply blew up.

"You damned spoiled good-for-nothing," he shouted. "You're the most selfish little bastard that ever walked in a pair of shoes."

"Erik," said Karin warningly, but he wasn't listening.

"Who do you think you are, you damned fancy piece, tearing around the islands like an idiot without a thought for anything except your bad nerves. Bad nerves! For Christ's sake, that's no worse than Karin's bad heart, is it? You'll just have to learn to live with your nerves, just as she has to live with her heart."

Isak raised his hands and held them out toward Erik as if begging for mercy, but nothing was going to stop Erik.

"What do you think it's like for Karin's heart when she has to be worrying about you all the time? Not to mention Ruben, who'll soon crack up if this goes on much longer. Or Mona."

Erik was so furious now, his voice failed him.

"I've finished with Mona," whispered Isak.

"Shut up!" shouted Erik so loudly the cups rattled. "Do you think you're some kind of god, who can just finish with someone? You belong, you two, we all belong, and it's only you who's so bloody stupid you can't take it in and take some responsibility."

Isak thought it was coming back again, the obliteration, and he was slipping away, but Erik did not take his eyes off Isak for one second, and the rage in them forced Isak to stay, the rage and something else.

Despair.

Isak loved Erik, and admired him.

"Please," he said.

"Please nothing," shouted Erik. "I'm damned well going to make a man of you."

"Erik!" It was Ruben shouting now, his voice so loud that for a moment Erik's rage subsided. But Olof intervened.

"Go on, Erik," he said. "You're quite right."

Erik's voice had gone back to normal as he leaned forward toward Isak.

"I'll get a job for you at Götaverken, boy. On the factory floor, where your father's money can't buy you out of trouble. You've got to grow up now, Isak Lentov, and I'm going to see you do."

The kitchen was silent until Karin spoke. "Have you had anything to eat, boy?"

"There'll be nothing to eat here until the boat's taken up," said Erik. "Come on, Isak. We'll get her up before she sinks."

Five minutes later, the spotlights were on in the boatyard and Erik appeared in the kitchen.

"We need help."

Ruben went with him. Maria stopped Erik for a moment in the doorway.

"Good, Erik. And for God's sake, arrange for that job."

"You can rely on me," said Erik, giving Karin a long and satisfied look.

Isak did not sleep much that night. He stood in the window of his old room, just as anguished as before.

But he was real.

Again and again he came back to what Erik had said, that he would have to live with his nerves just as Karin had to live with her heart.

Hell, he would, too.

The next day he phoned Mona.

"Dare you?"

Erik started planning for Götaverken at breakfast the very next morning.

"School papers are no use," he said. "Bad enough with middle school exams, but of course, you'll have to show some school papers."

"But what if they ask what I did after middle school exams?"

"You've been working here at the yard, for Christ's sake. Of course, you'll get a reference from me."

It was true Isak had helped Erik at the boatyard during his years at senior high. With Karin's help they managed to word a reference that evening, so that without lying they could make it out to be a year's work.

Isak worked on the boat, which fortunately wasn't as badly damaged as he had feared the night before. Two boards had to be replaced, but there was plenty of mahogany at the yard these days.

"You'll have to pay for it gradually," said Erik. "You'll soon be earning some money."

Isak took that as a joke, but Erik didn't look as if he was joking.

"Are you still angry with me?" Isak asked.

"No, I got most of it out of me, I suppose. What I wanted to say really was only that you have to take responsibility, even if everything inside you is bloody awful."

"You've never been going mad."

"Yes, I have," said Erik. "Most people probably have. But as I said, you have to live with it."

"Yes, I got that," said Isak.

Ruben phoned the yard.

"How's it going?"

"Better, I think," said Erik.

"So it was good you got so furious?"

"Yes, they said so, the doctors."

"Eriksberg is advertising for apprentices in the paper today."

"To hell with that," said Erik. "The boy's going to Götaverken. The yard's known for its good spirit."

"I didn't know that."

Erik managed to bite back the words on the tip of his tongue, that there's quite a lot you don't know, Mr. Lentov.

"Things are turning now, Ruben," he said instead. "I can feel they're turning."

For the first time in ages he heard Ruben laugh.

"You told me that once before, Erik. Do you remember?"

"No," said Erik. "Was I right?"

"Yes, very much so."

"You see?"

"Apply to the machine shop," said Erik at dinner. "The yard's screaming for people, and most of all for turners."

* * *

At the personnel office everything went smoothly. They accepted his qualifications, nodded, and asked a few questions about Larsson's boatyard. Fine double-enders.

"Things are a bit bigger here, and not so much timber," they said.

Then there was a medical, breathe in, breathe out, never had heart trouble, asthma, TB? Good, fine blood count, next please.

The form to fill in was the worst, but Isak filled it in. There were several alternatives for religion, Lutheran, Catholic, Jewish, other faiths.

He put an X next to Jewish.

No lies, Karin had said.

Completed military service? There was only yes or no there, but Isak wrote in a firm hand: *Exempt. Nationality: Swedish. Place of Birth: Berlin.*

A few hours later, his papers had gone to where they should have gone and come back again, his name was called in the waiting room, and the man behind the counter said that it would be all right if he started on Monday at seven o'clock as an apprentice to Egon Bergman in Machine Shop 2.

He was told the rates of pay, and when he looked surprised, the man behind the counter said that mostly depended on the agreement he would be given after a month or so.

Isak didn't say that he had never reckoned on being paid.

He was frightened as he left the place, but it was a tangible fear in his knees and stomach. On the ferry back, it rose to his throat and he could find words for it.

"If I don't cope with this, that's the end of me."

"Whatever happens, I'll stick with you," Mona had said the evening before. She was unshakable. But he couldn't live on her strength.

You can't rely on women, he thought.

The thought surprised him so much, he stopped for a moment by his bicycle. Was he crazy, he who had had Karin for so long, as solid as a rock?

But once she had almost died on him.

Isak, he said to himself, a person doesn't let you down because she's ill.

And Mona. He knew with his whole being that she was like Karin, like the very bedrock.

He was ashamed.

Maria always went on at him that he should tell her his dreams and try to remember strange thoughts. He didn't dream, but now he had a strange thought to tell her, he thought as he cycled to the ferry and then set off home, to Erik and Karin, to tell them he'd gotten the job.

But when he got to Karl Johansgatan, he turned his bicycle into town. Ruben, he thought. Must tell Dad first. Ruben was pleased, but Isak could see the anxiety was still there in his eyes and that he was thinking just what Isak was thinking—would he cope?

"There'll be good men and certainly strict discipline there," Ruben said, but when he saw the anxiety in Isak's face he wished he hadn't said it.

"Isak," he said, trying to put his arm around the boy. "It'll go well. You've always been good with your hands. And if it's too hard for you, we've still got Chalmers waiting for you. Afterward, you'll easily get . . . a less demanding job."

Isak took away his arm.

"Dad," he said. "We don't usually tell lies. You know perfectly well that if I don't manage this, then that's the end of me."

"No!" cried Ruben.

But the pain in the boy's eyes went right into him. Isak noticed and managed to feel guilty before turning on his heel and running through the office and out to his bicycle.

Mona was on duty at the hospital the weekend between Isak and his great Monday. That was good. He wanted to be alone. He took out his boat and sailed close to the wind between Vinga and Nidingen, taking in no sail despite the fresh wind beyond the skerries.

Almost without thinking, he searched for a boat with a patrol service flag, with Simon on board. But there was nothing military as far as his eye could see, and he didn't dare go into the prohibited waters.

I'm childish, he thought. This is mine. For the first time I'm alone and must sort it out myself.

Bylund's face appeared on the surface of the water astern, that sniffing nose, those quivering nostrils, but the next moment, Isak was heading straight for Böttö lighthouse, knowing the wind was too great to jib, and that Erik would have shouted at him, but he managed, and by the time he got the boat up into the wind again, he thought he would sort it all out even if Egon Bergman was like Bylund.

The world was perfectly real to him and what was pouring salt into his face was only seawater, he thought as he sailed in toward Långedrag and moored. He cleaned every nook and cranny of the boat so that no one could say anything except that everything was in its place, shipshape, neat and tidy.

When he got back he called Mona at the hospital. Yes, he was fine, no, he wasn't nervous.

They had already eaten at home, but Karin heated up some meatballs and he wolfed them down and went to bed early and slept.

Slept all night.

At half past five, Erik woke him, Karin made sandwiches, got half a cup of coffee into him, and packed a rucksack with his lunch, overalls, and reinforced shoes. At half past six, he put his bicycle in among a thousand others at Sänkverket, and at twenty to seven he was one of a hundred sleepy men, packed like sardines in a barge, being hauled over to the great shipyard on the other side of the river.

He could feel the quiet friendliness even on the barge, but he didn't dare believe in it.

The shipyard appeared in front of him, freeing itself from the morning mist. On the right along the shore were the slipways where the huge ships grew, and beyond them he could see the two docks, enormous, one of them unimaginably huge.

Railway tracks, workshops, warehouses, a jungle of larger and smaller buildings.

How would he find his way?

"I'm to go to Machine Shop Two," he said to the tall man nearest to him.

"Behind the joinery shop and across the tracks," he said, scarcely even awake yet.

"You can come with me," another man said. "I work there. New, are you?"

"Yes. I'm to be apprenticed to Egon Bergman."

"Onsala," said the man, who was large and fat.

Isak didn't want to ask what he meant, but he looked up into the man's face as the barge reached the quay, and met a pair of pale blue eyes embedded in fat, inquisitive and slightly amused.

"My name's Tich," he said.

"Lentov," said Isak.

"Turning?"

"Yes."

Isak realized the man was economic with words, so he trotted after the fat man, past the joinery and into the machine shop, and caught a glimpse of an endless world of steel and machines, before going up some stairs to a changing room. He was given a locker, changed quickly, and the moment they were on their way down the stairs to the workshop, the horn sounded.

Over five thousand men started up simultaneously, and for a moment Isak thought he would drown in the noise.

"You look almost grown up," said Onsala. "I'm mostly used to little kids," he went on. "Fifteen-year-olds who can't control their fingers."

He had very blue eyes deeply embedded in a narrow intelligent face, a smile flitting occasionally over it, lighting it up from within.

But not often.

He was twenty-eight, a passionate turner, proud of his skill, famous on the floor for his precision, his ability to maintain even tolerances of thousandths of a millimeter. He was getting extra pay at the moment for training apprentices, but he probably hadn't chosen the task for the money. He liked teaching and could feel a quiet happiness when he occasionally had a boy with intelligence in his hands as well as that rare passion for being exact.

When Isak was allowed on the lathe itself after an hour or two, and the machine delivered his first flanges, Onsala knew he was in luck this time.

Machine Shop 2 was chaos, but around Onsala and his lathe and his pupils was a circle of comprehensibility, security, in fact.

They had to shout that first morning.

"They're testing a diesel in the assembly shop," he bawled. "It'll stop in an hour or so, then we'll be able to speak like human beings."

Isak nodded.

"What was your name?"

"Lentov."

"Lento?"

"No, Lentov," shouted Isak, for he wasn't going to lie about his name, Jewish and known in town.

"Tovv," he shouted so loudly that it cut through the noise all the way to men on the other lathes.

Someone laughed.

"Hi, Tovv," someone shouted.

One of those rare smiles slid across Onsala's face.

"That happened quickly this time," he said.

Isak didn't grasp at once that he had been rebaptized and, with his new name, the Jew had gone.

A week later, he realized that in this place Jewishness meant nothing whatsoever, neither good nor bad. He could have been called Moses and had a hooked nose without its being of any significance.

He understood that the day when Onsala told him to go to the molding shop to fetch a load of pig iron.

"It'll be a heavy and filthy job," he said. "But you have to learn everything from the bottom, lad."

"Ask for the Jew," he called after Isak as he ran off.

Isak managed the trick of not stopping as he ran, and was pleased he had his back to Onsala.

In the molding shop was a very tall man with a pink complexion and chalk-white hair above a young face. An albino, thought Isak, like that priest at school.

"I was told to ask for the Jew," he said, keeping his voice steady.

"Then you've come to the right place, for that's me," the man said with a huge grin.

Isak laughed, thinking about Tich, the fat giant who had shown him the way on his first day and was a highly respected borer.

Onsala was not much of a one for praise, and as far as was known, no great words had ever passed his lips. He expressed his satisfaction in grunts, and he often grunted at Isak.

Isak's defeat began to lose its grip on him. The terror was still there inside him and let itself be known occasionally, but in the daytime there was little room for it and at night he slept heavily, exhausted. Two evenings a week, he went to Maria, and though they seemed to be getting nowhere, he was beginning to enjoy it.

"You'll be a good turner," Onsala said after a fortnight. "I hope you'll stay."

I'm going to work here all my life, thought Isak. But then he remembered.

"Dad wants me to go to Chalmers," he said.

"But then you need school qualifications."

Isak knew he ought to tell the truth, that he already had, and it wasn't anything very remarkable, just spending hour upon tedious hour in classrooms. But he was glad he said nothing when Onsala went on.

"God, lad, how I would have liked to have gone. But you know, there wasn't any money, and now it's too late. If you get the chance, take it. Chalmers . . ." and there was a world of longing in his voice. Isak was ashamed.

Otherwise conversation proved to be no problem. He knew the talk from Karin's kitchen and Erik's yard. Both there and here there were lively and occasionally heated political discussions. But here the borderline was sharper between social democrats and communists.

Isak joined the union.

He bought books and read them, to Ruben's extreme surprise.

Slowly a realization of the importance of money grew in him. It had been as obvious as the air before, but here it was a matter of life and death.

It started in the lathe shop. In his beginner's eagerness, Isak found it hard to keep to a regular pace. But knowledge of the negotiated pay rates for piecework was just as important as skill, and incomprehensible shame befell anyone who couldn't keep up. He soon had that in his very bones, like all the rest. He adapted, learned rapidly. There would be a row if the rate was poor and the work filthy and heavy.

No mistakes were made in the great boring mill where they made cylinder linings a meter and a half in diameter. But at the older lathes where they made nuts and bolts of every size, misfortunes could arise. Helge Eskilsson wrecked a whole consignment one day, and Isak was astounded at Eskilsson's fierce disappointment, the anger that found an outlet in ferocious swearing.

But when he was told that Eskilsson had to pay for the lot himself in lost piecework, he understood it better. Helge had four kids at home and a big mortgage on a recently purchased house in Torslanda.

"During the war," they often said. Isak kept hearing how every lathe had run for three shifts and how they had poured out shell cases. And about manliness, honesty, and the cruiser *Oskar II*, always on constant repairs in the great shipyard.

"Good heavens," the old men said. "They would have fallen apart out of sheer terror if they'd even caught sight of a German submarine."

One day, shortly before midday, as he was walking across the tracks to Onsala with a new drawing, he was stopped by a young man not much older than himself.

"Hi there, aren't you Isak Lentov?"

Isak didn't recognize him. But the man, who worked for the transport foreman, went on with Isak to the turning shop and Onsala, and said they had met in the national service. He had driven the ambulance the day Isak had broken his arm and gone to the hospital.

At the midday break there were a lot of men in the hut where they ate, and Onsala said, "Then you've done your military service, have you, Tovv?"

It didn't turn silent, for there was nothing strange about the question. But Isak thought the world stopped, time had ceased, and he remembered Karin's words, *Don't lie, don't lie.*

"No," he said. "I was called up, but then I was ill."

"So I suppose they're waiting to get their claws into you again, now that you're better?"

"No, I was exempted."

"What was wrong with you?" Onsala didn't sound suspicious, but perhaps worried.

He likes me, thought Isak.

Suddenly and for the first time voluntarily, Isak told the whole story, the whole appalling story.

"Yes," he said. "You see, I'm Jewish. I grew up in Berlin . . ."

The entire hut was quiet now and time stood still. When Isak got to the end, about how he had recognized the Nazi in Bylund, the sergeant, and how he had had a nervous breakdown, you could have heard a pin drop.

The silence frightened Isak. Oh God, he thought, Israel's God, why do I talk so much?

But then he could feel the compassion in the air, warm and strong there between the walls of the hut. Then, in the end, Tich spoke.

"Dang it, take my sponge cake."

They usually laughed at Tich and his packed lunch and his cakes, but this time nobody even smiled. It was as if they thought Tich had said and done the only thing that could be said or done at that moment.

When the horn sounded, some of them came over and shook Isak by the hand. And when they went back to the machine shop, something happened that had never happened before. Onsala put an arm around one of his apprentices.

That afternoon at Maria's, he told her what had happened and how he had suddenly told them everything. She was pleased.

"Good, Isak, that's one step."

"They were so bloody nice."

"I can see that," said Maria, but even she was surprised. "People are often nice when you meet them singly," she added. "But in groups, people are often much worse, much more afraid."

"Not in the machine shop."

"What's next?" said Maria. "I mean in the promotion stakes?"

"You don't really become anything more than a skilled turner, and that's fine and has great prestige."

"So they don't compete?"

"No." Isak told her about the rates of pay and the unwritten laws around them.

When his session was almost over, he remembered that strange thought about not being able to trust women.

"It was the day I got the job," he said. "I knew it was idiotic, but it stayed like a thorn in the flesh that all women are untrustworthy."

"What did you think next?"

"I thought about Karin and Mona, and they're as loyal as rocks."

"But there has been another woman in your life, before Karin?"

A wave of heat raced right through him and his face flared.

"Mama . . . but I never think about her."

"No, I've noticed that," said Maria. "But she's there in your memories."

"No, I remember nothing."

Maria leaned over her desk and looked him straight in the eye.

"Why did your grandfather beat you? Why were you running away that day in Berlin?"

He did not look away, nor did the question upset him. He has asked it himself, thought Maria.

"I don't remember," said Isak.

"Something happened to you there with your grandparents,

often, I suspect. This terror of madness you have was there before the assault on you, I'm sure of that. You understand both of us have to tackle this?"

"But the thing is, I simply can't remember."

"Do you never go to see your mother?"

"No. Mona does sometimes, and she wants me to go with her."

"You do that, Isak."

Isak considered why he didn't want to, that he certainly did not want to, but Maria said, "You don't dare."

"That's true. It's bad enough with Iza, and I have to see her sometimes."

"Why?"

"Hasn't Ruben told you that they're like twins, her and my mother?"

"No," said Maria. "Perhaps he's never seen it."

"Oh, yes he has," said Isak. "But Dad's the kind of person who thinks everything's his fault, all misfortunes."

How clear-sighted he is, thought Maria.

"Simon's the same," said Isak. "Sometimes I think he's crazier than I am."

"Maybe you're right there," said Maria. "But this is about you. Have you never considered that your mother can't do you any harm any longer, that she's just a confused old woman, and you're a strong adult?"

Isak started fumbling for a handkerchief, which he didn't have, so he borrowed one from Maria, who said nothing, not a word of consolation.

By the time they parted, Isak had decided.

"I'll go with Mona to see her," he said.

"Good, then come back to me."

"I promise."

Isak and Mona said nothing to either Ruben or Karin, just slipped away early on Sunday morning and via trams and buses went all the long way out to Lillhagen mental hospital.

Isak was looking straight ahead as they walked down the corridors, unwilling to see any lunatics at all. Olga had a room of her own and was dressed, perfumed and smart, bracelets tinkling as always as she sat there playing with her dolls.

Dressing them and undressing them.

She recognized neither of them, but he was prepared for that. Mona had told him she recognized only Ruben and only in glimpses.

Mona had thought Isak would feel pity and tenderness, and he himself was relying on Maria's words that he would no longer feel fear. But when he met Olga's eyes, which were flickering as always, he was seized with a rage that took possession of his whole being and was in no way possible to control.

"You bloody witch," he said.

Olga presumably didn't understand the words, but she felt the unease in the air and turned her attention to the doll. Wrenching at it roughly, she said, *"Mein süsser, süsser Knabe."* My sweet, sweet boy.

Her mouth was smiling, but she whimpered as she pulled the doll's hair, pinched it, and went on prattling in that strange voice, complaining and at the same time satisfied.

Isak knew he had to get out, and he was through the door and out in the corridor when he heard Mona calling, "Wait for me in the grounds. I'll be with you soon."

He sat down on the grass under a tree, feeling the strength of his anger. God, to behave like that, and what would Mona think, and what would Ruben say if he ever found out. Not to mention Karin.

When Mona came, she was neither angry nor reproachful. Her eyes were sad, of course.

"Straight to Maria now," she said.

She was at home, thank goodness. Isak was heading straight into unreality, the world blurring, and the terror in him felt like it would kill him if he didn't get away.

Mona went up with him and told Maria briefly what had happened. Maria was pleased and took Isak into her room.

"At last, we're on our way," she said.

She held his gaze in such a grip that he couldn't free himself.

Step by step and quite mercilessly she took him back to Berlin and his early childhood. Isak could feel her strength and knew he would die now, or dare.

"I recognized her," he said. "I recognized her face, her look, and those nostrils sniffing. She's like Bylund."

"Yes."

"I was so angry I went mad and raced around the apartment screaming, and she couldn't get me to be quiet. She pulled my hair and pinched me and complained, but all the time she was pleased. And then . . ."

"Then?"

"Then I disappeared," said Isak. "I disappeared just as I did in the army. But then . . ."

"Then?"

"Then Grandfather came home and beat me."

"Your mother was horrid," said Maria.

"Yes!" He shouted it out, and it came back again, that great anger that made everything real, and he shouted that he would gouge her eyes out and cut off her breasts and stick a pole up her cunt.

Maria encouraged him. "Good, Isak. Just give it to her."

The pain was unbearable, yet it *could* be borne, and the world was perfectly clear.

Isak had begun to see, at last.

TWENTY-FOUR

*T*he heat was quivering between the skerries. The men guarding the long coast in this land of darkness usually loved the sun but now had to learn to fear it. They had always sought it, learned to preserve every ray of sunlight, but now they huddled like flies on a flypaper in the shade of a sail they had slung between themselves and the merciless heat.

Every morning the sun rose, and by midday, mirrored by the sea, had vastly increased in strength, mindlessly beating down on them, heating up the rocks and jetties so they burned their feet, with not a tree to shade them, nor a green blade to rest their eyes on.

It was August and they were having a heat wave.

"The whole damned Kattegat will boil soon," they said. The sea was seething with jellyfish, so they had to clear the bay of the slimy monsters for a quick dip, a minute-long cool, and even the sea evaporated like smarting salt on their bodies, increasing their pain. On the day they shared their last tin of Nivea creme, two red-haired men were taken ashore to sick bay.

It was easier for Simon than for most of them. He just turned dark brown and leathery.

"You look like some bloody desert sheikh," a man said one evening, and Simon had laughed, a dazzling white smile in all that brown. But he was thinking about his distant ancestors and how they wandered in the Sinai deserts, and the leathery skins they developed to survive under a sun even more merciless than this one.

To the surprise of his friends, he read the Bible in the evenings, and that gave him an undeserved reputation for being religious. Then a parcel from Ruben had arrived containing a history of Israel in two volumes. So Simon spent his evenings with Isaiah and Jeremiah, Ezra and Nehemiah in a fruitless attempt to distinguish between myth and history.

But his dreams were all of trees, mysterious earthly giants, their tops providing protection and shade. Tall aspens drew lacy patterns against the sky, ancient oaks presented strength and wisdom, and wide-skirted spruces invited rest in birdsong and sighing of forests.

When he was awakened by the shrieking gulls and curses from his companions and saw the sun begin its threatening journey across the sky, he thought that as soon as he got some leave he would go walking in the forest by the long lake where Inga's farm was wedged in on a ledge in the hillside.

The night the thunderstorm came, they all went mad and ran naked out of their huts onto smooth rocks and stood there letting their skin, hair, mouths, and eyes slake their thirst. They stayed relishing the downpour until they grew cold, and one man said, "Christ, how marvelous. Never again will I ever complain about the cold and the dark."

Simon would repeat that statement to himself many a time in December when it was pitch dark at three in the afternoon, the sea roaring and the icy wind whistling straight through his clothes into the very marrow of his bones.

Simon had been on leave twice now, the first a feast when Karin had cooked all his favorite dishes. He had planned to come on the Saturday morning, but had the chance to get away on a boat heading for Nya Varvet on the Friday afternoon. So he found Karin alone in the kitchen with a bowl of green peas in her lap. He went straight across to her and laid his head on her apron, breathing in the scent of her and feeling her hands running over the back of his neck.

Simon thought that this business of regressing had its delights after all. At least for a while. Then they looked at each other and he saw that a great deal had changed, that she was smaller than he remembered, older and more worn. He was filled with a great tenderness, an almost painful need to look after her and please her.

Bird of sorrow, he thought, the good bird of sorrow.

Karin saw that the boy in front of her was now an adult, that there was a hardness and a strength that made her feel shy. A man, she thought, and there was both alienation and sorrow in the thought.

But then she pulled herself together, told herself she was silly, and what had she expected, wasn't it just what she had tried so hard to achieve, that Simon should become an independent adult?

The weekend after the thunderstorm, Simon obeyed his dreams about the trees and phoned from the quay to Karin.

"Mom, I thought I'd go and see Inga."

He could hear from the silence that there was fear in it, but then her voice came back with all her usual confidence.

"Do that, Simon dear."

"I've got a lift with a guy who lives in the same direction and his brother's going to meet him by car."

"That's good, then, Simon." Then, after another silence, "Should I phone and warn her?"

"Yes, perhaps you'd better," said Simon.

They dropped him off beyond the village store.

"Can you find your way?"

"Of course."

"We'll pick you up at about five on Sunday."

"Great. Bye, then, and thanks."

Then he walked along beneath the leafy foliage, and the great trees calmed him.

Be, he thought, don't do.

He saw the trees had been scorched by the heat, some leaves already fallen and glowing like fairy gold in the moss. The long preparation for winter had begun, the trees slowly shutting off their circulation systems to enter the sleep where they would live only in their dreams.

He came to a glade, a clearing in the forest where they had spared an oak out of respect for its stature and great age. It was hot. Simon took off his uniform jacket, rolled it up into a pillow, and lay gazing up into the tree, the top still dark green, almost impenetrable.

The tree was at peace with itself, the kind of peace all living creatures have when they accept what is mysterious.

He slept for a while in the shade before going on toward the lake and the house where Inga was waiting for him. She had had time to clean up, and everything was neat and tidy. She turned bright red when he appeared on the edge of the forest.

"You'd like some coffee, wouldn't you?" she said.

Inga had known for months now that Simon knew, and she had many a time imagined their meeting and how they would be able to talk about what had happened.

All through his childhood, she had distanced herself from him, afraid, glancing out of the corner of her eye at that quicksilver little boy. But when Karin and Erik had been there last spring and told her that they had told Simon, she had torn all that down, just as you tear down boarding when it no longer provides shelter from the wind.

She was grateful for the months between then and now. She had needed the time to imagine what would happen next. But she hadn't realized that he would be so adult, so handsome, and so like . . .

Over coffee, they talked sluggishly about the weather, the heat wave and the rain that had come too late. She had gotten rid of the cows and told him about that. And she had gotten a job at the school, in the school kitchen.

"That's a long way to walk," said Simon.

"Yes, but not too bad." She cycled until the snow came and then she took the kick-sled. They plowed the road nowadays.

He saw she was pleased to have the job and enjoyed the people she met and the company. There was no bitterness in her, no sorrow, either, as with Karin, more a sense of wonder in all her earthiness.

It started clouding over and the wind brought with it a touch of autumn chill, so they went in.

"The leaves are turning already," Inga said. "Did you notice?"

"Yes." He thought about the fairy gold in the moss and smiled his new white smile in all that brown. When she drew in a sharp breath, he gathered up his courage to ask.

"Am I like him?"

"Heavens, yes," said Inga. "If he was standing there beside you, I'd find it hard to tell you apart."

But then she saw that was probably not true. Simon was sturdier, taller, had more strength and was less of a dream. There was a tension in the air between them, and yet it was a relief that he had dared to say what they had to talk about. Inga sought an outlet for her unease by busying herself, splitting kindling and lighting the kitchen stove.

"It's cold, don't you think? I've some dough setting, so the heat from the stove'll be just right."

Simon wasn't cold. He looked around the cottage as if seeing it for the first time, sensing the security and comfort always found below low roofs in old houses. He thought with surprise that it was beautiful here, the light trickling through the mullioned windows and dancing on the rag rugs on the wide floorboards.

She lit the tiled stove in the front room, too, while she was at it. It was now so hot, he had to take off his uniform jacket and sit down in the rocking chair in his shirtsleeves.

"Did he often come in here?" he said.

"Oh, no," said Inga. "Father and Mother were both dying in this room. We never came in here. We met by the stream. It was such a blessedly warm and lovely spring," and as she said it, her calm returned and she sat down at the table and started telling him.

She found the words. They came as they should and as if she had thought it all out through the summer she had been waiting for Simon. Then at last she came to their last evening.

"I realized he was saying good-bye, for his violin was so sad that evening. So I wasn't really all that surprised when he never came back."

The melancholy in her voice was like a thin blue note.

"Nor sad?"

"Yes," she said. "But then I'd known all the time, you see. We two were not created for each other. He was too grand for me."

Simon saw how she had bowed to the ground, taken on the yoke just as all peasant women had always done, humble and grateful for what had been.

"He wasn't really of this world," she said. "For a while afterward, I almost believed I'd dreamed it all. But then you began to make yourself felt."

"Did much time go by before you realized you were with child?"

"Yes, a long time. I probably didn't dare take it in. I was big and heavy in November when Karin came, and I suppose I only really took it in when she told me."

You're with child, Inga, Karin had said. Even today, Inga could hear her and feel the terrible fear as she was forced to admit it, the shame of the child growing inside her.

Denied, thought Simon. But he wasn't surprised. He could remember it from his dreams in his childhood. Denied, then abandoned between the tiled walls of the hospital far away from the trees, the sighing in the treetops, and the light over the lake.

"I had a letter afterward," said Inga.

"I know, but Erik made you burn it during the war."

"Erik couldn't make me," she said, as firmly as the ground she stood on. "He phoned in the spring of 1940 and was quite hysterical. I thought to myself that if the Germans come, then I've plenty of time to hide the letter in the crack in the oak behind the barn. But the Germans didn't come. So it's still in the bureau, where it's always been."

Simon's heart thumped.

She got out the key and unlocked the old-fashioned bureau, pulled out a drawer, and took out a brass container with a lid.

"I put the letter in this when I thought perhaps I'd have to hide it in the oak."

She couldn't get the lid off. They had to go out into the kitchen to fetch a knife to pry it open. German stamps, postmarked March 4, 1929, in Berlin. Opened, never read.

"I didn't know the language. We couldn't speak to each other, " said Inga, and Simon wondered why life is so incomprehensible, so unfathomably sad.

"I've got the attic room ready for you, and made the bed up there," she said.

He thought what a lot she had done since Karin had phoned, cleaned the place up, ironed her best blue dress, kneaded the dough for bread, and made up the bed in the attic.

"Go on up," said Inga. "You should be alone when you read it. You can read German, can't you?"

"Yes," said Simon.

He went up the creaking stairs and lay flat out on the crocheted bedspread, the letter on his stomach. Heavens. His mouth was dry, so he went down again for a drink of water and stood there for a while watching Inga putting the risen dough into the oven.

"You haven't got a beer, have you?" he said.

"Afraid not, no," said Inga. "I didn't have time to go to the shop, and I hadn't really thought of you being a man and wanting beer."

They had to laugh at that. Inga found some fruit juice, black currant from this year's crop. So Simon had the taste of childhood in his mouth and the childhood smell of freshly baked bread in his nose as he plucked up his courage and read the letter up there in the attic bedroom.

It was a love letter, full of romantic words. Siren of the woods, my siren of the woods, he called her. He hoped to come back in the autumn and had applied for the job at the college. But he had to know if she was expecting him, that she was longing for him as much as he was for her. Would she write, send a sign of life. A thousand kisses, Simon Haberman, an address in Berlin.

Disappointment kept coming in spurts as he read. At the same time he asked himself, what had he expected, what had he hoped for? The Jewish violinist couldn't know that his love had borne fruit, that there was a little boy.

Simon covered his face with the pillow and let the tears come. They stopped a while later, but his melancholy was still as great as the sea, he thought.

When he went over to the washstand to wash his face, he found the water in the can yellow and stale. So she had put the room in order a long time ago, had been expecting him for a long time.

Inga was in the kitchen, her cheeks glowing, but otherwise she was pale, very pale. He sat down at the kitchen table and began translating the letter for her.

" 'Siren of the woods'. . . I'm not quite sure, but I think it's siren of the woods."

Then all that about longing, love, kisses. And begging for a reply.

"But why didn't he come?" Inga's voice was scarcely audible, her hands over her face, but he could see her shoulders shaking.

"He was waiting for a reply," said Simon.

"But he knew I wouldn't understand what he wrote."

"Perhaps he thought you'd find someone to translate it for you." Simon's voice was bitter as he went on reading.

" 'Write to me, give me a sign of life so that I know you exist, that you're not just a wild and beautiful dream.' "

"Heavens," said Inga. "Who would I go to? You must see that no one could know. The shame, Simon, I would have died of shame."

"Because of me," said Simon.

"Yes," said Inga, and when Simon got up and left the cottage, she ran after him.

"You don't understand, Simon," she cried. "You'll never understand what it was like in those days."

He stopped and turned halfway around.

"No, I don't suppose I will."

"Things were so good for you, Simon. Things were so good for you with Erik and Karin."

Karin, he thought with wild fury. Karin could have had the letter translated, could have written to Berlin and told him about the child.

But then he knew she had never wanted to, that she wanted to leave the letter unread while she looked after her baby and tried to think as little as possible about the father of the little boy with those unfathomably dark eyes.

"I'll take a walk in the forest for a while. I'll be back for dinner."

His voice was shriller than he had intended, charged with anger not directed at Inga, but at Karin, and he tried to smile to hide it. But Inga had already turned back to the cottage.

He climbed up the hill and sat gazing over the lake, now a dull blue, in perfect agreement with his melancholy. But the trees were silent, and he knew their peace was not for him, that he belonged with the thousand uneasy questions seeking answers in vain.

On the way back, he thought that if Haberman had really meant what he said in his letter, he could have gotten help translating it from one of the many Swedes in 1920s Berlin.

Inga was waiting with meat soup, which she knew he liked, freshly baked bread, and beer. She had cycled all the way to the store and bought a few bottles.

He gulped it down, but it was only pilsner and gave him no relief. Neither of them slept much that night.

He told her over coffee in the morning that she should keep the letter. "It's to you. I'll write a translation on the back."

But she said she had been thinking all night. "I know you'll laugh," she said. "But I want it said that I've come to believe that all this happened for your sake, so that you would come into the world."

She's crazy, thought Simon, but he didn't laugh, so Inga found the courage to go on.

"I like to think you chose us. But we two, him and me, we were so incompatible. If he could have talked to me and found out what a simple person I was, he would never have fallen in love with me, nor even looked at me. We were from different worlds, Simon."

It's true, he thought. She's right. They could never have become a family. But then his eyes hardened and he thought that if she had married him, then the man would have survived, saved from Hitler and the extermination camp.

But he didn't say so, and he remembered the man in his dream, the man who had gone down the hill with his violin, heading for death because he wanted to die.

"You would've known he didn't really belong on earth if you'd heard him playing," said Inga, as if she'd been listening to his thoughts. "They were no tunes, Simon, not the kind of fiddler's squeals we used to dance around to. It was as if from heaven. I'd no idea a violin could sound like that."

"Do you know what he played?"

"Yes, I once heard his music on the radio, and I imagined he was there, playing, because it was an orchestra from Berlin. The person who'd written the music was from Finland, but I've forgotten the name now."

"Sibelius," said Simon.

"Yes," she said. And he would have given anything in the world to have a violin, to get it to sound again in her mind, some wild yearning music by Sibelius.

But he had no violin, nor could he play.

He gave her a warm hug before he left, then stopped at the edge of the forest and waved, and as he ran along the forest track so as not to miss the lift that would take him up to the main road, he was thinking that what Inga had told him was more comforting than anything else he had ever heard.

I think it was for your sake all this happened. You wanted to come into this world. You chose us.

Perhaps I'm going nuts, he thought. Such a crazy, incredible, foolish idea.

But it comforted him.

He had a moment at the jetty while he was waiting for the boat fetching them, so he phoned Ruben.

"His name's Simon Haberman," he said. "And the address is in Berlin. Can you look into it, Uncle Ruben?"

"Of course. I'll let you know."

"Thanks."

I know it's pointless, that he went to the gas chambers, Simon thought. All the same, you have to give what is rational a chance.

Jewish congregations all over the world were working on constructing a network between the dead and the survivors. It took Ruben only a week to find the information. Simon Haberman, violinist with the Berlin Philharmonic Orchestra, had been deported with his sister in November 1942 and sent to Auschwitz in May 1944.

The sister had died earlier from her privations.

He was unmarried and there were no living relatives.

Simon was sixteen when he had died, thought Ruben. For sixteen years the man could have known he had a son in Sweden. He had undeniably had every right to know.

For the first time, Ruben felt a grudge against Karin. She had been part of that injustice, he thought.

There was a letter waiting for Simon when he got back to camp, postmarked Stockholm. He knew it was from Iza, that she was extending her claws to get him now.

She enclosed a photograph. She was slim, lovely, made up like a film star, and she was looking at him with eyes burning with hunger.

"Phew, what a bird," said the boys. "What a vamp. Where the hell have you been keeping her?"

"In Stockholm," said Simon, seeing his stock going up in their estimation.

"Going to see her?"

"Yes. She says she wants me to."

"Getting engaged to her?"

Simon gazed at the man who had asked the question, then answered bluntly, "I sincerely hope not."

As usual, they couldn't understand him, and there was much head-shaking. Bengtsson with the pale eyes and so much longing in him gave him an embarrassed grin.

"If you escape, then perhaps you'd let me know. For here's one who'd gladly step in."

Laughter rolled around the hut, leaving no space for Simon to explain.

Whatever he would have been able to explain.

TWENTY-FIVE

Simon was standing by Ruben's bookcase reading about spiders in the 1935 encyclopedia.

". . . distinguished by an enlarged, usually undivided rear abdomen, connected like a stalk to the thorax and equipped with four or six poison glands . . . has claws (fig. 2) on the tips of which are the ducts for the poison glands . . . The four pairs of legs have comblike toothed claws. . . . The main part of the nervous system consists of brain. . . . Sexual organs are in pairs, the ducts merging into a passage flowing out at the base of the abdomen. . . ."

He looked at fig. 2 and shuddered.

Nocturnal, he read. Predators. Poison of unknown composition. Those indigenous to Sweden are all harmless.

But there was a European species, the tarantula, whose bite could injure humans although the effect of the poison was limited to the immediate area around the bite.

Not a word about the females eating the males on coupling.

He was waiting for Isak, who had taken his driving test and was to drive Simon back to camp in Ruben's car. It was autumn, yellow leaves swirling off the trees, and the air on the sea horizon bright and crystal clear.

Most of the boys were on harvest leave or having a few extra days for domestic reasons, as it was called. Simon went to Captain Sjövall and stood at attention, but there was a slight jokiness over the ritual as he applied for three days' extra leave for domestic reasons.

"What's the Larsson family up to?" said Sjövall.

"I have a girl in Stockholm," said Simon.

"That won't do," said Sjövall.

"She's ill," said Simon, and it was true in a way.

Sick fiancée, Sjövall wrote, and that was that. Simon said nothing at home, and on Wednesday morning, he was on the express to Stockholm, trying to remember what he had read about spiders.

The illustration had lost its force.

Isak's fault, he thought, remembering the quarrel they'd had in the car, beginning with Simon saying almost in passing that he was going to see Iza in Stockholm the next weekend.

Isak had been strangely upset and told Simon loudly that he was mad, heading straight for perdition with his eyes wide open.

Simon had been frightened not only by his outburst but also by the speed they were going, for within a few minutes Isak had Ruben's old Chevrolet tearing along so fast, Simon had shouted at him to calm down for God's sake before he killed them both.

Isak had slowed down and said nothing. They had driven into the parking lot in front of the barracks at normal speed and with ten minutes to spare. Isak had then used those minutes well, telling Simon about Olga and the conclusion he and Maria had come to.

"You're free to choose if you want the kind of life Ruben had had with a mad wife. He had no peace from her until she was taken to the hospital," Isak had said. Then he had added, "But you've damned well no right to bring children into the world with a mother of the kind Iza would be."

Isak had been almost tearful, and Simon had sat there as if struck by lightning.

"For Christ's sake, I'm not marrying her, am I?"

"If she can get you to give her a kid, she will. Her chances of marrying are few, because she frightens the life out of any normal man. If she gets her claws into you, she'll never let you go."

"Claws in which are the ducts of the poison glands," Simon had said.

"Simon, are you going mad, too? Perhaps you should talk to Maria, as well. Maybe you'd get sick leave."

Simon had looked at him and attempted a laugh.

"I'll think about . . . everything you've said. And it was great you wanted to tell me about your mother."

He had realized what it had cost Isak. But then he had simply had to go.

Now he was on the train trying to conjure up his old image of Iza as the evil but real person. But he felt childish.

Like someone playing with emotions.

Isak is more adult than I am, he thought as the train stopped at Skövde. For a moment, he considered getting off and waiting for the next train back. But he stayed where he was. I must conquer her, he thought.

Conquer my image of her, he corrected himself, and was so ashamed he flushed. A girl opposite him looked surprised, so Simon went to the toilet to wash his hands, then to the restaurant car for coffee. He stayed there, watching the landscape rushing past and being swallowed up by the train.

Iza met him at the Central Station in Stockholm and was the same, the same as ever. The famous psychoanalyst in Switzerland had not touched her. She talked of the city as if she owned it.

"Göteborg's a dump in comparison," she said.

As he stood in her window looking out over the city, Simon had to admit it was magnificent.

Ruben had bought her an apartment up on the heights of Söder. The sun was shining on Strömmen's waters, the palace, and the thousand roofs, although it was well into October. Simon thought how strange it was that no one in Göteborg ever talked about Stockholm, the capital, or that it was beautiful. But although he'd never been there, he also reckoned he knew it quite well from Strindberg, Söderberg, and several hundred other books he'd read.

Most of all he wanted to go on a voyage of discovery, walk along Drottninggatan up to Blå Tornet, stroll along Strandvägen, take the ferry to Djurgården and see those famous oaks.

But Iza said, "Now let's make love."

Simon looked down into her face and thought about spiders. Come into my parlor, said the spider to the fly.

But that didn't increase the temptation, and anyhow he had been quite wrong about the love life of spiders.

"I'm hungry," he said. "Have you any food at home?"

Iza, never able to wait for anything, was furious, stamping her foot and swearing. When that didn't help, she turned melodramatic and wept.

"Here I am, having waited for months for my lover, and all you want is food," she said.

But Simon was already out in the scruffy kitchen. He opened the refrigerator and found a tin of corned beef and a few slices of stale bread.

"Come on now, let's eat." Then he said, nastily, "Since when did I become your lover?"

That brought on a flood of tears, and Simon found to his surprise that he was quite unmoved. She noticed his coldness, abruptly stopped crying, and there was a gleam of pleasure in her eyes as she said, "I've bought a bottle of wine."

Almost amicably, they ate and drank, quite like friends, until she said in her usual feverish voice, "So you haven't come to make love to me, then?"

"No, mostly to see the place and find out how things are for you."

"You're joking?"

"Maybe."

"How cruel you are," she said, her eyes narrowing with expectation, her mouth wet with desire.

Simon finished his wine and then they were in bed, and randy as he was after months out in the islands, he had plenty to offer her, or so he thought. He had no need to hold back, either. She didn't want tenderness, just endurance and hard hands.

But he couldn't satisfy her. She wanted him to hit her, and he thought about the spider's ducts merging into its abdomen, but all he could manage was to slap her, and wild now, she went off to fetch a whip she had in the wardrobe, and he lost all desire as well as his erection.

Feeling sick, he went into her bathroom and threw up, blaming the tinned stuff they'd eaten, but he could feel his whole body contracting with loathing. After his stomach had emptied itself of its contents, he washed, pulled on his trousers, and went back to her.

She was lying stock-still on her back, staring vacantly up at the ceiling.

"You're nothing but a little shit, Simon Larsson," she said.

You may well be right, he thought, but he said nothing because her despair was obvious. He crept back into bed again and lay close to her. Her body again caught fire and was soon burning with devouring force. He let himself be swallowed by the fire, hook, line, and sinker.

They stuck it out for three days, loving, hating, weeping, sleeping for a moment or so, getting up occasionally to eat. He went down to the dairy for bread and butter, and she made no attempt to pay for it. He realized his money would soon run out.

She sucked his blood, cracked his bones, and he let it happen, as if paying off an old debt.

And she hated him for that. She wanted him to feel everything, everything she had had to endure. She humiliated him, hitting him, tormenting him, and he didn't resist, he complied with everything. She screamed out her contempt.

As dusk fell on the city on Saturday afternoon, he fell asleep, away from his own and her despair. She woke him with the whip.

"Hit me," she shouted.

But he couldn't. He simply got out of bed and was free, rid of them all, Karin and Inga, Mrs. Ågren and Dolly. He had met them all and knew they couldn't be conquered.

Just as on the first day, Iza lay stock-still in bed, those vacant eyes on the ceiling.

"Go away," she said. "Go away now. I never want to see you again."

He showered, put on his uniform, and walked straight out into this cold and dark alien city. He had five kronor, seventy-five öre in his pocket. He knew that, because he had counted it on his last trip to the dairy. Not enough for a hotel room.

He had a return ticket, so he could make his way to the Central Station and take the first train back to Göteborg. But as he walked down Katarinaberget, he decided to take a look at the city after all, at least the old part, Gamla Stan. There was no frost yet, so he could probably walk the streets for one night.

He crossed Slussen, walked along Skeppsbron, and turned into the narrow alleys, icy winds whistling between the tired old buildings. He was cold, mindlessly cold as he stood there in Stortorget trying to feel the wingbeats of history, but simply froze.

I've no heart any longer, he thought, just a pump in there moving the blood around and keeping it warm.

But his feet took him toward Kornhamnstorg, where the cafés looked cheaper. He stood outside one, reading the menu in the window and calculating that he could afford two cheese sandwiches and hot cocoa for two kronor, twenty öre.

"Hey, my lad, you do look pale," said the waitress in a singing north-country voice, and Simon saw she was like Mona, but older, and even more motherly.

He tried to smile, though not very successfully.

What was most important at that moment was to be allowed to stay there in the warmth for a few hours.

He took small mouthfuls at a time, chewed them thoroughly, sipping at the cocoa and swallowing carefully. Slowly, his heart started up again, the warmth spreading from his stomach down to his feet, where it turned around and made the long journey back up to his head.

Once his brain began functioning again, the relief he had felt in Iza's bedroom vanished and his thoughts became of the very worst kind.

God in heaven, what a bastard he was. For years, he had fantasized about the girl, the evil in her that would make him real. He would use her, a thousand times, to participate in her reality and make it comprehensible.

Because he had wanted evil, but had never dared it himself.

He thought about Mrs. Ågren all that far back in his childhood, how he had been attracted to her in order to hate her, how he wanted to cut off her breasts and gouge out her eyes.

In his imagination, always only in his imagination.

His stomach turned over again. If he didn't calm down, he wouldn't be able to keep the food down.

Bylund. He thought about Bylund and eventually realized that they were really rather alike, but the sergeant was the more honest.

No tears, and he was grateful for that, for the café was filling up with people. He would pay soon and get up and go.

Bylund had coped, he thought. Bylund with his quivering nostrils would have been able to give Iza everything she wanted. He could move from fantasy into action.

But he had almost killed Bylund.

The memory gave him a little strength. He managed to swallow the next mouthful and feel it settling in his stomach.

He tried to remember how it had arisen, his attraction to Iza. He had been there in the sanatorium, looking at this girl, fat and ugly then, and he had thought she was the first person he had ever met who was ruthlessly honest in everything she said and did.

That was true, she is.

Then he remembered staring at the numbers on her arm, and time had stopped.

She possessed reality, he had thought.

There were many descriptions of the camps now, written by survivors. They didn't describe only the evil and the suffering, but also the way in which what was unfathomable made everything unreal.

They did not survive if they left any room for compassion, someone had written. And without compassion, the world becomes unreal.

They take on the guilt for the executioner's crimes, Olof had said.

Iza?

No, he didn't think she felt any guilt. But to be real, she had to be tormented.

I'll try to write to her.

What should he put in the letter?

Real people are decent, he thought. Reality is to know you can trust each other. Like Karin and Erik. Ruben, Inga, yes, she also possessed reality.

Not that dreary musician, who had made love for a few weeks in the forest and then vanished, only to make himself known a year later with a silly letter.

Thousand kisses.

God Almighty, how disgusting.

Simon gave a lot of thought to his dream about the fiddler heading for his own destruction.

The same attraction to evil as his own?

I have it in my genes, he thought, inherited, like the music.

Death?

I can walk to the station, slip out onto some track, and throw myself in front of an express train.

But he knew he couldn't do it. Because of Karin.

He hated her for that.

Then he knew he didn't want to die.

The only thing he really wanted was to go straight home to her, put his head on her lap, and tell her everything.

But he couldn't do that.

He had to be alone in what had happened.

Alone, that's what it was to be an adult.

For the first time he realized that he was now an adult, and the thought was unbearable.

TWENTY·SIX

"You're looking pretty awful."

A man was sitting opposite him at the table now, a middle-aged man with friendly, slightly slanting brown eyes. "You ought to get some proper food inside you."

"No money."

"Can I get you a bowl of soup?" said the man.

The waitress had been keeping a worried eye on Simon and now almost rushed to bring the hot soup.

Simon ate it gratefully, thinking vaguely that perhaps he'd met this man before.

"Name's Andersson."

"Larsson."

They shook hands, the man's hand strangely broad, warm and dry.

"Have you deserted?"

"No, no, I'm due back in Göteborg. Been on leave."

"And having a fling around Stockholm, I suppose?"

"Mm," said Simon with a grimace, though he had to smile at the glint in those brown eyes. "I've got a return ticket," he said.

"You can come with me if you like. I'm taking my truck down to Göteborg tonight."

Simon considered this was more than he deserved.

"My dad had a truck for years," he said. "Maybe that's why I recognize you?"

"Mm, probably when you were a child," said Andersson. He paid for the sandwiches and the soup, ordered ten more cheese sandwiches, no, five cheese and five with liver pâté, please.

"We'll need them," he said, hauling two thermos flasks out and having them filled with coffee.

"Let's go, then."

They walked up the hill toward Slussen, turned off toward Södra Station where Andersson's truck was parked, loaded and ready. It was almost ten now, but the streets were a restless and perpetual stream of people.

"Stockholm's becoming the kind of city that never sleeps at night," said Andersson.

Simon nodded, but with little interest in Stockholm now, only in staying as close to this driver as possible. The man was surprisingly small, a whole head shorter than Simon was.

The green Dodge was heavily loaded and had tarpaulins roped over the back. There was a half-meter-wide ledge behind the driver's seat, on it a thin mattress, a few old blankets, and a large and surprisingly soft pillow.

Andersson jerked his stubby thumb at the bunk.

"You need some sleep, Larsson. I'll wake you at dawn somewhere in central Sweden."

Simon slept like a child, enveloped in dreams, rustling grass, and bright safety.

He woke at dawn as they left the asphalted trunk route and drove onto a minor road. He lay there remembering where he was, sat up, met those slanting eyes in the rearview mirror, and felt looked after.

"Thought we'd take a turn up toward Omberg and have some breakfast in the green up there on the holy mountain," said Andersson.

It was no longer green, but a mild autumn sun was just coming up over the Östagöta plain and the wheels were rustling through a carpet of reddish-yellow leaves.

"Beech," said Andersson. "Just fallen."

Simon looked at the pillar-straight trunks along the roadside. He had never seen beech trees before, only read about them.

"What do you mean by the holy mountain?" he said.

"Omberg," said Andersson. "One of the eight holy mountains of the world, mentioned in the secret scripts since time immemorial."

"You're an Östagöta man," said Simon, laughing.

"Maybe so," said Andersson, and Simon reckoned they were probably worse than Göteborgians.

"I've lots of evidence," said Andersson with a laugh. "Look over to the east, right out over the plain."

Simon looked at the windows of red-painted cottages winking sleepily in the sun.

"That's where Queen Omma kept her marsh people once upon a time," said Andersson. "They were magical people who knew the mystery of life and celebrated it with great feasts every time the moon was on the wane."

"You made that up," said Simon, but then remembered reading about the Dags Mosse excavations of a special Neolithic pile-dwelling.

"They drove in over a thousand piles," said Andersson, nodding. "Then put a floor on them. Not a very big job. Those were the days when giants still walked on two legs on the earth."

Simon envisaged the giants yanking Omberg's huge beeches straight out of the ground, snipping off the roots and slicing off branches, then running the trunks between thumb and forefinger.

"We'll take a piss with the old monks," said Andersson, as the Alvastra ruin loomed up against the dawn light.

Andersson stopped the heavy truck, switched off the engine, and put on the hand brake.

"You have to take her gently," he said. "She's not so young any longer, and she has her whims, the truck, I mean."

They walked toward the ruin and stood there with their backs to a monument each, Oskar II's and Gustaf V's contribution to the history of the monastery. Simon watched the slanting rays of the sun creep through the arches in the nave of the church, and sensed those wingbeats of history he had missed last night in the old city.

"Just think," said Andersson. "Imagine a long line of monks jogging through Europe, one after another as if on a string. With them they have all kinds of seeds of medicinal plants, cuttings for apple, pear, and cherry trees, all to become the ancestors of this old heathen country's cultivations.

"Imagine," he went on, "them making their way through the primeval forests of Småland, praying to their God every morning that this wilderness would come to an end before nightfall, when the wolves started howling among the trees. Then one day they are at last here and start building a church and a monastery."

Simon glimpsed the gray Cistercians, the men of Saint Bernhard, among the remains of the pillared hall.

"What courage," said Andersson. "All they had to put their hopes in was a letter from an old woman called Ulfhild. She'd killed off several husbands, married Sverker the Elder, and was sitting here at the royal demesne as queen."

"They probably put their trust in God."

"Yes. Thy will be done. That's the thing called trust, and it achieves miracles."

"Overcomes matter and moves mountains," said Simon.

But Andersson laughed when he said that quite a number of horses and men had probably been involved when the monks moved the mountain from the limestone quarry in Borghamn to build their church.

They washed in the rainwater in the piscina in the north cross-aisle, where once the monks had also washed their hands.

"I wonder," said Andersson as he put his truck into first gear and they started crawling up the hill, past the elaborate woodwork of the tourist hotel, and Simon gasped at the view and Lake Vättern. "I wonder if Ulfhild's guilty conscience was the reason for her bringing the monks here."

"Probably politics," said Simon, memories of school and discussion of the works of Heidenstam coming back to him. "Wasn't it only God who gave power to anyone in good standing with the Catholic church?"

Andersson smiled, the kind of smile that showed he had more to say but was keeping it to himself. Because there were no words for it, or just for the pleasure of secretiveness.

He's like an old Chinese man, Simon thought.

"Anyhow," Andersson went on. "It wasn't long before church bells began to resound over the mountain and frighten away Queen Omma and the giants."

"Where did they go?"

Simon was truly enjoying the moment, the man, the mountain, the view, their conversation, a kind of healing settling over the torments of the day before.

"They went to another reality where things were good," said Andersson, his voice so definite it was as if he had just been to see them.

"That's good," said Simon, and they both laughed.

"Down on your left is Rödgaveln's cave, the entrance to the mountain king's palace," said Andersson, but Simon had no time to see the precipice before they were running downhill toward Stocklycke meadows, guarded by great oaks. There were larches, too, flaring against the sky, but the truck swung sharply to the left by the tourist hut and started climbing again, up Örnslid out to a precipice where you could see the Västra Väggar.

They stopped.

"Not afraid of heights, are you?" said Andersson.

Simon shook his head, speechless from the magnificence. Just as the Rock of Gibraltar meets the Mediterranean, Omberg met Lake Vättern, but here it was forested and grandiose as up in Norrland. The lake was a brilliant turquoise, the sun reflected in the water and enveloping the hills in a shimmering blue-green.

"What a light," said Simon.

"No talking," said Andersson, taking his lunch box and blankets with him over to the very edge of the precipice.

I'll send him my poem about the sea, thought Simon as they sat over generous sandwiches and coffee.

"The water's green because the giants wash their filthy long johns in it," Andersson said, swallowing his last piece of bread.

Simon exploded with laughter, so loud it echoed in Omma's prehistoric fortress several kilometers away.

Andersson smiled his secretive smile, the sun warm now, then stretched out on the blanket and pulled his cap over his eyes.

"Isn't it odd," he said, "that all knowledge from outside tries to make you believe you're nothing but a fly-spot in the universe? But what comes from inside yourself insistently says you're everything and have everything."

Simon hadn't given that any thought, but he pondered for a moment before answering.

"Something biological, I suppose, some instinct for survival persuading you you're so damned important."

"No," said Andersson. "It's science, bloody well much better to rely on science."

He knocked his cap off, propped himself up on his elbow, and looked at Simon.

"Close your eyes, lad," he said. "Switch off your brain and go inward, to the hall of the mountain king in your own heart. There you'll hear the truth about whether you were born in vain."

Then he lay down and fell asleep, and Simon did as he had said, closed his eyes. The second movement of the *Symphonie fantastique* came to him and almost immediately he was beyond the images and out in the whiteness . . .

He was brought back to earth again by Andersson gently putting his hand on his shoulder.

"We must get on, lad. Well, did you hear the truth?"

"Not hear," said Simon. "More like feel."

"Good, then let's go."

From Borghamn, they made their way back to the main route, where the wheels quietened on the asphalt and Andersson began to whistle. Simon tensed, out of habit prepared for the worst, but not a note was off as Andersson whistled the melody of the second movement of the Berlioz.

It had been a morning of such wonder that Simon had ceased to be surprised. That was as it should be, that Andersson had also heard the music that had rushed through Simon's head up there on the mountain.

Once they had Jönköping behind them and started climbing the Småland Highlands, Andersson was told the whole Iza story.

"D'you see what a bastard I am?"

"That's a bit much," said Andersson. "I'd say you were one of those poor devils who go through life paying off old debts of guilt. You must stop that, for there's no guilt except in your imagination."

Simon said nothing at first, he was so surprised. But then he collected his wits for a question.

"So there's no point in trying to pay it off?"

"No, you can't. There's no valid currency. It's obvious, if the debt of guilt doesn't exist, there can't be anything to pay it off with."

"I see what you mean," said Simon, "but . . ."

"You're fantastic," said Andersson, and Simon heard he was teasing. "Otherwise it usually takes your whole life before you've paid off the installments."

Simon stared out over the mosses in Bottenaryd, thinking so hard his face was all screwed up. His internal burden, that which he usually called guilt, didn't exist.

"Then I suppose it's sorrow," he said almost to himself.

"Sorrow," said Andersson, "is generally self-pity."

"Now you're being bloody awful," said Simon, but he had to laugh, and at that moment it was true, at that moment Andersson's words applied.

"It's only the moment that exists," said this long-distance truck driver.

"But, good God," said Simon.

"Exactly," said Andersson. "God is the God of the present, accepting you as he finds you. He doesn't ask what you've been, but what you're like at this moment."

He put the gear into neutral down the hill at Ulricehamn.

"You're probably also one of those idiots who think they can control life," he went on. "That's why you're drawn to what you call evil. You imagine that if you understand how it functions, then you'll be able to defend yourself against it and escape being afraid."

Simon drew a deep breath. That was true, he knew that, and it hurt and was good at the same time.

Then Andersson's voice came back, gentler now.

"What are you afraid of, lad?"

"I don't know," said Simon, but the very next moment he knew, an old terror moving deep down inside him.

He told Andersson about Inga, about being abandoned before Karin came. Andersson nodded.

"The body has its memories," he said.

It was raining as usual as they approached Borås, so Andersson rolled up the window and after some jiggling managed to get the windshield wipers going.

"There's something remarkable about infants," he said. "About their minds. Have you ever looked into the eyes of a newborn baby?"

No, Simon hadn't.

The rain stopped abruptly in Sjömarken.

"Have you any children?" said Simon.

"A whole lot, scattered all over the world."

"In America?"

"Yes, there and elsewhere."

"So you've none left here at home?"

"Yes, I've a boy in Sweden," said Andersson, his mysterious smile sunnier than ever as he added, "A bloody fine lad."

According to the clock, six hours had gone by before they bowled down the Källebäck hills into Göteborg. But for Simon the journey had been short and he would have liked to stay there in the truck with Andersson forever.

"Here we are, then," said the driver, braking in front of the Central Station in Drottningtorget. "Off you get now, quickly, as I'm a bit behind time."

"Can I have your address?" stammered Simon as he stood on the pavement and Andersson was closing the door.

"See you sometime, lad. We'll meet again, don't you worry."

He was taking his load to the ship bound for England and the load had to be stowed on board before five o'clock. Simon watched the truck disappearing down toward the quays.

He felt horribly lonely.

But he went into the station, checked his money, still only five kronor and seventy-five öre, and picked out some coins.

Karin answered.

"Hi, Mom, all's well with me. Is Isak there?"

"No, he's gone to the cinema with Mona."

Simon tried to think, gaining time by asking a question.

"You all right?"

"Yes, fine."

"Mom, can you tell Isak I managed all right, that it's over now?"

"What are you talking about, Simon?"

He could hear ears flapping and thought, Oh, hell.

"A joke, Mom, a bet."

"Oh, I see." Her voice had a touch of acid in it now. She didn't believe him.

"Mom!" he shouted. "Money's running out, but I've never felt so well in all my life, do you hear!"

That she did believe, and she laughed, and then they were cut off.

When he came into town the next Saturday, he spent hours in the central truck depot, going from driver to driver, asking after Andersson, a little guy with brown eyes who drove a green Dodge.

No, no one knew Andersson.

"Some cowboy, probably," they said. "Lots of them around in the trade."

TWENTY-SEVEN

*E*rik brought Karin her coffee in bed in the mornings. At first it embarrassed her, but it soon became a habit. A need, in fact, to be allowed to stay in the warmth of bed with fresh coffee and the morning's thoughts, those, too, often new and good.

This early spring, her thoughts were mostly on Simon, at present happy and harmonious, despite the fact that the cold and winds out there couldn't have been very cheering.

One day in February when it was snowing and she had switched off the bedside lamp to be able to see the snowflakes in the early morning light, Mona knocked on the door.

Of course, thought Karin, it's Wednesday and her day off.

"Can I come and sit with you for a while?"

Mona crept up onto the end of the bed and pulled a blanket around her.

"Would you like some coffee?"

"No, thanks. I've already had breakfast." Then, very quickly, as if to get it over and done with, "Karin, I'm pregnant."

Karin felt her heart behaving oddly for a moment, but she was used to that and more or less ignored it. Thoughts raced through her head, contradictory emotions within her, primeval female fear of giving birth, tenderness toward the girl, anxiety, and most difficult of all, that old sorrow over her own childlessness.

Envy, she thought. I'm envious.

Then it struck her that she would have a grandchild.

That wasn't strictly true, but anyhow that joy was the strongest of all.

"Heavens, how wonderful," she said, then added with a laugh,

"I ought to have known, with so much love in such a cramped little bed, and only a little rubber thing to resist it."

Mona had told her about the pessary and shown it to an astonished Karin, who had said that she would never have relied on such a thin slippery rubber thing.

Mona had been offended on behalf of the pessary, but she could tell Karin now that she hadn't used it in a long time, because she wanted a wedding. And children.

Most of all, she wanted to leave the nursing school.

"You'll be a grandmother, Karin," she said.

"Almost like one, anyhow."

Then they got lost in chatter about a boy, no, a girl. Mona said, "I'm almost certain it'll be a girl. We'll call her Malin."

"Why?" said Karin, who thought it an ugly old name, smelling of poverty-stricken old Sweden.

"That was my mother's name," said Mona, so there was nothing to add.

"Does Isak know?"

"No, not yet."

"You must get married."

"Mm. Have you heard the hairdresser is moving into town? I suppose they can't stand the gossip about Dolly any longer. So I thought we might be able to rent the three-room apartment above the Gustafssons'."

"That'd be good," said Karin, thinking that, after all, life was kind. She would have Mona and Isak as neighbors. And the girl. Karin had already begun to think of the unborn child as the girl.

"Maybe you would ring Gustafsson and ask."

"Of course," said Karin.

But then they came to all the worries, Isak and Chalmers.

"We can live on a student loan," said Mona. "Silly, when you think about Ruben, but all the same, it'll have to work."

Her eyes were appealing to Karin, who shook her head. At work, Isak had become aware of the connection between money and self-esteem. He was careful to pay his way at Karin and Erik's, and he had told Ruben he would pay Maria's fees, quite an expense, as he realized he would need to go to her for many years.

They had sometimes been so hard up, Mona had had to borrow tram money from Karin.

Karin realized Isak's attitude was good for him, but she occasionally felt sorry for Mona.

They sat there in bed listing silently in their heads, sheets and towels, duvets, covers, beds, furniture, saucepans, plates . . .

"It'll have to be as simple as possible," said Mona, but when Karin said they would have to look at what they had stored down in the basement, Mona had to look down to hide her embarrassment.

"There can't be much there," said Karin, remembering they had thrown most things out when they had rebuilt the house. "Pity about your training," she said, because she had been pleased when Mona had passed her nursing exams.

"Oh, well," said Mona. "I don't want to be a nurse."

"But it's good to have a profession should anything go wrong," said Karin, then the next moment realized there would never be any shortage of money in Ruben's family.

Yet she sighed without knowing why.

Before Lisa came, Karin rang Gustafsson, and he said no, they hadn't promised the apartment to anyone, yes, that would probably be all right.

While Lisa was cleaning, Mona and Karin went for a walk along the shore. It had stopped snowing and a pale winter sun had dared emerge, painting the ice around the jetties a golden yellow.

"It's important you tell Isak," said Karin.

Mona went into town that afternoon and stood on the quay watching the barges coming across the river with the men from Götaverken. He was in the first one and was pleased though slightly worried to see her.

"Come and meet Onsala."

Mona shook the tall man's hand, and then the two of them were alone on the quay, and she saw the question in his eyes.

"Let's go," she said.

Isak wheeled his bicycle while trying to put one arm around her shoulders.

"Nothing's happened, has it?"

"Yes," she said. "We're going to have a child."

Isak let her go, and the bicycle, which fell with a clatter onto the road, while he stood stock-still letting his delight fill him.

"Heavens, how wonderful," he said, just as Karin had.

He went back to Sänkverket and locked up his bicycle for the night, then, taking Mona's hand, said, "We'll go and tell Dad first."

They flew through town, at least until they were approaching Ruben's entrance, then reality returned to Mona.

"What'll he say?"

"He'll be pleased."

Even so, Isak was surprised to see Ruben's delight as they stood in front of him, very young and rather scared, and Mona said, "We're expecting a child."

His joy rose from great depths, from thousand-year-old sources, the joy of blood, the joy of the family. Mona seemed to understand that, as she said, "It'll be a Jewish child. We're going to be married in the synagogue and I'll convert."

Ruben did something unexpected. He lit the menorah, put his arms around Mona and Isak as they faced the quiet flames, and read a long prayer in Hebrew.

The ancient prayer affected both them and the child listening, the words incomprehensible, but containing a peace that went beyond all reason.

A little later, Ruben phoned Karin and asked them to come and have dinner with him that evening, as he had something important to tell them. He could hear the laughter in her voice when she replied that they would try, she and Erik, but not until he had put the receiver down did Ruben realize what she had meant.

She knew all right, his Wise Norn.

At dinner, Isak said, "Dad, I think I'll stay on at Götaverken. Chalmers can keep it as far as I'm concerned."

Mona looked down to hide what she was thinking, but Erik's eyes gleamed inquisitively and slightly maliciously. Now they would see how deep that went, the classlessness Ruben always espoused. He wouldn't agree to his son becoming an ordinary worker, not unless he meant it seriously.

"I'd almost realized that, Isak. You like it there so much," said Ruben, then, turning to Erik, he went on, "Isak is working his own lathe now, a tremendously intricate machine."

Erik was surprised, but then he banged his fist on the table so hard, the glasses jumped.

"Well, damn me . . ."

"Don't swear," said Karin, which startled him, as she wasn't that bad at swearing either. But then she was perhaps thinking about the child inside Mona.

"Isak," said Erik. "You know nothing about what lies in the future, the way you get worn out, ruin your back, and rheumatism sets in. Not to mention damaging your hearing, and the wretched wages. I've worked on the shop floor and I know. In the long run, you can't stand the filth and the noise. And the lack of freedom," he added. "That's the worst."

Isak was about to say that he'd seen quite a lot now, but he still preferred the hard work to becoming some fancy engineer.

"Isak needs practical experience," said Karin as a diversion. "Even if he is to start at Chalmers. It won't do him any harm if he stays on a few years, so they have some order in their lives when the child is small."

She told them about the Gustafssons' apartment.

"Isn't it rather uncomfortable?" said Ruben.

"No, they've put in central heating and a bathroom."

Isak was thinking God was good and he would go to see Gustafsson that evening, and Mona and Karin were thinking about sheets and linen, furniture and mattresses, plates and cups and other necessities.

None of them said anything, so when Ruben raised his glass to Karin, she could see in his eyes that he had had a good idea.

Mona told them she was going to convert to Judaism. Erik looked surprised, but Karin nodded. She knew why.

No one gave a thought to Mona's father.

They broke up early so that Isak would have time to see Gustafsson. He came back half an hour later and said it was all arranged and he was to sign the rent agreement on Saturday.

It was going to be more expensive than he had expected, and Karin gaped when she heard the sum.

"Gustafsson probably piled it on," said Erik when he and Karin were on their own. "Figured rich Lentov's son could afford it."

Karin nodded, but said there was also a housing shortage, so they ought to be grateful.

The next day Mona went to the superintendent of the nursing school with her resignation. She told her the truth, that she was pregnant, and the stern lady just said curtly, "Well, Mona, you would have been expelled anyhow."

As the girl filled in the necessary papers, the superintendent talked about how uncivilized the young were, and had the child a father, oh, so there's to be a marriage and could she ask who the lucky man was?

Mona smiled gently at her as she said, "Ruben Lentov's son."

"The woman looked as if she were about to choke," said Mona when she told Ruben, who smiled and thought that here was at least one child who was proud of him. They were having lunch at a restaurant and Mona loved him for his beautiful words.

He took out an envelope.

"This is a gift to my daughter-in-law," he said.

"But Isak?" she said.

"Isak has nothing to do with our friendship," he said, his eyes glittering.

Mona smiled as she put the envelope into her bag. On the tram journey out to Karin, she resisted the temptation to open it, but thought worryingly that it looked thin and they would need a lot more. Rugs, Ruben had said. She knew a place where they had wonderful rugs.

Back at Karin's, she took out the envelope, which appeared even thinner than she had remembered.

"You open it," she said. "I don't dare."

Karin firmly took out a knife and slit open the envelope, which contained a piece of paper.

"A check, I think," she said. Neither of them had ever seen one before.

"It says ten thousand," said Karin, and Mona had to sit down to stop herself from fainting.

They collected their wits over a cup of coffee before going to look at the apartment, where the hairdresser's wife had just started packing. So many roses, thought Mona. How ugly. But the rooms were lovely, large and light, and the kitchen as spacious and pleasant as Karin's.

"You see," said Mona as they stood in the bedroom window overlooking the Larssons'. "We can wave to each other."

"Awful furniture and terrible wallpaper," she said when they got back. "We'll paint every room white."

Karin had never liked her neighbors, but she had always admired their home with its stylish furniture and crystal chandeliers, so she was surprised.

"What are you going to do?"

"White walls, white furniture, white curtains," said Mona.

"That sounds . . . light," said Karin.

"Not too much, but expensive furniture," said Mona. "Lots of flowers."

She was happily dreaming, and Karin realized she had had those dreams a long time.

"It's to look like a country parsonage," said Mona. "And the kitchen'll be like yours, with bright rag rugs on the floor. No chandeliers and stuff like that."

Karin realized she ought to feel flattered, so said nothing about how she had always longed to have a crystal chandelier.

They heard Isak whistling in the drive, out of tune as usual, and Mona looked guilty. He noticed at once.

"What have you gone and done?"

He was joking, but was slightly scared when Mona said they'd better go upstairs and have a talk.

"If you need any help, give me a call," said Karin, also a little anxious now.

But a moment later, she heard Isak laughing, then he suddenly came flying down the stairs, hugged Karin, and imitating Ruben's slightly drawling voice and slight accent, he said, " 'Tell Isak he has nothing to do with our friendship.' He's a cunning old Jew, Dad is."

Isak was relieved, and Karin and Mona simultaneously saw that his head was full also of lists, sheets, linen, furniture, china.

TWENTY-EIGHT

A few weeks later something occurred that would go down in family history as the Saturday everything happened.

But for Ruben it did not start so well.

"Your niece is on the phone."

Ruben hid a grimace. "Not mine, but my wife's niece," he said wearily, though he knew he was being foolish.

The voice was as urgent and feverish as usual, and she wanted some more money.

"I'm starving," she said.

But he had become hardened to Iza over the years, and remembered Olof Hirtz saying he must limit the girl.

"You know you have to manage on your allowance," he said.

She was purring like a cat when she spoke again. "Simon spent a week here, eating like a horse and living it up in town and all that."

Ruben's heart sank, but his voice was steady when he answered her. "When was that?"

"A while ago," said the voice evasively, and he knew she was lying, but perhaps not about everything.

"I'll send you a hundred," he said. "How are things going at college?"

"Fine," she said. "Thanks, Uncle dear."

That was Saturday morning. He phoned Karin to ask whether Simon was coming on leave as usual that weekend.

"Yes, we're expecting him."

"I'll pick him up."

Ruben was angry, but knowing his anger would protect him from anxiety, he stuck with it as best he could: Damn the boy.

Simon was waiting on the jetty for the boat to take him to the mainland. The wind was off the sea, northwesterly and cold as cold. But it didn't come from town, so it carried no message of Ruben's fury.

Simon was in a good mood.

He had been on guard duty over the dark sea that night, monotonous and tough, but he was used to it now. At first he had almost wished for war, hostile ships on the horizon, snipers on the skerries. Then you could fire and raise the alarm and make a hell of a noise.

Some of the men had done that and been reprimanded by Sjövall, then teased for weeks afterward by the men who had been dragged out of their beds by the alarm and had felt fear gripping at their entrails.

Simon had gazed at the skerries all that long night, thinking they knew he was there watching them. They have their life in eternity, he could see, nothing had influenced them since the end of the Ice Age ten thousand years ago. But then he reckoned they had a different calculation of time, and a conversation with an atomic scientist had assured him that a dance went on inside the stone.

"I believe you," Simon had said, trying to imagine the rhythm in the granite, the way anything that feels no fear would dance. Then he had been relieved and had managed a few hours' sleep before the time came for kit inspection and transport ashore.

Ruben watched the boy coming toward him, tall and happy, his big smile white in the weatherbeaten face and an intensity in his movements.

He's an adult and has a right to a private life, Ruben thought, but it was already too late.

"You're angry with me," said Simon.

"Well," said Ruben. "Jump in."

Simon didn't make it difficult for him. He was just as usual, open as a book wanting to be read and understood, and not to be blamed for the text being rich and complicated.

"Iza phoned," said Ruben, putting the car into gear and easing his way out.

Simon flushed scarlet, then went into retreat and nothing was said for a while. Simon felt exposed, as if Ruben had torn off all his protective disguises and revealed his innermost and worst fantasies.

"Why did you go?"

"Because I was like a child, playing with emotions."

Another long silence.

"I imagined she could make me feel real," he said at first. Then, "But I failed. I just made it worse for her." He tried to tell Ruben about the spiders, the desire for obliteration, but couldn't, and heard himself how sick it sounded.

"Lots of guilt, too," he said. "Idiotic fantasies of participating in her destiny."

Silence again as he searched for words.

"I couldn't do anything for her."

"No, Simon, no one can."

"It's awful."

"Yes."

"I'm dead ashamed."

"You're not going again?"

"Never."

Ruben was greatly relieved, but he had to tease a little.

"But you ate all her food and lived it up in town and spent all her money."

"That's a lie," said Simon, and he told Ruben how he had been out on the streets with five kronor, seventy-five öre in his pocket, and had to count the öre before daring to go into a café for a few sandwiches.

Ruben laughed.

"Can't we stop for a while, then I'll tell you something," said Simon, so Ruben maneuvered the car into a parking slot.

Then out came the story about Andersson, and Omberg and Alvastra, and the giants washing their long johns in Lake Vättern.

"He said the most amazing things, you see, all the time. I've been happy ever since I met him."

Ruben felt almost jealous, but he, too, was taken by the story of the mountain king's hall in your own heart and how everyone knows that he hasn't lived in vain.

"But best of all was all that about guilt," said Simon. "He said it doesn't exist, that it's about crimes that have never been committed, so can never be atoned for."

"I've often thought that, too," said Ruben. "But it's not true. People have always betrayed, hurt, and neglected."

"Not you?"

"Oh, yes. I betrayed Isak when he was small. I hurt Olga by marrying her, because it wasn't her I wanted. Not to mention my parents, when I didn't make them come with me to Sweden."

"How could you have made them?"

"It would have worked if I'd wanted it."

"Andersson said that God is the God of the present, and he only bothers about who one is now."

"I can't make it that easy for myself," said Ruben, but Simon was trying to remember other things that had been said in the truck, and didn't hear.

"Anyhow, you can't settle things, there's no valid currency with which to pay off the debt of guilt."

Ruben stared at Simon. That's true, he thought. It's horribly true.

"What else did he say?"

"That most people go on paying meaningless installments throughout their lives, wondering why the debt never gets smaller."

"I'd like to meet Andersson," said Ruben.

"You can't," said Simon, and he told him how he had searched all over the depot for the driver. "Absolutely no one knows him."

"Strange."

"Yes."

They looked at each other in amazement, shook their heads, and finally went on into town.

"How's Mona?"

"She's fine," said Ruben, who then had to listen to how one should look into the eyes of newborn babies, for there was lots to learn there.

As they turned off toward Långedrag, Ruben said, "You haven't long to go before freedom now."

"Six weeks," said Simon. "We're counting the days."

"I'm going to America at the end of April, then back home via London and Paris. I'd thought of asking you to come with me, if it interests you?"

"If!" cried Simon. Then he added, "Why do you want me to come with you?"

"I thought it'd be fun . . ."

Simon laughed. It was true. They had fun together, he and Ruben. This wasn't about paying off some old debt to Karin. This was about him, Simon. Ruben's face lit up.

"On one condition only," he said. "And that is you stop calling me Uncle. You're too old for that."

"And you're too young, Ruben," said Simon as they drove up to the house by the boatyard.

A large confused meal awaited them. Breakfast, lunch, and dinner all in one, Karin said, for no one had any time to cook more than once a day. The parlor had been turned into a sewing room, clouds of white muslin at one end around Karin's old sewing machine, and at the other end a table laden with scale drawings, color cards, paper models of furniture, and heaps of leaflets.

"A bridal dress?" said Simon, looking at Mona in all that white with some surprise.

"No, silly," she said. "Curtains."

Simon knelt down before her. "The holy virgin," he said, "you are not married." But then he put his head against her stomach, said, "Hello in there," and looked up at Mona.

"A girl," he said.

"Yes," said Mona. "Of course it's a girl."

"Those two are quite crazy," said Isak.

"Pregnant women do go a little crazy," said Karin.

"Yes, I've heard that. And Simon's always been crazy."

They ate standing up in all the muddle, and Simon said as if in passing that when he was discharged he was going to go to America with Ruben.

There was surprise and jubilation. But Karin said that would kill her, and wasn't it enough with a wedding and setting up house and a birth without a trip to America in the middle of it all.

"Mom," said Simon, rather anxiously. "You don't have to worry about my trip."

"Simon," said Karin. "I know there's something magical about uniforms, they grow apace with the boys inside them. But here at home, we don't know any of those conjuring tricks and I don't think you have a single garment you could get into."

They laughed. They had laughed every Saturday at Simon's attempts to get into his civilian clothes, which in the end looked as if someone had cut the sleeves off the shirts and the legs off the trousers. Not to mention his jackets bursting at the seams when he tried to get them on.

"There are a few days between to arrange for some clothes," said Ruben. "But you must have your passport, Simon. Have you got one?"

Simon nodded. He had acquired one in his last year at school with some kind of adventurous idea that the world was once again open and perhaps . . .

"That's good," said Ruben, thinking about the spirit of McCarthy hovering over the passport authorities like everything else in the United States.

Simon and Isak were then dispatched to the apartment next door to take some more measurements, in the kitchen this time. Simon stood looking out of Dolly's old room, and Isak said you could see right into the top floor at home from there.

Simon nodded. Yes, he knew you could.

The room had been painted all white, as Mona had decided.

"I don't have a chance to think anything," said Isak when Simon said it was almost dazzling.

They went back to the big living room.

"Isak," said Simon. "There's something I want to tell you."

"Something else?" said Isak with mock horror. They had been discussing Iza and his Stockholm visit, so that was clear between them.

But not mentioning Bylund had been worrying Simon.

He lowered himself down until he was sitting on the floor. Isak did the same.

"You know," said Simon, "I almost killed Bylund."

Isak's eyes widened and he went hot all over. Now he wanted to know everything.

By the time Simon got to those front teeth in a pool of blood in the corridor, Isak could no longer sit still, so he got up, staggering as if drunk, and started dancing around the empty room.

"You know, I've always been rather good at fighting," said Simon with mock modesty, and Isak stopped in the middle of his dance, remembering his first meeting with Simon, that small boy knocking down the tall son of a landowner in the school yard.

He wanted to say he loved Simon, but had to make do with "I'll say," and his voice was full of admiration.

When they got back, Mona commented on what a long time it had taken, and Karin said a letter from Stockholm in a brown envelope had come for Simon.

Simon was scared, and could hear it in his own voice as he said far too quickly, "Where is it?"

"Yes, you may well ask," said Karin. "In all this muddle."

They turned over white clouds of muslin, crawled under tables and sewing machine, but the letter had vanished.

"It'll turn up," said Karin, and Simon groaned inwardly. Hell, he thought, Iza's on the warpath again.

He exchanged looks with Isak and saw that he was thinking about what he'd said in the car last autumn. If she can get you to give her a kid . . .

Four months ago now, he thought. It couldn't be possible.

But he was uneasy and slipped out to the boatyard, where he

found Ruben and Erik in the partitioned-off space that served as an office. Erik was looking worried, as Simon had noticed earlier, and he forgot his own worries.

"What is it, Dad?"

"Things are difficult for Erik," said Ruben. "It's all doing rather too well."

Erik had to laugh, then they counted up the orders stacked in great piles at the yard, which had long since grown out of the space available.

"I don't want to get any bigger," said Erik. "There's something sick about everything having to grow bigger. Why can't I be allowed to build three or four double-enders a year, just as I've always done?"

"Because your customers will go to a competitor who has a larger capacity and shorter waiting times," said Ruben, as he and his lawyer had been saying to Erik frequently during the winter, making Erik equally angry each time.

"There's land going out at Önnered," said Simon.

"Yes, I know, for Christ's sake. I've already got a sea site in Askim," said Erik. "But it'll all be such a hassle, Simon, a whole lot of people and keeping accounts and papers and nothing but troubles."

"You'll have to appoint a manager," said Ruben.

"Ruben Lentov," said Erik. "We've known each other—"

"Dad," interrupted Simon. "What about Isak? He's got Erik's business sense in his very bones."

Erik stopped, and all three thought about how they had laughed over the years at Isak and his ability to buy cheap and sell dear, empty bottles, football stars in toffee papers, and all manner of other things.

"Do you think he'd want to?" said Erik.

But Simon said, "What about Chalmers, Dad, your dream for Isak, never for yourself?"

Erik had to laugh.

"You're a genius, Simon."

"I know," said Simon. "I am not without talent."

Ruben was pleased. If all went well, then as soon as Erik's self-esteem allowed it, Ruben could transfer his capital in the yard to Isak.

Then the boy would be secure.

But the three of them sat there thinking about Götaverken, the basis of all Isak's self-esteem.

"We must ask him," said Erik.

"I'll go and get him," said Simon.

Isak came and was as surprised as he was interested.

"What an amazing day," he said. "Can I have time to think it over? I must ask Mona what she thinks and all that."

But he had already decided, and as he left he said, "How long is that business course?"

"I think you'd manage with a year or two," said Ruben.

It was late by the time Simon got up to his room, and there was the letter, neatly placed on his desk, a large brown envelope, just as Karin had said.

He tore it open, then shouted aloud and raced downstairs like a madman. Ruben was still there, which was just as well, and Simon fell into his arms and went on shouting.

"They've taken it! They're going to publish it! My sea poem."

Karin had to sit down, her cheeks scarlet and her eyes glowing with pride.

Her boy had become a writer. A book was coming out with his name on the jacket. He had read the long poem to her and she knew it was beautiful, that it sang of the sea and was as incomprehensible as the sea was.

Erik was also beaming with pride.

But Ruben, who had had the poem typed out and had sent it in to the publisher, was not so surprised.

"Let me see the agreement," he said.

Simon was to have four hundred kronor, the first money he had ever earned in his life.

It'll be enough for some clothes, he thought.

TWENTY NINE

*N*ew York, New York, beat the great heart of the city, and Simon enjoyed the very sound of it. Everything was there in rapid succession, life and death, tears and laughter, fear and trust, cruelty and compassion. A melody freed itself from the rhythm, rose to the skies, took strength from the beating of that great heart, and became obscene and arrogant, laughing over the rooftops.

A young song, full of hope, New York, New York.

There were moments when Simon, now twenty, felt old, a tired stranger from an aging world. But he mostly felt in tune with this city that heightened his feeling for life.

"It's fantastic," he said to Ruben over dinner at the hotel, and that applied to everything, even the food.

Ruben nodded, thinking how good his trip had been, thanks to Simon. Look, see that, have you ever seen, listen, taste—everything also became new for Ruben, a man of conservative habits who on his own would have visited the famous art museums and possibly gone to the Met.

He had been there before the war and had been pained by the noise, the crowds, the shameless prostitution and wretched poverty amid all the greatest abundance in the world. Now he was enjoying it, like Simon, with all his senses and found he almost longed to leave meetings, even meetings with old friends in the publishing world.

"It fits," said Simon. "And yet it doesn't. You see, I've been here before."

He told Ruben about school and the boredom that used to come over him, and how he learned to fly, describing in detail how he had trained himself to find the point of intersection between two lines in the right side of his brain to be able to escape between his temple and skull.

Ruben laughed.

"I often came here," said Simon. "It looked just as it does, more or less, but I missed the essence of it, the intensity, the rhythm."

Ruben drank to him with the mellow California wine he found rather sweet, resisting making a speech to thank Simon for making their trip such an experience.

They had crossed in the *Stockholm*, eight restful days in pleasant luxury for Ruben. But Simon found friends among the officers and crew and disappeared down into the clattering heart of the ship to plague machinists and engineers with his questions.

Although the bridge was a prohibited area for passengers, he had spent all their last night there, looking out with tense expectation for the famous outline of the Statue of Liberty and the skyscrapers. At dawn he had awakened Ruben and made him come and look.

Ruben said nothing about having seen it before, but went with the boy, only to realize that he hadn't really seen it before.

Their last days before departure had gone quickly. Simon was discharged and had to be equipped, so he went from shop to shop with Mona trotting beside him, offering advice, it was said. But she chose the clothes. It was to her credit that he always felt correctly dressed on the trip. He himself would have bought clothes that were either too simple or too showy.

They had had a wedding, too, a simple ceremony in the synagogue, then dinner at Henriksberg afterward. None of Mona's relatives honored the ceremony with their presence, although they did come to the dinner. Ruben escorted Mona's aunt to the table, and as hostess, Karin looked after Mona's father. In both instances, there were few topics of conversation.

Afterward they all went to look at the apartment, now so pleasing and right that Simon stopped teasing Mona about her mania for interior decoration.

"I wouldn't be surprised if there weren't an artist hiding inside you, my dear," said Ruben.

On their last evening in New York, Simon and Ruben went up the Empire State Building and gazed out over the giant city with its thousand noises and tens of thousands of lights. Simon was sorry to be leaving, but found some consolation in that they were to fly across the Atlantic the next day.

But the flight was a disappointment, and Simon had to admit Ruben had been right when he had said flying was a dull way of seeing the world.

"Duller than walking," said Simon, who loathed going for walks.

But London received them with sunshine, a rather weary old lady, badly scarred by the war, but faithful and loyal.

After catching up on sleep at a hotel on the Embankment, they felt their spirits rise again and they had a large lunch.

"I've got a lot to do here, and not much time to spare," said Ruben.

"I can manage on my own," said Simon.

"This city isn't as nice as it looks, Simon. It's larger and more dangerous."

"I'll get a bus to the British Museum," said Simon, which is what he did, and from then on he saw very little of London. Over four days, he became a familiar figure to the attendants in the department of antiquities, the Swedish boy they had to go and look for at closing time.

Ruben's evenings were taken up with Simon's descriptions of the immense treasures, the incredible collections from Greece and Rome, Egypt and Mesopotamia.

"British imperialists were certainly not afraid to loot," said Ruben.

"No, but there are differing opinions on that," said Simon. "A whole lot of opinions. But at the moment I'm just glad they're here, assembled all in one place."

Then they crossed the Channel, spring came, and it was warm, almost hot on the train. Ruben's eyes glowed as they thundered into

Paris, another elderly lady, more sensitive, elegant, and sharper than London, but also shabby and exhausted by the war.

"This is the city of my youth," said Ruben. "The city of my dreams, where I came across practically everything that was to prove decisive, music, art, the great spirits."

Rebecca, he was thinking. We met here one spring.

"Strindberg," he said, then seeing Simon's surprise, he went on. "Not personally, but his books that I found in German, cheap, at one of the stalls on the banks of the Seine."

The next day, Ruben had a meeting and Simon was going to the Louvre. They agreed to meet in the entrance hall of the museum at three o'clock in the afternoon. Ruben was there on time, but not Simon. By four o'clock, Ruben was worried. He should have told him this city was more dangerous than London.

Then Simon appeared, and from a distance Ruben could see something had happened. He was white in the face, as if he'd seen a ghost.

"Uncle Ruben," he said. "You must come with me."

As Ruben hurried after him up the stairs and through the long galleries, he wondered why Simon had suddenly reverted to his habit of calling him Uncle, the first time on their trip.

In one of the galleries of antiquities, Simon stopped in front of a half-meter-high statue of a little man looking at them with centuries of inscrutable wisdom.

Gudea, Ruben read, Sumerian divine king, twenty-second century B.C.

"It's him," said Simon, "the man I told you about, the man who was there all through my childhood and who came back in the Berlioz symphony."

Ruben could feel the hairs on his arm standing on end and thought about Strindberg again, the writer who had given him an interest in Swedenborg and Sweden. But not even Swedenborg would have understood this.

Ruben looked from Simon to the statue, from the boy's scared eyes to the calm and superior oriental eyes of the statue. Finally he said in a voice not as steady as he would have wished, "However unfathomable life may be, Simon, we are here now. In these bodies that require food and rest."

To his relief, he saw that the boy was able to laugh.

They ate in silence, unable to appreciate the good French food at this expensive restaurant in the Champs-Élysées. They had planned to do Paris by night, but silently agreed to return to their hotel room, and Ruben was pleased he had booked a double room, rather than two singles. They showered, put on their pajamas, and Ruben took a cognac, though he still couldn't get his thoughts into any kind of order, or subdue his anxiety over Simon, who was still very pale.

But after they had lain there for an hour or so, gazing at the ceiling, Ruben's mind, the logical part of it, started working again.

"I was thinking about a famous parapsychological study I've read about," he said. "It began with the hypothesis that people under hypnosis could remember what they thought was a previous life. Among many others, there was a man who spoke in resounding Latin."

"Oh, yes," said Simon with interest, sitting up and switching on the lamp.

"Long strings of words, always the same. But it was remarkable, all the same, because the man was an American and lacked any education in the classics."

"Yes."

"Well, they tried to chart the man's life, everything he had been involved in, major and minor. Gradually, he remembered, in connection with a dramatic break with a woman he loved, sitting for hours in a library, utterly beside himself with despair. To be left in peace, he had borrowed a book, opened it, and stared without seeing at two pages containing that particular text he had quoted by heart under hypnosis. It had passed his consciousness but become engraved on his subconscious."

"Yes," said Simon.

"It strikes me," said Ruben, his voice steadier now, even more convinced, "that this is what has happened to you. Sometime when you were tired or so small you don't remember it, you saw a picture of that statue in the Louvre."

"And the picture made a great impression on my subconscious, you mean?" said Simon in a voice full of doubt.

"Yes," said Ruben. He told Simon he had recently seen a picture of Gudea in a book, a German book on archaeology by someone called Ceram, which was being translated into Swedish.

"Have you got a copy?"

"Yes, in German. You can borrow it as soon as we get home. What I mean is that this is a famous figure, reproduced in a great many contexts. Have you the catalog of the Louvre prehistoric collections?"

Ruben was eager. Simon leapt out of the bed and found it. In fumbling French, they read about Ernest de Sarzek, a French diplomat, who had excavated at the foothills in Lagash and found the statue, which was then loaded onto a ship and sent to the Louvre.

It had aroused tremendous attention in its day, because it confirmed that a culture had existed that was older than that of the Assyrians, even older than the Egyptians.

"When did de Sarzek live?" said Simon.

It didn't say in the brochure, but Ruben guessed the end of the nineteenth century.

"In the 1880s, I should think. If you would just calm down, I'll see if I can remember more from Ceram's book."

Ruben had a good memory, so after only a moment or two's silence, he spoke again.

"This is how it was," he said. "For a long time in various scientific indices, largely linguistic, it was guessed that there had been an unknown people before the Semitic high cultures in Mesopotamia, before Sargon. The Gudea find proved that they were right and the Sumerians entered history."

Simon was interested. His color had come back, and he suddenly remembered that amazing day at school when war broke out and the young teacher had said, *History begins with the Sumerians.*

"What I want to say," said Ruben, "is that the statue is well known, and has probably appeared in Swedish newspapers in connection with some article on the arts pages or some report on archaeology. You have seen the picture and, being who you are, it has come to influence your imagination, your dreams, and gradually your inner life."

He was on safe ground now, and his assurance affected Simon. When they awoke the next morning to make their way out to the airport and the plane to Copenhagen, the mystery had lost its hold on their minds.

Back at home, Simon found the time to read Ceram's book, which he found endlessly exciting. When Ruben invited him to dinner with Olof Hirtz, Simon told the story of how they had found the divine king of his dreams in a diorite statue in the Louvre.

Olof looked strangely surprised at first. Ruben noticed, but then recounted his theory of the picture that had been stored in Simon's subconscious, and Olof nodded, almost enthusiastically.

"Write about it, Simon," he said. "Write a poem, or why not a long short story about a day in childhood, a perfect day, as if created to form a lasting pattern in the child's emotional life. The sun is shining, there's a mildness in the mother's voice. She takes the child by the hand, strolls past the kiosk on the shore, and buys a magazine. They sit in the sand, and the tall grass on the edge of the shore sways in the wind and the shore meadow is endless, from the perspective of the little child. The mother is enjoying the warmth and leafs absently through the magazine, keeping an eye on the little boy digging canals in the sand and getting water to run from the sea into them.

"She is half asleep when the boy comes back to her, sees the magazine lying open beside her with the article on Mesopotamia. He can't read, but the pictures transfix him, the lion with a man's head, the canals, the temples and towers rising above the sea of grass. Most of all, the child sees the picture of the divine king with his strange round hat and gentle features that match the peaceful day. The boy is so small, he has still not yet begun to put memories into his computer bank, so everything goes into his subconscious, all colored by the beauty of the day, his mother's love, and the warm light over the river."

Simon laughed.

"Write it yourself," he said. "You, who's so sure."

"But I'm no writer."

"Yes, you are, you've just proved it," said Ruben, and they all laughed.

But Simon reckoned he would never write that story, even if the synopsis was good and the explanation reasonable, credible, in fact.

My friend, Andersson the truck driver, would never swallow it, he thought.

THIRTY

*T*he professor was a small man with inquisitive eyes and a smile that flitted back and forth across his innocent face. The Historical Institute in Göteborg was known for its vitality, and it was said that students there became more gifted than they were by nature. Anyhow, both intelligence and imagination were required of students, and most lived up to expectations. Students with a need to assert themselves soon transferred to Nordic languages after a term or two, where their chances of being in evidence were greater.

Simon had a brief talk with the professor, telling him that after his first degree, he wished to specialize in hieroglyphics.

"That's good to hear," said the professor with a swift smile. "Most are so fixated on the Aesir and Vikings."

His smile came back again.

"Sweden is not exactly a good place for Assyriologists," he said. "Perhaps you'll go to London, all in good time."

Apollo danced over the Elysian fields in Simon's dreams.

He was now sleeping at Ruben's in Isak's old room. There had been trouble at home over that, and about money.

"I'm getting a student loan, Dad."

"No, you bloody aren't. No child of mine is going to owe anyone money as long as I can afford to keep them."

The temperature in the kitchen rose. This was more than about money, on both sides.

"It'll be much more expensive than school."

But Erik had forgotten about his mutterings over the school fees long ago.

"Be ever so grateful, just as it's always been," Simon said to Karin when they were alone together.

"It's silly to get into debt unnecessarily," she said, and Simon could see she was sad, so he said nothing more. He had to agree slightly, particularly as Ruben had been drawn into the discussion and taken Erik's side.

"You can keep your independence in other ways apart from money," he said. Ruben himself had accepted help from his family when he had started building up his business in Göteborg. But then he realized that was a Jewish tradition.

Simon asserted himself by saying he wanted to leave home.

Erik was furious, having presumed everything would be the same as before now the boy was to be studying again. But Simon remembered only too well how you were made to eat Erik's bread not only once, but twice when at his table, so he persisted, and received unexpected support from Karin.

"You seem to have forgotten what it was like being an adult and having to live with your mother," she said to Erik.

"Mothers are different," said Erik. "And also, I was earning a living and contributing with money that was damned well needed."

"There you are," said Simon.

But Karin said that was enough, and they both saw that she was near to tears. Erik disappeared with his tail between his legs, and Simon stayed to console her, but nothing was sorted out.

Everything was just as it had always been.

There were no apartments to be had in Göteborg now, and the rooms to rent through college went to students whose parents didn't live in town. Ruben suggested that Simon should rent a room from him, and he protested forcefully when Erik, scarlet in the face, flared up again.

Ruben pointed out, "That's no more than fair. You've had Isak living here for years."

For once Erik could find no reply.

Ruben had been much taken by Mona's efforts at interior

decoration, so had his apartment redecorated. The walls were painted white, the velvet and plush were thrown out, and he had the same kind of white curtains as Mona had at the windows.

Even the old suite of big leather sofas was ignominiously carted off to the dump, to the astonishment of a sanitation department employee, whose wife was delighted. Ruben's apartment now had neat, pale blue Carl Malmsten sofas, a white dinner table, and grace-ful chairs.

"Looks like some manor house in Värmland," said Karin, who had once been to Selma Lagerlöf's Mårbacka in her youth.

The oriental rugs survived and glowed like jewels on the newly scraped parquet flooring, and the old glass-fronted bookcases had never even been at risk.

"You'll soon be able to see how much good art you have," said Simon. After endless discussions, Ruben and Mona had rehung the colorful paintings on the new white walls.

Simon told him how, as a child, he had stood in front of those incomprehensible canvases and tried to understand them. He could now, at least sometimes.

When his Victrola arrived and was placed against the white wall in his large room facing the courtyard, Mona said it was hideous.

"I've never noticed how ugly it was before."

"I can forgive it," Simon said with a laugh.

He was secretly pleased to be going to live with Ruben. At a lec-ture on scientific methodology, there was a reddish-yellow ponytail in front of him, the sun shining on it, making it sparkle. He couldn't remember seeing it before, so he waited with some excitement for the girl to turn her head. When she did so, he was disappointed, a long neck, an extremely high forehead in a narrow, pale, freckled face. He smiled slightly as they got up after the lecture, and he found she was almost as tall as he was, and had a generous mouth and large gray-green eyes.

Klara Alm had noticed Simon on the very first day, his good looks, but also something else, an unease that was not the usual kind, as if he were constantly preoccupied with the mystery of life and expecting fantastic answers to appear at any moment.

As usual, she had twin thoughts. The first was, There goes the course's Don Juan, and the second, He'll never even look in my direction.

She was wrong on one score, for although girls flocked around Simon at first, he was friendly to them all but no more than that. He hasn't even the sense to be flattered, she thought with surprise.

But she was right on the second score. He never even noticed her.

Now he was smiling at her. How intense he is, she thought, then was afraid of sweating, of damp patches under her arms.

A few days later, Simon asked one of the girls about Klara and was told she was going to be a doctor.

"She's already got her first degree," said the girl. "So she's probably just having a break with a little humanities before going on."

That surprised Simon. Klara must be older than she looked.

"She's very clever," the girl went on. "She passed all her final school exams privately when she was only sixteen. The intelligent and ice-cold kind, you know."

Simon disagreed, for Klara Alm did not seem cold, but he did wonder what she was afraid of.

Then he forgot her until the day he found her again over coffee when Nordberg, the witty son of a dean, was holding court as usual about the necessity for a Marxist view of history, even of the Greeks.

Klara suddenly flushed scarlet with annoyance and got up so quickly, the coffee splashed about in the cups.

"You're making things too easy for yourself," she said. "I think you should distinguish between private and political revolution and settle your puberty argument with your father, if rather late."

Then she left and there was a lot of laughter. Nordberg said furiously that she was a bloody bitch, but Simon got up and followed her out.

"You're not scared," he said when he had caught up with her in the hall.

"No," she said. "But I'm stupid. They'll label me right wing now."

"And you aren't?"

"No. I largely agree with him. But he's so certain and second-hand, if you know what I mean. He gabbles off Marx and charges it with childish aggressiveness."

"The new revolutionaries pick the bourgeoisie's fruits from the tree of knowledge and pay with money from capitalist fathers earned in a more or less honest way," said Simon, laughing.

"You're really intelligent," she said.

"Why shouldn't I be?"

"Well, you know," she said. "Good-looking boys . . ."

"You're wrong," he said. "It's pretty girls who're stupid."

"Of course, I forgot," said Klara. "As you may have gathered, I'm very intelligent."

"Are you warning me?"

"Maybe."

"You needn't bother," said Simon, and she reckoned she already knew that. He was just amused by her malice. But Simon went on. "You see, I'm a genius, so you can't threaten me."

She was idiotically pleased, but her laugh sufficiently disguised her pleasure.

As they walked across to the cycle stand, Simon told her about his father.

"He was a truck driver, politically extremely clear-sighted, about everything except the Soviet Union. Now that you can't close your eyes to the fact that the workers' paradise is a police state, he's lost interest in politics in general."

"So you're working class?"

"Yes. That is, things have changed a bit," Simon said. When he saw she was curious, he went on. "Dad was unemployed, like so many coming out of the army, so he started building boats, sailboats. Now he's got a yard of his own and stacks of problems and employees."

"From communist to capitalist. That sort of thing must also mean political vacuum," said Klara.

"Mm. He's a good man," said Simon.

"Understandable," said Klara, "that you've got a great dad, I mean."

"What do you mean?"

"Well, you're the kind of unusual guy without a big need to assert yourself and overdo things."

Simon was more than surprised.

"Well, I am a genius," he said. "But I'm unfamiliar with the psychological jargon, so I find it a little difficult to keep up. What about a beer, and you could teach me?"

As they cycled down toward the Avenue and on toward Rosenlund Canal and the Fish Church Market, where there was a pub, she thought she would make a stupendous effort and be nice, and be herself.

"Tell me about yourself," he said once they had got a beer each and were sitting looking at each other across the table.

She heard what he was saying.

Who are you?

"My father owns a sawmill in Värmland," she said, naming the place. "My mother ran away with another man when I was eleven, and it still hurts. But I can understand her, because, well, he's difficult, you know, my father, he drinks."

Simon tried to hold her gaze, but she held it back, as if it were quite alone inside those gray-green eyes.

Simon made an effort to understand what it would be like to have a mother abandon you when you were small, then thought about how angry he had been with Karin when she seemed to be dying. But then he realized there was no possible comparison.

Klara started telling him about her studies, and her eyes lost their emptiness and met his again. She forgot to be anxious, and it occurred to Simon that she was beautiful.

"I've thought of becoming a psychiatrist," she said. "But at the moment I'm obsessed with the ancient mythologies. They were something else, as well. They had a psychological function, almost therapeutic. Do you know what I mean?"

"Yes," said Simon, and she could see his interest was genuine, as if suddenly faced with fantastic answers to what he had always been looking for.

"The popular sagas especially," Klara went on. "The way they contain a whole lot of difficult emotions that children have, but mustn't have, and must never talk about. You know, cruel fantasies, violence, that kind of thing."

Simon's heart beat faster. The girl was giving him a piece of the truth that would make him freer, but she was unaware of it, and she went on.

"I'd thought of concentrating on the Greeks and Mount Parnassus and trying to find the connection between all those gods and the forbidden fantasies of humans."

Simon sat very still. This is my girl, he was thinking, and for a moment he could hear the truck driver's laugh echoing between the tiled walls of the pub.

Then Klara said that a great many people had had the same ideas before her.

"Writers?"

"Yes, but scholars, too," she said, and she started talking about Carl Gustav Jung, the collective unconscious and archetypes, the hero, the wise old man, the great mother, and the holy child.

"He researched the myths and found common foundations in all cultures," she said. "If you want to know something about mankind, you have to look at their myths, he thought."

I've always known that, thought Simon.

"You can borrow some books," she said.

Somehow they made two beers last a whole hour, then they ordered two more and four sandwiches. When they eventually left, Simon said something about how strange it was that horrible fathers had wonderful daughters.

"I know another. She's married to my best friend," he said, and Klara felt faint.

They parted company in the Avenue, and it was already dark as they cycled in different directions, both feeling as if they had a secret together.

Simon was glad Ruben was away. He needed to think.

Thoughts were racing through his head, one after another. This wasn't love, by no means related to what he had seen happen between Isak and Mona. There was no light around Klara. The two of them would never be luminous.

She was not a nice person. She had said so herself, and he had both seen and heard that. She was prickly when she retreated into herself. Plain, too. Tall and flat as a board, and those horrid freckles on her face and arms, even on her hands, though her hands were also lovely, secretive, with long fingers and soft pads on the insides, the lifelines deep crevices.

And when she smiled . . .

No, he'd forget it all. That was easy, as there was nothing to forget.

Yet his last thought before falling asleep was that when he was with her he was with himself.

He dreamed he was walking along the shore and Life came toward him and had golden reddish hair and an apple in her long-fingered, freckled hand.

The next day when he was sitting next to her at a lecture, Simon asked her if she liked music.

"Yes," said Klara.

"I've got two tickets for the Concert Hall on Saturday. They're playing Nystroem's *Sinfonia del mare*."

He had no tickets, but he would have time to get some.

"Would you like to come?"

"Yes, please," said Klara, keeping her eyes closed so that he wouldn't see how pleased she was.

"I heard it at its premiere," said Simon. "It made such an impression on me, I wrote a long poem."

She looked up again in surprise, and he couldn't resist the temptation.

"Bonniers is going to publish it."

Then the lecture began.

In her tiny apartment in Haga, in a block due for demolition, Klara went through her clothes and decided nothing would do. But it was only Saturday morning, so she would have time to run down Linnégatan where there was a shop window she had often gazed into and dreamed of a different and more beautiful Klara.

She bought some nylons and the first high heels she'd ever had, as he was taller than she was. Then she remembered a boy at an anatomy lecture telling her she had a delicious backside, so she tried on a very tight skirt.

"Fits as if welded to you," said the assistant, who then brought a green silk blouse with wide sleeves and a collar like a shawl to play with around her neck.

"But I've no bosom," said Klara, seeing the silk clinging to her and revealing all, and hating the woman who had made her mention what was so painful.

But the assistant just smiled and said that was easy to fix, and before Klara could blink, she had bought a padded bra.

"I must be crazy," she thought.

Then she washed her hair and rolled it in a towel to get a thick pageboy, then hoped she wouldn't break out in a cold sweat if she felt anxious.

"Klara Alm," she said aloud to herself. "You will not have any anxiety tonight."

Before dressing, she made the bed up with clean sheets, then last of all she darkened her fine long eyelashes. When Simon came as agreed at half past six, he beamed as he looked at her.

"You're awfully pretty," he said.

She thought it would be quite good to die now, before everything got spoiled.

"You know, people at home say that I have the nastiest tongue in the village."

"You're not plain any longer," said Simon. "So perhaps your tongue will be nicer."

"That's the question," said Klara, as if about to cry.

He kissed her.

But they were on time for the concert and the music worked its magic around them, and fortunately, she said nothing afterward.

They walked through town and Simon told her about the Indian women washing their children at the source of the river and about the wave wandering across the Atlantic, only to be smashed to pieces on the rocks of Bohus.

"When I heard the symphony for the first time, I thought the wave couldn't die because it never became personal. Do you understand?"

"Yes," she said. "I also think personality is largely a defense. That's why mine is strong and pronounced."

He kissed her again, right on her mouth, right in the middle of Hamngatan.

Simon had never dreamed a girl could give herself to him with such trust. She was so willing and innocent, so naked and childishly open, he was near to tears. He went home with her and gave her enjoyment and satisfaction. She bled a little and he understood, feeling that was also a gift.

At two in the morning she went into her kitchen to wash under the cold-water tap, then came back in a blue bathrobe.

"I'd quite like to die now," she said. "But before I do, I'll play for you."

She got out her flute, and Simon wanted to cry out *No, please don't, Klara, don't*. But she sat at the end of the bed and played Carl Nielsen's flute solo from "The Mist Is Lifting," slightly tentatively at first, as if she were out of practice, but soon increasingly surely, richly, and warmly.

Simon lay still in bed so long afterward, she had to ask him, "You didn't fall asleep, did you?"

"Don't be silly," said Simon. "You're no amateur," he added.

"I've had the best teaching you could get in Värmland," she said. "From a Jewish flautist in Karlstad. He had been in the Berlin Philharmonic. He got out of Germany, then earned his living teaching music. He was wonderful. Thanks to him, I survived when my mother left."

Simon pondered on hidden otherworldly connections.

"I was allowed to keep my mother," he said. "Perhaps that's why I never learned to play the violin."

"Did you want to?"

"Klara, it's a long story and I probably haven't understood it yet."

But what about Simon Haberman, violinist in the Berlin Philharmonic?

"Is he still alive, your teacher in Karlstad?"

"Yes."

"One day we'll go to see him," said Simon. Then they went to sleep.

They awoke on Sunday at about twelve feeling very hungry. They found a pub down in the harbor open on a Sunday and ate herring and salt brisket. Simon ordered two schnapps, and as they drank to each other with the fiery spirits, Klara said she had never tasted anything so good before.

For a fortnight, they were wide open to each other and remained in paradise. Then Simon said that he did have a family and Ruben and Isak, and that she must come and meet Karin.

He saw she was scared, but he knew nothing of the demons now released in her heart and making their way to her head, where they at once started taking over.

But as he left, saying he would pick her up on Saturday, he could feel the wall between them.

THIRTY-ONE

Simon had to call Karin to tell her about Klara, but he delayed, blaming Klara and her reluctance. On Friday morning between two lectures, he conquered his reluctance and dialed the familiar numbers.

"A long time since we heard from you, Simon," he heard her warm voice say with delight. "Where have you been?"

"Well, you see, Mom, I've met a girl."

"Oh, yes." The voice seemed to come from a long way away, and he wanted to explain, say she was a strange girl, fragile and tough at the same time, plain and pretty, and I think I love her, whatever that means, but she's terrified of you.

But he didn't, of course.

"I was thinking of bringing her out tomorrow so you can get to know her."

"That'd be nice, dear."

That wasn't what Karin had wanted to say, either, but she was pleased she had said it and that her voice had been much as usual.

"She's a doctor," said Simon. "I mean, she'll soon be qualified."

"Heavens," said Karin, then there was a silence until she added the usual. "We'll be having dinner at two, as usual on Saturdays. I'll get some turbot and cook something really good."

"We'll be there. Bye for now."

"Bye." She wanted to say something more, but couldn't think of anything. He wanted to say something else, too, but couldn't.

"Give my love to Dad" was all he could manage.

"I'll do that, Simon."

Angry with himself and uneasy because of that, Simon went

back to the lecture room. Karin replaced the receiver, leaned against the wall in the hall, and thought about her heart.

But it was beating calmly and firmly.

Determinedly.

After all, she had known it would happen. Sooner or later, Simon would meet a girl, just as Isak had, and Karin tried to find some consolation. She might be a girl like Mona. But at the thought, Karin had to go back to the kitchen, sit down, and speak seriously to her heart.

"There, there," she said. "There, there, calm down and beat as you should, slowly and decisively."

Her heart obeyed, and Karin dispatched the thought of Mona, because what followed was the knowledge that if Mona had been Simon's girl, Karin would have detested her.

She looked around the kitchen, at the security, remembering another kitchen, smaller and shabbier, with the smell of poverty in its walls, the nasty smell from pissing in the kitchen sink because the privy was three floors down in the courtyard. Another woman sat there, her hand on her heart to stop it from breaking, and in front of her was Erik with his arm around the shoulders of a young girl, a lovely girl, her straight nose pointing up in the air and brown eyes flashing as she said, "That's the point, the old are to die out to make way for the young."

There's a price for everything, Karin thought, but the memory of her mother-in-law helped her. She had her pride, and she would never be like Erik's damned mother. No, she would be the best of mothers-in-law, just as she had been the best of mothers and no one would ever have the slightest idea what that would cost her.

Her heart thumped, ice in her breast now. When Lisa arrived a moment later, Karin put on the coffee and said, "Just think, Simon's got himself a girl."

"How nice," said Lisa, and those alert eyes of hers, always seeking out dust and secrets, were gleaming slightly with excitement. "Who is she?"

"A doctor," said Karin. So it had been said and she could enjoy Lisa's surprise and smile.

"Oh, my goodness. But then he's always been a bit superior, hasn't he?"

Karin realized there would be the usual talk now, that same old routine of the Larssons and their rich Jewish friends, their boatyard and the boy who'd gone to school and university to study ancient history. The Sumerians . . . she could hear the snorts when they said that Simon was spoiled and thought life was nothing but a game.

"What's her name?"

"Heavens, I forgot to ask. You see, I was so surprised."

"Well, I suppose you thought you'd have him for the rest of your life," said Lisa, smiling to take the edge off the malice.

Karin flushed with annoyance and got up to go, reluctant to give Lisa the satisfaction of seeing her anger. She went to the boatyard, found Erik in the drawing office, and spoke quickly to have it over and done with.

"Simon's met a girl. She's a doctor. They're coming tomorrow."

Erik dropped his pencil and compass and took off his glasses.

"That's good news. God in heaven, Karin, what fun," he said, and she could see his delight was quite genuine.

"Is he in love?"

"I presume so," said Karin, her smile wide and almost natural.

Erik went back with her for some coffee. This had to be celebrated, and he kept talking about the game of life when one was young and in love, and how he had really hoped Simon would fall in love. Then he laughed loudly and said he had always hoped for a doctor in the family, and "Christ, yes, Erik Larsson always gets what he wants. When the boy doesn't want to be a doctor, then he gets hold of one. Smart."

Karin joined in the laughter, but frozen ghosts went through the room when she saw his delight and thought about the girl he had once loved, the one his mother had frightened off. Erik had grieved so much, he had fallen ill with TB and been admitted to the sanatorium.

Then Karin thought so intently about her decision to be a good mother-in-law that her face closed up completely.

"Goodness, how serious you look," said Erik. "Not jealous, are you?"

"Of course not," said Karin, her eyes flashing.

"I was only joking," he said to extract himself. "You know that." She smiled, an unfamiliar false smile.

Jealous, an ugly word, she thought as she went off for her usual walk, not a word suited to her sorrow, which resembled another sorrow after another loss long ago.

Petter, she thought, he had the sense to die. Simon was betraying her. But she couldn't hate him, only the girl. No, not the girl, either. Suddenly she thought about how she had always detested doctors, superior people with power over life and death.

She went to the fish market for her turbot and added half a kilo of shrimp for good measure. The girl would have a princely welcoming dinner and no one would have any complaint against Karin. She wanted no truths that day, so she avoided the oaks on her way home. She took the roundabout way across the old wild garden where she had played with Simon when he was small and thought no one would ever love him as she did.

Over coffee that evening, Erik was the nervous one. Did Karin think the girl was upper class? Suppose she was snooty? Would they have to mix with some idiotic business family?

"I don't know," said Karin. "But Simon is usually a good judge."

Erik almost snapped back, but as he could never stand not knowing, he rang Simon, but he wasn't there. Ruben answered, and he knew a little more, though he hadn't met the girl.

When Erik came back to Karin, he had calmed down.

"The girl's called Klara Alm, daughter of a sawmill worker who married money and took over the sawmill up there in Värmland."

"Sounds good," said Karin.

"Hm," said Erik. "The father drank, apparently. There was a divorce. Klara's a clever girl, but hasn't had an easy time."

She was coming closer now, the girl, and Karin was not pleased.

But then Erik said that Ruben had said that Simon had hardly been home for two weeks, and he was besotted with love.

Erik laughed with satisfaction, so full of his own delight he didn't notice Karin stiffen, that blessed chill returning to her.

Klara had fought her demons all night. And lost, she realized the moment Simon came to pick her up, standing there in the doorway filling the entire shabby apartment with his intensity.

She agreed with the demons, both the one saying that she was silly to have anything to do with a man like that, and the other whispering, God, how ashamed he will be of you.

Klara was in a black sweater, which made her look paler than usual, her freckles standing out in her white face, and she had rings around her eyes the same color as the sweater. She could see he would have liked her to change into something nicer, but she was grateful he didn't say so. The black sweater would hide it if she started sweating.

They walked to Järntorget and took the tram to Långedrag. He attempted to talk to her about school as they went past it, and anything interesting on the route that had been his for so many years. But she wasn't listening, absorbed as she had been all night in what he had told her about his family and his wonderful mother, whom Klara already disliked. In the end he grew angry and told her she looked as if he were taking her to the slaughterhouse. She didn't reply to that, either, just thought, Now it's started, and I'll harm him, as I have to.

As they walked from the stop down to the river, he tried again, telling her about Äppelgren saving him when he was small and had gotten lost. This time there was a little response, and she listened.

"Why did you run away?"

"Run away?" he said. "I suppose it was to do something, get away in that way inquisitive youngsters do."

But there was a question in his voice, and she realized he had never really asked himself why before, and she had knocked the first fragment out of the picture of that wonderful childhood, and she ought to turn on her heel and run before she destroyed too much for him.

It all went as badly as Klara had feared. There she was, standing like a beanpole in the kitchen doorway while he greeted his mother, and she could see the tie between mother and son was so strong it would suffocate them both. Then she looked at Karin and to her despair saw that she was not only good, but also something much worse.

Beautiful, thought Klara. And intelligent, she thought as those wise eyes fell on her, saw straight through her, and rejected everything.

"Nice to meet you, and welcome," said Karin, but then it became uncomfortable for her, too, this plain redhead with clammy hands and Simon looking frightened.

This is crazy, thought Karin. My boy and that . . .

But then Erik came in from the boatyard with rolls of drawings under his arm and his usual naturalness.

"My, what a tall fine girl you are," he said, looking brightly at her, and the paralysis gave way and Klara was able to smile and be nice. Simon hugged his father and laughed.

"She'll soon be a qualified doctor," he boasted.

Everything could have turned then, for Erik said, "My goodness, what a girl," and Klara's smile broadened. But then the demons told her that Simon was ashamed, so he had to use my education, and the next moment Isak came and was so frightened of Klara, he disliked her on sight and was unable to hide it.

He vanished off into the boatyard with Erik's drawings, calling over his shoulder that he would get started and they should come when they had time.

They were to survey what had to be done before the boatyard was moved.

Erik looked surprised, but soon trotted after Isak, so the three of them were left alone in the kitchen again, with Karin laying the table with a newly ironed cloth and their best china.

The turbot and shrimp was good as always, but Klara ate it as if it were cardboard and found it hard to swallow, the sweat pouring off her.

Back with Mona, Isak said Simon had brought a peculiar bird back, tall as a crane, plain and stiff and snooty as hell. So Mona had to go and borrow some sugar. More lovely and pear-shaped than ever, she could easily have stepped out of a Renaissance painting as the expectant Virgin Mary.

Klara disliked her because of that gentle maternity and because she was so friendly and natural. But Mona went back home to Isak and said that Klara wasn't arrogant.

"She's just frightened, you must see that."

No, Isak couldn't see it, and anyhow it was idiotic, there was nothing to be afraid of here.

"I'd be dead scared if I were Simon's girl and was to meet Karin for the first time," Mona said.

After dinner, Klara went with Erik to the yard, and that helped a little. It was drafty and cold there, so all the sweat dried. Erik was proud of his boatyard, and Klara genuinely thought that the two almost-finished double-enders were handsome.

In the kitchen, Simon appealed to Karin in his despair. "She's scared, Mom, can't you see?"

"Yes, I can see all right, but what can I do?"

"Take her with you up the mountain, Mom, look at the view and talk, you usually . . ."

So when Klara came back from the yard, Karin said decisively, "Would you like to go out for a while, Klara?"

Klara nodded and went as if she were going to a court of law that had already decided she would confess every crime and find every verdict just.

They sat on the mountain, and Karin pointed out the fortress and talked about the sea, saying there were good and bad points about living so close to it. In the end, Klara couldn't stand it any longer.

"Why are you going on so like this? Why don't you just say it? You think I'm horrible and should go to hell."

"No, what are you saying?" said Karin.

"I'd agree with you. I don't think I'm worthy of him. And I know I'll ruin his life."

Karin felt vindicated, but concealed it.

"I can't dislike anyone I've never seen before," she said.

"Nicely put, but you've probably seen enough," said Klara, now hopelessly delivered up to her demons.

"Klara, dear," said Karin. "Perhaps you could begin by telling me a little about yourself."

"Me," said Klara. "I'm the plain daughter from the sawmill, with the nastiest tongue in all Värmland."

"How did you become that?"

"Maybe when my mother disappeared with another man when I was small. But I don't know. I'm probably nasty by nature."

"Did you never hear from her again?"

Karin's question was routine, and she found it difficult to hide the satisfaction in her voice. She was not very successful, and both of them sensed it. Klara laughed scornfully, but nevertheless replied.

"No, not even she was able to love me, as there's been no sign of life from her since."

"You'll have to go and find her now you're grown up," said Karin, as if that were the simplest thing in the world, and the girl thought about her mother's phone number in her notebook she had been trying to call for three years.

"That's good advice," she said.

"You must dislike yourself a lot to be so angry with other people," said Karin.

"Of course," said Klara. "It's called projection in the jargon."

"Are you trying to impress me?"

"No, I know that wouldn't work."

"I find it difficult with people who don't like themselves," said Karin. "They let other people pay such a high price for it."

"Of course," said the girl. "I understand perfectly well that you hoped for a better fate for Simon. We are agreed on that. Rely on me, Karin, the great mother. It'll soon be over now, this brief love story."

She turned herself into a statue, distantly gazing out to sea without seeing. Understanding this was the girl's way of keeping back her tears, Karin felt guilty and annoyed.

"Are you trying to blame me?"

"No," said Klara. "The good mother is always blameless. She has to be to survive."

That hurt, like a knife, but Karin managed to keep her voice steady.

"You're probably the nastiest person I've ever met," she said.

"I told you so," said the girl, but she looked frightened as she looked at Karin and saw that she was ghostly pale and had her hand clutched to her heart.

Simon had told her about the coronary.

As they walked down the mountain, Klara knew she had to get away from here quickly before she destroyed too much. As soon as they got into the kitchen, which was full of people, she went around saying good-bye, thanking Karin for the meal and apologizing that she had to get back home and study for her exams. "You can rely on me," she said quietly to Karin.

Ruben Lentov was there, and she held out a clammy hand.

Simon went with her to the tram, and they didn't exchange a single word on the way.

"I'll come up to your place for dinner at five tomorrow," he said when the tram arrived. "Perhaps both of us will have calmed down by then."

All that Sunday, Klara paced around her gloomy apartment in Haga thinking about the promise she had made to Karin. She was as miserable as anyone could be. At half past four, she opened a can of mushroom soup and made some sandwiches—then he arrived on the dot.

He tried to smile, take her in his arms, but she pushed him away.

"Was it that awful?" he said.

"No, of course not," she said. "They were all as great as you'd said. Erik is nice, and Isak pleasant and Mona terribly sweet, not to mention your mother, who's fantastic. The Great Mother who allows herself to be worshiped in her temple, modestly turned into a kitchen."

"Shut up," said Simon, but Klara couldn't stop herself.

"Even the rich man was there, prepared to kiss the ground the Great Mother walks on," she said.

"Who are you talking about?"

"Ruben Lentov, that typical representative of the cultured Jewish capitalist class."

Simon was sitting very still, but his eyes were burning.

"I've never understood how anyone like you could be a psychiatrist," he said. "You haven't the slightest sense when it comes to people. But I didn't know you were anti-Semitic."

There was something in her face appealing for mercy, but it was too late.

"Let's take one thing at a time," he said. "Karin is no great mother, because she's never been able to have children. That's the great sorrow of her life."

Then he went on, very slowly, "I am adopted. A Jewish child. My father was a typical representative of the Jews who were gassed at Auschwitz. You would have done well there, among the executioners," he shouted, then he left, slamming the door behind him so hard that it was strange the old building didn't collapse on the spot.

Klara took four sleeping pills, then stopped.

THIRTY-TWO

The next morning Klara woke feeling sick and with a thumping headache, but that didn't matter, it was better than anguish.

She called the Historical Institute and told them she was giving up the course. They reprimanded her and told her that the term's fees would not be refunded.

Then she dialed the hospital number and asked her supervisor if she could start her residency now.

"You're a month behind," he said curtly, but he liked her for her quick intelligence, so he added that it would probably be all right.

"I'm glad to hear you've gotten all those psychological fantasies out of your head," he said curtly.

She spent all Monday writing a letter.

"Simon. I'm a horrible person, and you should be glad things between us are over. But I am not anti-Semitic and I don't think I would have been among the executioners in Auschwitz, where your father died.

"That is, I hope not. For who knows . . ."

Then she got in a muddle again, but no matter. She never sent the letter, and on Tuesday morning she was at the back of the crowd on the internal medicine rounds, her gaze even more distant than ever.

But she was listening, and the fact was, the more she closed her heart, the clearer her mind became. The demons had been calmed for a while. They were quiet.

Simon had never believed it could hurt so much, the sheer physical pain in his chest. The air was clear, the September sun shining mildly over town, but his world was gray. He could bear that. But the evil replacing the guilt that had plagued him all through his growing years, that was unbearable.

It wasn't guilt this time, he told himself. He didn't regret a word he had said, on the contrary. The only thing that gave him any solace was thinking of worse things, nastier words that he ought to have said. Fascist bitch.

He sometimes thought there was something wrong with him, with his relationships with women. First Iza, and now this bitch who was even worse.

He remembered his fantasies about the evil that would make him real. That sat inside him now and life had never been so unreal. Ruben spoke to him, but Simon couldn't listen. It was the same at lectures. The damned pain inside meant he couldn't hear.

Every moment, he tried not to think about Karin.

Ruben phoned Erik to say he was worried.

"You don't die of that," said Erik. "But it can make you ill."

Ruben remembered Erik once saying he had gotten TB after a love affair in his youth.

"We must do something, Erik."

"No one can do anything. But it's a damned shame. She was a nice girl, unusual."

"What happened, Erik?"

"Well, you tell me."

A fortnight later, Simon developed a temperature and then nothing could be hidden from Karin. She arrived at almost the same moment as the doctor, whom Ruben had sent for. He told them Simon had pneumonia.

"It's no longer dangerous," the doctor said, after giving Simon antibiotics. But to be sure, he wanted the boy admitted to the hospital.

Karin went in the ambulance with him.

Simon lay in Sahlgrenska Hospital, dreaming again that he was running after a girl in a sea of grass. She was long-legged and slim, elusive as a ray of sunlight, and he caught her, knowing it was

Klara, but when she turned around, it was Iza laughing at him. Then he heard a flute and saw the mist was lifting from the river, but he didn't want to go there, didn't want to see that it was Iza playing and laughing in his face.

Karin sat with him throughout the night, and for the first time in her life prayed to God for atonement and forgiveness. And she prayed that she, Karin, was not to blame.

Things went well, particularly after the doctor on duty had examined him and said he would soon recover. They trusted this new drug, and no doubt that trust was more reliable than nightly whimpering to a God she didn't believe in.

Karin was given coffee, and she reasoned that the girl was insane and would have destroyed Simon's life, so what had happened was just as well.

Then Simon started calling out in his sleep. Karin thought he had stopped breathing, and her fear was so great, only God, who had to be appeased, existed, and she heard her mother again saying *poor me, poor me*, and she saw herself in her mother-in-law's kitchen saying *the old have to die to make room for the young*. She realized that with those words she had made a pact with the Devil, and now he had come to demand his own.

He hadn't come himself, Karin thought. He'd sent a girl, a witch who had crushed her self-esteem, which was what the boy lived on. So he had to die.

Karin wept aloud in despair, and Erik was there, and Ruben, saying she had to take care of herself. Then her old cardiac specialist came, summoned by Ruben. He examined Simon and said he would soon be back on his feet again, the drug had worked, his temperature was down, then he gave Karin an injection, and she never remembered how she got home. Fourteen hours later she woke in her own bedroom as Erik brought her tea in bed and told her Simon had slept well all night and his temperature was now normal.

She dozed all morning and thought about that God she didn't believe in and how strangely great his power was. As far as the Devil was concerned, she realized she had met him in her own heart, that he was within her just as in everyone else, only unusually repressed and hidden.

She lay there remembering how she had fallen ill when peace came, ill from all the evil that had been revealed that terrible spring four years ago.

She also remembered all the dreams she had had at the cardiac unit, and she dwelled for a long time on the memory of Petter and the night he had come to her in her sleep, wanting to say something to her, but she had been too tired to listen.

I didn't want to, she thought.

She knew now that what Petter had said was that evil exists within people, within everyone, and that not until that is clear could it be understood and fought against.

So she got up, looked up Klara Alm's number in the directory, and phoned.

The girl's voice rose with surprise, and with something else, as well.

Joy, thought Karin.

"I know you two have put an end to it, and you may be right in much of what you said to me about good mothers," said Karin incoherently. "But the thing is, Simon is so terribly ill, I thought you, as a doctor, might be able to—"

"Is Simon ill?" Klara's voice was shrill.

"He's in Sahlgrenska." Karin told her which department and the ward number.

"I'll go at once. And I'll phone you back."

Klara took a taxi, then regretted it as it would have been quicker to cycle, but she got there in the end. White coat, right expression. The ward sister was polite, but kept her distance when, looking as if about to cry, Klara said she wanted to hear what the situation was for private reasons.

She's in love, poor creature, thought the nurse, but not unkindly as she took out the case sheet.

Lobate pneumonia. The antibiotic had taken; he had been

X-rayed after a drop in temperature. No remaining patches on the lung.

"You can look in on him," said the nurse, and Klara felt braver when the sister added that he would probably be asleep and she was sure Klara realized he shouldn't be awakened.

He was in a private ward, fortunately, and he was asleep as the sister had said, and goodness, how handsome he was.

She stood there gazing at him for a while, and as if he had felt her presence, he opened his eyes and said, "Go to hell, you Fascist beast."

As she turned around to go, she bumped into Ruben, who must have been standing there for some time, watching her and hearing what Simon had said.

Then the tears came. She stood quite still, but it was no use this time, the tears poured down her face. She was scarcely aware of the big handkerchief he took out, but she did feel his warmth as he wiped her face, comforting her. "There there, Klara dear, there there."

She pulled herself together and tried to say something, tried again, then finally succeeded.

"Would you tell Simon that when my mother left, the only person I loved and who bothered about me was a Jew who played the flute."

"I'll remember that," said Ruben. But he was annoyed with Simon, Klara could see that as she left.

She went home, trying to calm down, then phoned Karin.

"I've been to see him," she said. "I saw his case notes. He's in no danger and he'll be discharged in a few days."

"Thank you," said Karin. "Thank you, my dear."

"I'm very sorry," said Klara in an unsteady voice. "I hope you'll forgive me . . . for what I said . . . about good mothers . . . it made you so miserable."

"Don't take it back," said Karin. "I've thought about it, and there is some truth in it. But mothers are necessary all the same, aren't they?"

"Karin, I'll phone her."

"Do that, and call me if you want to talk."

"But Simon . . . ," said Klara.

"This has nothing to do with him," said Karin, adding quickly as if afraid of changing her mind, "Simon is a difficult creature, and always has been. He'll never find a nice pretty girl, the kind mothers-in-law dream of."

"Then I'd be suitable."

"I think so," said Karin. "I can see you'd be really damned suitable."

Her voice was shaking. Klara could hear it, and understood.

"This isn't easy for you, Karin," she said.

"No," said Karin. "Life is difficult to understand in general. And, Klara, there's something else you don't know about Simon. He never gives up."

"He's probably given me up," said Klara. "I acted crazy, you know."

Karin put down the receiver, knowing she still disliked the girl, but also that there was a grandeur about her. Klara is the only person I've ever met who has seen my Devil, and whom I'll never be able to deceive, she thought.

Klara wasted no time wondering, or even taking off her overcoat. She made a call to Oslo.

"May I speak to Mrs. Kersti Sörensen?"

"Speaking."

"This is Klara."

It was as quiet as if the earth had stopped in its orbit, not even the sound of a car from either Oslo or Göteborg. God made time cease, thought Klara. Then she heard her mother crying.

"I hoped you would make contact. I've dreamed of it over all these years."

"But why didn't you telephone?" Then the world stood still again until her mother's voice came back.

"I didn't dare. But I know you're studying medicine at Göteborg. I'm proud of you."

"Mother, why did you never contact us when I was small and needed—"

"But I wrote, Klara. I've great piles of letters your father sent back unopened. I contested custody and spent all the money I inherited from my mother on lawyers. But it was hard in those days. I hadn't a chance. I'd been unfaithful."

"Mother!"

"We got as far as making your father transfer my share in the sawmill, the money, to you. In exchange for a promise that I would never try to make contact again."

"Mother!" Klara was crying now.

"You were so intelligent, Klara. I wanted to assure your education, and I knew how stingy he was."

"But I've had to beg for every penny. And I took out a student loan."

"Phone Mr. Bertilsson the lawyer, in Karlstad. Do that, Klara. If you give me your address, I'll send you those old letters."

"Have you saved them?"

"Yes, I thought . . . they'll give you some idea of what things were like, how I felt, you see."

The operator interrupted to say their time was nearly up.

Klara gave her address.

"Be seeing you, Mother. I'll come at Christmas."

"That'll be lovely."

It was lucky for Klara Alm that she still had some of her anger, her great anger, over the next few hours. She got hold of the lawyer at home in Karlstad, and he confirmed with some surprise that there was an account in her name and that it had been there ever since the divorce.

"How much?" said Klara.

"About twenty-five thousand," he said. "It will have accumulated, of course, so it should be about thirty by now."

She phoned the sawmill and could already hear from his voice that he was drunk.

"You're a great bloody shitty bastard," she said, and put down the receiver.

But then she forgot the money, because of her mother, because of that voice she recognized, that was full of so much pain and love.

I've got a mother, she thought. I, too, Simon, have a mother who cares about me.

Two days later the letters arrived from Oslo. Klara phoned the hospital to say she was ill, an autumn cold, she said.

Then she read the letters and wept, and went on reading.

Until she knew them all by heart. Then she phoned Karin and told her.

"That's wonderful," said Karin. And Klara could hear her voice had its old strength back.

As if she had obtained redress.

THIRTY-THREE

Sprawling in an armchair at Ruben's, Simon now thought the worst was over, his love affair and the pneumonia both healed. He could no longer be really happy. Happiness was only for the innocent.

But one evening Ruben told him he had happened to hear what Simon had said to Klara that afternoon at the hospital.

"I was dreaming," said Simon.

"Unfortunately that's not so," said Ruben, and Simon could see he was really angry.

"I was delirious."

"You called her a Fascist. After everything that's happened, it is unforgivable to hurl words like that about. This is about decency, Simon, respect for the dead."

Simon drew a sharp breath at the fury in Ruben's eyes.

"For Christ's sake, you don't even know what she said."

"I know what she told me, after you'd gone back to sleep, and that's enough. She asked me to tell you, and it was so important, I even wrote it down, word for word."

He took out his wallet, found the note, and read it out loud.

"When my mother left, the only person I loved and who bothered about me was a Jew who played the flute."

Now we're off again, thought Simon.

There was a long silence.

"That man knew my father," he said.

"Simon Haberman?"

"Yes."

Simon had only one thought in his head, and that was that the pain inside him had been guilt after all. As it had always been.

"I'll write and ask her to forgive me."

"Do that," said Ruben.

He spent two days on the letter, filling a whole wastepaper basket with earlier attempts.

"Klara," ran the letter he finally sent. "Please forgive me for the hideous things I said to you. Naturally I know you're not a Fascist. Simon."

He received a reply.

"Simon. Thank you for your letter. I can understand your reaction because I was so damned awful myself. Klara."

But this did not lessen Simon's torment. His sense of guilt gnawed at him, and there were moments when he had some inkling that this concerned someone else apart from Klara, but he rejected the idea.

They struggled on apart all that autumn, determined and industrious as they had always been. Simon began to take an interest in politics and joined the endless discussions among Ruben's friends on the young state of Israel. Occasionally he thought he would go there. But he wasn't a Jew on paper, and no one had any use for his idiotic education in a country fighting for survival.

After the Christmas holiday was over and Mona had given birth to a daughter, Simon sensed what happiness was for the first time in many months. As Andersson had instructed him, he looked into the baby's eyes, and they were as unfathomable as Simon's own realization that he had acquired a sister.

The day before Christmas Eve, Klara flew to Oslo, her suitcase full of presents for her mother and the young siblings she had never met.

Christmas turned out not to be simple. Kersti met her at Fornebu Airport, and they had no words for what they wanted to say to each other. They fumbled for words for days, but got no further than chat about the occupation and how much better, despite everything, food had gotten, and so on.

Her half siblings said in fluent Norwegian that they had always heard about how amazing she was, and she realized she had not come up to their expectations.

The new husband was another alcoholic, but kinder, not so destructive as Klara's father. But Klara could see things were not good for Kersti.

Kersti suggested that Klara should do something about her lovely hair, and with some giggling, they went to an elegant hairdressing salon in the city center. Klara had her hair styled and permed, ending up with the bangs she ought to have had all along.

"I don't recognize you," said Kersti.

Klara kept looking into shop windows and anywhere else where she could see her reflection.

They met Kersti's friends.

"My daughter. She's studying medicine in Göteborg."

She was proud of her, and that was good for Klara.

The day before New Year's Eve, she flew home and on the plane realized she hadn't even given Simon a thought for a whole week. She was on duty at the hospital on New Year's Day, and that also felt good.

Returning was difficult, and she found she hated her dirty old apartment, now icy cold and dark.

A rat's nest.

There was a parcel for her and she at once recognized the handwriting stating *Dr. Klara Alm* on it. He's teasing, she thought.

But she opened it and it was his book, with *To My Love* inscribed on the flyleaf.

She swore a long string of foul words.

But her anger did not do the trick, and it was almost as if she had mislaid it in Oslo. She sat on her bed with the book in her hand. Perhaps she had known all along there was no way out and that she had had to go to Norway because of Simon. So as not to destroy him.

She was so cold by now she was shaking, so she got the kitchen stove going to get rid of the chilly damp. Then she unpacked, went down to the corner shop and bought bread, butter, and coffee, avoided the fish looking at her with eyes that had been dead for far too long, and bought pork chops so that she had some food for the New Year.

She didn't really like pork chops.

She kept thinking he shouldn't have used that word, that it was wrong. They had never talked about love. Now it had been said, the word standing there like a house, making it painfully real. Demanding. They would have to go into that house now, and live there.

It took almost two hours to get it warm enough for her to crawl into bed, though she still had to keep on her woolly mittens as she lay there reading the sea poem.

> *at last realizing*
> *the truth can only be found in what is unspoken . . .*

Exactly, Simon Larsson, you should have thought of that before writing that dedication. Words make everything final. Reality is something else, constant movement, impossible to capture.

She read the poem over and over again, and just before she fell asleep, the thought occurred to her that she could have written it herself.

If only she had been able to write.

With that came words for the knowledge that had grown freely in her subconscious—that she and Simon were very alike.

She slept all night, and when she lit the stove the next morning, she knew what she was feeling was happiness, just that and nothing else.

No more duplicity.

This must be what people call serenity, she thought, remembering how suspicious she had always been of the word. She had never understood it, but she recognized the feeling, so she must have possessed it before. As a child, before her mother had left. And in music, inside the notes when you could let go and the flute could play by itself.

She was also calm when she phoned Ruben's apartment, and he

answered. She gave her name and asked to speak to Simon. She could hear he was pleased, but Simon was not at home. He was with his parents, preparing to celebrate the New Year.

"Oh," said Klara, disappointed. She did not want to phone there.

"You wouldn't like to have lunch with me, would you? I've wanted to talk to you for some time," said Ruben slightly shyly, unusual for him.

"I'd love to," she said, though she figured there wasn't much to talk about any longer.

"Can I come and pick you up?"

"No, for goodness' sake." Klara felt slightly faint at the thought of Lentov here in this scruffy apartment. "I'll come to your place," she said.

"Take a taxi, then we'll go and find a place that's open."

"Food's not all that important as far as I'm concerned," said Klara.

"Nor me. Then I'll see what I can find here."

She brushed her newly curled hair so that it crackled, and found the skirt and green silk blouse she'd worn to the concert with Simon. As she was putting on mascara she told herself there would be no crying that day, nor any sweating, either, she thought in the taxi when she realized she had forgotten deodorant.

Ruben let her in. She remembered how kind he had been at the hospital and thanked him for the handkerchief. He smiled, saying how furious he had been with Simon, and also that he had passed on her message.

"I knew that when I got his letter," she said.

At first they were rather stiff and silent, but then Klara spoke.

"I've read the sea poem," Klara said. "Now I know we're very alike, Simon and I."

He nodded, and at last she knew what the very special quality about Ruben Lentov was. Presence, she thought.

"That was what I wanted to talk about," said Ruben. "And of course, this peculiar thing called love that is so difficult."

"That word scares me," said Klara.

"Never mind the word. Let's talk about how unusual it is, this thing called love, which most people confuse with unsatisfied needs."

"Not me," said Klara, then went on defiantly when she saw his mouth twitching. "I mean, if I was able to confuse my dissatisfaction with love, I'd be in love all the time."

They were both able to laugh at that, and Ruben agreed with Erik that this was an unusual girl. Klara was thinking how wonderful Ruben was and whether she dared tell him so. Then she did.

"You're a wonderful person, Mr. Lentov."

He blushed like a schoolboy and asked her to call him Ruben, so that he could go on calling her Klara.

He offered her some sherry and went out into the kitchen to forage for something to eat. When he came back he said decisively, "I'd thought of telling you something I've never told anyone else."

At first he had to search for words that would describe Rebecca, the girl he had loved and whose sister he had married.

"Rebecca and I were made for each other," he said. "Maybe I'm romanticizing. No, I'm not. We were meant for each other. But she wanted to escape from Judaism, and I saw how strong her longing for freedom was, and let her go. To a German officer with an aristocratic name that would guarantee her a place among the Aryans."

He paused, and so did Klara.

"I was wrong on both counts," he went on. "The grand German name was no help when the Gestapo came. She died in a concentration camp with two of her children."

Klara realized she had been wrong about the mascara, but also that the mess on her cheeks didn't matter.

He told her how they had met in secret at a restaurant in Paris, the city he loved.

"I had such noble ideas," he said, then added with sudden heat, "God, how much harm those ideas caused, that idiotic decision to give her up and go against the will of God and nature. Harm to her, and to her sister, whom I brought here with me, and who went mad with fear and lack of love."

"And to yourself?" whispered Klara.

"Yes."

Klara retreated into the bathroom to splash cold water over her face and was calmer when she came back.

"Please don't repeat this to anyone," he said. "Not even to Simon."

"I promise," she said.

They had another glass of sherry before he spoke again.

"I have to be out at the Larssons' by five. Do you think you'd dare to come, too?"

"Yes," she said.

In the car, he told her about becoming a grandfather, about the child just born, adding, "They say she's like me."

"Here I am," said Ruben when they got there. "And I've brought a surprise with me."

Karin stared at Klara as if she didn't dare believe her eyes, but then came joy, despair, anger, then happiness again.

"Perhaps we oughtn't expose you to such shocks."

"Happiness can't be harmful," said Erik, hugging Klara so hard it hurt, and Klara was thinking she must find out exactly what was wrong with Karin's heart.

Simon was out with Isak practicing driving in Erik's car. Mona was cooking, laying the table, and watching over the turkey in the oven. The smell was delicious.

"Take the babe away so that I can get some kind of order into things," she said, and Klara found herself with a newborn infant in her arms. She gazed at the tiny face, then at Ruben, and said solemnly, "Yes, it's true. She does look like you."

"The doctor says so, so it must be true," said Mona.

Karin and Klara took the child into the old parlor, its walls and curtains now white, the old oak furniture still there, looking slightly shamefaced in all that white.

Klara told Karin about her mother and the new husband, another alcoholic.

"Can you imagine," said Karin, "why life is so difficult?"

"No," said Klara, and both of them gazed at the baby lying there, so simple and good.

Then they heard the car, and Karin looked nervous.

"Klara," she said. "It might give him a frightful shock. Run up-stairs and we can prepare him a bit."

Klara handed over the child, her heart beating so fast it hurt, but there were no demons in her fear as she went upstairs.

"The door on the right," called Karin.

She went into Simon's old room, permeated by him through and through, and her knees felt so weak she had to sit down on the bed.

When Simon came into the kitchen, Karin was speechless, see-ing only the thin face and anguished eyes, and she wondered what on earth to say.

Happily, Erik found the words.

"The amazing Ruben Lentov has brought you another Christ-mas present, Simon. It's up in your room. Prepare for the worst, for it's even better looking than the Victrola."

Simon laughed, saying Ruben should stop giving him presents, and anyhow he'd already had one from him. He started off toward the stairs, but Karin stopped him.

"A drink, Simon?" she said. "That's soothing."

Ruben didn't know whether to laugh or cry. Mona chose to laugh.

"Mom, you're off your head," said Simon.

He went on upstairs and the house held its breath, but despite the quiet, they could not hear a word.

Only a door closing.

"Let's forget about them until dinner's ready," said Mona, and began clattering about with pans again.

Simon stood by the door, staring at the girl on his bed. Then, quietly, he went over to her and without a word started undressing her, the silk blouse, the tight skirt, the nylon stockings, the bra, the lot. When he had finished, he lay down beside her and made love to her just as he had done in a thousand dreams over the last six months, fiercely and solemnly.

"Thank you," she said afterward, but he put a finger over her mouth.

"Have you brought your flute with you?"

"No."

"Tomorrow," he said. "You're to play for me."

Only a moment seemed to have gone by when Mona knocked on the door to say that no one can live on love and they had been waiting almost two hours for dinner.

Simon laughed.

I'd forgotten what a big laugh he has, thought Klara as she dressed.

They came downstairs hand in hand and said practically nothing all evening. It was difficult to look at them, they seemed so naked, stripped to their very souls. Only Karin dared steal a long look at Simon, and she saw what she already knew, that she had lost him now and that he was happy.

As midnight struck, they raised their glasses to them.

"To your love," said Erik. "Cherish it, for God's sake."

THIRTY-FOUR

At six the next morning, Klara almost frightened the life out of the sleeping household. "Simon, I'm on duty—I have to be at the hospital before seven, and I haven't any shoes. Are there any trams?"

"You were going to play the flute for me," said Simon, but then he saw the seriousness of the situation and woke Erik, who pulled his trousers on over his pajamas and went to get the car.

Karin found a pair of comfortable shoes, blessing the fact they took the same size.

"Karin," said Klara, ashamed over the fuss she was causing. "Say it straight out. You're angry and think I'm careless, forgetting the hospital and work and everything."

"I just wonder how long you're going to go on deciding what other people think," said Karin. "I might possibly think you're silly for not understanding that anyone can lose their head after an evening like yesterday's."

"I'm not sure I've found my head yet," said Klara.

"All the worse for your patients," said Erik as he brought up the car.

The following week, Klara moved out of her shabby apartment into Simon's room at Ruben's. They talked, and by Twelfth Night they had talked so much, as Simon said, it was enough for a lifetime.

At Easter he went with her to Oslo to visit her mother. Not anxious at all, thought Klara, sure that he would take Kersti by storm, which indeed he did.

When spring finally came, they paid a quick visit to the sawmill, largely so that Klara could show him off along the road. He understood and willingly stopped to kiss her here and there, wherever the windows were close together.

Her father was worse than Simon had imagined, crude in his language, with hatred in his eyes, as if driven by demons and wrecking all attempts at friendliness. He scared Simon, who recognized him for what he was.

Now that Simon had a driver's license, they had borrowed Erik's car to drive there, and on the way to Karlstad he said it.

"You play your father's game when your demons get you."

They had planned a visit to Joachim Goldberg, her old flute teacher, writing first and asking him if he remembered Simon Haberman.

"I'm the nervous one this time," said Simon as they got there and climbed the stairs to the apartment, where Mrs. Goldberg was waiting for them with coffee and cakes, and the old man received Klara with great warmth.

"I'm afraid I have to disappoint you," he said to Simon.

There had been over thirty Jewish musicians in the Berlin Philharmonic, and Goldberg could only vaguely remember a shy violinist called Haberman.

"He was one of the faithful who stayed behind, refusing to believe that what was happening all around us could happen," he said.

On their way home, they stopped at Trollhättan and spent a while looking at the ruined waterfalls, and were soon quarreling furiously about everything and nothing. Then they were silent down through the valley.

They married on Midsummer Eve in 1949, in Oslo, where Kersti arranged a wedding that grew larger and more elaborate than any of them had wished for. Simon's family came. Karin liked Klara's mother from the first moment and stayed on for a few days in Oslo to visit the cousins she had sent food parcels to all through the war. To her dismay, she soon realized that they disliked her, the rich relative from the protected neighboring country.

"You couldn't carry on a conversation without the German trains being rammed down your throat," she told Mona when she got back.

THIRTY-FIVE

*K*arin was sitting in the kitchen with an old pan on her lap. It had never been much, but was now bent and buckled after many years of use, and one handle was loose.

She was looking at it with some surprise, remembering how pleased she had been with it when she had seen it in a shop and dreamed of all the good soups she would make in it. She must have done so over the years, but once dreams are fulfilled, she thought, they are seldom noticed.

"Out with you," she said, heaving it into the large garbage bag in front of her.

This was one afternoon during the hot summer of 1955 when it was so hot it was impossible to be outdoors. The kitchen was cooler than the shade under the trees, as at least there was a slight cross draft in there. Karin kept finding it difficult to breathe.

She and Lisa had decided to use the hot afternoons to clear out cupboards and throw out all worn-out things.

Karin had always found it difficult to throw things away, but now she found it almost a pleasure, old black-handled cutlery, the metal soup ladles she had always disliked, the silly flowery coffee set her brother had given her when she had married, they all went the same way, thrown into the sack in the middle of the floor.

Lisa sighed, now and again objecting, and she cried out when the coffee service, cream pitcher and all, started going the same way.

"Take it if you like it," said Karin, stopping for a moment. But then they both sighed, because they knew how full Lisa's cupboards were, too.

They were bothered by this modern abundance and hadn't the slightest idea how to deal with it.

On Thursday afternoon, the sky clearly became aware of the earth's torment and its own mercifulness. The heavy clouds massed, thunder rolled, lightning flashed, and the rain poured down over sea and land. The soil drank, slurping it all up quite without gratitude, as the soil always does, the sky thought sulkily, and it turned gray and cold without producing any more water, although the ground had by no means slaked its thirst.

The evening after the downpour, Karin didn't feel like going to bed, so stayed in the garden breathing in the cool air until she found she was cold and realized that now that it was sufficiently cool, she would sleep well.

The next day the sky was again morose, but Karin was pleased, as she could now go out and roam around as usual. She slipped slightly guiltily up the path at the back of the house, afraid someone would see her and follow her.

She wanted to be alone with the hills and the sea, the river and the yellow meadows. She headed straight for the old bathing place and stood thinking it wasn't all that long ago since Simon had taught her to dive there.

Time runs out through your fingers, the faster the older you get, she thought.

No one could bathe there any longer, for the water stank and was brown and oily. Karin looked over at the new houses, boxes cheekily perched on the hillside, which in a few years had ruined the landscape that the sea, the river, and the hills had spent centuries shaping. She had never imagined prosperity could become so ugly. She had dreamed that when the welfare state was complete, people would escape the oppression that follows poverty, and now it was here. Everyone was better off, and that was good, indeed wonderful. Worries over survival no longer ravaged, and the other anxiety, the one that is always down there in the depths, could be dulled by material things. Thousands of new desires that no one had envisaged before were suddenly there, and almost all of them could be satisfied in this new and ugly abundance.

I'm like some old reactionary, Karin thought, scolding herself. In those ugly boxes ruining the landscape, people have good housing, hot water, and proper drains running straight out into the sea to mix with the effluent from the great industries along the river.

She turned away, took the path across the meadows where they were soon to stake out for new houses, and she thought, Well, I won't be seeing those houses, anyhow. Just what she meant by that, she didn't know, but when she got to the oaks and sat down to rest, she suddenly felt she wanted to tell them about the old pan.

"You see," she said to the trees, "it was such an old pan, it had served its purpose. It used a lot of current and wouldn't stand flat on the stove any longer."

The oaks listened and understood.

But when she went on to tell them how ugly the pan had become, buckled and crooked, the handle loose, they didn't agree with her. It had had a faithful old beauty, the oaks thought, and Karin reckoned there was something in that.

Then she talked about Simon, as she usually did, and the other children, about how well things were going for them and what a lot she had to be grateful for.

For the fourth year in succession, Simon was at the University of London, and he must be doing something important, because he had a government grant for it. Year after year the money came, which enabled him to return to those strange signs on old clay tablets from Mesopotamia.

Karin didn't know what was so important about them, or why people struggled to understand a language that no one had spoken for thousands of years.

It was a mystery, like prosperity and ugliness.

I must be getting old, she said to the oaks, and they laughed at her, so she had to admit that that wasn't true, either, she was only fifty.

She ought to think about things she understood, the oaks considered, so she went on for a long spell being pleased that things between Simon and Klara were all right. Klara was now in Switzerland and would soon finish her training.

They didn't see all that much of each other, but that was probably good for them and their love.

Karin's thoughts dwelled for a while on Klara, the girl who knew more about her than anyone else, but to whom she would never be close. Respect, mutual respect, was what existed between them.

She had stopped being ashamed of what had happened when Klara had come to see them for the first time. That had been a difficult time, and Karin had walked alone in the hills realizing she was not all that different from her own mother-in-law.

Most important of all in Karin's life, even more important than Simon, was her image of herself as a good wise woman. The great mother, as Klara called it. Karin could laugh a little at it now, and think it wasn't really all that bad an image, better anyhow than the usual one women create from feelings of inadequacy.

Whatever it's like, you strive to make the image of yourself into the truth, and the good wise Karin had been good for the children. What it had been like for her was debatable, for she had worked hard and over the years become rather worn and buckled, like the pan she had thrown out.

Klara had a profession. She had what Karin had always wanted. She wasn't dependent on a man for survival.

And yet she was more dependent on Simon than Karin had ever been on Erik.

That was surprising, but it was the same with Mona and Isak, that marriage so full of demands. They shared everything with each other, understood everything about each other, leading to disappointments, inevitably. She could see it clearly with Isak and Mona, how their despair grew on both sides until they renewed their efforts, their quarrels, to be able to get closer. Instead of leaving things alone, thought Karin, who could never be persuaded that a man and a woman should be able to understand one another at a deeper level.

She had tried to say that to Mona.

"We come from separate worlds."

But Mona wouldn't listen, although for a while she was able to subdue her expectations when reminded of the fragility of the ground Isak stood on.

Malin came running up the slope from the house, the blessed child, Karin thought, as she always did when she saw the child, her great gravity and great joy.

Simon called her little sister, but that couldn't be because they were alike. Where he was as eager as fire, she was as calm as the trees. Where he was bursting with questions, she was rich with knowing. Karin sat down and took the girl in her arms.

"Malin, six years old and light of my heart," she said as an almost formal greeting. Then as usual, she ran her fingers through the child's thick hair and nuzzled at the back of her neck, smelling her special strong fragrance.

"You smell as if you'd come from the sky," Karin said.

"I saw you leaving and was going to run after you," said the child. "But then I thought you wanted to be alone."

"Good," said Karin. "And now I don't want to be alone any longer. Now I want to be with you."

"What was it you had to think about?"

Well, what was it? Karin thought for a moment, then, surprising herself, said, "It was that old pan I threw out yesterday. I thought I had to think through it."

Malin didn't think that strange. She shared Karin's sense of loss.

"Couldn't you have given it to me? I could have played with it in the sandbox."

"But you've got so many fine new buckets."

"But I love old pans," said Malin, and Karin had to make an effort not to laugh.

They walked hand in hand down the hill and into the big new garden.

The garden, yes. Despite the gray sky, it lay there in all its magnificence in front of them, the serious morello cherry tree, the strawberry beds now picked clean for the year, the soft lawn creeping up to all the trees, the aspen trees by the hill farthest down toward the river, and the spruce hedges which weren't up to much yet, but would provide shelter from the northeast wind in a few years' time.

Karin sat down on the old deck chair on the wooden jetty by the pond, looking at the man-high Turk's cap lilies curling their dark purple perianths in and out, their fiery red plants insolently sprawling. They were about to go to seed and would go on pleasing Karin with their elegant seed cases that could be dried and put into vases indoors.

Malin was sitting quietly at her feet, feeding ladybugs with aphids.

"I don't like captured animals," said Karin. "Put them on the roses, dear."

"Soon," said the child, looking over at the heavy roses by the pond, now badly affected by the heat and the downpour.

When Karin leaned her head back, she could see the old apple trees on the edge of the old garden, the garden she and Erik had laid out once at the beginning of time. They were Akero apples, gnarled old things, and they would provide a good crop.

I won't bother to preserve them this year. Mona can have what she wants and the birds can have the rest.

Malin was quiet as if thinking Karin wanted to be alone with her thoughts again, happy thoughts now, on the garden and everything it had given her.

Secret joy at first, then when the boatyard had moved, Mona and she had had an idea. All that early spring, when Malin was a baby and was handed from one pair of arms to another, or slept on a cushion on the kitchen sofa, they had drawn plans and fantasized. Mona had dreamed up a wild meadow of oxeye daisies and columbines, cornflowers and poppies in the south-facing corner. Karin had contributed with a fine kitchen garden with strawberry and raspberry beds. They would have creeping plants and primroses in the rock garden for pleasure in spring, and brilliant blue gentians for the autumn.

"Sedums," Karin had said soberly.

"You know," Mona had said. "There are twenty different species of wood anemones, purple and yellow. And white, but double like little roses."

No, Karin hadn't known that, and she had thought anemones should be white and ordinary for the short time that was theirs.

They had begged gardening books from Ruben, and their dreams had taken on a faster pace, soon out of control. Then they had had to persuade Erik, not an easy task, indeed almost the most difficult.

"You'll just work yourself into the grave," he had said. "Anyhow, I'd need to get something from the land."

"You talk like a capitalist, you bloodsucker," she had shouted at him, so angry the right word wouldn't come to her. Exploiter.

He had been furious, too, but since her heart trouble, their quarrels had never really taken off, and he had, as usual, taken his rage off with him to the workshop.

Only Isak supported them at first, agreeing that it would be marvelous to have a garden right down to the river. Ruben had shaken his head and been inclined to agree with Erik. How would she and Mona be able to look after such a large garden? He had also been thinking about ownership, too, and that Isak and Mona only rented from Gustafsson.

No one knows what would have happened if the Gustafssons hadn't died so conveniently, the old man first, then a few months later his old wife, who had complained about her husband for sixty years but had not been able to live without him. Their heirs hadn't wanted to live in the big house with all its awkward angles and leaded windows. It would cost a fortune to modernize, to straighten out those angles and put in panoramic windows. So they were only too pleased when Isak put in a reasonable bid. Mona was noisily jubilant, Karin quietly in her heart.

They didn't get very far that summer, but got people to come with machines to clear and level out the boatyard land and had load after load of manure brought there before the frosts came. Trees and bushes were planted before the winter, which was spent on alterations to the Gustafssons' house. There had been eight rooms and two kitchens at the start, but now there were only six rooms, for Mona was not afraid of pulling down walls to create light and air around her.

The old kitchen on the upper floor had become a weaving room. Mona had taken a course and learned to weave, while Karin looked after Malin.

By the time the garden had been laid out, Mona was pregnant again and had sat there, large and clumsy, in the rock garden, her stomach getting in the way of her trowel. Erik had employed a man, an old gardener, who came once a week and did the heavy work.

The twins had arrived the following winter, two boys who were totally unalike, one dark as night, Jewish, introverted and thoughtful, the other fair, happy, and apparently simple and uncomplicated.

"Like my father," Mona had said.

"Now, shush," Karin had said, appalled, but Mona had just laughed, hugged her blond baby, and said that she loved her father, after all, and the fact that things had gone wrong for him was due to his upbringing and his heritage.

"You know," she had said, "my grandmother was an absolute devil."

"Like my mother-in-law," said Karin. "I wonder how they came to be what they became."

Golden years, heavy with sweetness and the same kind of confidence as when Simon was little, Karin thought.

She took Malin with her back to the house. Lisa had gone for the day, and Karin and the child decided to make a cream cake to go with coffee in the evening. They beat the eggs and sugar, strewing flour all over the kitchen floor, whipping the cream, and having fun. They put the cake into the oven and forgot it, so it was slightly burned, but not so bad that they couldn't trim off the burned bits.

"You'll have to sweep the floor," said Karin. "I'm a bit tired."

Malin swept, and as she was the kind of person she was, it was properly done.

When she left, she said, "You aren't miserable about your old pan any longer, are you?" and Karin replied no, she probably wasn't.

The sky had overcome its bad mood by Sunday, swept away all the clouds, and had the sun playing freely with trees and people. Ruben came to dinner with Isak and Mona, as he usually did on Sundays. They sat in the garden and chatted, he and Karin, and she told him about the pan she had thrown out, but couldn't get it out of her mind.

"It's strange," she said. "I hadn't even seen it for years, so I can't be missing it."

Ruben told her about the rabbi who said you should live every day as if saying farewell to everything, all your possessions and all the people you loved. If you managed to do that, then life would be real, the rabbi had maintained.

Karin gazed at Ruben, much taken by his story. A shadow flitted through him and he regretted what he had said, without really knowing why.

Just before going to sleep that night, Karin thought she was probably beginning to learn, freeing herself of people and things.

The pan was only a beginning, and that was why it had been on her mind.

Perhaps it was true that life had become more real after the downpour and something new had grown inside her. No, not new, it had probably always been there, but had been hidden behind her worries over the children and all the unpredictable things that can always happen in life.

She slept like a child at night, more soundly and better than for a long time. Her walks in the hills became freer, and she had fewer memories and found more pleasure in observing things.

"I think I'm beginning to stop thinking," she said to Malin one day.

"That's good, isn't it?" said the girl. "Thinking mostly just muddles things."

"Yes, you may be right there," said Karin, looking at this new person who had just started thinking instead of just being.

Karin sat beneath the oaks for a long time, regretting that she had always hurried on, done everything in her life to get it quickly over and done with. What had she done since, with the time when she hadn't been working?

She couldn't remember.

But the oaks comforted her as usual. They knew, as she did, that it was silly to grieve over things that can never be undone. As she walked back, she had no memories and was feeling strangely free.

"You're very quiet," said Erik. "You're feeling all right, are you?"

"Oh yes," said Karin. "I've never felt better. The only thing is, you see, I've stopped worrying."

"Then there's nothing to talk about, do you mean?"

"Yes, and not much to think about, either."

"You could say it's about time you stopped worrying," said Erik, but Karin could see there were suspicions in his eyes.

But she didn't bother about that, either.

He can take it as he likes, she thought.

Erik and Isak were going to America at the end of November to look at yards for small boats. They were both worried about the trip, Erik most of all because he couldn't speak the language, nor could he stand being at a disadvantage. But he couldn't admit that, not even to himself.

He wanted Karin to go, too, but she had said bluntly that she hadn't the energy for such a long journey, thinking, You can't keep hanging on to my skirts all your life, Erik Larsson. The time's come for you to stand on your own two feet.

It rained in September, but at the beginning of October came the Indian summer, mild and golden. Karin had found a place along the shore where the reeds were so high, they hid everything except the sky and the river. She could sit there for hours and just look.

She had never been so clear-sighted as she was now that she had freed herself from all her ideas about what life ought to be like.

She knew now what it was and how it should be lived.

That day, Tuesday, the waxwings came, a whole flock of them on their way south. They came down all around her, and she looked at the orange stripes on their wings and their funny heads with those defiant crests, and again she heard their song, that strange song halfway between joy and dark sorrow.

She was surprised, all the same, when she became conscious of her insight, and realized this was what all the signs had been pointing at, and the great freedom had prepared her for.

As quietly as she could so as not to disturb the birds, she lay down and made herself comfortable, lying there calmly, paying careful attention to the way her heart was slowing down. Then it gradually stopped beating altogether.

THIRTY-SIX

Mona threw out the tea that had been sitting for too long and was now cold. "It's idiotic to worry," she said, aloud this time.

But then Malin came in crying, saying she had been on the hill at least a hundred times to meet Karin.

"Why doesn't she come, Mamma?"

That made Mona take her worry seriously. She phoned Lisa and asked her to come and see to Malin for an hour or two.

Then she took the paths she knew so well, walking calmly at first. She's probably sitting somewhere, perhaps has fallen asleep, so I mustn't come running and frighten her.

But then all reason left her and she ran, beneath the oaks, over the hills, across the meadows, along the shore. That took her an hour, then another, but no trace of Karin.

As she turned back again, she had a small hope that Karin would be there in the garden with Malin as usual. But in her heart, she already knew.

Isak was at home, fortunately. Erik was at the yard, so that was good. She asked Lisa to stay, and she and Isak ran down toward the shore.

"I've hunted everywhere. Perhaps she's fallen into the water."

Isak's eyes had darkened with fear. Together, they ran along the river shore, then in among the reeds, and there she was, lying quite peacefully, as if asleep.

"Karin," called Isak, relief in his voice, but when she didn't answer, he looked at Mona and understood. Not wanting to, he grabbed her by the shoulders and shook her.

"Mona, it mustn't be true. Tell me it's not true."

But it was. They stood there holding hands like children, without tears, but when Mona freed herself and picked some of the last flowers of the summer to put them in Karin's hands, and both could see that she was already rigid, Isak cried out in horror. Not despair, for that hadn't reached him yet, and at that moment he was unable even to imagine the great grief to come.

White to her lips, Mona told him they had to keep calm. One of them should stay there to keep guard while the other went home to phone for a doctor.

"I'll stay," he said, for now that his fear had found an outlet, he wanted to be alone with Karin for a while, to talk to her as he always had done when things had been difficult.

"Heavens," said Mona. "When will Erik be back?"

"He was working on a blueprint, wanted to get it done," said Isak.

Mona ran, first to Lisa to ask her to stay and put the child to bed. Malin looked wide-eyed at her.

"She's gone, Mamma? She has, hasn't she?"

"Yes," said Mona. "Malin darling, you must be a clever girl now."

"Yes."

Mona ran to the Larssons' house, and found to her dismay Erik's car in the drive.

"I was worried when Karin didn't answer the phone," he said, although he didn't look worried, but happy as usual, and Mona thought, What shall I say, what in heaven's name shall I say? Help me, God.

"Karin's . . . ill," she said. "We must get hold of a doctor." She rang the old doctor who had looked after them over the years, holding firmly on to Erik's hand as she told the doctor that he must come at once, that they would wait on the road outside the house and show him where Karin was.

"Let go, Mona!"

Erik shouted with anger, but without letting go of his hand, she eased him down onto the kitchen sofa and knelt down beside him.

"She's dead, Erik," she said.

She could see he didn't believe her.

"The doctor'll be here soon, won't he, with his injections."

Then the doctor was there and everything went very quickly. Erik leapt into the car and shouted at the doctor to get the syringe ready, and when they came to the end of the road, Mona ran ahead along the path. The doctor could see at once that it was too late. But not Erik. He threw himself over Karin and shook her furiously.

"Wake up, woman, wake up."

It was terrible. Isak had to use all his strength to pull Erik off and take him to the car, where the doctor gave him an injection. Erik's rage was obliterated in darkness.

"We'll take her home," said Mona. "We'll hold a wake over her at least until Simon gets back from England."

That was what happened. With shaking hands, Mona made up the bed with Karin's best linen. Isak saw to Erik and the telephone.

Ruben first. Isak could almost hear him shriveling at the other end of the phone, then his voice disappeared.

"Dad!" he yelled. "Dad, we mustn't give way now. You must get hold of Simon!"

Ruben's voice came back from nowhereland, brittle at first.

"I'll do that, then I'll come on out."

Ruben set to work, pausing long enough to think that Simon should not be told over the phone and making a call to Zürich instead, from where he heard Klara's calm voice. Klara turned icy cold with the effort of not showing she was upset and simply said she would take the evening plane to London, then she and Simon would take the first flight to Torslanda the next morning.

"Take care of the boy," said Ruben.

"How in heaven's name can I do that?" she cried, the ice gone, fear dissolving it.

But she managed to get a seat and sent a telegram to Simon from Zürich Airport. "Meet me at Heathrow this evening at eleven o'clock. Your Klara."

When Simon received the telegram he was pleased. He had

little time to think until he was on the airport bus, but then it struck him that this was not like Klara. Something must have happened to her.

The moment she appeared, coming toward him in the main hall, he saw that her gaze had retreated in that way she had when things were difficult. But her voice was calm.

"Watch for my case, will you? The ordinary red one, you know. I'll go and get tickets for tomorrow."

"Are you already going back tomorrow?"

But she didn't answer, simply sitting very close to him on the way back to London, and by this stage Simon knew they were heading for something unfathomably great and desperate.

He was frightened.

"Klara, can't you tell me?"

"Not here, Simon."

When they got up to his room, she told him. It couldn't be postponed, nor could it be done carefully.

"Karin died this afternoon."

She saw him also die, standing in front of her, more and more rigid for every minute that passed. After a while, he began to shudder with cold, so she got him into bed and lay down beside him. He said nothing, but occasionally in the night she could feel him crying and the tension in her gave way a little.

In the morning, he mechanically got dressed and went stonily with her to the taxi and the plane. As they fastened their seat belts, he opened his mouth for the first time since the evening before.

"I hope we crash."

"We'll make it," she said. "We have to, for Erik's sake."

Then Simon was able to think about Erik, and that shook him out of his paralysis, at least a little, at least for a moment.

The plane landed neatly at Torslanda, where Ruben's car was waiting for them, one of his employees at the wheel.

Göteborg was shamelessly the same as ever.

* * *

In the garden by the river, Erik had gone berserk, his fury such that it could move trees and shift boulders.

It wasn't possible. No one could bloody well treat him like this.

Isak stayed with him all night, trying to hold him when things were at their worst, and at dawn the doctor came with some tablets.

Ruben and Mona sat with Karin. Malin, too. She appeared in her white nightie at three in the morning, and simply sat down beside them as she looked at Karin.

She was the one to say it, what they had all known, that Karin had been on her way ever since the rain when she had thrown out the old pan.

"She wanted to be on her own," the child said.

Lisa came and made coffee and breakfast, saying they had to eat. Mona found it hard to swallow, but Ruben drank cup after cup of black coffee and was unusually alert, which only increased his torment.

Mona went back to the children for a while, telling them Lisa was going to be with them for the day, speaking so seriously they made no protest.

Then she went back. Fortunately, Erik was sleeping, and the doctor had said that he might have accepted it and would be more resigned when he awoke.

He'll never be resigned, thought Mona. Not deep down, anyhow.

Then Simon was there. And Klara. At last another adult, thought Mona as she hugged Klara and both were able to cry. Mona whispered into Klara's ear that they had all gone mad here, worst of all Erik, whose mind seemed to have gone.

Simon went straight in to see his mother, then sat there as the candle burned down and no one would ever know what he thought or what he said.

Erik was calmer when he awoke, his rage returning only when he caught sight of Simon, and said what he had been saying all night, that it was unfair and no one should treat them like this. Si-

mon said the same, shouting that Erik was bloody well right, and
Klara sighed with relief.

Toward midday, the undertakers came, and as the hearse drove
away with Karin's body, the road was lined with weeping neighbors
and silent children. Not wanting to watch the hearse leaving, Ruben
went into the garden, thinking as he stood there like a statue that
she was dead now, the second woman he had loved, and he had no
right to mourn this time, either. He decided to go home, for there
he would be able to shriek like Erik.

Klara saw him heading for his car and she sensed an injustice
had been done to him. She hesitated, but only for a moment, then
she phoned Olof Hirtz at the hospital.

He was also shaken by Karin's death. And worried about Ruben.
He said he would go and see him as soon as he was finished for the day.

"Jews seldom take their own lives," he said, though if that was
meant as some consolation to Klara, it failed. She put down the receiver and made a supreme effort not to scream.

Gradually things settled down and they spent the week doing
what had to be done for the funeral, making it so splendid that
Klara thought Karin would have been ashamed. "Ashes to ashes,
dust to dust."

Simon was still inside his rage and kept thinking, It isn't true,
this is all one great lie, a life is much more than a spadeful of soil.

Inga was among the family mourners, but it was Klara who
had the idea, got Inga alone, and asked her.

"Could you possibly stay with Erik for a while, until he's over
the worst?"

Inga said she would.

Mona insisted Isak and Erik should go to America as had been
arranged. When Erik came back from America, Inga had moved
into the house by the river and locked up the little house by the
lake. They were cousins and had always liked each other. She became his housekeeper, keeping the house clean and tidy, and Erik
away from the drink.

She was kinder than Karin, more compliant. Through her, Erik gradually regained his equilibrium and was able to take control of his life.

But he was never joyful again, that childish joyfulness that had been the gift of the gods to Erik. That had been lost that Tuesday in October down by the river.

THIRTY-SEVEN

*F*rom the air, they could see the coast of Norway outlined against the blue sea.

"It's strange, but in the midst of chaos there is strength," said Simon.

Klara had just admitted to herself how tired she was, but she forced herself to pay attention.

"Does that surprise you?" she asked.

"Yes. You see, I've always believed that if she didn't exist, I wouldn't exist. *Believed* is the wrong word . . ." He fell silent.

"If Karin died, then Simon would, too?"

"Something like that, not thought out, but just obvious, like the ground or the night."

"But it wasn't true?"

"It was at first, when you came and told me. But not any longer."

Klara stayed at the student hostel at Queen Boswell for a week, silently at his side as he took up his thesis again. She sat next to him in the gigantic British Library reading room and thought about Karl Marx sitting there day after day doing his research. Perhaps there had been no room for anything except *Das Kapital*, perhaps Marx had forgotten his wretched finances, his deceived wife and poor children.

Klara looked at Simon, envying men for their ability to do one thing at a time and become totally absorbed in it.

One evening when they were having a meal at one of the little Indian restaurants in the student area, he started talking again.

"It's like being born again," he said. "In great pain."

Klara drew in her breath sharply and took a glass of water, tears in her eyes from the spicy chicken.

"I realize that what makes it different now is that you exist," he said. "I won't be abandoned this time."

Klara gazed into the distance, and he laughed when he saw it.

"Hello there, come on out."

She did, and the tears in her eyes couldn't be blamed on the spicy food.

"I've had an idea," she said. "But I'm slightly scared to talk about it."

"Try anyhow," said Simon.

She told him about the little Volkswagen she had seen, red with a canvas hood. She had gone to look at it while Simon was at a lecture that afternoon.

"It's secondhand and not very expensive. And we've got the money."

She had feared a long conversation on cheaply bought consolation and other involved matters, but she had forgotten Simon could be surprisingly practical.

"I'd never dare drive in London."

"Yes, you would. We'll try tomorrow."

The next day they took the red Volkswagen out on trial, and Simon had to have all his wits about him to get through the jungle of traffic. It was fun.

"Well?" said Klara as they parked the car outside the showroom and he wiped his brow.

"Yes," said Simon, and she saw he was pleased.

"You need it. Everything here is so far away."

"I think about getting out into the country occasionally," he said. "Parks are not quite the same thing."

The car gave luster to the days they had left before Klara had to return to Zürich. "This is crazy," said Simon. "I really ought to be ashamed of having such fun." Klara refrained from saying she knew that, that it wasn't the car in itself freeing them, but the driving and all its demands for total presence.

So she left, and he was unprepared for the loneliness and guilt waiting for him in the hostel room. It had only been delayed a while, waiting for Klara to go, and it began quietly so as not to frighten the life out of him.

Why wasn't I at home? I could have gone along the shore with her and kept her hold on life. The last time, she wanted to live for my sake.

At first, his reason told him what the doctor had said, that if a heart is worn out, then it is.

"Anyhow," he said aloud to the guilt, "that's not true. I couldn't make her take pleasure in life, not always. Not even often. She pretended most of the time, and you know it."

But with those words he exposed himself to guilt, which could attack right to the heart of a child.

It was my fault she wasn't happy.

Then they came over him, those thousands of old thoughts about what hurt him so, that his mother was always sorrowful. When they had said what they had to say, silence fell and the chasm opened. His fear was so great, his mouth turned dry, the sweat pouring off him and his heart thumping so it seemed to reverberate against the walls.

There was half a bottle of whisky on the bookshelf and he drank it down, giving himself sufficient distance from the terror so that he could think again and remember Klara had said she had left a box of pills in his desk drawer.

"Only if things are unbearable," she had said.

They were that now, so he took two and fell asleep as quickly as if he had been knocked unconscious. When he awoke in the morning, the place inside him where guilt lived was silent, and that was much more important than his headache.

J. P. Armstrong was lecturing and nodded at Simon as he arrived.

"I'm sorry," Armstrong said.

It was an acknowledgment of Simon's loss, very English, but enough, so Simon was almost able to smile as he thanked him.

Klara called that evening and at once heard what the situation was.

"You mustn't take those pills every day, Simon, do you hear?"

"You've no idea what it's like."

"I'll come back."

"No!" cried Simon, flinging down the receiver.

He hated her, just as he hated Karin, these women, one after another admonishing you, then abandoning you.

But an hour later he called back.

"Forgive me," he managed to say.

"You're probably right," said Klara. "But promise me you'll phone before you take any more pills."

"They'll be very expensive pills," said Simon, and both were able to laugh at that.

As he went up to his room, he thought, You bloody guilt, you mustn't do that, behave badly to Klara.

He was frightened as he lay down on his bed and remembered his sudden hatred toward Karin and Klara. Black hatred had always existed within him.

Had Karin seen it?

Of course she had, said the guilt, twisting the knife now placed right in his heart.

He didn't sleep at all that night, but some sense returned after the panic and he succeeded in largely keeping a grip on it.

In the morning he sat down at his desk and took out his notes.

Hieroglyphics, Sumerians, a vanished language to be resurrected, how idiotic, how unfathomably idiotic. That a grown man could occupy himself with such nonsense, that was insane.

He started to laugh and went on until he was crying and had to lie down again. When guilt twisted the knife yet again, he admitted everything.

Karin, I know you would have been pleased if I'd become something sensible in life. I could have been a doctor by now, Mom, and how proud you would have been if I had been a surgeon saving lives at the hospital. You'd have thought your life had been worthwhile.

Perhaps you would have wanted to go on living?

They were not easy thoughts, but Simon had learned from the night that thoughts are at least better than wordless guilt, the chasm that swallowed you up. The discovery interested him, in the end so much, he sat up and was almost free of guilt because he had to think so hard.

He had often considered how limited words were and now he needed them to survive. Put a name to the ogre and it cracks. It really does. Perhaps it was because of the ogre that words had to be found.

When Klara called, he told her about what he had been thinking and she laughed.

"What do you think psychotherapy is?" she said. "My job is one long search for words that can free people."

"I'm often terribly stupid," said Simon.

"No," said Klara. "But you are so total."

He didn't understand what she meant by that, but he assured her he was feeling better.

Then he returned to the casts of clay tablets on his desk, fragments that would show what in the great *Gilgamesh Epic* had been borrowed by Babylon from Sumerian times. It was difficult, but he conquered the clay tablet bit by bit and was charmed by the story of the *Huluppu* tree by the Euphrates that saved the goddess Inanna from drowning in the river. She took the shoot to her garden and tended it carefully, for when it grew she planned to make a bed out of its timbers.

But when the *Huluppu* tree had grown to its full height, it couldn't be felled. The serpent, whom no one can charm, had built its nest at the foot of it, and in the treetop lived Lilith, the demon, also the evil woman in Jewish legends.

He translated. Inanna's bitter tears over everything that had happened to her *Huluppu* tree, how she eventually had some help from Gilgamesh, who killed the serpent and drove Lilith into flight. But Inanna made no bed. She made a drum out of the tree.

It was strange and comforting.

Naming the ogre filled his mind. He thought about Samuel Noah Kramer, the American who had come to lecture in London.

Simon hunted out his notes.

Early Sumerian scripts consisted of lists, long repetitions of birds and animals, plants and trees, species of stone, stars, all distinguished by their visible characteristics. There was order in the Sumerian universe, and the gods made visible in their art had definite tasks.

All transcendental qualities were lacking, Kramer had said. It had been a fact-directed culture, and yet the most religious that the world knew.

The old people, who called themselves the dark ones, had thought the only way of controlling the world and its unfathomable forces was to name everything it contained.

In the beginning was the word. It created the world and overcame fear.

Out of that insight, magic was born, Simon thought, and eventually natural science, which largely had the same function.

That evening he wrote a long letter to Klara telling her what guilt had said about him, his betrayal and his inability to make Karin happy. He wrote like a child, not bothering about how he phrased it, and nor did he care about the answer. But his heart thumped when her reply lay there one day.

"Simon, I told you on the phone that you are so total in everything, particularly when it comes to Karin. But you have an adult mind. Can't you see how childish and egocentric your relations to her are? A Freudian would call it an unresolved Oedipus conflict. Can't you see that you weren't everything in her life, perhaps even not the most important thing? As far as her sorrow is concerned, that was there long before you came into the world . . ."

He refused to read any more.

For once his anger came immediately, rising like red-hot iron through his body and exploding in white fury in his head.

He hadn't asked for a diagnosis. He had long distrusted psychology, even if he had been fascinated by its interpretations, by its supreme inclination to put words to what no one could possibly know anything about.

What did Klara know, what could she know, feel, understand about a relationship such as the one between him and Karin!

She did what so many people do when faced with what was incomprehensible—found a few phrases and distanced themselves.

"Early on and quite unconsciously, you took the blame for her sorrow onto yourself . . ." Of course. On a conscious level, I've known for years that her sorrow existed before me. But deep down that simple fact changes nothing.

How could Klara have any idea about the fine thousand-threaded network of sorrow and guilt, intimacy and merging that had always existed between him and Karin?

Always, thought Simon. It was primeval, decreed by fate, woven together through the centuries.

Karin had not talked much, and she knew that the most important things in life couldn't be talked about.

He flung the letter down on his desk, sparks apparently coming from his hand, heard the telephone ringing down in the hall, and thought, There she goes, phoning again, and God, how I hate her.

But the call was not for him, so that gave him a breathing space. He had to get out of the building before she called, that bloody marvelous psychoanalyst who understood nothing.

He ran toward New Oxford Street, caught a double-decker bus at Tottenham Court Road, then as dusk fell, gazed out of an upstairs window at the city and the people moving about.

Gazing without seeing.

But when he got off the bus and joined the crowd, the never-ending stream of people, he did take them in. A thousand destinies on their way to fulfillment, a thousand ways, lives lived and ended according to some unknown pattern, only just imaginable.

Outside Harrods in Brompton Road, a large Indian in a gray jacket was staring into a shop window displaying kitchenware, saucepans, cutting boards, knives, and toasters. He was totally absorbed, as if amazed at the thought that the objects in the window spoke a secret language and possessed knowledge of the soul of westerners.

Simon wanted to shake the man and tell him there was nothing to understand and they were all superficial.

For that matter, have you ever heard of an unresolved Oedipus conflict? he wanted to ask. Without understanding? Yes. Then I can tell you that there is nothing to understand. Like the kitchenware.

He was attracted to dark-skinned people. Some black youths were in a queue outside a cinema. Simon joined them, keeping as close as he could, as if wanting some of their strength, people who still knew they were bearers of great destiny, that which can never be contained inside the skin and never described by man.

The flashing white laughter of the men knew more about life than any damned psychologist, Simon thought as he turned abruptly away from the ticket office and ran out again, refusing to sit still and let entertainment rid him of his rage.

He was real.

As Karin had always been. The sorrow had made her real. She was courageous enough never to look for words that would free her. She had always known that life shouldn't be explained, only lived. Endured.

And a price had to be paid for that.

He ran straight into a prostitute, stopped and looked into her white face with its red mouth, painted like a wound of despair, and tried to see right into her eyes, into the knowledge she had when she fulfilled her destiny, which was to go to the bottom, sink into the depths where shame would obliterate her.

"What a nice boy," she said, and there was no mistaking her surprise, but he was determined. This evening he was going to sink with her.

He shut out all the details of the dirty room, the slack fleshiness of her no-longer-young body, the absurdity of the situation. Only superficial. He wanted to reach her despair and be scorched by it.

Naturally he did not succeed. He smiled, she smiled, they made love, almost coldly. He paid, left, wanting to wash but rejecting the idea, wanting to be down in the filth. He wanted to be in reality.

Afterward he went to the nearest pub and got so drunk he had no idea whatsoever how he got back home. But when he awoke in his own bed the next morning, he found two notes saying that Zürich had phoned, at seven o'clock and half past nine.

She was probably worried now. Serves her right, he thought.

But he felt ill at the university and telephoned after the last lecture.

"Thanks for your letter," he said coldly, savagely.

"Simon, please be sensible. You must—"

"I must nothing," he cried, but before he hung up, he managed to say he would write.

He did so, still in anger, iron that had cooled.

"I regret I opened up to you, and I think you should take all those grand words about Oedipus and stuff them up your ass. You've understood nothing, neither about me nor the myth of Oedipus . . ."

It was crude, but he thought it funny, so he sent the letter and felt even worse the next day when he phoned her and asked her to tear up the letter without reading it.

No, she wouldn't, she said, but they managed to talk to each other on minor matters in tones of voice that would assure them that all was well between them.

That night he dreamed he was lying in bed and becoming weightless, rising, floating up to the ceiling, through the dirty gray fog over London and up into the blue sky.

In the daytime, he was utterly absorbed in the origins of the Sumerians, the mystery that could be solved only through the language. But the language was like no other, neither Indo-European nor Semitic. He was fascinated by the scripts of the Hittites, the first Indo-Europeans in the Middle East. With them, the clay tablets had a familiar resonance, although the words were long and incomprehensible. But there was something, a rhythm, an inkling of a tune that related to him.

At the beginning of December, Ruben came to a book fair in London. He stayed over the weekend and they drove out into the country and found a coaching inn with a long history and a warm interior. On Sunday they roamed around the countryside, across fields and through clumps of bare trees. It was misty.

"I'd like to talk about Karin, about what she was like at the end," said Ruben.

It was hard going, but Simon needed to know as much as possible about what she had thought and felt.

Ruben told Simon about their conversation about the old pan, the first time he had had any idea that something new was taking shape in Karin's mind.

"I quoted an old rabbi, who used to preach that one should live every day as if saying good-bye to everything, people and things. It made a tremendous impression on her."

Simon looked at Ruben in surprise.

"Then Mona told me Karin's walks were getting longer and longer," Ruben went on. "I was rather worried and one day I asked her what she thought about on her long walks. She said she had stopped thinking and was free of both emotions and thoughts."

Simon had to stop on the path to be able to take in properly what Ruben had told him.

"There was something strange about her, something new," Ruben went on. "When I got home that evening, I tried to work it out, make out the expression in her eyes."

"And?"

"I came to the conclusion that Karin was happy," said Ruben. "What was new was a happiness. For the first time since I first met her, she was without sorrow. You know that there was a sorrow in her?"

"More than anything else," said Simon.

"I thought so."

"Do you think she knew she was going to die, and that was why?"

"I don't know. Perhaps she knew, but not consciously. I don't think she had ever thought about it."

Simon wept, but that didn't matter in the mist.

"I've thought a lot about it," Ruben went on. "That there is a deeper meaning in death than that the body is annihilated, that it's about psychologically coming to an end. Everything I have lived through, all my knowledge, my happiness, and my suffering, my memories and strivings are toward an end. The familiar, the family, children, home, ideas, ideals, all that you have identified with is to be left."

Simon thought about the wave dying against the Bohus rocks and having to give all its experience to the great sea before it could be born again.

"That must be what death is," said Ruben, "this relinquishing. And I suppose that's what all fear of death is about, don't you think?"

"I presume so."

"I wanted you to know," said Ruben again, "that Karin died free. She left everything and was happy before she went."

After Ruben had gone, sorrow came to Simon, great and melancholy. But where it was, guilt couldn't be. They excluded one another.

In the end he decided he had inherited Karin's sorrow.

This is her country, he thought. Here was where she lived and worked. It is large and lonely, but not unbearable. One can live here and carry out daily tasks with care.

THIRTY-EIGHT

Klara and Simon went home for Christmas, meeting at Kastrup Airport, then taking the train.

Things weren't easy. The days went sluggishly by, as heavy as lead, as long as Karl Johansgatan. But they all got through them as best they could for the sake of the children, as they kept saying.

Klara and Simon had his old room in Erik's house. Erik's rebellion against fate was over. He had shrunk and grown milder. Simon thought it awful, for his dad had always been big and vital.

A stillness had come over Isak and Mona.

Klara had completed her studies and had been given a post at the psychiatric clinic at Sahlgrenska Hospital, where she had no use for what she had learned with the Jungians in Zürich. Simon had only two exams left in London and would be back in March to complete the writing of his thesis at home. They were on a list for housing, but Ruben had his eye on a ninety-year-old widow who had a three-room apartment in Majorna.

One wet day at the end of February, J. P. Armstrong asked to speak to Simon in the handsome room where the professor had assembled his books and casts of Assyrian lions. In his youth, Armstrong had taken part in Sir Leonard Woolley's famous excavations of the royal tombs at Ur, but he was a specialist in Assyrians.

"The University of Pennsylvania have a dig going in Girsu. The Eninnu temple."

He smiled when he saw Simon's interest.

"One of their men has fallen ill, the script expert. They've asked us if we can send a replacement down there quickly, so I thought I'd ask you whether you would be interested."

If the Sumerian sun-god had stepped down from his sky and spoken to him, Simon couldn't have been more surprised, and if Inanna herself had invited him to her love nest, he couldn't have been more pleased.

"You've practically finished here, and by the way, congratulations on the results. Perhaps it might amuse you to see it all from a slightly more down-to-earth viewpoint," said the professor.

Amuse, thought Simon. This was Gudea's temple of fifty gods outside Lagash, and *amuse* was a very English word to use for the jubilation he felt.

"I'm really very grateful, sir," he said, and that was a lot to say here, but the professor smiled graciously.

Then everything went very quickly, visa, money, tickets. Simon managed to pack up his thesis and send it to Sweden. The car had to stay where it was in the hostel yard. He called Ruben, who was genuinely pleased, Erik realized you couldn't refuse such an adventure, and Klara was miserable.

"It'll be only a few months. They stop when the hot weather comes," said Simon.

"Look after yourself," said Klara, and he thought angrily that she was getting more and more like Karin, the guilt maker.

"You must see I have to take a chance of this kind."

"Of course I do."

If she says "dear boy" I'll go mad, thought Simon, as always hating this eternal obliterating understanding. Then Klara's angry voice came back.

"I suppose I have some right to be downhearted," she said.

Then it was over and they both laughed, but the last thing she said down the telephone was that damned "Look after yourself."

He flew to Basra, Iraq, which with intermediate landings took thirteen hours, so he was almost asleep when he registered at the English colonial hotel that looked like a stage set at the back of the airport. There was a park on the other side of the building, and he could hear the rustling of the wind through the palms outside his window.

At eight the next morning, David Moore burst in saying, "Hey, boy, now life's serious, waiting for you outside in the form of an old jeep." He was so American he could have stepped out of a western.

"Have I time for a shower?"

Simon could hear he sounded rather English, and he noticed David's eyes narrowing with dislike as he said that God knows how Her Majesty Queen Victoria's plumbers had managed the job in this mausoleum, but a shower could perhaps be produced out of some rusty pipe. Simon laughed, got out of bed, and held out his hand.

"Larsson," he said. "I'm Swedish, so you can't annoy me with imperialism, colonial hotels, gentlemen, or anything British. Innocent, you see?"

David Moore laughed so heartily he had to throw himself down into an old wicker chair, which creaked and creaked.

"A Swede. From the University of London. Didn't they have anyone else?"

The thought pleased him.

They had a large English breakfast, and then Simon and his case were packed into the jeep. David carefully fastened the hood and taped over a crack by Simon's door.

"Will it be cold?"

"You'll soon find out."

Within half an hour, they were out of town, taking the road north, and Simon remembered Grimberg's words: *Mesopotamia is a land of the dead and great silence. The Lord's restraining hand weighs heavily over it.*

As far as the eye could see was desert, sand in treacherous dunes. Here and there, the road disappeared under flying drifts, but they drove around for a while and soon found the way back.

"Not all that unlike snowdrifts," said David. "I suppose you're used to that?"

Simon laughed and got a mouthful of sand. The hot wind blew the sand into the vehicle, into his eyes and mouth, under his collar, down his back and stomach, where it mixed with sweat and itched.

They stopped at an inn on the quay of the marsh town of al-Shubaish and rinsed the sand off their faces in filthy water.

"Don't think you can get a beer," said David. "The prophet Muhammad decides drinking habits here. And don't rinse your mouth out with water, for Christ's sake. You'll have to use a Coca-Cola."

The inn was a hovel of reeds about to collapse. But they had Coca-Cola, and the drink cooled him and banished the grittiness from between his teeth.

"I usually bring the young rosy-cheeked ones here," said David Moore. "It's a useful place for romantic fools. You can see how people live in the same conditions as they did in the days of the ancient Sumerians."

He waved a hand along the jetty and Simon gazed at the marsh people's pointed canoes, the same as the famous silver canoe in Mes-Kalam-Dug's tomb in Ur. But he mostly watched the men poling and the emaciated children in the canoes, their eyes covered with flies.

"There's everything here," said Moore. "Malaria, leprosy, tuberculosis, bilharzia. Take your pick. Conditions include oppression of women, cruelties of various kinds, vendettas, and the enchanting habit of female circumcision."

This was Simon's first encounter with destitution, and he was unprepared for the shame he felt, a burning sense of how tall and well-fed, white and educated he was.

"Not far from here is the Garden of Eden," said David Moore. "Nothing surprises me any longer except man's ability to lie."

Simon looked away from the woman passing them on the quay, timid as an animal, so thin that her pregnancy looked grotesque.

"Are you Christian?" said Moore.

"Officially I'm Lutheran," said Simon. "But Scandinavia is fairly secular."

"Any better for that?"

"I don't know. Perhaps more energetic."

"The British were here for years and years. But do you think they did anything else but mix quinine in their drinks and guard the oil route to the sea?"

They hired a canoe, and Simon was ashamed when the green dollar bill changed hands and it was clear this was the greatest thing that had happened to the marsh Arab, who smiled a strangely gentle smile.

"Apropos quinine," said David. "There's quite a bit of the delightful anopheles here."

"What's that?"

"The malarial mosquito."

It was a distinctive world they poled their way through, a world built by people thousands of years ago from the clay of the delta. Here and there were houses similar to those on ancient Sumerian reliefs, constructed of bundles of reeds bent into curved arches.

"They should bring in bulldozers and drain it, spray with DDT like hell, send the kids to school, build a hospital, and take the veils off the women," said Moore. "Then we'd be being useful instead of digging about in piles of ruins in the desert."

"Why did you become an archaeologist?"

"Because I was a fool, like you."

When they got back into the jeep and were unable to speak because of the sand, Simon tried to suppress those pictures of children. The thought of the inescapable matter of his religion occurred to him. Had Moore seen he was Jewish?

"What religion are you?" he said.

"Me?" said David Moore. "I'm an orthodox Jew."

As they crossed the main road and the Euphrates to continue north toward Tello, David Moore said, "The old man has great expectations of you. His name's Philip Peterson, our own little professor from Pennsylvania, and he happily believes every damned shard we've found is going to reveal great secrets."

"What?" said Simon, appalled.

"Yep, for instance, where the capital of Akkad was, the much-lauded and vanished Agade. There's a chance our friend Gudea was behind leveling it to the ground."

"Hardly," said Simon. "The mountain people, the Gutians, did that."

"When it comes to Mesopotamia, you can never be sure. Someone sticks a spade in the ground somewhere and the course of history is changed."

"Yes," said Simon, thinking about how he had seen pictures of that war the first time he had heard the Berlioz symphony.

Then they were there and Moore introduced him.

"To avoid any misunderstandings," he said, "this is Simon Larsson, a Viking from Sweden. He has been honoring London for only a few years with his presence."

They all laughed, and Peterson was relieved. He was a man of about fifty, a stable man, and Simon liked him from the start.

They were just exposing the scribes' district, and it looked as if some mad giant had thrown smashed walls at the moon. A large tent had been erected for sorting all the shards that had been found.

"I hope you won't be disappointed, sir," said Simon.

"For God's sake, my name's Philip," said the professor. "What do you mean? You're a Sumerologist, aren't you? A script expert?"

"Yes."

He was given a mug of thick, American canned soup, and then there was nothing else to do but to go straight into the tent, where the fragments had been arranged in orderly rows.

Most of them were lists of stores, but they knew that already. So Simon had time only to glance at the ruins of the Eninnu temple before sitting down in the tent, thinking it couldn't be this hot even in hell.

They didn't stop until darkness fell so swiftly it was as if someone had turned out a light. Peterson looked hopefully at Simon, who shook his head.

"Haven't seen anything except the usual so far."

A man who hadn't been there at lunch came up to him.

"Thackeray," he said. "English. Grandson of the writer. I'm the doctor at this cowboy camp. I hope you didn't let that damned Moore drag you around the marshes."

"Did I have any choice?" said Simon.

Thackeray groaned. "I hope you're a lucky man. If not, you've got about ten days."

"What are you talking about?"

"Malaria."

He handed him a box of quinine tablets. "Dissolve four tablets in boiled water every morning and evening," the doctor said, and left.

"It's not a dangerous illness," said someone at the table, a comfortably charming man from New York. He had a mop of bleached hair and was called Blondie. But five men had caught it so far and had been flown home with high temperatures.

"But that's crazy," said Simon.

The man opposite him laughed and told him this was the place a famous warrior referred to when he said that survivors should envy the dead.

After a few days in the heat and sand, Simon knew what he meant.

Nor was it any better when, day after day, Simon had to disappoint Peterson. Their mood lightened one day when Simon was given new fragments and saw at once that they were different, much more interesting. With fluttering heart, and Philip Peterson leaning over his shoulder, he translated.

"He cut the thongs of whips and switches and put pieces of the wool from a ewe onto them. The mother did not scold her child. No one opposed Gudea, the good shepherd, who built up Eninnu."

Almost simultaneously they recognized the text from Gudea's famous cylinders in the Louvre. What they had found were copies, not originals.

Peterson was inconsolable.

Twice Simon went up onto the walls of the temple. They were only vast dead piles of ruins—mute, with no sign of life, not even a whisper of Gudea.

Though Simon hadn't really known what to expect, his disappointment was as great as Peterson's.

Late in the evening of the tenth day, when Simon was alone in his tent, he felt the first shivers. He knew that he now had only an hour before the fever would take possession of him, and he ran over to the ruins and climbed to the very top.

The moon was out.

"Gudea," he said. "For the sake of the merciful god."

He was so cold his teeth were chattering, but he got what he wanted. A man was standing on the wall, waiting for him.

THIRTY-NINE

*H*e could only just make out the intimation of a mysterious smile, a reinforcement of the gentle wisdom in those half-moon-shaped eyes.

When Simon asked the question he had pondered over ever since childhood—What are you doing in my life?—the smile grew broader, becoming a laugh ringing around the walls, multiplied by the echo. Simon could feel the fever taking over his body, and he wanted to scream with rage and despair, for he was so close now, almost at the answer to the mystery that had concerned him all his life. But this damned malaria would now prevent him, and would soon obliterate his mind.

He could feel himself falling, then hitting something outside the wall, leaving him on a ledge where the desert wind cooled his fever but increased unbearably the pain in his leg.

The next moment, Gudea held out his hand, a small hand, with a strange firmness in its grip, and Simon took it. Light as a feather, the hand lifted him over the top of the wall. The temple was resurrected before his very eyes, the golden bulls decorating the walls between the pillars in the great market square, and the ziggurat rising to the sky, both heavy and light at the same time, a vast testimony to man's unity with God.

It was light, the sun flowing over the temple that was a whole city, glorifying the magnificence, its reflections in blue azure, dark diorite, white alabaster, but most of all the gold covering the ceiling and walls, shimmering, warm gold.

Simon was dimly aware that outside the walls, the night and the desert were as before, and that Steven Thackeray had found him, got hold of people and a stretcher, splinted his broken leg, and done everything that had to be done. But Simon forgot the darkness and reality in the stunning sights of the interior of the temple city, mostly because of the man who had been there in his dreams and whose secretive goodness now filled Simon's mind.

"What did it sound like, the language you brought back to life?" Simon asked.

Gudea smiled that almost indiscernible smile, and this time Simon thought there was a touch of sorrow in it.

"It's not as you think," Gudea said. "It didn't concern the Sumerians' language in itself, but something much greater. Sumerian existed in the scripts and prayers, but my dreams were about its origins. There was an ancient language, the oldest in mankind, a language that could be spoken to animals and trees, the sky and water."

He sighed, and there was no longer any hesitation, but there was sorrow in his smile as he went on.

"In spoken Sumerian, there were still the remains of the very first language. I thought I had the key to it. I would be able to resurrect the connection. But it was too late, the way to the great reality was closed and our songs could not open it. The Sumerian language had lost its power and had to borrow from Akkad words and expressions not needed in the old days when everything was still simple and unified.

"Perhaps," he added, "it was the last attempt made on earth to get man to participate again."

Then he laughed.

"Now the great God is nonetheless making a new effort with every child that is born, an attempt to establish wholeness. A few years at the beginning of every life, man is still able to communicate with everything that lives, with the rivers and the skies. Then most of that is lost."

Gudea threw out a hand, and oaks grew in the market square, Simon's oaks from the land of childhood, and in front of them was a little boy with rage burning in his eyes, calling out his separation, measuring, judging, evaluating, and naming the trees.

Simon screamed with pain and somewhere someone stuck a needle into his arm and the wild torment receded.

"Nevertheless you ought to realize now," said Gudea, "that anyone who judges loses reality, that whenever a judgment is made, the wholeness escapes."

Then he took Simon's hand.

"We have to start by going to see the God, he who lives in our hearts and never tires in his striving to resurrect the pact."

Simon saw the sorrow had gone from Gudea's face and the half-moon eyes were full of confidence.

They went into the temple at the foot of the tower, and Simon was astonished by the size and strength of the hall. But when he turned his eyes to the God awaiting them at the end of the hall, Gudea stopped him.

"No one may look at him without being destroyed. You may look at him only with your heart, in the temple where he is always waiting for you, and which knows no limits."

They both fell to their knees, side by side, and the world vanished, the great desert around the ruins and the golden temple in the sun. Simon stayed behind until Gudea put his hand on his shoulder, a light touch full of tenderness that Simon recognized.

"Now you are to greet Ur-Babar's daughter, Nin-alla, the high priestess of the moon-god and my wife."

Simon followed Gudea, who was a head shorter than he was, up the ziggurat's wide staircase to the first level, from which he could look over the brilliant temple city and out into the darkness beyond the walls.

Gudea then led him onward, a hundred more stairs, until they came to the temple of the moon-god at the top, high up as if hovering above the ground.

"The priestess is asleep and may not be awakened until the next new moon," said Gudea. "She needs all her strength to guide the silver ship across the skies."

Simon bowed to the sleeper, whom he knew well, and whose red hair was plaited into a fine wreath around her high forehead.

On the way down the staircase they heard a violin playing, a tune of wild beauty.

"Yes," said Gudea, "you must listen to our violinist, the one you chase like the wind but you can never find."

Then Simon knew it was Haberman playing, and he ran after the sound, but it mocked him, disappearing among the pillars in the great palace. Only once, for a brief moment, did he catch a glimpse of the back of the player, and it was just as he remembered it from his dream, timid, fleeing.

Now I'm lost, Simon thought. I'll never find my way out of this palace with neither beginning nor end. And he cried out his fear, and at the same moment the tall Aron Äppelgren leaned over him, just as it should be, and he was lifted up onto the bicycle. They walked as usual across the meadows back at home, and Aron imitated all the birds and teased the great gulls, and Simon laughed just as he had as a child, and wet himself just as he had done when he was small.

Then he remembered where he was.

"Gudea," he called.

"But I'm always here," the gentle voice said quite close to him, and Simon knew there was nothing to be afraid of.

Then they were standing in a Bedouin tent, the dark cloth devouring the light, and it took a while before Simon's eyes were sufficiently used to it that he could see the woman bowing to them in the middle of the tent.

"I was childless," she said. "It is a fate worse than death in our people. So you can understand my joy when Ke Ba, the priestess, came one night and asked me to look after the boy she had secretly given birth to.

"But you know," she went on, "Gatumdu's priestess cannot be with child. Her womb is open to many men and gives great joy to the chosen, but the seed belongs to the goddess and cannot grow in the womb of the priestess.

"So when Ke Ba became with child, she knew the child was the god's own and dared not talk about it to the priests of Akkad, who would have destroyed the holy child."

Simon nodded.

"So," she went on, "Gudea had to grow up here with me, and he gave my life value and became a blessing to all his people."

Simon looked for a long time at the woman, for there was something about her he recognized. But not until they bade her farewell and he saw the walls of the tent open up to the great Nordic forest did he realize that it was Inga speaking to him and that the long lake was there, blue and cool in the endless desert.

But then they were already back in the temple and Gudea said he wanted him to meet his mother, the great Ke Ba.

He took Simon to another golden room with glowing blue walls and a ceiling covered with gold.

A woman was waiting in the center of the room.

"I'll leave you alone," said Gudea.

And Ke Ba, who had given birth to the child but had not been allowed to keep it, turned slowly around and her warm brown eyes met his.

"Mother," he said. "Karin, my darling mother."

She smiled her wide old smile, and he thought, God, good God, I'd forgotten how beautiful she was, and he recognized every note in that firm voice as she said, "Simon, my boy."

They just stood there holding hands, and the joy between them was so great that it split the walls of the room. Then she said with all the old challenging force in her words, "I don't like this guilt you torment yourself with. You were a joy every single day in the house by the river. Nothing you did, do you hear, should have been different."

"Mother," he said. "Why did you die?"

"I chose to go when I thought I had done what I could, Simon. I had a good life, but I didn't want to stay lying about getting old."

He opened his mouth to protest, but she saw and laughed.

"I'm joking, Simon. There was something you didn't know about."

She told him about Petter and the waxwings, and at last he saw it, the source of the sorrow in her heart.

"Life is great, Simon," she said, "much greater than we imagine."

He looked around and the infinity of the plain met that of the sea, and behind Karin were the forests, the deep forests, and above them the sky without end.

Then an unease came over Karin, and she said just as she had over all the years, "Simon, we're wasting time, you must hurry."

"Run," she said, hanging his satchel of schoolbooks over his shoulder.

"You'll be on time," she said. "Put your best foot forward."

He nodded. He was safe. She cared for him as she had always done. He would be there on time.

But he turned around at the kitchen door as usual, and she was standing just as she should be by the stove, laughing.

"Hurry, boy, hurry now."

FORTY

*H*e got there on time and he opened his eyes to a gray sickroom one ordinary Swedish afternoon and heard voices outside the door, blessed Swedish voices.

I'm home, he thought, not really all that surprised, for somewhere he had been aware of injections and stretchers, planes and white coats, Klara's face leaning over him, cool hands turning his pillow and wiping his forehead, Ruben's eyes anxious, Erik's fearful.

He was sad, not wanting to return to the reality so many people think is the only existing one.

Karin deceived me, he thought.

But at the same moment, he knew she had done what she had to.

After a while, it was clear the voices outside the door were talking about him.

"We can't let it go on like this. He seems to be in a state of confusion that has nothing to do with malaria," a young voice was saying.

"Concussion and fever, that's a good enough explanation," said an older voice. "His relatives have assured us he's quite stable, not neurotic. And his wife is a psychiatrist and she's not worried."

"But he's been hallucinating for two weeks—between attacks of fever, as well, when he ought to be calm."

That was the young voice again, and Simon tensed. He was not frightened, but he had an inkling of danger and found time to think before the voices moved away. I must take a stand against my visions, not give way any longer.

Put your best foot forward.

The next moment he was aware that his other foot and leg were in plaster, and he was dimly able to remember he had broken it falling off the wall.

He tried to sleep. Images appeared, but he drove them away and awoke before he was in midstream. He rang the bell by his bed, and the night sister came.

"Could I have a sleeping pill?" he said. "I can't sleep."

He could see she was surprised, then a harassed duty doctor appeared to take his pulse and told the nurse to take away the drip in his arm and give the patient a cup of gruel.

"Welcome back to reality," the doctor said, then left.

Simon smiled, ate the gruel, took the pill, and had a dreamless night.

The next morning, the ward doctor was there, the owner of the young voice, and Simon found they knew each other from student days.

"Hi, how're things?"

"All right, thanks, just tired."

Per Andersson looked at his temperature chart, now going down, took his pulse and listened to his heart. Simon realized all this was to conceal the fact that the doctor was curious.

He talked about malaria and told Simon his recovery would be quick and his leg was healing nicely.

"Make sure you get up and exercise it, preferably today," he said.

Then he had to go, but he turned around in the doorway, no longer able to curb his curiosity.

"Who is Gudea?"

"A Sumerian king, one of the last."

"What was special about him?"

"Well, he built a great temple and tried to blow life into the Sumerian language, which had been almost extinct. His name means *Called*. Why the hell are you interested in him?"

"You've been raving about him for nearly two weeks now."

"Have I?" said Simon, pretending surprise. "Not that strange, I suppose. My thesis is on him and I've had a high temperature."

"We thought it peculiar. Lasting hallucinations aren't part of the picture."

"Really," said Simon.

"For a while I thought you were almost obsessed," said Per Andersson.

"Obsessed," said Simon, his surprise now genuine. "Does the medical world believe in that kind of thing?"

"There are more things in heaven and on earth," the young doctor said, then left, apparently almost disappointed.

Simon stayed where he was—he had survived, he would probably survive in the future, too. But he felt no satisfaction over his victory and there was little joy in him.

Klara came and, yes, he was pleased to see her.

"You can be frightening, Simon," she said quietly.

"I didn't mean to be."

"Did you meet him, Gudea?"

"Yes, at least in my dreams," said Simon, fearing she would start talking about Jungian prototypes or something else tiresome he hadn't the energy to defend himself against. But she just sat there holding his hand until he fell asleep.

On the third day, she had to ask him.

"He didn't take away your will to live, did he, Simon?"

Then she saw he was weeping, but he couldn't tell her that it wasn't for Gudea but for Karin, and because she had gotten him to run from the kitchen.

Erik came for a while, but he could see Simon was tired and hadn't the energy to talk, so he just sat there, his eyes glistening.

"I've been so bloody worried."

"You needn't have, Dad. After all, you taught me to fight."

They managed a laugh.

Ruben came with flowers and books. He brought Malin with him, and it was good to see her.

In the corridor they were talking about giving him antidepressants, but Klara objected.

"He'll manage without," she said. "All he needs is time." But Simon knew she was worried.

A few days later, Dr. Per Andersson appeared.

"We've got an Englishman here," he said. "He's something of an expert on malaria."

There were more than usual on the round the next day, white coats all over the place, including a small man who spoke meticulous English.

Per Andersson stammered out Simon's case in his clumsy English.

"We were worried about the patient for a while, as he was hallucinating almost continuously for several days."

"That happens occasionally," said the Englishman. "Excuse me," he added as he pulled back Simon's eyelids with a practiced hand and shone a light into his eye.

"No sign of any lasting damage," he said, looking at the case sheet. "A fall, too, probably concussion in combination with fever."

A jolt went through Simon, his whole body alert as he recognized the hand, that touch. He stared at the stubby fingers, raised his eyes to the face above him, and saw into the eyes smiling their secretive smile. It couldn't possibly be the same man, Simon thought, and yet . . .

I am mad, Simon thought.

Warning bells rang—watch out, watch out, for God's sake.

But as they were about to leave, the whole lot of them, his need to know overcame his fear.

"Forgive me, sir, but haven't we met before?" he said.

His English was almost as good as the man's, so he hadn't been at the University of London for four years for nothing. And he knew his voice was quite steady.

The Englishman turned around and came back to the bed, looked at Simon, at the chart with his name on it, then, with surprise, and almost cheerfully, he said, "Simon Larsson, of course. I very well remember that morning on Omberg."

Not one of the doctors standing around could have possibly placed the name, but they all looked surprised and the consultant said, as people do, that the world was a small place.

Simon could feel laughter rising in him.

"Do you think the giants still wash their long johns in the Vättern, sir?"

"Of course," said the man, his eyes glinting, and the laughter leapt from Simon and exploded, so that Simon thought it was probably echoing in Queen Omma's fortress as it had once before.

They all laughed, most of them uncertainly, some thinking that typical English humor was rather trying when it was so obscure.

But the man turned to his colleagues and said in an apologetic voice that they must understand he had spent a day with this young archaeologist and had made it quite clear to him that his mission was to search for the hall of the mountain king.

"Do you think he listened to me?" he went on. "No, he went straight to the malarial marshes of Iraq and the ruins in Lagash."

They all nodded, not understanding, their smiles becoming more and more strained, but Simon persisted.

"How are your children, sir?"

"I've had some trouble with my son, but it's better now," he said. "And now I have a little daughter."

"Congratulations."

"Thank you."

With that, he put his hand on Simon's shoulder, and great force came from it as he said, "We'll meet again, Simon Larsson."

Then he was gone, but his joy and a great security remained and struck root in Simon's heart, right in the mountain king's hall.

He recovered astonishingly quickly, ate like a horse, slept like an innocent child, and had gentle friendly dreams.

Klara came to fetch him on the day he was discharged.

"I've got a surprise for you downstairs," she said.

There was his car, the red Volkswagen that had been shipped over from London.

"I can drive if your leg makes it difficult," she said.

"You do that."

It was good to see the world again, so full of experiences and realities to enjoy. The others were waiting in the house by the river mouth, and he took Malin into his arms.

"Karin sends her love," he whispered.

She nodded, not at all surprised.

The table was laid at Mona and Isak's, and as Simon limped through the big garden, he noted that spring had begun her work. The blue anemones were out and competing with the blue of the scillas under the aspen trees.

As they sat down and raised their glasses, Simon said, "Here's to Karin, to her memory."

They drank to her, and Simon felt her sorrow had lost its hold now, on all of them.

At dusk, Simon went up the hill, across the meadow toward the oaks in the land of his childhood—to renew the association.

Simon's Family

MARIANNE FREDRIKSSON

A Reader's Guide

"This is a work of imagination and must, with both humbleness and boldness, obey the laws of fantasy."
—JOYCE CAROL OATES

A Conversation with Marianne Fredriksson

Q: What strikes me first and foremost about *Simon's Family* is the awesome abundance of historical and psychological references and themes: World War II and the Holocaust, the Sumerians, the Oedipus complex, the nature of reality, animism. I could go on. Few authors, I doubt, would be able to navigate such rich and varied depths with your skill. What led you to some of these interests? Why do you think you are able to piece together such a cohesive story from them?

MF: A person is a far more complicated being than our culture is prepared to accept. He or she has a lot more depth, and his or her life has totally different dimensions, than our upbringing and culture allows. The problem is that we see only what we have been taught to see.

I have also written novels with motifs from the Old Testament—*The Book of Eve, The Book of Cain, The Tale of Norea*, to mention a few of them. These books demanded some research. What I learned from my studies was that the biblical stories are variations of myths thousands of years older. They were handed down from people to people in ancient Mesopotamia, all the way from the oldest culture we know of—the Sumerian.

This roused my all-absorbing interest in the myth—the mysterious and eternal symbol of an original view of the human life. Then I stumbled upon a Swiss historian who soon fascinated me. He didn't divide the time according to the old model of Stone Age, Iron Age, etc. Instead, he spoke of the magic age, the mythic age, and following that, the logical age—where we are now. It hit me powerfully that, even today, each child repeats these stages. Every very small child lives in a magical world until he or she reaches the mythical age, when life is dominated by the fairy tales—of the hero, the princess, the Tomnoddy, who always brings home the victory and so on. Then, finally, the child is put in school and is told that one plus two equals three and that this is the only reality.

After a while, usually in middle life, we start to suspect that, somewhere along the line, we have suffered a great loss. And then the longing for reestablishing the child we once were can come upon us.

Q: I asked you in a previous conversation about your first book, *Hanna's Daughters* (Ballantine Reader's Circle guide to *Hanna's Daughters*), if you ever uncovered any interesting stories in your own family history. Your reply was that *Simon's Family* was, in fact, the novel that contained autobiographical elements. So, I can't resist asking what aspects of this novel are autobiographical.

MF: It was like this: I had reached a point in life where I wanted to go back and re-create my childhood. Not the family stories, not the pictures in the family album, but my personal experiences, feelings, memories. But there was a problem. I couldn't bring the little girl who I once was to life. She refused to take form. The months went by and life was miserable. One day someone said, "Write about a boy." And so Simon was born. And because he was a boy, he let a lot more of his feelings out and was more aggressive than the little girl who had been me. But the foundation was the same: a strong sense of being an outsider and a great loneliness.

Q: Like *Hanna's Daughters*, *Simon's Family* is full of characters who possess uncanny intuitions that border on the mystical. Are these people extraordinary in life, or do you believe that as human beings each of us carries within ourselves the ability to transcend reality? In Simon's vision while in the Iraqi desert, Gudea tells him that God makes an attempt to establish wholeness in every child that is born. "A few years at the beginning of every life, man is still able to communicate with everything that lives, with the rivers and the skies." Why do you think that certain people, like Simon and Karin, never lose that oneness?

MF: No, the people in the novel are not extraordinary. The sad thing is that only a few people ever dare to open up to the magic/mythical dimension that is a part of our legacy.

Q: Karin starts out as the most simple and accessible character in many ways. Yet as the story progresses, she becomes one of the most complicated and elusive. Do you agree? What does Karin represent for you?

MF: We all play our roles, and probably we have to, to allow the social play to continue. It is important to play them well, but it is more important that we don't confuse ourselves with the roles we play.

Karin plays for understandable reasons (her own childhood, the time, spirit, etc.) the role of the good mother and the loving wife. She does it well. She is more genuine in her interpretation of the role than most of us. But women are also people of intelligence, ambition, striving to develop the self, to influence and to be seen. Karin didn't take these sides out on the husband or the children, which is common in many families. She didn't become dictatorial or a martyr. She lived her part—and denied her aggressiveness. Until the day when Simon's girl showed up, the combative Klara, soon to be a doctor. And then I think Karin's denied aggressiveness rose up from unknown depths within her and struck Simon and Klara. We all have, as I already mentioned, many depths—and the most dangerous are those we've refused to see throughout the years.

Q: Referring back once more to our prior interview in *Hanna's Daughters*, you stated that the mystery of women for men lies in sexual fear, "the man's fear of being absorbed." (*Hanna's Daughters*, p. 353) If I had to choose the most overt theme of this novel, it would be the complicated feelings that men have for women. Simon, Isak, Eric, Reuben . . . each of these men is tormented in some way by the women, or the memory of the women, in their lives. Tormented and yet nourished. You obviously have strong feelings and ideas about this. Can you elaborate a bit?

MF: I think that the small boy's total dependency on the almighty mother is part of the explanation. The baby girl is, of course, also dependent. However, she doesn't have to break from her mother until her teens.

Q: I wonder if *Simon's Family* prompts a different reaction or touches a different nerve in Europe versus the United States. While every country is haunted by the long, historical shadow of the Holocaust, I can't help thinking that it casts an even darker one in Europe, where so many countries lost great numbers of Jewish people. Do you have any sense of a different reading of the novel from these two continents?

MF: Perhaps the long, bloody history of Europe leaves its mark on the people here. Every new hell gives rise to a collective horror. Every picture from the wars in the Balkans gives rise to the feeling that man is incomprehensibly evil. The Holocaust is the foremost symbol. Here, we had to witness a Western industrial nation use all its technical knowledge to build well-equipped factories where they rationally and systematically murdered millions of people.

Q: Although you don't make specific references to Taoist philosophy, there seems to be a close affinity with its teachings at work in this novel—in particular, the notion of living in the present moment and the idea of other realities and planes of existence. Is this purely coincidental, or is this another interest of yours?

MF: I have always been interested in the history of religion. Through the years, I've studied Taoism, Buddhism, Hinduism, Christianity, and Judaism. They point out different paths to insight, but at the core their messages are the same. Hinduism says, "You are it." Jesus says, "Heaven is within you," and "Only he who receives the Kingdom of Heaven as a child can enter in it." [Translated from the Swedish edition of the Bible]

Q: Simon is one of those rare characters whom writers dream of creating. He is so distinctly himself and yet always unpredictable. He embodies so many profound ideas about life and still never comes across as pedantic or contrived. Can you tell us more about how you conjured him up? As you mentioned, he is a loose characterization of yourself.

MF: That's right. I wrote about myself and dared to be open and ambivalent because I could hide behind another person.

Q: It must have been a struggle to create a mate worthy of Simon's complexity. Now that you've done it, I cannot imagine anyone other than Klara fulfilling that role. There is a lot that links them together. What, in your opinion, is their most significant tie to each other?

MF: The most significant tie between them is that they both felt they were strangers in this world.

Q: Both *Simon's Family* and *Hanna's Daughters* have become number one international bestsellers. These two books are about very different situations. True, they both deal with wartime angst, but that alone does not make a bestseller. What do you think is driving the success of your novels?

MF: Almost all of the experts have different answers to that question . . . "A good storyteller," "An irresistible touch of the mystical," etc. Personally, I have no explanation. I am just endlessly happy and surprised.

Q: You must get inundated with fan mail from your readers. What are some of your favorite questions and comments about your work?

MF: Yes, so many letters that the piles of bad conscience constantly grow. The most common phrase I hear from fans all over the world is "You have given words to something I have always known but couldn't express."

Q: The stark beauty of the Swedish landscape added to the ethereal quality of the novel. Was this otherworldly, dreamlike dimension of the novel a catharsis for the heavier themes of the Holocaust and psychological abuse?

MF: No, the depictions of nature have nothing to do with psychology, the Holocaust, or other measurable phenomena. Rather, it is religious. The Swedish people are the most secular in the world. The churches are empty. But according to a recent study, around fifty percent of Swedes say that they experience God in nature. I am one of them, although I wouldn't choose the word "God". My wanderings in the great forests and along the shores give me a rich spiritual experience.

Q: **I've asked you before about your favorite American novels or authors. You've cited Kurt Vonnegut and Toni Morrison. At that time, you'd also fallen in love with James Salter. What are you reading these days? I won't limit you to any particular country—although at least one American novel would be appreciated.**

MF: Wonderfully enough, I have made a new literary discovery that has helped me through the long winter—the work of Joyce Carol Oates. What an author! I hope you are proud of her. Other than that, I mostly read nonfiction.

Q: **What does this bestselling international author have in store for her readers?**

MF: The hardest thing about being an author is the waiting. This winter is a long wait.

Reading Group Questions and Topics for Discussion

1. This novel is so richly textured with various themes and ideas about life, spirituality and art. What, in particular, touched or interested you the most? Why?

2. What do you think is the most significant, overt theme of this novel?

3. Simon is an extraordinarily complex character. If you had to describe the essence of him, how would you do this? If *Simon's Family* were to become a movie, which actor could you envision playing the role of Simon?

4. Why do you think Simon had such a drive for self-punishment in relation to women?

5. What are your feelings about Karin? Is she authentic in your eyes? Or was she, like Klara, simply forcing an image of herself as the good mother?

6. How did the mystical aspects of the novel—the personified oak trees, the visions, the uncanny intuitions—affect your reading experience? Have you read other novels of this style before?

7. We might call Simon's experience listening to music an "out-of-body" one. Has there ever been a time in your life when you felt that you transcended your conventional perception or state of reality?

8. Simon talks about a desire for evil to "make him real." Do you understand—or can you relate to—this notion?

9. The novel touches on various psychological terms related to the Holocaust—persecution mania, survivor guilt. Have you ever heard of these conditions or do you know of people who have dealt with them?

10. Ms. Fredriksson states that most people do not "dare to open up the magic/mythical dimension that is a part of our legacy." Do you agree with that statement? In your opinion, what does opening up to magic and myth entail?

11. Karin's memory of the waxwings helps her through difficult times in her life. Is there a particular memory or symbol that you turn to for solace?

12. If you had to choose just one passage from this novel to entice a friend to read it, which would it be?

ABOUT THE AUTHOR

MARIANNE FREDRIKSSON's novels have sold more than two million copies in her native Sweden. *Simon's Family* is her second U.S. publication; *Hanna's Daughters* was her first.